THE BALKAN NETWORK

GREGORY M. ACUÑA

GMA

Copyright © 2019 by Gregory M. Acuña

All rights reserved.

No part of this book may be reproduced in any form or by any electronic or mechanical means, including information storage and retrieval systems, without written permission from the author, except for the use of brief quotations in a book review.

Cover Design by: 100 Cover

http://100covers.com

❦ Created with Vellum

For my Family

Introduction

On March 27, 1999, after four nights of sustained aerial bombardment by NATO aircraft, the Serbian 3rd Battalion of the 250th Missile Brigade shot down the invincible U.S. Air Force F-117 Stealth fighter using a Soviet-made SA-3 surface-to-air missile. The pilot ejected safely from his crippled aircraft and landed deep in hostile territory. Serbian military and paramilitary forces rushed to his location from all quadrants. The propaganda value of shooting down and capturing an American F-117 pilot was enormous. Remarkably, NATO Combat Search and Rescue forces extracted the pilot near the Serbian town of Ruma, sixteen miles from his last known GPS location.

On May 2, 1999, Serbian forces shot down a U.S. Air Force F-16 fighter with a Soviet-made SA-6 surface-to-air missile outside the city of Novi Sad. The pilot ejected from his crippled aircraft and landed in the forests of Fruska Gora National Park. Once again, NATO Combat Search and Rescue forces extracted the F-16 pilot thirty miles from his last known GPS location.

Given the geographical constraints of the Vojvodina

Introduction

region of Serbia, which was deep inside enemy territory, it would have been extremely difficult for the downed pilots to evade enemy capture had there not been a network of friendly forces established in the area. These rescue operations are documented historic events; however, many details were omitted due to their highly classified nature. What follows is a work of fiction and offers a possible explanation as to why these two pilots were successfully rescued within hours of being shot down.

Chapter 1
JANUARY 1945 JASENOVAC CONCENTRATION CAMP

At precisely six in the morning, Ustashe prison guard Vera Curic—a large, heavyset woman wearing a grey, well-pressed uniform—walked slowly to the women's political prisoner block. This facility housed *enemies of the state*. Once inside the cellblock, Curic shouted in Serbo-Croatian, "Walsh, get up! Walsh, come forward!"

Jasenovac was not one camp but a cluster of five detention centers. Collectively, this facility was the third-largest concentration camp in all of Europe. A few minutes earlier when Curic first approached the dilapidated structure, she caught whiff of the stench—a combination of body odor, vomit, excrement, and rotting blood. Because of the never-ending stream of female prisoners that overwhelmed the prison's capacity, the system had to be simplified. The female prisoners had to forgo bathing and changing clothes. Most slept nude or slightly clad; it was easier to clean a naked body. Curic knew that to enter this facility was to pass through the gates of hell itself; that is why she took her time and walked slowly into the structure. When she entered, she placed her hand over her nose and mouth to keep from breathing the stench. In front of her were eighty-three women crammed into a hut built for seven. All slept five or six to a bunk stacked- up three high. At first glance, the women in the political block would never be recognized as human beings. Most were lice-infested skeletal creatures with shaved heads and sullen faces.

A frail, semi naked figure appeared from the shadows and whispers upon hearing Curic's command. She looked sixty years old but was only twenty-six. The young woman could barely stand, too fragile from weeks of intense manual labor and dysentery. She approached Curic and said in English, "It's Lieutenant Walsh! I'm a British officer."

"I don't care who you are. Komendant Huber will see you, now!"

Walsh knew that when called to see the SS camp administrator, nobody returns. In a way, she felt this was *it* and that this was her release from hell. Stalling for time, she switched to Serbo-Croatian, "It's cold outside; I need to get more clothing on."

"No, the Komendant will see you immediately!"

Walsh reluctantly went out into the cold winter morning—Curic behind, poking her with a cane. As they made their way to the camp headquarters, Walsh caught sight of two Ustashe officers and a private standing next to SS Sturmbannfuhrer Huber. Curic stopped and shoved Walsh toward the men and shouted, "Get on your knees whore!"

Reluctantly, Walsh dropped slowly to the ground.

Huber unfolded a small piece of paper, a telegram from Gestapo Headquarters, Berlin, and read the simple decree in English.

"By order of the Fuhrer, British political prisoner Penelope Walsh is to be executed at once!"

He lowered the order and watched as the private walked over to Walsh and drew his small-caliber pistol from his holster. He circled behind her and pointed the gun to the back of her head. Surprisingly, despite the despair of certain death, the young woman felt no fear. She had accomplished her job and done it well. Soon the Red Army and Tito's partisans would advance on the camp. She smiled inside knowing the Soviets would be issuing Huber's own execution orders within weeks. She thought about her young daughter left behind in England and knew the child would be in good hands. Then she looked into the eyes of each of the three officers in front of her. She had contributed to the Allied victory. None of the V-1 rockets she helped destroy would reach their targets. Huber gave a nod, and the private fired one shot to the back of her head. Death was instantaneous.

Chapter 2
NOVI SAD, SERBIA DECEMBER 1998

It was three in the morning near a wheat field. Milan Belic, a CIA contract operative, was waiting in his Hugo sedan. He was a short, stocky man in his late sixties, with broad shoulders and muscular hands. Fieldwork was difficult at his age, but he had no choice but to do the work himself. The end of the Cold War had taken its toll on human assets in the former Eastern Bloc countries. Belic was the last CIA asset still working inside Yugoslavia. The U.S. military was preparing to launch a massive air assault and needed valuable information on military targets.

It had been a cold and lonely night as he pulled down his knitted stocking cap over his head. The overcast skies were perfect conditions for covert activity. Belic's job on this assignment was to provide sniper cover and transport back across the border into Croatia for a team of U.S. Special Forces. Two hours prior, a U.S. Air Force C-130 flying over Bosnia-Herzegovina, dropped three Navy SEALs from high altitude. The Navy SEALs were on a special reconnaissance mission gathering information on a large formation of Serbian heavy armor positioned against the Danube River. U.S. intelligence was trying to determine why a large armored division was in a position unable to mobilize during an attack. The Navy SEALs discovered the reasons and completed gathering data on the target area when Belic's radio cracked to life.

"Roper One, this is Dagger Six. We're ready."

"Copy, Dagger Six, stand by for extraction."

Belic reached into his overcoat, took out his personal cell phone, and made a local call. Someone answered after several rings, and Belic spoke in Serbo-Croatian, "The team acquired the information and is waiting extraction. No change to rendezvous point."

The anonymous voice replied in Serbo-Croatian, "Monitor the situation. Call me if something changes."

At his field headquarters, near Backa Palanka, Domonic Slavo was awakened by one of his "Young Tigers" (paramilitary forces). Slavo was in his early thirties, slender of build with long, greasy, brown hair worn in a ponytail—too long for military regulations. Slavo was not part of the Yugoslav Army (JNA) but was with a special detachment of paramilitary forces. His specialty was tracking down and killing enemy fighters, especially NATO airmen. It didn't matter what nationality, as long as they were a threat to the JNA or paramilitary. He hunted them as if it were sport. Slavo's weapon of choice was the latest version of the Russian-made Dragunov sniper rifle, fitted with a laser sight and night vision scope. The weapon was a gas-operated, semiautomatic rifle with an effective range of more than one mile. The weapon was always in his possession.

"Sorry to wake you, sir, three enemy fighters parachuted in and landed near our mechanized deception area. Initial reports indicate they could be the NATO Special Forces you've been waiting for."

"Get me an off-road vehicle to make the trip to the countryside."

Belic, now using a night vision scope on his rifle, was monitoring the movement of the three Navy men. The SEALs were using a handheld GPS with beacon, enabling them to navigate directly to his location. Once the rendezvous was complete, they would travel through the countryside and cross the border into Croatia at Backa Palanka. He would disguise all the men as Orthodox priests in long, black, hooded robes.

The SEALs were moving to the rendezvous point as they were trained—stealthy and professional using the wheat fields as cover—when Belic noticed an unmarked Land Rover moving quickly along an access road. The Land Rover was traveling at high-speed and moving to the location of the SEALs. Belic keyed his radio, "Dagger Six, this is Roper One. Be advised, there's an enemy vehicle moving toward your position; standby."

The stalking Land Rover stopped several meters from the SEALs' position. Slavo's plan was simple. He knew the NATO Special Forces were Navy SEALs—some of the most highly trained warriors in the world. He would never be able to engage them single handedly in a firefight and win. He had an alternate plan. They had advance knowledge of the rendezvous point thanks to the Serbian counterintelligence apparatus. Three of his Young Tigers were already waiting in *spider holes* near the known extraction point. All they had to do was wait for his order, and they would emerge from concealment and take out the men from the flanks. Slavo dismounted from the vehicle and aimed his rifle at the navy men, then made his phone call.

The SEALs realized they were out of range to engage using their Heckler and Koch 9 mm MP5 submachine guns. They would need to move closer to the Land Rover and their target. Belic could now see the disadvantage and tried to call off the engagement, but it was too late. A halo of blood and brain matter engulfed the area near one of the SEALs. Then, two more bursts. The SEALs were hit in a hail of automatic gunfire from the hidden paramilitaries.

Belic keyed his radio, "Dagger Six, this is Roper One, do you copy?" There was no response. Belic noticed the Land Rover moving toward the downed men. "Dagger Six, this is Roper One, if you hear me, key your mic!" There was still no response.

Slavo and his three paramilitary men now stood over the bodies of the bullet-riddled men—his plan was a success. The U.S. servicemen, though superbly trained, were all too predictable. He knew they would focus their attention forward and to the rear and not notice the hidden fighters emerging from the flanks. The four men dragged the bodies and placed them in a pile. Next, Slavo reached into his utility vest and took out an antipersonnel mine. He placed the mine under the lifeless bodies, armed the fuse, and hid for cover. The explosion could be heard for miles.

Belic swore under his breath. The operation was a complete disaster. The casualties were unfortunate but a reality of war and espionage. Several minutes passed as he watched Slavo and the three paramilitary men return to the Land Rover and drive away. Belic reached into his coat pocket and took out another phone. This was a secure satellite phone used for encrypted communications. He pressed the numbers he had committed to memory and placed a call to his handler. The National Security Agency spy satellites routed the call to an undisclosed location somewhere in the United States. A voice answered on the other end and spoke in English, "This is Preacher, go ahead."

Belic screamed into the phone, "I have three men down. It was a complete ambush! They were waiting for us. You've got to come up with a better plan if you want that information."

There was a moment of silence as the NSA satellites scrambled the transmission.

"The Pentagon is run by a bunch of imbeciles. This was the JCS's idea, not ours."

"How did they know our location?"

"The Serbs aren't stupid. They probably saw the parachutes dropping from the sky. Navy SEALs are not covert operatives!"

"Do we have enough time to try something different?" asked Belic desperately.

"I can get a lot done without the idiots from the Pentagon and Langley. I'll meet you at our cutout when the plan's operational. In the meantime, stay low and recover the bodies using standard operating procedures."

Belic secured the call from his handler, got out from his vehicle, shouldered his rifle, and then walked through the wheat fields. He made his way slowly to the downed men. It took him several minutes to reach the location chugging in the soft earth. He was stunned by what he faced as he arrived. All he could see were blood and body parts strewn about. There was not much to recover. As he shined his flashlight over the surrounding carnage, something caught his attention. He picked up a U.S. military cell phone with a sat-com cable adaptor. The device was still functioning. He placed the phone in his overcoat and continued to recover the bodies.

Chapter 3
JANUARY 1999 EMERYVILLE, CALIFORNIA

University of California Professor Emeritus Josef Kostinic was dropped off at the Emery Cove Park at precisely nine in the morning by his personal assistant. Kostinic was in his eighties and lived alone a few blocks away at the Emery Apartment complex for seniors. Celeste, his beloved wife for over fifty years, passed away several years earlier. He often took outings along the bay to get exercise and fresh air. He was dressed in a dark, charcoal-colored suit with white shirt and red bowtie, his thinning silver hair combed neatly under his fedora. He sat down at his usual spot, gazing across San Francisco Bay. This was one of his favorite places to reflect and reminisce.

The aging professor heard a car approach from behind and come to a stop. A man in his late seventies approached the bench and walked toward Kostinic, keeping his back to him. Waiting to make sure no one was around to hear their conversation, Harold Mattingly, United States Undersecretary of Defense for Intelligence, turned around and spoke. "It's been a long time, old friend, thank you for meeting me on such short notice."

Kostinic stood up slowly. He had difficulty standing on his own despite using his cane. He reached out and shook Mattingly's hand, "This must be extremely important for a personal visit all the way from Washington."

"I received confirmation NATO and the European Union agreed to support ethnic Albanians in Kosovo and protect them from the Yugoslav Army and Serbian paramilitary forces. They've also stepped up the timeline for intervention, trying to prevent another ethnic cleansing by the Milosevic regime. We brought in a reliable asset out of retirement to head the overall network, but we still need an organizer for the Serbian circuit."

The two men sat back down on the bench, Mattingly assisting Kostinic. They continued to gaze across the bay before Mattingly spoke. "I recall you set up a circuit inside Yugoslavia in 1943 and helped coordinate the rescue of hundreds of Allied airmen shot down returning from the Ploesti oil fields. To this day, that mission was one of the most remarkable and successful events of World War II. There is no one alive who knows more about setting up covert networks inside Yugoslavia than you. Can you help us again?"

"What could I possibly do at my age to help?"

"Organize the network for starters."

The two men basked in the sunlight, then Mattingly continued, "We can't rely on our usual assets. As you're aware, the geopolitical situation inside Yugoslavia has become very complex. Local sources are unreliable. Loyalty is changing daily. We can't trust anyone anymore. We don't know the difference between Croatians, Bosnians, Bosnian-Croats, Serb-Croats, or just plain Serbs."

"Sounds similar to the political situation we were thrust into back during the war."

"Precisely, I'd like to go back to the way it was in 1943

using OSS-style military operatives, but it's essential we find someone whom we can trust, perhaps someone new to our profession."

"What sort of timeline do we have?"

"I need to start assembling the team by the end of February."

"That doesn't leave us many options."

"Yes, I know. We're running out of time."

The two men continued to look across the bay, watching the sailboats. Finally, Kostinic stood using his cane. "Come, let's go for a stroll. There's a lot to talk about if I'm going to help you organize the Balkan network."

The two men walked slowly on the paved walkway around Emery Cove, the cold wind blowing off San Francisco Bay, cutting through their aging bodies like a knife. They did not walk far. Kostinic stopped along the path, looked to the University of California campus, and closed his eyes. Finally, he uttered, "I don't recall if I ever told you this, but I'm truly sorry about Penelope. I tried my best to save her. I was nearly killed myself during the rescue attempt. This could be very painful, bringing up events from our past. Are you sure you want my help?"

"That was a lifetime ago, Josef, and, yes, we desperately need your help. As far as Penelope is concerned, there's been someone to fill the gap." Mattingly quickly changed the subject and asked, "Is there someone you know?"

Kostinic nodded his head still looking at the University of California campus.

"Perhaps there *is* someone? He fits your requirements. However, it's been a long time since I've been in contact with him. He was an undergraduate student of mine here at Berkeley, one of my best and brightest students. He could do well, but I'll need your help in locating him. I do believe he's still on active duty in the Air Force."

Chapter 4
FEBRUARY 1999 NORTHERN CALIFORNIA

United States Air Force Captain Daniel A. Radivich was at the controls of his aircraft over the skies of Northern California. The giant C-5 Galaxy transport of the Air Mobility Command (AMC) was on its final leg home. Dan was a handsome man at six feet, with brown hair, a chiseled chin, and brown eyes. He was a native Californian, born in the beachfront community of Oceanside, just north of San Diego. He was a typical Southern California youth, learning to surf and play beach volleyball. He attended Oceanside High School where he played football and baseball. He attended the University of California, Berkeley, where he developed a deep passion for history and geography. During his studies, he made the decision to follow a career in the military as a pilot.

Dan's first assignment was an HC-130 pilot stationed at Hurlburt Air Force Base, Florida, assigned to the Special Operations Command. While at Hurlburt, he learned about combat search and rescue (SAR). After spending four years at Hurlburt, Dan transferred to Travis Air Force Base in California to get back to his native state.

The Balkan Network

It had been a long, ten-day trip to the Pacific for the thirty-three-year-old pilot. There were plenty of miscellaneous items he needed to work out once he entered his mandatory three-day crew rest period. The Air Force nurse was his first priority. They had met at the Officers' Club the day before he left on this trip. It seemed like every time he met someone he liked, he had to fly off the next day.

"It's a beautiful night," said Dan to his copilot. "I never get tired of seeing the lights of San Francisco and the Mendocino coastline."

The C-5 made its final descent and approach into Travis over the Napa and Sonoma valleys and landed on schedule at 8:30 PM. The post flight duties for a C-5 always took an eternity—one of the things that bothered him most about being an Air Force pilot. Why couldn't he just set the parking brake and go home as most airline pilots do? Finally, one full hour after landing, Dan and his crew were on the crew bus, heading back to the squadron for debriefing and post mission reports. As the crew bus pulled up in front of the squadron, Dan noticed Lieutenant Colonel Boyd Parker, Squadron Commander for the 75th Airlift Squadron, standing in front, waiting for the crew. He was dressed in civilian clothes. This seemed odd to Dan because normally the commander was never at the squadron this late in the evening, especially on a weekend. The trip went flawless, no delays or problems on the mission.

Parker came up to Dan as he unloaded the last bags from the crew bus.

"I need to speak to you in my office when you're done. No hurry, Dan, just finish your duties."

Dan could tell this was urgent by the tone of Parker's voice."

"I'll be right there, sir."

Dan was perplexed. He didn't think he violated any regulations or procedures. Perhaps Parker wanted to talk to him about future assignments. He was coming up for another reassignment and knew that squadron commanders were under enormous pressure to fill these vacancies. Dan was not in the mood tonight to talk about future assignments that would take him away from California, so he took his time debriefing the crew and completing post mission reports.

When the last crewmember left the squadron, Dan leisurely made his way down the hall to Parker's office. As he approached, he noticed the door slightly ajar—someone was in the office with Parker. Dan thought he'd better knock and report in a military manner in case it was someone important.

Dan knocked on the door and walked in slowly. He noticed two men dressed in civilian clothes standing off to the side. Both men were in their mid-twenties, with military-style haircuts, and were dressed in poor-quality, inexpensive suits probably purchased at the local base exchange (BX). Dan saluted Parker, "You wanted to see me, sir?"

Parker returned the salute, "Take a seat, Dan. This is Sergeant Rudy Perez and Sergeant Steve Evans, US Army Intelligence. They're here on behalf of the Defense Intelligence Agency in Washington. Dan, I don't know how to put it any other way—we're here tonight to talk about your next assignment."

Dan took a seat in one of the chairs in Parker's office.

Sergeant Perez interjected, "Captain Radivich, we've been ordered to hand-deliver your new orders. You're wanted at the Pentagon. It seems you have a special skill that's needed."

A sudden alarm went through Dan's mind as he realized his ability to speak Serbo-Croatian and German fluently would be of use now that there was a real war going on in the former Yugoslavia.

Dan was the son of an Eastern Orthodox theology professor—his mother and father both from Yugoslavia. They had immigrated to the United States back in the early sixties during the communist days under the Tito regime. Dan's father was a former Serbian Orthodox priest but left the church when he came to the United States.

Even though Dan was born in the United States, he spoke Serbo-Croatian and English at home and thus had become fluent in both languages. Dan's father was a full professor at the University of San Diego, and his family made frequent trips to Yugoslavia, traveling extensively throughout the country, visiting monasteries and churches.

Parker sitting at his desk went on, "Dan, I want you to know that as your commander, it's my duty to inform you that you are being reassigned to the Pentagon, effective immediately. This is a temporary, three-month assignment. You're still assigned to the 75th Airlift Squadron. Your assignment to the Pentagon is classified *top secret*. You are not to discuss this assignment with anyone. In fact, that's why these two men are here tonight—and to arrange your transportation back to Washington."

"Did you say, tonight, sir? What about my crew rest, what about my truck, what about my personal life?"

"As you know Dan, I have the authority to waive your post mission crew rest. However, these two men have assured me that your crew rest will be honored so you can get some rest before you leave for Washington. Your private vehicle will be safe here in the squadron parking lot for now. In fact, why don't you leave me your keys just in case we have to move it?"

Dan handed Parker his car keys.

"As far as your personal life, I can't comment on that; you'll have to handle that as time allows."

Sergeant Perez spoke up, "Captain, we have our orders, and we have a schedule to keep. We've been told there will be arrangements for your personal life within the next few days. I have two documents for you to sign. The first is acknowledgment and acceptance of your orders; the second is a confidentiality statement. Please sign here, sir."

Dan read and signed the two documents then handed them across the desk to Parker. Parker gave both documents to Perez along with Dan's medical, personnel records, and his Isolated Personnel Report Card (ISOPREP). Combat Search and Rescue forces use the ISOPREP card to authenticate the identity of downed or captured aviators. An airman can only have one ISOPREP card on file to prevent the information from being compromised.

"I'll make sure these get safely to Washington. Do you have your bags in the building?" asked Perez.

"They're down the hall in the loading area."

Parker said, "Dan, I'll get your personal bags. You can change into your civilian clothes here in my office instead of using the bathroom. Again, you are not to speak to anyone about this assignment. If someone from your crew should still be in the building or come back to the squadron, we don't want anyone to know that you're being transferred out in this manner."

As Parker left the room, Perez said to Dan, "We don't have a *need to know*, so we don't know anything about your new assignment. Please don't ask us any questions because, frankly, we don't know. We've been tasked to hand-deliver your orders and secure your crew rest and transportation back to Washington, that's it."

Evans stood up, "I'll bring the car out front. I think we're about finished here."

The government vehicle drove off the squadron parking lot at 10:32 PM and headed for the north gate at Travis Air Force Base. His reassignment and transfer had all happened so fast that he didn't have time to think about the seriousness of the situation. He realized Parker was just doing his job and probably followed scripted instructions from the two Army men. Reality hit Dan when he noticed they were traveling eastbound on I-80 toward Sacramento. Dan presumed they were going to Sacramento International Airport and thus rested his head against the side of the window and closed his eyes. He hadn't realized how tired he was. Just before he dozed off, he heard Evans mumble to Perez, "I've called ahead, and everything is on schedule tonight. It'll be tight, but we'll make it."

Twenty-five minutes later at the Amtrak station in Davis, Sgt. Perez awakened him, "Let's go, Captain, you've got a train to catch."

Dan muttered, "Where are we?"

"The Amtrak station in Davis. Have your ID cards ready so we can get your ticket."

Dan heard the sound of a train horn in the distance as the Amtrak Coast Starlight from Los Angeles to Seattle approached the platform.

"Is this some kind a joke? You can't be serious. I was expecting a night at the Sheraton before boarding a plane to Washington." The three men walked hurriedly to the ticket counter.

"We have a reservation for Dan Radivich," Perez told the Amtrak agent.

The Amtrak agent, a heavyset man in his mid-fifties with gray hair, looked at Dan over the top of his silver reading glasses.

"Can I see your ID?"

Dan took out his driver's license and handed it to the agent. The agent looked down at his computer terminal and spoke without looking up.

"Here's your ticket to Seattle and your follow-on tickets to Chicago and Washington."

Dan turned around and looked at the two Army sergeants, "This is a mistake. It'll take me days to get to Washington by train."

"We have our orders, Captain. We don't care how long it takes you to get to Washington. We're here to make sure you're aboard this train *tonight*."

The Amtrak agent interrupted, "The train will be leaving in ten minutes. You'd best be getting to the platform."

As the Amtrak Coast Starlight came to a full stop, Dan could see the conductors getting off the train and direct the few waiting passenger to their respective cars. Sergeant Evans helped Dan with his bags. The three men walked up to one of the conductors. Evans said, "Just one boarding for Seattle."

The conductor, a young woman with an innocent face and long hair tucked under her conductor's hat, said, "Can I see your ticket please?"

Dan handed her his tickets.

"Right this way, Mr. Radivich. You'll be in the second sleeper car on the first floor."

"At least I'll be able to get some sleep tonight."

As Dan approached the sleeping car, an elderly, distinguished-looking man stepped off the train holding a large brown envelope and motioned to Dan, "Are you Daniel Radivich?"

"That's me, and who are you?"

The Balkan Network

"I'm here to escort you back to Washington. Are those the two men that brought you here?"

"Yah, they gave me a ride from the base."

The distinguished looking man looked at the two Army men. "I'll take over from here. Do you have something for me?"

Sergeant Perez handed him Dan's records and ISOPREP card. "Everything is here, sir, just as you requested."

"Thank you. You two men are free to go."

"Have a safe trip, sir," replied Perez.

The elderly man got back on the train. Dan grabbed his bags and gave the two army sergeants a polite nod.

"Your compartment's right next to mine, Dan," said the elderly gentleman.

Dan entered the sleeping compartment and was surprised to see the bed already made. The elderly man stepped in then closed the door.

"Before we go any further, let me formally introduce myself. My name is Harold Mattingly. You can call me Hal. My official title is Undersecretary of Defense for Intelligence. I work specifically with the Defense Intelligence Agency in Washington."

Harold Mattingly was in his late seventies, tall and slender, with thinning white hair, and surprisingly well dressed for train travel in a dark-blue, pinstriped suit with white shirt and red tie. His face was long and narrow with a thin white mustache trimmed neatly over his lip. He wore a pair of gold-rimmed reading glasses that hung on his nose.

"I'm here to brief you on your new assignment in Washington. Can I take a seat?"

Dan nodded his head and motioned to the seat in the compartment. "Okay, sir, you definitely got my attention.

I'm sorry for being rude and disrespectful; I had no idea who you were. I'm all ears now."

"First, my apologies for the rush, but we wanted to make sure you were onboard this train tonight. Second, I was told to make sure you get some rest, so we've arranged this sleeping compartment for your trip. I understand you've already had a long day."

"That's right; I've been up for almost twenty hours now."

Mattingly looked at his watch, "The train leaves at exactly eleven thirty-three. The Amtrak attendant has already turned your bed down. You can sleep anytime you want."

At that moment, Dan heard the train horn, and the Amtrak Coast Starlight pulled slowly away from the station. As he looked out his compartment window, he saw Sergeant Perez and Sergeant Evans give him a final wave.

Mattingly continued, "Before you turn in for the night however, I need to ask you for a few personal belongings. I need your driver's license, military ID card, credit cards, ATM cards, cell phone, and your military passport if you have one."

Dan handed Mattingly his whole wallet and cell phone and said, "Keep the change, don't worry about me leaving or jumping off the train. I'm too tired for those heroics."

"Don't forget your passport."

"Sorry, I almost forgot. I'll have to get it out of my flight suit pocket." Dan fumbled in his suitcase, found his passport, and handed it to Mattingly.

"Thank you, Dan." Mattingly placed the wallet, passport, and cell phone inside the large brown envelope he was carrying, then sealed it. "You'll get your personal belongings and military records back in due time. Have a good night."

Mattingly left the compartment and closed the door behind him. Dan could hear the adjacent door close and muffled voices from inside. He brushed the thought off and took a long, hot shower in the small washroom and then climbed into bed. He was surprised to find the bed comfortable, and with the rocking motion from the train, had no trouble falling fast asleep.

Chapter 5
SERBIA

Half a world away in Belgrade, Yugoslavia, Milan Belic, the owner of the Overland Airfreight Company, was locking his office door. This had been a slow week. The war in Bosnia and now neighboring Kosovo was challenging the airfreight business. Most commercial aircraft were still banned from Serbian overflight. This meant aircraft had to traverse around Serbia, thus increasing the cost of shipping. Since business was slow, he could concentrate on his other job: overseeing locations of Serbian anti-aircraft missile sites near and around Novi Sad. As usual, there was nothing new to report to CIA Headquarters in Langley. The Serbs had positioned the surface-to-air-missile sites outside the city of Novi Sad along the Danube. In addition, two armored divisions were in position on the eastern side of the river waiting to cross into Croatia. All sites were functioning normally. There had been no changes since his last failed attempt acquiring information on the target area.

Belic took the elevator from his fifth-floor office to the ground floor and walked three blocks to his favorite restau-

The Balkan Network

rant, the Trandafilovic. It was well after eight o'clock when he arrived, and the establishment was crowded for the busy dinner hour. Belic approached the maitre d', "Same table and location please."

The maitre d' nodded politely, "Right this way, Mr. Belic."

Belic sat down and ordered his typical meal for the day, which consisted of grilled pork cutlets and tomatoes. Just before he finished his meal, another man about Belic's age sat down next to him and spoke in Russian, "Good evening, Milan, do you mind if I join you tonight?"

"Not at all, Yuri, have a seat; I was getting ready to order dessert. I wondered when you were going to pay me a personal visit after our failure last month. I take it you have a new plan?"

Yuri Pavol worked at the US Embassy in Belgrade as a defense attaché using the codename Preacher. Pavol was not his real name, but the only name Belic knew him by. He had worked as Belic's CIA handler during the Cold War and retired in 1991. Now the United States and NATO were planning an attack on Serbia and needed information. The U.S government asked Pavol to come out of retirement and organize the network.

The two continued to speak in Russian because it sounded similar to Serbo-Croatian; however, no one would fully understand their conversations if overheard. "Tell me, Milan, do you think you could have the report by tonight? My boss is expecting activity in your sector shortly, and he wants to make sure there are no surprises when he places his order."

"I'll have the report sent in on time. I don't foresee any changes in the foreseeable future."

"Good, I thought so. Yes, we have a new plan in place.

Everything is proceeding on schedule. By the way, what do you recommend for dessert?"

The two men finished their meal then Pavol said, "I'm leaving for Bosnia tonight. I'll be coordinating activities from there. If you need to contact me, use my primary number." He rose from the dinner table and said, "I think you can take care of the bill. After all, we're paying you handsomely for your efforts. Have a good evening, Milan."

After dinner, Belic returned to his apartment. The coffeepot and breakfast dishes were still in the sink where he left them that morning. He sat down at the small kitchen table and took out his laptop computer from his briefcase. He removed a cell phone from his coat pocket and connected it to the laptop with the cable adaptor. He turned on his computer and typed in a number on his cell phone. Within seconds, a message appeared on his computer screen that read, "Central Intelligence Agency, Secure Sat-Com Data Link Established." He transmitted his report to CIA Headquarters, then removed the cable adaptor and cell phone from his laptop and turned off the computer. As he was about to get ready for bed, he heard a ring from the cell phone on his nightstand and answered it.

"Good evening, Vecili. I've transmitted my report to Langley. Everything is proceeding as planned. I should have your requested information in the next few weeks."

Twenty-five miles away, outside the city of Novi Sad, Serbian paramilitary leader Vecili Vorchek secured his phone call with Belic and looked across the evening sky. Vorchek was with a special paramilitary detachment of the JNA, handpicked by Milosevic personally, to carry out the most secret and brutal details of the JNA. Vorchek gained his reputation during the 1991 Battle of Vukovar in eastern Croatia. He was appointed head of the Serbian paramilitary force and established a base in the Serb-popu-

The Balkan Network

lated Croatian suburb of Borovo-Selo. It was there that Vecili took control of all JNA forces in the Battle of Vukovar and integrated his paramilitary forces into the poorly motivated conscripts of the JNA. The results were remarkable. Although his troops were relatively untrained, they made up for this with a xenophobic dedication to the cause, thanks to Vorchek.

Vorchek thought to himself, *all the tanks and antiaircraft batteries are functioning normally.* As he walked over to one of the Soviet-made T-54 tanks, he moved it several feet to the left then another foot to the right. All the fake T-54 tanks and fixed SA-2 antiaircraft batteries were made of plywood and cardboard. These *dummies* were painted with a special metallic paint that gave off a much higher heat signature than wood or cardboard. When American spy satellites detected these dummies, they would give off a heat signature similar to real tanks and missiles. In addition, the special paint allowed the heat signature to dissipate slowly, giving the illusion the vehicles and equipment were real.

Vorchek looked at his assistant, Domonik Slavo, "We're ready to sting like a bee. It won't be much longer until we have the NATO scum in our grasps. It's payback time for Bosnia."

Vorchek selected Slavo to be his special assistant. His job was to track down and kill enemy fighters. Slavo also played a key role in the Battle of Vukovar: he commanded the Young Tigers. In November of 1991, Slavo, with his paramilitary and regular JNA forces, launched a successful amphibious assault across the Danube near the city of Ilok. He met Vorchek's forces and spearheaded an assault on Vukovar.

Vorchek dropped his cigarette and crushed it into the ground. "As usual, you can use any method to find the

NATO filth that flies over our skies and kills our people. Our traps are ready to be sprung."

"Four of my Young Tigers are in place along the Croatian border. They're on the lookout for more U.S. Special Forces."

At the same time, at 36,000 feet over the skies of Bosnia-Herzegovina, the E-8C JSTARS aircraft using the call sign Wizard 86, was on patrol. The E-8C Joint Surveillance Target Attack Radar System is an airborne command, control, and reconnaissance platform. Its primary mission is to provide military commanders with real-time tactical information. The E-8C is a Boeing 707 commercial aircraft, extensively modified with radar and communications equipment. The most prominent feature is the twenty-seven-foot-long, canoe-shaped ray dome under the forward fuselage that houses the side-looking phased array antenna. The radar and computer subsystems on the E-8C can gather and display detailed tactical information on ground forces. The information is relayed in real time to the Army and Marine Corps. ground stations, and so this information can be processed immediately.

Onboard Wizard 86, working his radar console, Captain Jud Anderson, USAF, pointed his radar antenna toward Serbia and watched movement of ground forces. The latest version of the JSTARS radar included an enhancement that could pick up passive radar returns to anyone with interrogation equipment. This feature allowed the JSTARS to monitor locations of human assets twenty-four hours a day. Captain Anderson activated the passive radar system onto a target working in the center of Belgrade. The target reply indicated the asset was that of a U.S. intelligence operative. The asset was moving away from the city toward the Bosnian border. Captain

Anderson switched his com-link and talked directly to the JSTARS airborne commander, Colonel Frank Owens.

"Sir, we have positive radar contact with the asset in Belgrade. He's moving toward the Bosnian border. The network is starting to take up positions."

"Thank you, Captain, let me know if you encounter any problems with his signal."

Chapter 6
OREGON

At nine in the morning outside Klamath Falls, Oregon, Dan woke up from his deep sleep. Everything seemed like a dream. One moment he was coming home from a ten-day trip across the Pacific, and the next he was onboard a train headed across the country. Dan slept on the lower bunk and opened the curtains to let in the sunlight. It was a beautiful winter morning, and he could see the snow-capped ridges of the Cascade Range in the distance. He had never traveled on an Amtrak train before, let alone slept on one.

He took another long, hot shower and put on the wrinkled clothes from the night before. It occurred to him he had not eaten anything since leaving Yokota Air Base more than twenty-seven hours ago and he was very hungry. Dan heard a knock on the compartment door. He opened the door and let Mattingly in. "Good morning, Dan. We let you sleep in for a while and didn't want to wake you until we heard movement in the compartment. How did you sleep?"

"I never heard or felt anything."

"I'm glad to hear that. Can I have a seat?"

"Sure, make yourself comfortable."

Mattingly sat on the edge of the bed, "Now that you've had some rest, let me pick up where we left off last night. Your assignment to the Pentagon is classified *top secret*. As you know, there's a war going on in Yugoslavia. The military doesn't have a lot of people who can speak or read their language. We need your help in putting together a team who can speak and read Serbo-Croatian."

"I think I can help you with that."

"There's a possibility we may need you inside Yugoslavia. This part of your assignment is dangerous; in fact, you could get yourself killed. If you have any reservation about this assignment and the possibility of using you overseas, you can get off the train in Seattle. We'll give you back your personal belongings—get you over to SETAC where you'll board a commercial flight to Washington and be assigned duty at the Pentagon working in the language translation department. If, on the other hand, you agree to the complete assignment, with the possibility of using you overseas, we'll continue our journey by train to Chicago and Washington. The choice is yours, but you must decide before we get to Seattle."

Dan paused for a moment realizing the seriousness of the ultimatum. "So, let me get this straight. If I don't agree to go along with you and your *complete* assignment, then I'll be assigned scribe work in the dungeons of the Pentagon?"

Mattingly, nodded his head in acknowledgement, "It's officially called a quarantine."

"That doesn't sound pleasant, nor does it seem like I have a lot of options in the matter."

"That's precisely the point, Dan. As you were told by your commander, you have special skills we are in desperate need of."

"Hal, can I ask you something?"

"Sure, go right ahead."

"What exactly do you mean by potentially dangerous?"

"That's a fair question. As I told you, there's a real war going on now in Yugoslavia and has been for some time. You can speak and read Serbo-Croatian fluently, Latin and Cyrillic; you've traveled extensively to Yugoslavia throughout your life; you've studied the history and geography of the region—not to mention you're a highly trained military officer. At this point, I can only give you sketchy details until you give me your decision. Let's just say we may need you where your talents are the strongest."

Dan couldn't resist asking, "So, because I speak and read the language, does this assignment involve covert activity inside Yugoslavia?"

"Possibly, but we won't know until we get to Washington, and we won't know until you give us a decision."

Dan contemplated what Mattingly said. "I thought the CIA does all that cloak-and-dagger stuff. Why can't they do the work? They're supposed to be the experts in this field. I'm just a pilot, not a spy. I don't know anything about intelligence work."

"The military doesn't have any spies, and you're in the military. Dan, you are correct, the CIA does all the cloak-and-dagger stuff. Here at the Pentagon, we like to call it tactical assistance or threat analyses, *TA* for short. We may need you to provide the Defense Department with TA. That's all I can say."

"TA, that's a new one," Dan said sarcastically. "Can I ask you another silly question?"

"There's no such thing as a silly question from now on."

"Can I get something to eat before I make my decision?"

"By all means. Your meals are included in your train fare. I've already had breakfast, but if you'd like, I'll accompany you to the dining car. I could use another cup of coffee."

"Great, please show me the way, sir."

The two men walked to the dining car and took a table near the rear. Once comfortably seated, Dan ordered breakfast from the menu while Mattingly ordered another cup of coffee. Dan was beyond being hungry and now ravenous. He devoured the eggs, bacon, and pancakes he ordered. The two hardly spoke to each other during breakfast—when they did, they limited their conversations to small talk. Dan got the impression Mattingly's mind was already somewhere else or thinking about someone else. He could see that Mattingly had cold, steel blue eyes and deep wrinkles on his face. He didn't notice them the night before, but maybe it was because it had been late and he was very tired. After eating his breakfast, Dan, speaking quietly, said, "Mr. Mattingly, what's your background? How did you end up working in your present occupation?"

"I served in the military during World War II. Back then, I was a nineteen-year-old private assigned as a clerk and courier for General Eisenhower's staff. After the war, I went back to school and earned my degrees. Eventually, I got a job as a teacher of history and political science at Stanford University. At Stanford, I was introduced to several people who were consultants to the U.S. government—mainly Soviet Geopolitical Doctrine. One of my colleagues was asked to work for the White House National Security Staff during the Eisenhower administration. I was asked to join the team, mainly because I'd worked with Eisenhower before during the war. Once you get in the inner circles and do good work, one job leads to another."

Dan remembered reading about people like Mattingly

who spent their whole lives working behind the scenes within the United States government. He didn't say another word and pondered his limited choices. He thought this could be his way of getting out of the Air Force flying business and into the areas where he had a deep passion, namely geopolitics. As he finished breakfast and had one last cup of coffee, he looked into Mattingly's eyes.

"Should I call you Doctor Mattingly?"

"Hal will be fine."

"Okay, Hal, I'll do it. I'm with you one-hundred percent. I'll help the Defense Department with whatever they need me for; even doing work overseas. This must be extremely important for you to go through this much trouble to get me this far."

"Thank you, Dan; we knew we could count on you. With that said and done, there is someone I'd like you to meet; please follow me."

This did not come as a surprise to Dan because Mattingly spoke all along as if someone else was working with him. Mattingly got up from his seat and walked out from the dining car. "Right this way, Dan."

The two men walked back to Mattingly's compartment, knocked on the door, then entered. As Dan adjusted his eyes to the bright light in the compartment, he realized he recognized the figure seated against the bright window.

"Dan, I do believe you already know Professor Kostinic. We boarded the train together last night in Emeryville."

Mattingly continued and addressed the seated figure, "Doctor Kostinic, I have good news: Captain Radivich has just agreed to join our venture."

Dan could hardly believe his eyes. Seated in front of him was his old college teacher. He had Kostinic for several classes as an undergraduate student. Kostinic was well into his eighties: small, frail in build, five feet seven inches tall, thinning silver hair, and wearing dark horned-rimmed glasses. He wore a camel hair jacket, white shirt, and red bow tie, making him look like the typical academic. He seemed a little thinner than Dan remembered, but that was over fourteen years ago. Kostinic could barely stand to shake Dan's hand. Kostinic spoke in a low but soothing voice and said, "It's been a long time, Danny, do you still remember me?"

Dan shook his hand, "How could I forget you Professor Kostinic? I took four classes from you. I especially remember your exams."

"I recall you did very well on all of them if I'm not mistaken."

"That's because I re-created your lecture notes from memory and put them on paper almost word for word."

"That was my plan. I think you have something close to total recall. You remembered almost everything I said. I only gave As to the students that were listening and paying attention."

Kostinic was the last of a dying breed and the most unlikely person you would ever suspect as being a former secret agent. Before teaching at Berkeley, he spent time in the military during World War II. He had degrees in political science and geography, spoke fluent French, Russian, Ukrainian, and Serbo-Croatian. When he entered the Army in 1942, they found out about his unique skills and reassigned him immediately to the Office of Strategic Service, the wartime precursor to the Central Intelligence Agency.

As a young agent with the OSS, Kostinic worked behind occupied German lines in Yugoslavia. Kostinic spent the war years in various eastern European assignments. He was based in Cairo originally then moved on to Bari, Italy, where he was first a member, and later, chief of the Balkan Section Field Office. Dan also recalled that one of Professor Kostinic's jobs as an OSS agent during the war was setting up covert networks inside Nazi-occupied Serbia and helping downed Allied airmen escape to friendly territory. All the pieces of this intricate puzzle were starting to fall into place. Dan realized that one of the reasons why he left Travis Air Force Base in the manner he did was to be on board the train the same time as Mattingly and Kostinic.

"Have a seat, Danny, and make yourself comfortable because we have a lot to discuss. Can I still call you Danny?"

"Yes, by all means. Danny, will be fine, sir."

Dan took a seat at the table set up by the Amtrak service attendants as Kostinic continued. "Pretend this is just another one of my lectures except this time you can't take notes. You'll have to commit everything I say to memory, just like you did during my lectures."

Mattingly interrupted, "Dan, I need to inform you the Secretary of Defense has authorized me to use whatever resources we have to come up with this plan. That is why I have asked Professor Kostinic for his help. The Secretary has tasked me to put together a team made up of DOD personnel to insert into portions of the former Yugoslavia in preparation for the air campaign that is about to begin. Before NATO can send in their fighters and bombers, they need a human network in place. The NATO air armada will be enormous; well over a thousand aircraft will be flying over the skies of Yugoslavia at any given time. We need to have people in place on the ground in case one of our planes gets shot down. In addition, we may need to rely on that network to provide tactical assistance on the air campaign."

It was Kostinic's turn to talk.

"Let's talk about some of the peculiarities of this mission. Up to now, Danny, the CIA has always taken the lead in foreign, clandestine, and covert intelligence matters overseas. However, with the breakup of Yugoslavia into several countries, the CIA was left with no human assets in place. During the Cold War, the U.S. intelligence community did not consider the Tito regime a threat to the national security of the United States and thus had no need for human intelligence coming out of Yugoslavia. Most of the intelligence on Yugoslavia came from our spy satellites, other agencies, or the NSA. The CIA's only human asset during the Cold War was a contract operative by the name of Milan Belic. During the Cold War, he was the Pan Am station manager at Belgrade International Airport. With the demise of Pan Am back in the early nineties, Belic lost his job—and thus his cover—and was put out in the cold by CIA. The information he provided in the past during the Tito regime had been very good. The last we heard about Belic was that he set up shop in Belgrade as the owner of an air freight company."

Mattingly took a seat in the compartment and continued, "Because of this lack of reliable human assets in Serbia, the CIA has asked the Defense Department for help."

Dan sat up in his seat and listened intently as Kostinic spoke.

"Danny, let me give you an example of the importance of having a human network in place on the ground during wartime in today's environment. Most recently during the 1995 Bosnian Campaign, NATO lost a Luftwaffe aircraft to enemy fire. The crew ejected from their crippled aircraft and landed in Serbian-occupied Bosnia. They tried to evade but didn't get far. Serbian paramilitary forces captured the crew before SARs could get them out. The Serbs, still have a deep hatred for the Germans even some fifty-five years after World War II. The two German pilots were tortured, mutilated, and eventually killed."

Dan said, "I didn't realize the Germans lost any aircraft during that conflict."

"There's a lot of things that aren't public knowledge, Danny, simply because the U.S. and NATO didn't want to advertise their failures. They only glorified their limited successes. Remember the Air Force F-16 shot down over Gorazde?"

"Yah, I think the pilot even wrote a book about the incident."

"When he ejected, there was no human network in place on the ground to assist him. The military arrogantly thought they could get the job done with SARs alone."

Mattingly added, "The Marines tried to send a rescue team from one of the carriers, but they were unsuccessful. They arrived too late and the Serbs were alerted to the rescue maneuver, so the Marines called it off."

"Fortunately, Danny, the F-16 pilot evaded on his own until we could mount another rescue mission. It was shear overwhelming military force—three hundred aircraft, two carrier battle groups—and luck that rescued our F-16 pilot. We just got lucky that time."

"We can't leave anything to luck, nor commit forces of that magnitude." said Mattingly. "That's why we need reliable, friendly forces in place *that we can trust* when the air war kicks off."

Kostinic leaned closer to Dan and said, "Danny, when Hal asked me to help him provide assets for the DIA, I immediately thought of you. I can't physically go out in the field and set up these networks, so I want you to take my place. You have everything we're looking for: You can speak and read Serbo-Croatian fluently; you're an Air Force officer and pilot; you're an excellent marksman in small arms; you spent time in the Special Ops Command; you're a Desert Storm veteran; a graduate of the Air Force Tactics School at Nellis Air Force Base; you already know Serbia and Croatia. I'll teach you everything I know about being a field operative."

Kostinic coughed a few times then took a drink of water from a glass. "Danny, I can't do this work anymore. Will you take my place?"

After a few moments of total silence in the compartment, Dan finally spoke up, "I can see the seriousness of the situation and the lack of reliable assets in the area. I remember the troubles we had getting our downed pilots out of Bosnia, especially the F-16 pilot. What would you like me to do?"

"Help us select the team for starters," said Kostinic.

"Where would you like me to begin?"

"We knew we could count on you, Danny—we just wanted to make sure you fully understood what you were getting into and had no reservations about the potential dangers ahead."

Mattingly stood up and looked out the window. "You made the right choice, Dan. There is no one else alive who knows more about setting up covert operations inside Yugoslavia than Professor Kostinic. We do, however, have a time constraint. NATO has already committed assets for the air campaign, mainly American, British, German, and Dutch aircraft. They would like to start the air war within the next few weeks. The sooner we get the team together and in place, the sooner we can brief our aircrews on safe passage."

"So, Danny, do you have any questions for us?"

"No, sir, not yet, but I'm sure I'll have some as we go along."

"Good, let's get started. I have a lot of information to pass on to you if you're going to take my place. First, I want you to go over these files. We've searched the entire DOD database and came up with only a handful of individuals who can speak and read Cyrillic Serbo-Croatian. I would like you to narrow this list down to the most qualified individuals to work on your team. Remember, this will be your team and your responsibility. We've decided to set up your circuit as a team of six individuals: three couples, male and female. For security reasons, it's easier to operate behind enemy lines working as couples rather than individuals. I'll go over that in detail later."

Mattingly reached into the luggage rack, took out a briefcase containing several files, and handed them to Dan. "The train's scheduled to arrive in Seattle at eight thirty tonight. This gives you several hours to work on these files. If you want a break, just let us know. All we ask is that you do not leave the compartment with these files."

"No problem, I'll get on them right away. Can I have a glass of water or something to drink while I'm working?"

Kostinic asked Mattingly, "Hal, would you order us up some cold drinks?"

"Sure, I'll be right back," Hal said and left the compartment for the Club Car.

When Mattingly was out of the compartment Kostinic said, "That reminds me, Danny, under no circumstances must you or any member of the team drink scotch whiskey while inside Yugoslavia."

Dan thought to himself, *That's an unusual request.* "I don't even like the stuff. I'll take an ice-cold can of beer anytime over a shot of whiskey. Can I ask why?"

"It's because Milosevic is a scotch drinker. He only drinks the finest scotch whiskey, as do those in his inner circle. Drinking good scotch is generally associated with the Milosevic regime. We don't want to arouse any suspicion while in Yugoslavia, that's all."

"Okay, good enough, I'll make sure I don't drink any whiskey."

"Great, with that said, I'll sit back and look out the window. If you have any questions, just let me know. As you can see, my health is not what it used to be." Kostinic closed his eyes and drifted off to sleep with the rocking motion of the train.

Dan sat at the table and began working on the files. A quick glance showed the candidates came from a combined force of Army, Navy, Air Force, Marine Corps, Coast Guard, National Guard, and Reserve Forces from all over the country. He then separated the files between male and female then into officer and enlisted. At the top of the stack was the senior ranking officer, Lieutenant Commander Karoline Anne-Marie Koskov, United States Navy.

One hour later, Mattingly came back into the compartment with several soft drinks and ice. "I'm sorry for the delay. I had to make a few phone calls. I see Josef has fallen asleep. The cancer is eating him away slowly—too many years smoking cigarettes. He tires easily, but rest assured, he's still sharp. Did you know the Germans tried to surrender the entire German army in the Balkans over to Josef?"

Dan shook his head in disbelief. "No, I didn't know that. He never mentioned that in any of his lectures at Berkeley."

"It's true. General Neubacher's staff approached Josef as the senior ranking OSS officer in the Balkans and was prepared to hand over the entire German 12th Army over to the Americans instead of the British. When Josef sent word back to Bari that the Germans were interested in negotiating surrender, Churchill personally intervened and denied the request—presumably pressured by Stalin."

"He's full of surprises. I didn't know he was a statesman as well as a spy."

Mattingly continued, "Dan, there's more. I want you to know something about me before we go any further on this operation. I knew your father, Aleksandar. We go way back to the early days of the Cold War. We worked together for the U.S. government."

Dan was stunned to hear this piece of information. "My father never mentioned anything to me about doing work for the government."

"Your father probably never told you about a lot of things, Dan. Your father was a chaplain and a Marine Corps. Reservist at Camp Pendleton, am I right?"

Dan nodded his head.

"Did it ever occur to you, Dan, that there was a reason why a naturalized U.S. citizen from a former Eastern Bloc country was in the Marine Corps? Why do you think he took several unexplained trips overseas on a moment's notice? Why do you think your family made trips back and forth to Yugoslavia and Eastern Europe several times each year? Who do you think paid for the two Mercedes-Benzes your parents had in their driveway? How do you think your education was paid for?"

"I presumed it was all part of his research or in connection with the Marine Corps."

"Not entirely, Dan. Your father was asked to do certain things during the Cold War, and I might add, very sensitive things that are still highly classified today. He had the perfect cover. Let's just say not everything your father did was for research or the Serbian Orthodox church."

"I don't talk much with my father anymore. He left the University of San Diego and the Marine Corps. several years ago and is enjoying his retirement becoming somewhat of a recluse. He's still upset with me for joining the Air Force and not becoming an architect like he wanted me to."

"For obvious reasons, Dan, please do not communicate with him. We'll give you the opportunity to communicate with loved ones and family members, but for the time being, we have to keep the operation confidential."

"I understand," he said and went back to reading the files.

From the one hundred or so men and women in the files, Dan narrowed it down to thirty-five. All the candidates spoke Serbo-Croatian fluently; a few also spoke German, French, and Italian. After several hours, Kostinic woke up. Dan had just finished going over the files.

"Okay, Professor, I've narrowed it down to these thirty-five individuals. The main factors were age, physical fitness, and their ability to speak and read Serbo-Croatian—of course we won't know their true capabilities until we interview them." He handed the files over to Kostinic.

"Thanks for your work, Danny—that didn't take you long. We'll go over these files in detail later so I can start developing their cover names and stories." He placed the files back in the briefcase. "We'll make sure these get back to Washington."

The Amtrak Coast Starlight pulled into Seattle's Union Station at 8:30 PM. Mattingly was the first to get off the train, followed by Dan.

"Dan, please gather up all your luggage and stay here while I get Josef off the train."

Dan waited on the platform until most of the passengers had disembarked. The conductor helped Kostinic off the train and into a waiting electric golf cart. Dan could see that his old professor needed a lot of help just getting around and probably would not be around much longer.

Mattingly stepped onto the electric cart with Kostinic and said, "Meet us at the front of the station; we'll take a taxi downtown."

Dan followed the electric cart to the front of the station. Mattingly was already busy hiring a taxi when he arrived at the front of the depot. Dan helped the taxi driver load the luggage into the trunk then climbed into the back seat along with Mattingly. Kostinic went in the front and sat down with great relief. As the taxi departed Union Station, Mattingly turned to Dan and said, "We have a reservation for the Presidential Suite at the Sheraton downtown. Dan, you have the rest of the day off until tomorrow afternoon. Josef and I have a few things to take care of here in Seattle. Our train leaves the station at four-forty-five tomorrow afternoon. You'll be staying in our suite along with us. Consider this part of your crew rest. There will be three bedrooms, so you can come and go as you like. Be back here in time for the Amtrak Empire Builder to Chicago. Don't be late."

Dan was looking forward for some more rest and time to himself. Though he had been to Mc Cord Air Force Base in Tacoma, he had never spent time in Seattle. For starters, he'd find the nearest Laundromat.

Chapter 7
SEATTLE, WASHINGTON

After spending the day in Seattle and having a good night's sleep at the Sheraton, Dan boarded the Amtrak Empire Builder for Chicago with Kostinic and Mattingly. This time, Dan only had a Superliner Roomette. Hal and Josef continued to share the same large bedroom suite. When the train was well underway, Mattingly knocked on Dan's door.

"Put your game face on. Professor Kostinic has a lot of material to cover between here and Washington. We chose the train because it's secure and we can discuss classified information. Most importantly, we don't have to go through airport security. I brought some equipment that I need to brief you on. Besides, the train is easier on Josef—he can rest whenever he wants."

Dan followed Mattingly into his compartment. Once inside, everyone took a seat. Kostinic was seated looking at a large map of Eastern Europe taped to the side of the compartment.

"Now, let's begin," said Josef. "Overall, command responsibility for this mission is NATO Headquarters, along with the Defense Intelligence Agency. Lieutenant General James Hamilton is U.S. mission commander. General Hamilton will have command authority over the mission from DIA Headquarters in Washington. We will start the overseas portion of the mission from Aviano Air Base, Italy. From there, the circuit will be inserted into Croatia and eventually work its way into Serbia. Dan, you'll coordinate theater operations and you will be team organizer for your circuit. We chose to set up the forward operating base in Croatia because it's now a sovereign country and in close proximity to the Serbian border. Dr. Mattingly is our point of contact for training and logistics and getting everything we need for this operation. He has a talent for getting just about anything we need. For tactical reasons, I've given him the code-name *Finder*."

Mattingly spoke up, "Everyone on this mission will have a tactical name or call sign. Dan, you have the liberty of coming up with your own call sign. Just let me know what you want us to call you."

Kostinic poured himself a glass of water and continued.

"Danny, we're going back to the way it was fifty years ago during World War II. This mission will be planned and executed just like we did for the French and Balkan Resistance networks during the war. U.S. and British intelligence services had a series of covert networks working inside occupied France and Yugoslavia. Each network had a series of circuits. These circuits were then broken down into specific geographic locations. The same goes for our operations in the Balkans today. We'll have a Balkan network broken down into several circuits. I've given your circuit the code-name *Prospector*. You will conduct operations in and around the Srem district of Serbia. For security reason, each circuit will work independently from the other. That way, if one is penetrated, the others won't be compromised."

Kostinic closed his eyes and took a long pause as if reliving the past.

"One of the hard lessons we learned during World War II was that the circuits became too large as subcircuits combined with other subcircuits. This made it easy for German counterintelligence to infiltrate. We had too many people coming and going, and it was hard to keep track of all the agents. To further increase security, we'll limit our exposure by operating as couples, male and female, and in small elements."

Dan interrupted, "Professor Kostinic, isn't it dangerous for women to operate behind enemy lines like this?"

"Not necessarily in our case. In France during the war, SOE had an element consisting of husband and wife. They provided some of the best intelligence for the Allies throughout the war, and most importantly, the couple avoided the Gestapo and survived. In addition, if you'll recall from my lectures at Berkeley, my wife Celeste, and I spent several months as OSS and SOE operatives working deep inside Yugoslavia. We successfully avoided not only the Gestapo but the Ustashe as well. You have to remember, Danny, the JNA and their paramilitaries will be looking for highly trained special forces, not innocent-looking civilians speaking Serbo-Croatian. Also, the situation in Serbia is a lot more stable, and I might add, less hostile than Nazi occupied France or Serbia and should not be a problem. Finally, with our technology and satellite tracking systems, we'll know the location of our operatives twenty-four hours a day, seven days a week. That technology didn't exist back in 1943."

Mattingly said, "In addition, we'll have two carrier battle groups, the USS Carl Vincent and USS Nimitz on station in the Adriatic, along with NATO Combat Search and Rescue forces prepositioned in Bosnia. If any of our operatives should get into trouble, a rescue operation can be executed in a matter of hours."

Kostinic went on, "Let me bring you up to date about what's going on inside the former Yugoslavia. Hal and I have pieced together this information from our contacts at the Russian Consulate in San Francisco and from media journalists working inside Yugoslavia. As near as we can tell, no one within the U.S. government knows more about what's going on inside Yugoslavia than the two of us. It will be several years after the war before the CIA sorts out the mess. It started back in early 1991. Slovenia and Croatia declared their independence from Yugoslavia. Serbia responded by taking portions of Slovenia and Croatia by force. Serbian military forces took from Croatia what they decided were areas of Serbian settlement, namely Eastern Slavonia, a portion of Western Slavonia, and a large bulge of Krajina that curves around Bosnia and pushes toward the coast near Zadar. Belgrade had desires to acquire Zadar, thus giving them access to the sea; however, they were not successful in keeping the city due in large part by massive NATO and European Union support. All together, Croatia lost 30 percent of its territory to the Serbs between 1991 and 1992. In 1992, the conflict engulfed Bosnia-Herzegovina. It started out as a two-way conflict between Serbs and non-Serbs then later developed into a three-way conflict between Serbs, Muslims, and Croats with factional infighting in all three ethnic groups at one time or another."

Kostinic took off his glasses and rubbed his eyes then took another sip of water.

"Danny, not since World War II have we seen some of the most horrific atrocities toward humanity taking place

The Balkan Network

in Srebrenica, Bosnia-Herzegovina. I don't even want to discuss what happened there. These atrocities were committed not only by the Serbs but by Croatians as well. One group can't be blamed more than the other. Anyway, Croatian forces along with NATO support successfully intervened and recaptured areas controlled by the Serbs, which eventually led to a cease-fire and the Dayton Peace Accords ending the Bosnian war. The Serbs are still not satisfied with the outcome of the Dayton Peace Accords, and they have escalated hostilities into neighboring Kosovo. They're doing the same thing to ethnic Albanians as they did to ethnic Bosnians in Herzegovina. This has gone too far. The European community has allied with NATO to intervene and take control of the situation before it heightens into another ethnic cleansing operation. This brings us to the situation we're in today. NATO is ready to remove Milosevic from Kosovo by force."

Kostinic slowly stood up and moved to the map on the wall.

"Now that I've brought you up to date on the geopolitical situation, let me give you an outline of our plan. It will involve three phases. Phase One: The domestic stateside operation where we'll train and assemble the team. You'll help us select the military personnel needed for this mission. Phase Two: Setting up the Croatian forward operating base. Here, the team will establish a working base to conduct insertion operations into Serbia. Finally, Phase Three: Serbian Operations, where the team will set up locations inside Serbia and launch the tactical operations Hal discussed earlier."

Mattingly said, "NATO Headquarters believes the air war will last seven to ten days; after that, the Serbs will surrender. However, Josef and I think the air war will last much longer, perhaps as long as six months."

Kostinic pointed to a location on the map near the Croat-Serb border.

"As of this week, Serbian forces have decided to move back into portions of Eastern Croatia. Our sources inside Croatia have detected movement of forces along the Serb and Croatian frontier, mainly along the small finger of land between the Danube and Sava Rivers known as Slavonia. This area is where our NATO aircraft will egress out of Serbia once the air campaign begins. We don't know what the Serbs are up to. They've come across the border in small numbers, perhaps as few as four or five at a time; they could be doing reconnaissance work; they could be terrorists. Should you inadvertently encountering these forces while in Croatia, try to act normal and go about your business. We don't want any surprises."

Dan asked, "How can we tell whether they're Serb paramilitaries or legitimate Croatian military?"

"That's an excellent question, Danny. If our sources are correct, these Serb paramilitaries forces will probably be much younger, perhaps in their teens or early twenties."

Kostinic changed the subject and moved on.

"The easiest way to move within Serbia and Croatia is by working as couples. Traveling as couples is less suspicious and reduces the possibility of being stopped for questioning. The normal way of getting operatives and their equipment into the field is by airdrop. However, in this situation, it's too risky without a welcoming party to greet the shipments. We'd be doing a blind drop. Therefore, we've developed an alternate plan. We've learned the best way to travel and move around Yugoslavia is associated with agriculture and food production. The border between Croatia and Serbia is an open border to commerce, especially agriculture. No one likes to have their food supplies cut off, not even paramilitary or regular military forces, so

The Balkan Network

we'll develop the cover as European Union humanitarian relief and supply representatives while operating inside Croatia and Agriculture Inspectors while working inside Serbia. Hal has arranged three trucks with EU stamped on the doors. We'll move the team and equipment inside Croatia and Serbia using these vehicles. Danny, you're more familiar with the Serbian countryside now. Do you have any suggestions on transport once the team gets inside Serbia?"

Dan thought for a second then said, "Motorcycles and ATVs are used extensively now in the agricultural business. The motorcycle provides a multipurpose means of transport in all types of terrain and provides for a quick getaway. The motorcycle can also be hidden easier than a car. Most importantly it's better on fuel, which could be a problem inside Serbia once the air war starts. The ATVs could also be a valuable means of transportation on the farm roads."

"Do you have any ideas on makes and models?"

"I'll have to think about that, but it has to be lightweight and rugged at the same time. U.S. Special Forces use several different models. As far as the ATVs, Honda makes an excellent model called the Rancher."

Kostinic said, "Come to think of it, there were operatives inside France and Yugoslavia during the war that used captured German motorcycles as a means of transport, and they worked well."

Mattingly nodded his head in approval. "I'll incorporate them into the plan."

Kostinic continued his briefing. "Once the team sets up the forward operating base in Croatia, there are a few things we'd like the circuit to do before moving into Serbia. First, we'd like them to find an escape route back into Croatia. This is the most difficult and dangerous part of the entire mission because it involves land mines. The Croatians mined the border heavily during the 1991 War of Independence and the Siege of Vukovar. There is no definite border along the frontier in Eastern Croatia because it's mostly flat terrain. The only things that clearly mark the boundary are the land mines. Your team will have to search the area and find a safe route back into Croatia in case the primary extraction route is compromised or unavailable."

"How do we perform this?" asked Dan.

"We'll use metal detectors. We have state-of-the-art devices that are small, compact, and can detect explosive materials and metal up to three feet underground," replied Mattingly.

After briefing Dan for five hours, Mattingly told everyone to take a break and get something to eat. "I'll have dinner sent to the room for Josef and me. Dan, if you would like to take a dinner break, the dining car is still open. Remember to limit your conversations to small talk. We don't want any eavesdroppers."

After dinner, everyone met back in Mattingly's compartment and Kostinic resumed the training. He showed Dan maps, satellite photos, and detailed photographs of Yugoslavian air defenses.

"Danny, up to now, the Serbs have not turned on their sophisticated Soviet Air Defense radar systems during an attack, and we don't know why. It could be they learned something from the Iraqis. During Desert Storm, the first attack waves on Iraq came from surface ships and submarines in the Persian Gulf. The U.S. fired several hundred drones on Iraq from sea. The Iraqis, sensing an all-out attack from the Gulf, turned on all their air defenses and fired at the incoming drones. The results were disastrous. The Coalition countered with a huge air attack from

The Balkan Network

the west with a massive air armada, destroying practically every SAM site in Iraq and quickly establishing air superiority."

Dan absorbed all the information then took a can of beer from a bucket of ice, opened it, and took a long drink.

Kostinic continued, "In order for the Serbian SA-5 and SA-6 radars to work as the Soviets designed them, you have to turn them on and track incoming aircraft. NATO planners knew this back during the 1995 Bosnian Campaign. NATO F-16s tried to take out the air defenses, but they had no way of knowing where those sites were located. The Serbs used the highly mobile SA-6s, keeping their radars off during an attack. Eventually NATO made the wrong decision and assumed these radars were inoperative or defective and decided to send in their fighters and bombers without destroying Serb air defenses. The results were costly. Not only were the Serbian air defenses working, but it also appeared they deliberately left them off in hopes of luring NATO aircraft into a trap. At the last minute, the Serbs turned on their radars and were able to knock out several NATO fighters. This was how we lost the F-16 and Luftwaffe Tornado over Bosnia. The mobile SA-6 antiaircraft operators turned on their radars at the last moment, just as the NATO bombers were making their exit runs out of Bosnia."

Mattingly said, "Once the team is inserted into Serbia, one of our missions, Dan, is to find out why the Serbs are not turning on their radars. Second, we need to find the mobile launchers so we can take them out and carry out the air campaign over Serbia with complete "air supremacy," as the Brits like to call it."

Kostinic interrupted Mattingly, "Now for the disturbing news. We're not comfortable with this part of the mission and you have to be aware of the situation. The

CIA has requested all tactical information coming out of Yugoslavia by DOD personnel be forwarded to Langley. We've been told this information will be used to update their database."

Mattingly conceded, "I don't like this, but we've got no choice. CIA has the lead in foreign, covert intelligence matters; they dictate the rules."

"Is there a reason why you're not comfortable with this arrangement?" asked Dan.

There was silence in the compartment. Finally, Mattingly broke the hush.

"This is something new to CIA. They've always had total control of information in foreign operations. Since their existence, they've never let the military conduct foreign covert operations on their own. They're only letting DOD do this because they're up against a time constraint, and they don't have time to come up with their own assets. We don't mind sending the tactical information to Langley as long as it doesn't compromise the locations of our operatives. This is the part that's troubling to us."

"Can we trust the CIA? How will we know if we're being double-crossed?"

This time, Kostinic spoke, "The answer is, we don't."

Hal took a sip from a soft drink and chose his words carefully, "Josef and I have decided to pass the tactical information on to NATO first then wait up to six hours before we transmit to Langley. Langley will be expecting the reports because they'll get a copy of the tasking orders from NATO. The six hours will give us time to determine if our human intelligence assets have been compromised. Within six hours, any information coming from one of our field operatives can already be obsolete or invalid anyway."

Kostinic added, "It's a real legitimate concern, Danny; we'll just have to keep a close eye on the situation at all

The Balkan Network

times. The whole idea of having a human network in place is to provide real-time tactical information to commanders. This is different from anything the U.S military or the intelligence community has done in the past. Even during Desert Storm most of the information going back to Central Command Headquarters in Riyadh was out-of-date and provided useless information to commanders. Now we have the new updated JSTARS. The JSTARS will be on station over the Adriatic and Bosnia twenty-four hours a day. We can also communicate directly with them at anytime. With the JSTARS and our field operatives, we can provide military commanders the real-time tactical information they're looking for."

"How will we communicate directly with the JSTARS?"

Mattingly answered, "I'll get into that later when we have the whole team assembled in Washington, but to answer your specific question, we'll use secure cell phones and call them directly." Mattingly went on, "As you can tell, we still have a lot of details to work out. We need to move fast because our timetable is three weeks away, which means we need to get started now. We also don't have the time to thoroughly train our team. We'll have to do that as we go along. The good news is they won't need a lot of sophisticated training—mostly concealment and evasion and use of equipment. That's why we've got to get the team and equipment in place within the next few weeks. What's your thoughts on mobility, Dan?"

Dan replied, "I think the best way to mobilize the team and equipment overseas is by using Air Force KC-10 aircraft. We can fly nonstop from the East Coast direct to Aviano. The aircraft is reliable, fast, comfortable, and quiet—as much as I hate to admit it being a C-5 pilot—but it's the truth. The chances of having a mechanical breakdown in route are slim compared to using a C-17 or C-5. We also do not have to worry about customs or immigration. Once the team gets to Aviano, we can, if we have to, simply walk out the main gate of the Air Base and enter Slovenia and Croatia by way of Trieste. The KC-10 is large and spacious inside, and the team can rest while onboard. In addition, all our supplies and equipment can be carried onboard the KC-10. Once the team and equipment arrives at Aviano, we can move into Croatia by Air Force C-17s or NATO C-130s."

"Sounds like an excellent plan, Dan. I'll draft the tasking orders when we get to Washington. To save time we'll leave from Andrews Air Force Base. Once the team gets to Aviano, I'll make arrangements for the supplies and equipment to go into Croatia via C-17."

Dan added, "Once we get to Aviano, we could update our equipment and supplies and make any last-minute changes before we make the hop onboard the C-17."

Kostinic said, "Okay, Danny, you're already thinking like a seasoned operator. There's one more thing I need to brief you on in this segment, and it's extremely important. The team must look and act like native Croatians and Serbians, nothing Western European and especially American in their possession. This includes personal items like cosmetics, toiletries, and medications. Let me give you an example. During World War II some of our OSS and SOE operatives tried to wear clothing and accessories made in the UK or US; the results were deadly. Some of the operatives aroused suspicion simply because of the clothes they were wearing. One operative insisted on using his American-made shaving cream he'd been using for years. He was unfortunately arrested by the Gestapo. Once he was in custody, the Gestapo quickly determined he was an enemy agent. It didn't matter how good his German or French was, the Gestapo sent him off to a concentration camp where he was executed."

Mattingly said, "We don't want this to happen. To prevent this, each of the team members will be clothed and outfitted with accessories manufactured in Yugoslavia or Eastern Europe. The Defense Intelligence Agency has arranged for a specialist to help team members pick out specific clothing and accessories tailored specifically for him or her. Of course, the clothing is not foolproof. You have to use common sense."

Kostinic shook his head and recalled something in the past. "I once read a field report from an agent during the war that two fighter pilots were shot down over Serbia and hidden in a convent, only to be discovered by the Germans because their boots protruded from underneath their long black habits. All the airmen had to do was wear sandals or slippers, and they would have survived."

Dan got the point and took note of the personal items, "I'll make sure that no one on the team has any contraband. If I have to, I'll conduct a search myself before we send anyone overseas."

Chapter 8
ABOARD THE AMTRAK EMPIRE BUILDER

For the next forty-eight hours on board the trains, Kostinic and Mattingly continued their briefings on the operation. Dan absorbed the information and felt he could actually pull the mission off successfully.

Kostinic unfolded a map of the area and spread it across the table.

"Now, I need to give you a geography lesson on the Srem district, which is located in the heart of Serbia, along the Danube and Sava rivers. Once you're inside Serbia, you'll be assigned this territory."

Josef pointed to the Srem district on the map. "I'm working on securing safe houses in this area. You'll probably use a farm near the town of Kukujevci or Sid. This will be your home base," as he pointed to the area on the map. "From this location, you'll coordinate activities for your circuit. The Danube River to the north is a natural boundary and the Sava River to the south acts as the southern boundary. There are two major crossings over the Danube in the Srem District. The first is located in Novi Sad. The other is near the Serbian city of Backa Palanka and the Croatian city of Ilok. To the south, along the Sava River, the major crossing is at Sremska Mitrovica. NATO aircraft will target all these bridges during the first waves of the air campaign. The military objective is to cut off Serbian mobilization. Once the bridges are taken out, your team will be isolated from one another. Therefore, it's imperative we preposition our operatives in these areas before the air war begins."

Dan leaned closer to the map and studied the locations.

Kostinic continued, "Next, this area is one of the largest agricultural regions in all of Yugoslavia. They grow everything from wheat to flowers. Unfortunately, the area is flat with no terrain other than a small mountain range, which I'll talk about in a few minutes. The only cover is the irrigation canals or drainage ditches in the fields or low spots on the farms. Our satellites can't pick up the topography in such minute detail. You'll have to find these areas once your team is in place and before the air war starts so you can direct the downed airman to the safest hiding place. Also inside the Srem district are the Fruska Gora hills. These hills are strategically important because they offer the only high terrain for hundreds of miles. It's believed the Serbs will be placing most of their antiaircraft defenses in these hills. Here's the dilemma, located in these hills are several Serbian Orthodox monasteries. These monasteries have been there for centuries and are historic and religious monuments for the Serbian people."

Dan interrupted, "I know these areas. My father and I spent hours visiting these monasteries. Many of the monasteries are located in dense forest, are difficult to see from the main roads, and are practically military fortresses in themselves. If I recall, some of them were severely damaged during World War II. Most are still riddled with bullet holes."

"Precisely, Danny, we have to be careful in targeting this area because we don't want to destroy the monasteries —if we can help it. I've chosen you to lead your circuit in this area mainly because you're already familiar with the geography. I don't think there's anyone in the entire U.S. military that knows more about this area than you do. That's one of the major reasons I recommended you for this mission."

Josef handed Dan several photographs and satellite photos of the area.

"I want you to go over these photos and refresh your memory with this area."

Mattingly entered the compartment carrying a black duffel bag and placed it on the table in front of Dan and Josef.

"This is one of the reasons why we took Amtrak, Dan. I'm going to issue some of your equipment so you can get familiar with the items. You can brief the rest of your team later. First is a modified version of the Russian-made AK-47. It's called the Kalashnikov AKS-74U Assault Rifle. It was specially designed for Soviet Special Forces operating in Afghanistan during the 1980s. It's small, lightweight, and has a folding metal stock. When you take out the thirty-round magazine, the main weapon is small enough to fit inside a small backpack."

Mattingly handed the weapon to Dan.

"I want you to practice taking this thing apart and putting it back together again until you can do it in your sleep. Next, I want to issue this." He handed Dan a small 9 mm pistol. "This is a Russian-made Makarov automatic pistol, equipped with silencer. It holds a twelve-round magazine instead of the normal eight that's standard for

The Balkan Network

this weapon. These Russian models were specially modified for KGB use during the Cold War. I went to great difficulty in acquiring these weapons—thanks to our friends at the Russian Consulate in San Francisco. Both of these weapons are now standard issue for all Serb and Croatian military officers. The same goes for the pistol. I want you to become thoroughly familiar with this weapon because someday it could save your life or the life of one of your team members. Each member of your team will have both of these weapons issued to them later."

Finally, Mattingly reached into the duffel bag and pulled out the ammunitions for each weapon. "Here are four thirty-round clips for the AK-74 and three twelve-round clips for the Makarov. This should get you started. We chose these weapons because it's easy to get additional rounds once you're inside Yugoslavia. Ammunition is readily available from almost anywhere. The Serbs and Croatians use these weapons extensively, and they're practically impossible to trace. The Makarov pistol uses a 9.3 mm cartridge instead of the regular 9 mm casing used in the Beretta or Colt 9 mm automatics." Mattingly put all the weapons back in the black duffel bag and handed it to Dan. "You can sign for these later." Then he left the compartment.

When Mattingly was out of the compartment, Kostinic spoke. "Well, Danny, I've told you everything I know up to this point. I'll be staying in Washington for a few days before returning to Emeryville. I have some details and logistics to work out on my end, but I will be at the airfield to see you off. Before we go however, I want to tell you a story that I've never told you about during any of my lectures. It goes back to when I was a young agent in the OSS. Shortly before the end of the war, I was in charge of the Balkan field section. I was the organizer for the Alum circuit, a joint group of British and American operatives sabotaging German supply lines in Partisan territory. One night, two operatives were caught blowing up a crucial railway junction transporting V-1 rockets. Both agents were very young, nineteen and twenty-six years old and inexperienced. One was my OSS agent the other was a female, British SOE radio operator. The British insisted on having their own radio operators for all clandestine operations in the Balkans. Anyway, I was not with them that night because they had plenty of help from the Partisans. I was preoccupied with a higher priority mission."

Dan thought to himself, *The Germans discussing surrender terms.*

"During the meeting, I was interrupted with word that the couple had been arrested. I felt personally responsible for their fate. I should've never left them on their own. They were taken to Gestapo Headquarters located at a monastery in Chetnik territory for further interrogation. The female, being a civilian, was not protected by the Geneva Convention. The Sicherheitsdienst (SD) classified her as a terrorist insurgent. I was worried about her fate in particular because she was also a personal friend. Against direct orders from Bari, I assembled a team of Chetnik fighters and tried to pull off a rescue operation to save them, but we were unsuccessful. As we approached the monastery, a team of crack German SS commandos and the SD ambushed us. They were waiting for us as we approached the monastery. The rescue mission had been compromised by one of our most trusted and loyal Partisans who tipped off the Germans and Ustashe to our plan. Everyone on the rescue team was killed except for me. I escaped with my life only because I was lucky. After the botched rescue attempt, the two agents were taken to Jasenovac concentration camp where they were eventually tortured and executed. The British agent, Penelope Walsh, was Dr. Mattingly's fiancée. She held out and withstood extreme torture but revealed nothing about our network or radio checks. They were to be married as soon as she returned from her mission."

Kostinic looked out of the window and watched the Pennsylvania countryside pass by and continued.

"For her heroism, the British posthumously awarded her the George Cross. Mattingly was deeply in love with the woman, and he never got over her brutal death. That is why he has immersed himself in his work to this day. I regret leaving those two behind. Even some fifty years after the war, I'm still haunted by their murders. The agents were too inexperienced in the field and were no match for the Gestapo. Truly sad, Danny, I found out years later that Penelope had a young child, a little girl named Sarah."

Kostinic moved closer to Dan looking at him with teary eyes, "Danny, your team will be no different. The success of your mission depends on the safety of your operatives. No matter what the circumstances, you must promise me that you will not make the same mistake I made. Promise me that you'll never leave anyone behind."

Dan didn't hesitate, "You have my word, Professor. I'll bring everyone back if it's the last thing I do alive."

Kostinic leaned back in his seat and looked out the train window again.

"It's amazing and ironic how the world changes. The last time I organized a Balkan network, we were trying to help Allied airmen escape from the Germans. Now it's the other way around. Now we're trying to save the lives of German airmen. There's something I want to give you before you leave."

Kostinic reached into his briefcase and pulled out something wrapped in an old handkerchief. "It's a memento from General Mihailovich himself. He gave this Kama to me as I was boarding the last C-47 out of Yugoslavia in 1944. I want you to have it. It's the 'Credible Dagger'. I'm passing the baton on to you, Danny."

"Thank you, Professor. I accept it with honor and thank you for telling me this story about Penelope Walsh and Dr. Mattingly. I'll make sure the dagger is kept in a safe place." Dan thought about what Josef just said and realized why Mattingly appeared to have a lot on his mind. This mission probably brought back many painful memories.

* * *

ONE HOUR OUTSIDE WASHINGTON, Mattingly came back into the compartment and gave Dan his follow-on orders. "The train makes its final stop shortly. You'll be staying at the Best Western Hotel in Arlington. You can take a cab over there. We chose this hotel because it's within walking distance to the Metro station. Get used to taking public transportation. Tomorrow, go to the Pentagon shopping mall. There you will find a military clothing sales store. Buy a new set of uniforms. Here are vouchers for those uniforms."

Mattingly reached into his briefcase and took out the large brown envelope. "Oh, I almost forgot—here's your ID cards. Make sure you have your military IDs when you enter the Pentagon."

Next he handed Dan six one-hundred-dollar bills from his wallet.

"After you get your uniforms, there is a shopping center located at the mall. You can buy any personal items you need. Here's your allowance for those purchases. This should be enough."

The Balkan Network

Dan took the money and vouches and stuffed them in his pocket. Mattingly continued.

"Tuesday morning at eight o'clock sharp, you will report to the Pentagon main entrance in uniform. You will be given directions to your first appointment. You have a meeting with Lieutenant General James Hamilton at nine o'clock. The general wants to meet you and have a few words with you. After that, you will be directed to your next appointment. That's basically it; do you have any questions for either of us?"

Dan shook his head.

"Okay, you're on your own till Tuesday. Take the Metro to and from the Pentagon. Get off at either the Pentagon or the Pentagon Mall stops. Either one will get you close."

The Amtrak Capitol Limited pulled into Union Station on Pennsylvania Avenue at exactly 5:55 PM and came to a stop. Dan shook Kostinic's hand and said, "I hope this is not the last time we see each other. I'll do my best to remember everything. Thank you, Professor."

"You're welcome, Danny. Someday your life may depend upon it. Let me leave you with one final thought. The most productive activity an intelligence organization can do is penetrate other intelligence organization. The Serbs will be no different; don't wait until it's too late like I did. A collaborator can be anywhere." Kostinic released his grip from Dan's hand. "I wish I were going with you, but my health won't let me. Remember what I said about Milosevic and his inner circles. Protect your team and most importantly, don't leave anyone behind."

Dan grabbed his bags and walked off the train heading toward the depot. He looked over his shoulder and waved to Josef for the last time.

Chapter 9
WASHINGTON, D.C.

Dan woke up at six thirty the next morning at the Best Western Hotel in Arlington. He put on his workout clothes and went down to the hotel fitness center. The so-called fitness center was not much of a workout room at all. It consisted mainly of a treadmill and a few weight machines. Dan did his best to get at least a forty-five-minute workout. After that, he went upstairs to his room, showered and put on his last pair of clean clothes.

Dan found the Pentagon shopping mall and clothing store. He bought two sets of Air Force uniforms and civilian clothes to get him through the next few months. Then he returned to the hotel, dropped off his bags, and decided to head back to the city to view the sights of the nation's capitol. Dan spent the rest of the day viewing Washington. His first stop was the Washington Public Library. Once inside, he looked for everything on the former Yugoslavia. Since he was not allowed to take any notes on board the train, he needed to refresh his memory before he forgot too much information. He looked at an atlas and several books on the history and geography of the area. Next, he went to the periodical section and viewed all articles written during Operation Deliberate Force. After several hours in the library, he went to the Washington Mall. He spent nearly three hours alone at the Air and Space Museum before finishing the days sightseeing at Arlington National Cemetery. From there, he walked back to his hotel. It was after 7:00 P.M. when he returned to his room.

The next day, Dan woke up early, exercised, and dressed into his Air Force blues. He did not want to be late for his nine o'clock appointment with General Hamilton, so he left the hotel early and headed for the Pentagon. Lt. Gen. James Hamilton, Chief of the Defense Intelligence Agency, had an office on the third floor of the Pentagon. Dan had no trouble finding his way around. The halls and floors were clearly marked, and the directions the Army staff sergeant gave him at the main entrance were detailed and easy to follow. General Hamilton's secretary was busy at her desk typing on her computer. She never looked up from her screen.

"Major Radivich, you're a little early, but you can go right in. The general is expecting you."

"Thank you. By the way, it's *Captain* Radivich."

"The general said you can go in as soon as you get here," ignoring his remarks.

Dan knocked on General Hamilton's door and walked in. General Hamilton was seated at a large oak desk, and seated next to him hidden in the shadows was none other than Undersecretary of Defense Harold Mattingly. Dan saluting the general and replied, "Captain Radivich reporting as ordered, sir."

"Take a seat, Dan."

Dan moved into the chair and focused his attention at the general as he spoke very quickly.

"I'll get right to the point, Dan because we have a lot of work to do in a short period of time and you've already been thoroughly briefed. The U.S. military is getting ready to start the air campaign over Serbia. The Air Force plans on sending in over one thousand aircraft at any given time over Serbia. With an air armada of that size and with the air defenses the Serbs have deployed, we can expect to have some aircraft shot down. There's a good probability that our Combat Search and Rescue teams won't be able to get to our downed airmen in a timely manner. We need a backup plan to help the airmen escape and evade on their own until they can be rescued. That's why we need you."

"I'm ready for the job, General."

"Your task will be to pick the team necessary to help you carry out this mission. We will insert your team into places where we think our fighters and bombers will egress in and out of country, and you will wait there until called on. Once the air campaign begins, the Serbs will probably be redeploying their air defense assets. We need to know where these assets are, and we need this information in real time so our target information can be updated. Your team will help us track down these air defenses. The more we take out, the fewer chances they have of bringing down our aircraft. That's it in an abbreviated form. Do you have any reservation about your assignment?"

Dan shook his head and said, "no, sir."

"Alright, I do believe you already know Undersecretary Mattingly. He'll take over from here. Be safe, Dan. Oh, I almost forgot—effective yesterday at 1200 hours you have been promoted to Major."

General Hamilton reached into his desk drawer and took out a set of blue Air Force major's epaulets and gold major's leaf pin for his hat. "Here you go. Make sure you're in uniform before you leave my office, *Major.*"

"Thank you, sir."

Dan was stunned. He never expected a promotion. Dan slipped off his old captain's epaulets on his shoulders and replaced them with the new major's epaulets. He stood at attention, saluted the general, and left his office. Dan could not help but noticed that Hal Mattingly said nothing during the entire meeting. *He just sat there and did nothing*, Dan thought.

As Dan left the general's office, the receptionist handed him a sheet of paper with a schedule and office assignment without looking up from her tasks. "Here's your schedule and directions to your next appointment. I told you it was Major. Congratulations on your promotion."

"Thank you, ma'am, I appreciate that."

Dan glanced at the schedule and saw that his next appointment was with undersecretary of defense.

"Secretary Mattingly's office is two floors down on level B. You can take the elevator to your left as you walk out the door. Check in with Secretary Mattingly's personal assistant, Ms. Sara."

Dan found Mattingly's office without any difficulty. He entered his office and saw a receptionist seated at a desk. Unlike General Hamilton's secretary, there was no nameplate on the desk to identify the woman, and she was not busy typing on a computer. She had no papers or work on her desk, just a day planner and a cell phone. She was tapping her fingers on her desk as if she was anxious or annoyed. If smoking were allowed, she'd probably be inhaling a long drag.

Ms. Sara was middle-aged, approximately fifty-six, and dressed in a blue dress suit. She wore a lapel pin in the shape of a cross on her right side. Her black hair was streaked with grey. She made no attempt to color it. Had she done so, she would have looked much younger and more attractive than she already was. Her facial features were fine with thin lips, dark eyebrows, and deep blue eyes. She opened her mouth and spoke with a well-educated British accent. "Good morning, Major Radivich. Dr. Mattingly will be in shortly. You have a busy schedule today. You can go right on in and have a seat and wait for the undersecretary. Help yourself to coffee or juice."

Dan nodded his head and said, "Thank you, ma'am," then walked inside Mattingly's office. His office had a large conference table. There were files, pictures, maps, and yellow legal tablets strewn about. Dan grabbed a cup of coffee, took a seat at the table, and waited for Mattingly to arrive. Just as Dan was getting comfortable, he heard the door handle move, and Mattingly walked in.

"Good morning, Dan. How were your days off?"

"Just fine, sir. I took a walk around the city and played tourist for the day. I also had a chance to go to the library and do some research."

"Glad you enjoyed the sights of our nation's capitol. We need to move forward and make our final team selections. As we go through these individuals, keep in mind we're looking for someone that will be assigned on a covert mission deep inside Serbia. Thanks to you, Josef and I have narrowed this list down to twelve individuals. We'll select five candidates with one backup element. These twelve individuals are already here, and we've scheduled them for interviews this morning. The first one's in five minutes."

Dan recalled the files Josef gave him on the train.

"The first candidate on our list is Lieutenant Commander Karoline Anne-Marie Koskov, United States Navy. In fact, one of the reasons we chose to come to

Washington by train and why we stopped off in Seattle for the day was to make arrangements at Bremerton Naval Shipyard for Commander Koskov to be here today. Don't be fooled by her looks. She's a highly trained naval intelligence officer specializing in covert communications. We'd like to have her on our team, but we're not sure how she'll react under pressure in a combat environment. She's also the only officer other than you that we've selected from the pool."

"That's always a consideration in a tactical situation. I saw her file, and I did have concerns about her lack of field experience on actual intelligence missions."

"Let's find out," Mattingly called his personal assistant on the intercom.

"Sarah, have Commander Koskov come in as soon as she arrives."

Ten minutes later, there was a light knock on the door and Commander Koskov walked in. She was dressed in her black and white uniform with her light brown hair pulled back neatly in a bun.

"Good morning, Lieutenant Commander Koskov reporting as ordered, sir" she replied.

"Take a seat," said Mattingly. "From now on let's dispense with the military formalities. This is Major Radivich, you can call him Dan, and call me Hal. Dan will be working with me on this assignment and selection process."

Karol was an attractive thirty-four-year-old woman, five feet six inches tall. She had light brown hair with hazel eyes. Her breasts were full and firm, and she had a thin waist with shapely hips.

Dan found her very attractive.

Mattingly looked at Dan and said, "Karol has already been given a few details of our mission. She has similar qualifications as you. Both her parents were born in

Yugoslavia; however, she grew up in San Francisco. She can read and speak fluent Serbo-Croatian, French, and German. She's also traveled to Yugoslavia extensively."

"It's a pleasure to meet you two. If we're going to dispense with the formalities, call me Karol."

Mattingly said, "We asked that you come here today because we believe you have special talents and skills that we need. As you were briefed earlier, we are preparing for an operation inside Yugoslavia, which is potentially dangerous. We are also in need of an officer who can provide leadership to the team. Do you feel you're up for this mission?"

Karol responded, "I'm a U.S. naval officer. I will do whatever it takes to succeed on this mission."

Mattingly interrupted, "We've heard all that crap before! This mission is quite different from anything you've undertaken in the past. You'll actually be doing the dirty work instead of having your Navy SEALs do it for you. I need to know if you have the guts for this assignment."

Mattingly reached down and picked up a briefcase located under the conference table. He opened the brief case and took out a Beretta 9 mm automatic pistol.

"Have you ever seen one of these, Karol?"

"Sure, standard issue for all U.S military forces."

Mattingly placed the Beretta on the table and said, "Don't worry, it's not loaded. What about one of these?" as he took another pistol out from his briefcase. "This is a Russian, Makarov 9 mm pistol similar to the one used by both Serbian and Croatian military forces. This one *is* loaded." He took out the clip, pulled back on the bolt, and de-chambered a round. Next, he took out the twelve bullets from the clip, set them on the table, and put the unloaded Russian pistol on the table. He then walked quietly behind Dan and pulled out a thin nylon cord from inside his cuff link, wrapped it around Dan's neck, and pulled hard. Dan immediately reached for his throat and tried to pull the cord from his neck. Mattingly continued to pull on the cord until Dan started to turn red. Karol looked on with shock. Dan was starting to cough and gag and his face was now turning blue.

"What the hell are you doing?"

"We've got to know if you have what it takes to be on this mission. So what are you going to do about it, Karol?"

Karol tightened her fist, took a deep breath and said, "Take this you son of a bitch!"

She stood up and gave a backhanded karate chop across Mattingly's throat. He fell back, releasing the cord from Dan's neck. Before he could recover, Karol grabbed the gun, loaded the magazine, slipped it into the weapon and placed it to Mattingly's head, shouting, "Don't even breathe or I'll blow your fucking head off!"

Mattingly raised his hands, composed him, and said, "Well done, Karol, well done."

Dan still coughing and hacking said, "What the hell just happened?" He looked at Karol. "Obviously, she has some experience in close quarter combat and is good with a handgun. She could be very useful. Congratulations, Karol, welcome to our team."

Karol looked at both men, "Hal, I could have killed you in one blow if I had hit you one inch lower. And yes, Dan, I'm pretty good with a handgun, too."

Mattingly stood up, straightened his jacket, cleared his throat and said, "Well, I think that concludes this interview. By the way, each of the team members will have the opportunity to prove themselves just like you did, Karol. We've got eleven more interviews to do this morning. Would you two be so kind to help me straighten up the room so it doesn't look like we were trying to kill one another?"

They picked up the files and papers and straightened up the room to make it look like an interview room instead of a boxing ring. Mattingly put the pistols back in his briefcase and placed it under the conference table. Next, he handed Dan and Karol a yellow legal tablet, pen, and a stack of files.

"All the candidates you are about to interview have been prescreened, passed a preliminary background security investigation, and have been ordered to the Pentagon. In front of you are copies of their personnel files. The second interview this morning is with Air Force Staff Sergeant Naomi Markof, twenty-six years old. She can speak and read Serbo-Croatian, French, German, Italian, and Arabic. She works as an Air Operations Specialist at USAFE Headquarters at Ramstein Air Base, Germany. Dan, you and Karol will conduct the interviews. You will speak in Serbo-Croatian. Do not give a lot of details about the operation because we have not made our final selections. You are free to ask any questions you wish of the candidates; however, keep in mind we are selecting a group of people to be covert operatives. I'll sit here and watch for the most part because I don't speak the language. I will be taking notes on what I see."

Dan thumbed through the stack of files and found Naomi's file. He recalled selecting her from the preliminary candidates. This time her file contained her photograph. He was surprised to see that she was a very attractive young woman.

"Is she here now?"

Mattingly called his personal assistant again on the intercom.

"Sarah, as soon as Sergeant Markof is here, send her right in."

A few minutes later, Sergeant Markof walked into Mattingly's office. Mattingly was at the head of the conference table, and Dan and Karol were on the sides looking toward the door as Sergeant Markof walked in. She was dressed in her blue Air Force uniform and holding a black leather planner. She stood at attention, saluted Mattingly, and said, "Sergeant Markof reporting as ordered, sir."

Dan was stunned by her beauty. Karol noticed this as she watched Dan drop his jaw to the table. Her appearance was impeccable, even more so than in her photograph. She didn't have a hair out of place. Her blue Air Force uniform fit her athletic figure as if it were tailor made; she had on just the right amount of makeup and her fingernails were perfectly manicured.

Mattingly, too, was surprised at Naomi's appearance and didn't say anything for a few moments, then finally said, "Sergeant Markof, this is Major Radivich and Lieutenant Commander Koskov. They'll be conducting the interview in Serbo-Croatian. Would you please take a seat?"

Dan asked Naomi, "Sergeant Markof, could I get you a glass of water or coffee?"

Naomi replied in a soft, polite voice, "No thank you, sir, I just had an orange juice with my breakfast."

Immediately Karol gave Naomi a stern look and shouted in Serbo-Croatian, "Would you please take a seat, Sergeant! We don't have all day. We have several questions for you, so the sooner we get started, the sooner we can get finished and move on with the rest of the interviews."

Dan continued looking at Naomi with a big smile on his face. He composed himself and continued with the interview.

After several hours, Dan and Karol interviewed all candidates that morning. Dan already did most of the work back on the train and selected a highly qualified group of individuals. The group was narrowed down to five and consisted mostly of individuals who seemed older and mature but still extremely qualified. The deciding factors were physical fitness, age, and their linguistic ability. The ones that could speak and read the best, especially Serbian Cyrillic, were chosen. The candidates selected for the operation included, Lt. Cdr. Koskov, whom Dan code-named *Sutter*, after the street in San Francisco where she grew up. Next was Army Specialist Nicholas Bellou, a paratrooper from the 101st Airborne Division, Fort Campbell, Kentucky, code-name *Speeder*. Even though his language skills were not as strong as the other candidates, Dan discovered that he liked to fix and ride motorcycles— a big plus for this operation. Nick was the youngest of all candidates at twenty-two. He was short, five feet four, with a small build. He had brown eyes and light brown hair. Next was Air Force Staff Sergeant Naomi Markof. Her abilities with Serbo-Croatian were best out of everyone, including Dan and Karol; she had no noticeable accent. Her code-name was *Lombard* because of her good looks and tall, slender, athletic build. Naomi was a tall woman at five-foot-eight, brown eyes, and long brown hair. Next was Army, Sergeant Major Karen Criskos, thirty-six, from the Defense Language Institute in Monterey, California. She was intelligent and a fast burner, climbing to the top of the Army enlisted ranks in a short period. Her specialty was languages. She spoke excellent Serbo-Croatian, French, and German. Her code-name was *Eden*. Karen was medium height, five feet four, with short reddish-brown hair and blue eyes. She was in great physical condition with strong, lean legs and arms. Finally, there was Marine

Corps. Gunnery Sergeant Michael Karl from the 1st Marine Expeditionary Division, Camp Pendleton, California. Michael was a Marine sniper. He was the oldest of the candidates at forty-three, but his language skills were superb. Dan code-named him *General Grant*, or *Grant* for short. Michael was the stereotypical Marine. He had cropped blond hair with blue eyes and was in great physical condition. He had the body of a weightlifter. Dan gave himself the code-name *Specter*, to go along with his circuit as leader and organizer. He took the code-name from his days flying HC-130s at Hurlburt. These were the men and women Dan and Karol selected to be on the team. The rest were reassigned to the Pentagon but could be used as backups if the primary candidates were disqualified along the way.

Mattingly called all the primary candidates back into his office and had each of them sign a confidentiality statement acknowledging that they were now assigned to the Defense Intelligence Agency and they would have access to classified information. Next, he gave them their follow-on orders.

"You six have been selected to work on our team to do classified work inside Yugoslavia. Each of you has a special talent besides speaking the language. This mission is potentially dangerous, but you will not be alone. We will be in constant contact with the team, so if anyone should be in danger, rest assured you will have the support of the entire U.S. military. From now on, Dan, code-name Specter, will be team commander and help train you on your duties and assignments. We want you to use your tactical names that we've assigned to you, so please start using them. Tonight, you will check out of your respective hotels here in Virginia and report to the Billeting office at Bolling Air Force Base in Washington. You'll be staying there for the next several days. Tomorrow you will report to the Defense Intelligence Analysis Center at Bolling Air Force Base at 0800 sharp in uniform to begin your briefings. The Billeting office at Bolling will have directions to the site. Good luck to you. Except for Specter, you are all dismissed until tomorrow."

Everyone gathered their personal belongings and left the Pentagon for the day. Dan stayed behind and continued mission planning with Mattingly.

"Dan, you and I have a lot to talk about this afternoon. The first thing I want to tell you is that I pushed for your promotion. I knew Karol would be on the team, but Josef and I wanted you as team leader so I pushed for the promotion. It's a temporary, theater promotion. You'll revert to your regular rank at the completion of the mission."

"I'm okay with that, thanks for sharing that piece of information with me. It'll make it easier being in command of this mission with Karol and I having the same rank."

"There's something else I need to share with you. Pick up your belongings and come with me."

Mattingly led Dan down to the basement floor of the Pentagon. After passing several security checkpoints, they entered the Defense Department's Command Center. Inside the Command Center was an array of computers and video monitor displays. It looked like a typical command post with tactical displays of various geographical locations around the world. Officers and enlisted personnel were running around trying to look busy. They continued to a small section off to the side of the Command Center.

"Dan, this is the Balkan Section. The Defense Department monitors everything that goes on in the Balkans from this station." Mattingly then directed Dan to a tactical monitor found next to the bigger displays. "This is our Human Resources display. On this screen is the location of all our human assets in the field."

Dan looked at the display, and he could see small icons scattered all across Yugoslavia. Most of the icons were found in southern Croatia and inside Bosnia—a few were in Kosovo, but there were no icons inside Eastern Croatia or Serbia.

"As you can see from this display, we have no assets in place in these areas. That's why we need the team. I may also point out that we can monitor the location of our human assets twenty-four-seven. Tomorrow, I'll show you how we accomplish this." After showing Dan through the Command Center, they returned to his conference room where they continued to work on the logistics of the mission.

After Dan left the Pentagon for the day, Ms. Sara came into the conference room with a legal pad and scribbled notes. She had listened to all the interviews through a hidden com-link. She took a seat at the table. Mattingly pulled up a chair too and asked, "Well, what do you make of the team?"

"The weakest link is the young Army corporal. He didn't seem as motivated as the others, but I think Major Radivich is right. Specialist Bellou could come in handy fixing the motorcycles. We'll have to see how he does during the training exercise."

"What about the women?"

"You made the right choices. Commander Koskov would have made a good organizer had Major Radivich not agreed to join the team. My only concern is Sergeant Markof. She's young and beautiful, but is she brave enough?"

That night, Dan and Karol took a government taxi

from their hotel to Bolling Air Force Base and checked into the Visiting Officer Quarters. Nick, Naomi, Karen, and Michael had been staying at different hotels scattered all across the Washington DC area. Everyone checked out of their respective hotels and headed over to Bolling Air Force Base. When the team checked in at the Billeting Office, they were assigned rooms at the Visiting Officer Quarters (VOQ) and the Visiting Airmen Quarters (VAQ). When Dan and Karol got their room assignments at the VOQ, Dan asked Karol, "Would you like to get some dinner tonight? I think I owe you one after rescuing me from certain death. The Officers' Club is just around the corner."

"I was going to ask you the same thing. I'm starving. I can be ready in twenty-five minutes."

Dan took Karol's bags. "Let me help you with these."

The two officers took the small elevator up to the second floor, and Dan helped Karol with her bags to her room.

Karol unlocked her door and stepped in. "See you in twenty-five minutes. Just knock on your way down."

Exactly twenty-five minutes later Dan knocked on Karol's door and heard the deadbolt unlock as she opened the door. She was dressed casually in black leather pants with a white nylon blouse, and her shoulder-length brown hair was down. The leather pants were snug, and the blouse fit perfectly.

"Come on in for just a few minutes, I have to get my shoes on."

Karol sat on the edge of the bed, and Dan stood and watched her put on a pair of black, strapped shoes with high heels, making her appear taller.

"Dan, can I ask you something?"

"Sure, go right ahead."

"Did you have time to pack your bags before you left on this assignment?"

"Now that you mentioned it, no I did not. Two Army sergeants took me away from my last assignment late at night. I still have my B-4 bag packed from my trip to Yokota."

"What were you doing in Yokota?"

"Sorry, you don't know a lot about me. I was stationed at Travis Air Force Base as a C-5 pilot. I fly mostly in the Pacific theater. I just got off a ten-day trip when I found out about this assignment."

"I see, well, I didn't have time to pack a lot either. My commander told me to report to his office to talk about my next assignment. When I arrived at his office, Hal Mattingly was standing in the room with my boss, and then the next thing I knew, I was on a plane headed for Washington. I didn't even have my dress uniform with me, and I had to buy one at the clothing sales store here in Washington."

"It sounds like you were spirited away almost the same way I was. I had my Air Force flight suit, but I didn't think that would be an appropriate uniform to wear at the Pentagon, so I was told to buy some uniforms."

Karol changed the subject, "You're right. I don't know you very well, but I'm looking forward to working with you. By the way, when Sergeant Markof walked into Hal's office this morning, I thought your jaw was going to hit the floor."

"I couldn't help it; I wasn't expecting to see a raving beauty walk in. I read her personnel file before the interview; in fact, I selected her from a preliminary pool of candidates, but I never had any idea of what she looked like until this morning. Her language skills are flawless. I think she'll do fine on this mission and her good looks might come in handy."

"Well, she is a very attractive woman, I have to admit."

Dan asked, "Karol, I read your file in detail, but tell me a little more about yourself."

"Well, I'm currently separated from my husband. We're waiting for the divorce to be finalized. He's in the Navy and based in San Diego but spends most of his time at sea. He's a helicopter pilot. I met Tom shortly after my first assignment at Norfolk. We thought we had fallen in love. We were married within one year from the time we first met. Soon after we were married, Tom got orders for his first cruise. He was gone more than he was at home. After his first cruise, I transferred to Bremerton, and he transferred to Pearl Harbor. We were wrapped up in our respective careers. Before we knew it, we were perfect strangers to each other. So, Koskov is my maiden name. What about you, Dan? Married? Family?"

Dan looked at Karol, "No, I'm afraid not, no wife, kids, dog, or cat, just me. I'm a bachelor living in Northern California. Someday I would like to get married and have a family, but at this point, the right person hasn't come along. Usually when I meet someone, I fly out the next day. When I return home and make contact with them, I'm a stranger. Usually they've met someone else by that time and moved on."

"Yeah, I'm not into the single scene myself. You seem like an attractive, intelligent guy. Maybe the right person is waiting for you. Give it time, it will happen."

As Karol was ready to leave her room, Dan said politely. "By the way, from now on please don't use any of the perfume or makeup you have in your possession. We'll arrange for all the women to have special toiletries manufactured in Eastern Europe. It's a security issue."

The Balkan Network

"I never thought about that, but you're right. I don't even like the stuff I brought along with me anyway. I'll trash it when I get a chance."

The two left the VOQ and walked around the corner to the Officers' Club. If it had been any further, Karol would not have made it in the shoes she was wearing. The Officers' Club was practically empty that night, and Dan and Karol had no problem getting a table away from everyone. They ordered from the menu and polished off a bottle of California Chardonnay.

During dinner, Karol and Dan switched to speaking in Serbo-Croatian.

"Dan, I'm looking forward to going back to Yugoslavia. I haven't been there for over ten years, and I know it's changed dramatically. I knew there were many things happening in the Balkans, but much of what happened there was overshadowed by events in the Middle East and the fall of the Iron Curtain."

"You'll get all the details tomorrow when the entire team's together," said Dan.

"Fair enough."

"Let's get back to the Q, we have a busy day tomorrow," said Dan.

A few blocks away at the Non-Commissioned Officers' Club, the rest of the other team members were sitting down having dinner themselves. Mike and Karen, being the oldest and senior ranking, ordered from the dinner menu first, followed by Naomi and Nick. As Hal and Dan had told them, they all switched to Serbo-Croatian during dinner to get used to hearing one another.

Naomi was the first to speak up. "I don't like the name Lombard. They could have come up with something better than that. I'll bet Commander Koskov had something to do with it. She seemed like a real snip. If she'd asked me, I would have given her some suggestions like maybe Lombardi. At least that name is after a sports legend. What about you, Karen—do you like the name Eden?"

"No, not especially, but you have to remember the reason we have these names is security. As we communicate with one another, we don't want to tip off anyone who might be listening and who could intercept our transmissions. I was asked to provide linguistic support for this mission. In fact, Major Radivich asked me during the interview for some suggested code words to use. My advice is to leave it alone and live with it." Karen went on, "Naomi, since you're in a talkative mood, why don't you tell us a little more about yourself?"

"I'm a military brat. I lived everywhere and grew up nowhere. My father is American and my mother was from Ljubljana, which is now in Slovenia. My mother spoke French, German, English, Italian, and Serbo-Croatian. That's why I speak all five languages. We made a game of it as I was growing up. My mother would yell at me in one language, and I'd answer back in another. My father was in the Army. He was stationed in Stuttgart, West Germany, when he met my mother. She was working at the Post as an interpreter. My father had several tours of duty throughout Europe, and naturally, I took to the languages of the host country. When I grew up, I followed my father's footsteps, but I joined the Air Force instead of the Army. He still hasn't forgiven me for that."

"I could tell by your accent that you either grew up or lived extensively in Europe as a child. You should think about the DLI (Defense Language Institute)." Karen went on, "When I graduated from high school I took a trip to Europe—you know the kind of trip most high school students go on, staying in youth hostels and sleeping on railway platforms. It was supposed to be a six-week tour of the entire continent. I started out in Greece and worked my way up the Balkan Peninsula. I got as far as Dubrovnik, where I ended up staying for six months. That's where I learned to speak Serbo-Croatian. I traveled throughout Croatia and Bosnia, picking up German and French along the way. This background in languages gave me the urge to enlist in the Army. When the Army found out about my language skills, I was immediately earmarked as an instructor at the Presidio in Monterey. So here I am today."

"What about you two? You both have been quiet so far," Naomi said. "Can you tell us more about yourselves?"

Michael said, "I'm sorry, I don't have any exotic tales to share with you. I'm just a good old boy from Grand Rapids, Michigan. I grew up in a predominantly Serbian community. I played with all the boys and girls in my neighborhood that spoke Serbian or Croatian. I eventually picked up the language and the next thing I knew I was speaking fluently. I don't have any special skills other than being a Marine."

"Nick, what do you got to say for yourself?" said Michael.

"I'm like you, Sergeant Karl. I don't have an exotic story to tell you. My grandparents were from Yugoslavia. Both my parents worked when I was a child and my grandparents stayed home and raised me. I had no choice in learning Croatian because they spoke only a few words of English. My passion was riding dirt bikes and becoming a paratrooper. I joined the Army right out of high school. That's pretty much it."

"Sounds like we have a well-rounded group," said Karen. She raised her beer mug and said, "Here's to our success and a safe return."

The rest of the team raised their glasses. "To our

success!" Everyone took a long swig. After the toast, Karen said, "By the way, Naomi, where did you learn Arabic?"

"The Saudis. During Desert Storm, I was assigned to Central Command Headquarters at Riyadh as an Air Operations Specialist. I was the official Royal Saudi Air Force liaisons officer. They taught me the language."

The four enlisted members finished their dinner and walked back to quarters.

Chapter 10
DEFENSE INTELLIGENCE ANALYSIS CENTER

The next morning at 8:00 AM, the entire team met at the Defense Intelligence Analysis Center (DIAC) at Bolling AFB. The DIAC was a new, inconspicuous, redbrick, three-story complex with no windows. On the first floor, was a large multimedia-style classroom. Mattingly and Dan were already there setting up the classroom when the team arrived. At Mattingly's request, Dan was helping place books and pamphlets marked "Top Secret" at each of the six seats in the two front rows.

As the team members took their seats, Mattingly said, "Welcome ladies and gentlemen to the new world of Special Operations and our first day of academic training. For some of you, you might be thinking of Special Operations as Navy SEALS, Delta Operators, or Green Berets. The Defense Department has redefined Special Operations to mean any unconventional warfare requiring special skills and tactics. This is a new idea for the Defense Department, and we are in the early stages of its development. In future wars and conflicts, we'll have Special Operators working in many different fields, not just elite commandos. Overall command authority for this mission is with the Defense Intelligence Agency. As of yesterday, all of you have been reassigned from the Pentagon to the Defense Intelligence Agency. Once the air campaign starts, command authority will shift to NATO AFSOUTH in Naples. They will assign tasking and assume responsibility for your mission until one of two conditions exists: first is when the war is over and you are redeployed back to the United States. Second, if the mission is compromised, the Defense Intelligence Agency will assume command authority and bring you home. This mission will have three phases. Phase One: we will do our stateside training and preparation. Phase Two: insertion into Croatia and establish a forward operating base. Phase Three: Serbian Operations. Placed in front of you are your reading materials for this mission. As you can see from the cover sheets, the material is classified top secret, which means it does not leave this building. Therefore, you will study this material only in this building. The white books are unclassified, and you can take them with you back to quarters. The first order of business is to go over the ground rules. Except for Dan, each of you is here at your own free will. What this means is at anytime during this training period if you don't want to be here, just let me know and you'll be back at the Pentagon doing translation work for three months. I've got four people with your same qualifications at the Pentagon, waiting to take your place. Does everyone understand this?"

There was unanimous agreement in the room.

"Good, I thought so. Starting tomorrow, you will all wear civilian attire and will not address each other using military rank. Next, everything we do, we do as a group. This includes eating, drinking, and socializing, which you will not have time for. If one of you would like to go to the

The Balkan Network

gym and work out, then all of you will go to the gym and work out. Is that clear?"

Mattingly waited a few seconds before he spoke. "Good, the last thing I want to say is that everything that is said and done in this building stays in this building, no exceptions. That is why all of you are restricted to the base. You are not to leave the confines of Bolling on your own. Do I make myself clear?" Mattingly waited before speaking again. "Okay, now that I've laid down the ground rules, I'd like all of you to leave your personal belongings here and meet me outside. I have a military bus waiting to take you to Fort Detrick."

The team met outside the DIAC. Mattingly's personal assistant, Ms. Sara, was already waiting with a clipboard, stack of papers, and medical files. She spoke to the team:

"Ladies and gentlemen, could I have your attention for just a minute? For those of you that don't remember me, I'm Secretary Mattingly's personal assistant. You can call me, Ms. Sara. Today we're going to Fort Detrick to conduct your physical examinations. I've procured your medical records from your host units. I will keep these sealed records until we get to the medical facility." Then she told everyone to load the bus, and they departed.

The hospital at the Armed Forces Medical Intelligence Center at Fort Detrick looked like any other military hospital. Once inside, the team was directed to the third floor and a section marked "Physical Exams." Ms. Sara escorted the team to a waiting area and handed the receptionist at the window the stack of medical records and said, "These are the individuals you're expecting."

Karol was the first to be called. A tough looking Army nurse blurted out her name.

"Karoline Koskov, please come with me." The two

women walked into the examination room. Karol took a seat on the table.

"Are you taking any medication?" said the nurse.

Karol shook her head and said, "No."

"What about birth control?"

"No, I'm not on anything."

The nurse jotted a few notes down on her file and handed her a gown, "The doctor will be right in. You can get undressed including your underwear.

A few minutes later, an Army doctor came in wearing the rank of Major. She was a female about Karol's age and said, "Good morning, Commander, I'm Doctor Reed, I'm an OBGYN. I'll be conducting your physical exam."

Dr. Reed gave Karol a thorough examination, then she said, "You're in excellent physical condition; no children I see."

"I've tried to get pregnant over the years, but unfortunately I was never able to."

"I must remind you that should you become pregnant while in a designated combat zone, the U.S. military considers it 'dereliction of duties', and you could be subject to court martial. I'm sorry to be so candid, but that's my job here."

"I'm familiar with the directive, Dr. Reed; it's very similar to deployment on Navy war ships."

"You'll be doing classified work overseas and cohabitating. I can give you a prescription for a Serbian manufactured contraceptive, but it's best to abstain."

"I'll be fine."

Dr. Reed jotted some more notes on Karol's records then continued, "Should you be caught or detained, they'll probably give a detailed medical examination similar to the one I just gave you. That's when they'll discover you're not a local citizen. They can even determine if you're pregnant

The Balkan Network

or had any children. One of the reasons why we're conducting this examination is to update your medical records so we can identify you or your body."

The two other female team members received examinations similar to Karol's, except they accepted the Serbian manufacture contraceptives. The three men also underwent thorough medical examinations as well. When everyone finished their exams, Ms. Sara escorted the team to another section of the hospital marked Neurology. Dan was the first to go into the treatment room. Once inside the room, a nurse and a physician were waiting. The doctor injected local anesthetic into the back of Dan's head just above his neck hairline. A few minutes later, the doctor made an incision at the back of Dan's neck and placed a small electronic device no bigger than the tip of an eraser just under the scalp then sutured the incision. The whole process took less than five minutes after which time the doctor said, "The stitches will dissolve by themselves in a few days. You might experience some discomfort and itching. You can use hydrocortisone to help with the itching but only for the next four days. After that, you'll just have to get used to it."

The whole team had the small electronic devices placed under their skin and within a few hours, the team was boarding the bus heading back to Washington. Once back inside the DIAC and in the classroom, Mattingly continued. "You have all been fitted with a small, passive electronic locator. This device gives us the ability to track your location at any given time. This passive system bounces your signal to our satellites when activated. The interrogation signal lets us know your location within a few hundred feet. All the locating devices are functioning normally and you are now all under twenty four-hour surveillance. We can determine if you've left the confines of the base. I'd like to introduce you to the rest of our support system. Come with me."

Mattingly led the team down the elevator to a secure section in the basement of the building. At the end of the corridor was a door with an armed sentry. He showed the soldier his ID badge and said, "These are the individuals we've been expecting." Then he placed his ID badge on the card reader that opened the door and gave him access to the Defense Intelligence Analysis Center.

"This is the heart and soul of the Defense Intelligence Agency."

Dan noticed that this command center was similar to the one at the Pentagon except this one had more equipment, computers, monitors and personnel working the center, and the displays showed topographic and radar data.

Mattingly motioned the group to a monitor that showed all of Maryland and the District of Columbia. Each monitor in the room had an operator working the station. The computer operator monitoring the Washington area was a young female Navy petty officer. He leaned over and asked, "Would you zoom in on this area?" as he motioned to the area next to Bolling. Dan could see the small icons appear similar to the ones he had seen yesterday at the Pentagon. As the young petty officer was enlarging the area, Dan could see the icons had a small dialog box attached next to them. The Petty Officer clicked on one of the icons and a box popped up with Karol Koskov's information including her picture.

Dan said, "Karol, take a look at this."

Karol leaned over Dan's shoulder and saw the information. "Remarkable, I can't believe what I'm seeing. I knew we had passive devices, but I'd never seen them work until now."

The Balkan Network

Mattingly interrupted, "I wanted each of you to see this with your own eyes. This is what I meant when I said you will not be alone. We will have constant contact with you at all times. I also want to point out that when we communicate via our cell phones, which I'll talk about later, the transmissions are crossed-reference to make sure you are the actual person making the phone call. If we get a phone call and the passive radar beacon says you're in one place and the communications satellites say you're in a different place, we'll know something has happened to you. As you make the call, the icons should overlap one another."

Mattingly went on, "The information displayed in this room is in real time. When we get updates to our tactical information, we input that information so our displays will always have current information. I will be in this room almost the whole time you're overseas. All right, I think that's enough gizmos and gadgets, let's get back to work."

He led the team back to the classroom. Once inside the classroom, Ms. Sara was already waiting at the back of the classroom. Mattingly said, "Dan, why don't you take over from here?"

Dan stood up and addressed the team, "Our codename is the Prospector circuit. Let me go over our rules of engagement. Our number one priority is to avoid Serbian military forces. We will be traveling inside Croatia and Serbia disguised as couples to avoid any suspicion. However, if one or both of you should be apprehended by regular Serbian military authorities or Serbian paramilitary forces and detained for questioning, you are authorized to use deadly force to protect yourselves and members of the team. Does everyone understand this?" Dan waited a few seconds for everyone to grasp the seriousness of the directive then continued. "If you should be detained by Croatian civilian law enforcement agencies, you will cooperate to the fullest extent possible."

Dan looked at each of the team members then continued. "Good, now I must inform you that our timeline has been stepped up. NATO Headquarters believes the air campaign will only last a few weeks. Hal and I believe it will last much longer, perhaps as long as six months. Since this assignment could last that long, your TDY orders will be readjusted. However, we hope this mission will be over within a few weeks, and then we can all go home. Because the timeline is moved up, we can't train you thoroughly. We'll have to do most of our training as we go along. The classified pamphlets you have in front of you will give you details on our equipment, communication procedures, and most importantly, our escape routes. Please commit this material to memory. You will not be able to access this information once we begin the operation. Hal and I have already spent hours planning this mission so everyone returns safely. We'll spend the next three days here at Bolling for our academic training and then go over to Quantico to begin our field training exercises. These exercises are not difficult, and you will not be penalized for errors. They will, however, give us an idea of how you will react under pressure in a tactical situation. Karol has already done her field exercise, and she passed with flying colors. I expect each of you to do the same. Once our fieldwork is complete, we will go by military aircraft to Aviano Air Base then on to Croatia where we'll begin our operations and establish the forward operating base. From there we move into Serbia. Once inside Serbia, we'll receive our follow-one orders and tasking. That's basically it. Are there any questions?"

Naomi spoke up first, "Can you tell us what's involved in the field training exercise?"

The Balkan Network

"If I told you then it wouldn't be an exercise. You'd already know what to expect. I can tell you that each of you has a unique exercise tailored specifically for you."

"I guess you answered my question, too," said Mike.

Dan continued. "Let's get started. Please open your white books and turn to the first page. These are Serb anti-aircraft missiles. I'd like you to become familiar with each of these weapon systems. Now let's move on to page twenty. This is one of our biggest hurdles. Eastern Croatia is blanketed with land mines. Both Serb and Croatian forces planted them. The mines come in all shapes and sizes, some antitank and some antipersonnel. We have pictures and graphics of all known devices. Each of you will receive a portable metal detector. The instructions and operating procedures for this metal detector are found in the white booklet. Familiarize yourselves with this device because your life depends on it. Once we detect these explosive devices with our metal detector, we do have the ability to disarm the device. When we're in Croatia, please pay particular attention to road signs that warn travelers and motorists of the danger of land mines. The Croatians are doing their best to remove these devices, but it's been a slow process. The reason the land mines are so important is that we've chosen this area to be our escape route out of Serbia. We can't escape back into Croatia unless we know the locations of the land mines."

Mattingly interjected, "We'll talk about mines again during another block of training. Each of you was selected for our team based on your unique specialty and your linguistic ability. Time is limited, so we don't have the time to go through a six-month training program. I've paired each of you up with a partner. These partners are not interchangeable: Mike and Karen, Naomi and Nick, and Dan and Karol. As I mentioned earlier, from now on we do things together. I've arranged for all of you to have your meals at the mess hall. You will eat together as a group. This is important because we have to know what each of us likes or dislikes. When you're in Yugoslavia, you'll have to go to the store and buy food for your element. Oh, I almost forgot. Each of you needs to lose about ten to fifteen pounds. You'll be carrying backpacks and equipment fitted under your outer garments. You don't want to look like stuffed tamales which can compromise your identity."

After lunch, Mattingly had the team meet at the base riding stables. There, he had six motorcycles set up for the team to practice riding. The motorcycles were similar to the ones they'd be using on the mission. Nick, being the expert, showed each of the team members how to start and ride the motorcycles on the bridle track. Karol had no trouble riding the bike and was able to stay on the bike and ride around the course. Karen and Mike seemed to be naturals. Naomi being the indoor type, had the most difficulty riding the bike, but after several attempts, she was able stay on the bike and ride around the course.

After the riding lesson was completed, Dan spoke up, "I wish we had more time to practice, but unfortunately, we don't. We'll have to practice more once we're overseas."

"Naomi, I was amazed you actually stayed on the bike," Nick said.

Naomi thought to herself, *I'm going to show that little shit that I can ride just as well as anyone else.* Then she yelled, "You worry about yourself! What'd you expect for my first time on a motorcycle?"

Dan stepped between them. "Okay, you two, that's enough. Nick, I'm counting on you to keep Naomi out of trouble when she's riding."

"Yes, sir."

After class and training that day, the entire team went to the base gym and exercised. Karen, being in the best shape, encouraged them along.

Karol thought this was the best excuse to get into an exercise program.

After the workout, Dan spoke to the team, "From now on, I'll have the entire team get up early and have a morning jog before class."

Chapter 11
BOLLING AFB

Dan woke up at 5:30 A.M. got on his workout clothes, then headed down the hall and knocked on Karol's door. After a long pause, Karol opened. She looked like she just rolled out of the sack. Dan could only see her head peaking around the door. Even without makeup and her hair a mess, she was quite attractive to Dan. Her deep-green, half-open eyes were seductive as she looked at him.

"Give me a second, and I'll be ready. You can wait in here where it's warmer if you want."

Dan thought for a moment, then walked in. Karol had nothing on except a white towel wrapped around her waist. She walked into the bathroom with her back to Dan covering her breasts with her arms and hands. She didn't seem to mind if Dan saw her in this manner. Either that or she was still half-asleep and didn't realize what she was doing as the door closed. Dan could hear her brushing her teeth and putting on her running sweats and shoes.

A few minutes later, the two of them joined the rest of the team running around the base track, huffing in the cold morning air. Naomi and Karen were flying well ahead of

The Balkan Network

everyone else. Dan was running alongside Karol and said, "I want you to know something, Karol, since we'll be paired-up together. No matter what happens, I will not let anything happen to you. I plan on bringing everyone on the team back home safely."

"That's the kindest thing I've heard you say these past few days, Dan, thank you. I'm sure everything will work out fine. Don't forget we'll have the entire U.S. military looking over our shoulders," as she pointed to the sutures on the back of her neck.

Back in the classroom, Mattingly was already set up with his Power Point projector. He said, "I'd like to introduce you to some of the equipment that you'll be using on this assignment. We will communicate with the team via cell phones. Remarkable devices these cell phones; little old peasant women working in the fields have one. The cell phone coverage in all of Yugoslavia is quite good, in fact excellent in most areas."

He reached into his pocket and pulled out a typical looking cell phone except that it was slightly thicker than most.

"This is the device we'll use. It's an all-inclusive, multi-functional communications device. It's been specially modified by our friends at the National Security Agency. It's a regular Nokia cell phone used by most people in Yugoslavia except that it's been modified for satellite use and has a GPS tracking system in it. At any given time, we know where the call is being made. The GPS accuracy is within a couple hundred feet."

He removed the back cover of the cell phone. "This is a removable satellite antenna attached to the back of the phone. It is completely secure. No one in the world can intercept our communications except the NSA. You can also connect this device to a laptop and access the Internet from our satellites. If we need to talk to someone on the team, we just pick up the phone and call—it's that simple. The device acts like a walkie-talkie for short-range communication. It's also an aeronautical radio. You can communicate and monitor transmissions with aircraft. The GPS tracking mode allows you to monitor each others' positions using the satellite transmitter we implanted in your heads yesterday. Finally, it has a beacon and interrogation mode where you can send signals to search and rescue forces. Should someone be caught with the device, it will look and operate just like any other cell phone. Our satellites will reroute the call back to a local transmitter to ensure this."

Mattingly switched subjects, "Once the air war starts, all our tasking orders will come from NATO Air Headquarters in Naples. When they receive tasking from Brussels, they'll contact our operatives in the field and tell them what to do. As soon as our operatives acquire their information, they can call back and transmit the information in real time."

Mattingly went on, "Now that I've told you about the cell phones and communications equipment, let me introduce you to some of our field weapons. Each team member will be equipped with the cell phone, night vision goggles, laser designator, Makarov 9 mm automatic pistol with silencer and seventy-two rounds, and a Kalashnikov AKS-74U short barrel assault rifle with 120 rounds and a small backpack. We can get more rounds for the AK-74 if needed, but the weapon is basically for self-defense, not to ambush or fight off a brigade. We chose this Russian model because it's the same type weapon used by both Serb and Croatian forces. In fact, the possession of an AK-47 is quite common in all of Yugoslavia. You don't even have to worry about concealing the weapon because just about everyone has one in their possession."

The Balkan Network

Mattingly showed them a small device that could have passed for a CD player but in reality was a sophisticated metal and explosive material detector. "All the team members will have sufficient cash to live on. You will have to blend in with the local populous, so that means going to the store and buying food and gasoline just like any other person would." In the corner of the classroom were six black duffel bags with small index cards placed on top of them. Mattingly said, "Each of you is being issued one of these duffel bags. Inside you will find the AKS-74U, we'll just call it the AK-74, and four thirty-round magazines, the Makarov 9 mm pistol with six, twelve round magazines, Viking night vision goggles, metal detector, laser designator, secure satellite cell phone, and laptop computer. Please sign the hand receipt cards and take your duffel bag. You will have these with you from now on. I want you to become intimately familiar with each component. Your life will depend upon them. You'll have the opportunity to train using these weapons during the field exercises, but for now I want you to become familiar with the systems. Dan, would you please hand out the sacks?"

Dan went to the corner of the room and picked up the duffel bag with his name on it. It contained everything except the two weapons, which were already issued to him. He signed the hand receipt. He picked up the next one and handed it to Karol and then proceeded to issue each duffel bag to the other members of the team.

Mattingly continued with his presentation, "In this next phase of instruction, our objective is to give you training on escape and evasion in an urban environment. This afternoon we will discuss escape and evasion in rural and wilderness environments. Mike and Nick, you already know most of this type of escape and evasion, so we will rely on you two to help with this block of training."

Hal and Dan spent the rest of the day training the team on escape and evasion. This was accomplished by showing the team a film produced by the CIA that depicted agents evading enemy agents in the streets of Berlin. Next, Hal showed a film produced during the Vietnam War showing downed American flyers evading the Vietnamese in the jungles.

At the end of the training period, Mattingly said, "This concludes our academics training. Tomorrow we meet for our field training exercise to practice some of the techniques we've discussed and learned here in the classroom. Go to the base supply this afternoon and get a set of camouflage fatigues and combat boots. Supply personnel will have your names and will be expecting you. The rest of the equipment you'll need for the exercise will be issued at Quantico tomorrow morning. We meet here at 0600 hours sharp."

After the team was issued their equipment from base supply, Dan said, "I'd like everyone to meet back at my room after dinner, at 1800 hours. Bring your duffel bags and all the equipment with you. I need to give you some details before we begin the field training exercise tomorrow."

Later that night after dinner, Naomi was the first to knock on Dan's door, early. She was dressed in her fatigues. Dan said, "Come on in. You didn't have to wear your fatigues tonight."

"Well, I wasn't sure, besides I wanted to make sure they fit properly for the exercise tomorrow."

"Do you mind if I call you Lombard so we can get use to using the names?"

"Now that you mentioned it, I don't like that name at all. I could have come up with a different name if you'd asked me. I'd prefer you just call me Naomi."

The Balkan Network

"I'd like to call you by your first name, but I'm trying to get everyone to use their tactical names. Anyway, I know you take pride in wearing the military uniform but don't worry about the fit. In fact, we'll be issued Serbian or Eastern European-made clothing, usually designed as one-size-fits-all garments."

"Will I have a say in the colors?"

"I don't think so. Lombard … Naomi, one of the reasons why Karol and I picked you for this mission was because of your good looks. You can provide an element of surprise to an adversary if the need should arise. We paired you up with Nick because he's a good-looking guy about your same age, and I think that the two of you will blend in well. I trust that you two will look out after each other on this mission. By the way, where is Nick?"

"He was with me when we left the Q, but he forgot his duffel bag so he went back for it. I told him I'd go on."

Naomi knew about staying with Nick. The truth of the matter was she was attracted to Dan and she wanted to be alone with him for a few minutes.

Another knock on the door and Mike and Karen walked in.

Dan said, "I'm glad you two came together, come on in."

Karen dropped her duffle bag to the floor. "You said to stay together."

"Yes, I'm glad you listened."

Karol and Nick came at six o'clock, even though Karol only had to walk a few feet down the hall.

Dan closed the door to his room once everyone was inside and said, "I've asked each of you to be here tonight because tomorrow is a very important day in our training. Each of you will have a field evaluation exercise. Karol and I will coordinate the time and place for the exercise. We have several different scenarios to choose. At this point in time, we don't know which scenario you'll have. The purpose of this field training exercise is to see how you react under pressure in a tactical situation. Please keep in mind that the outcome of this exercise will help you and the team. When everyone has completed their exercise, we will have a debriefing session. If everything goes well, we should be back here by 1800 or 1900 hours tomorrow night. Do you have any questions for me?"

Nick spoke up, "Are we going to be doing any live firing with the AK-74 tomorrow?"

"Yes. That reminds me why I asked each of you to be here. Grant, would you show Eden how to work the AK-74? The same goes for you Speeder. Please give Lombard the rundown as well. I'll get with Sutter."

The team went through the motions on using the AK-74. Karol, being an intelligence officer and experienced working with Navy SEALS, had no trouble handling the weapon. However, Karen and Naomi, having no tactical experience, had trouble just holding the modified assault rifle. With some extra training, Mike and Nick were able to work with them and get them to load and unload their weapons.

After the team spent several hours going over the use of the weapon, Dan broke up the meeting. "That about wraps things up here tonight. Let's pack everything up and all get back to our rooms. We have a very busy day tomorrow." Dan walked everyone out of his room except for Karol. She stayed behind and helped tidy up Dan's room since it looked like a poker party had just broken up.

"Thanks for getting the team together to work on the rifles. Lombard and Eden definitely needed the extra training. You look tired, why don't you get some rest? We've got a big day ahead of us tomorrow."

"Yes, I'll do that in just a few minutes. Karol, there's something I want to ask you."

"Sure, go right ahead."

"Tomorrow, during the exercise, I'd like to put Naomi and Karen to the test, especially Naomi. I'd like you to come up with something where we could evaluate them in a combat situation."

"I think I already have something in mind, but we'll have to separate the couples."

"Yes, I know; that could be difficult especially after I've been telling everyone to stay with their partners."

"You and I'll have to find a way to separate first, and then we can work on the others."

Karol looked into his eyes and said, "Good night, Major. I'm looking forward to tomorrow."

"Let me walk you back to your room?"

"It's only a few steps away."

"Yeah, but I don't mind."

As Dan was walking Karol down the hall, he thought about her that morning in her room. For a second he thought about going back into her room but decided against it because they had such a long day tomorrow. *Perhaps another time*, he told himself.

Chapter 12
ARMED FORCES COMBINED TRAINING CENTER

Up to this point, the team had been given a lot of information in preparation for their assignment, everything from tactical intelligence and security to cooking Croatian food. Now it was time to start putting everything together. Grant and Eden were starting to bond. Lombard and Speeder developed a mutual respect for each other even though they both had powerful egos. Specter and Sutter were starting to develop an attraction for each other. The team met at six in the morning in front of the DIAC after breakfast. A military bus was waiting for them. Grant and Eden were dressed as instructed in their green, Battle Dress Uniforms (BDUs) with no rank or insignia and were ready with their duffel bags. Lombard and Speeder were up and ready to go, each with a tall, hot cup of coffee. Sutter and Specter were going through their duffel bags, making sure they had everything for the day's training. Hal Mattingly arrived at 6:05 AM in a black, government sport utility vehicle driven by Ms. Sara. They were both dressed in army fatigues with no rank or insignia.

Mattingly said, "Good morning, everyone, please take a seat on the bus where I'll brief you on today's training."

The team loaded their equipment on the bus, and everyone took a seat near the front of the bus. Almost instinctively, the team paired up instinctively and took seats next to each other.

"When we get to Quantico, we'll be met by the Army training specialists. They'll take us in the field to begin our first exercise. This should last until lunchtime. We'll take a lunch break sometime at eleven-thirty—at 1200 hours, we'll pair up and begin the evaluation exercise. Each of you will have an exercise and this should be finished by 1700 hours tonight. After that, we head back to base. You'll probably be exhausted after today's training, so we'll meet again tomorrow morning in the classroom for debriefing. That's it. I'm going ahead of the bus because I have a few matters to take care of before you get to Quantico. Regardless of what happens today, remember: it's only an exercise. Please take what you learn today with you." Mattingly turned and walked down the steps of the bus, said a few words to the bus driver, climbed into his SUV, and headed for Quantico. The rest of the team left Bolling just after 6:30 AM.

Later that morning at the Armed Forces Combined Training Center, two Army sergeants met the bus just outside the training ground at Quantico.

"I'm Sergeant Mike Mc Cullun and this is my partner Sergeant Steve Reems. We'll take you through the day's training. Please get all your gear off the bus and meet us down at the bottom of this hill.

Everyone assembled in the clearing, which functioned as a firing range. There were six targets set up on the range about twenty-five yards away. Mc Cullun and Reems briefed the team on the use of the small arms and each team member got to practice live firing of their Makarov pistols. Each team member got sixty rounds of practice ammunition to use with and without silencer. Dan and Mike were the best shots scoring 100 percent at twenty-five yards. Karol and Nick tied at 95 percent; however, Karen and Naomi had difficulty just hitting the target. After a few pointers from Sgt. Mc Cullun, both were able to hit some rounds on the target.

After the firing exercise, Sergeant Mc Cullun said, "I want each of you to get your other weapons out and loaded. We have a table set up over here with your MILES equipment."

MILES equipment is the military's version of laser tag. The MILES equipment uses an infrared device for scoring shots fired from another weapon loaded with blanks and gives the simulation of being hit by enemy fire.

Sergeant Mc Cullun attached the electronic device to each person's AK-74, while Sergeant Reems helped them put on the MILES vest. Next, they were handed a web belt with six thirty-round magazines fitted with blanks to load into their weapons. "These are your training rounds. You'll have the opportunity to use your weapons in realistic scenarios as you make your way to the objective area. Sergeant Reems and I will issue your instructions and stay about twenty paces behind as you make your way toward the objective. If someone should get hit from an enemy fighter, the MILES equipment will go off and you'll be a simulated casualty until we can unlock the system. Your leadership will direct you to the objective area. We will monitor and facilitate the situation and give you advice if we see the need to, otherwise you'll be on your own. Who's in charge of this group?"

Dan raised his hand and the whole group listened alertly.

The Balkan Network

"Okay, here's your objective. You are tasked with getting your group to the objective building that is located five kilometers to the east. You must get all members of your group to this blockhouse by 1130 hours. Once you get to the blockhouse, there will be an airman wearing a flight suit and carrying an ax. One of you will approach the airman and say these words, 'Good morning, can you tell me where the nearest farmhouse is?' The airman will respond with, 'Two kliks down the road.' If you do not get the correct authentication code, you can assume the airman is hostile, and you can take whatever action you see fit. Are there any questions?" Dan shook his head. "Good, now for the bad news. The area between here and the blockhouse has enemy fighters hidden in the brush. They could be anywhere, and their orders are to kill any enemy fighters coming through this area. You have ten minutes to plan this operation, then the clock will start. Do you understand?" Dan nodded.

"Okay, you have ten minutes. We'll be twenty paces behind monitoring the situation. Good luck."

Dan got the team together, "Grant, I need you to come up with a plan in a hurry, any suggestions?"

He spoke up immediately, "I've done something like this before. Eden and I will take point, you and Sutter take the center position, Speeder and Lombard will cover the rear and the rear flanks. We'll start on the high ridges first. The aggressors will probably be seeking higher ground as well. We'll be there to meet them. Once we get the high ground established, we can move to the lower areas and work our way to the blockhouse."

Dan took out a small topographic map of the area that Sergeant Mc Cullun gave him and showed it to Mike.

"Show me the ridgeline you're thinking about?"

Mike pointed to a small ridge located along a valley.

"This would be the one. If we move now we might be able to surprise them."

"Okay, let's get going. Everyone draw your weapons and follow Grant; do what he says and keep low and close to the trees."

The team gathered their gear and headed out. The area was wooded with tall trees and underbrush providing plenty of cover. Dan thought Mike had the right idea. A quick look at the terrain showed the higher ridges had fewer trees and fewer places to hide for an ambush but left plenty of cover for a team to evade. In less than ten minutes, Mike held out his fist for the team to stop. Immediately Dan and Karol dropped to their knees followed by Nick and Naomi. At that moment, a hail of automatic small arms fire engulfed the area. Grant had been right, they had obviously been surprised—the aggressors had no choice but to engage the team. Mike gave Dan a signal to come forward.

"Is everyone all right back there?" said Mike.

Dan nodded his head as Nick returned fire up the ridge. Mike continued to fire at the aggressor as he spoke to Dan.

"You and Sutter take the left flank and then up the ridge. The aggressors will be trying to do the same but they'll be going downhill. We've got the element of surprise. When you take the flank meet back here.

Dan nodded in acknowledgment and knew what Mike had in mind. He worked his way back to Karol's position, "Follow me and move fast. Remember: we stick together."

"I'm right behind you."

The two officers hurried down the left flank and into the brush. Nick and Naomi holding the rear flanks were firing in small bursts as Nick coached Naomi. This was Naomi's first time firing an automatic weapon and her aim

The Balkan Network

was high and left, but she kept the aggressors from making a clear shot at the team. Mike and Karen continued to fire in full automatic bursts at the Aggressors.

Nick shouted to Naomi in Serbo-Croatian, "I don't like this damn AK-74! I wish I had my regular M-16 or even a standard AK with longer range. Stay low and keep firing in small bursts till I tell you otherwise."

Meanwhile, a few feet away, Karol stayed within a few steps of Dan as they worked their way across the left flank and then up the hill to the aggressor's location. The extra exercise and laps round the base jogging track were paying off. Within a minute, Dan and Karol heard crashing and thrashing in the brush from the aggressors trying to outflank them. They took cover behind two large trees. Dan raised his weapon and nodded his head at Karol to do the same. Karol took aim and Dan yelled, "Now!" They stood up and emptied their thirty round magazines into the area where they heard the noises. The sound of MILES gear went off like a pinball machine. Dan and Karol quickly loaded another magazine then continued up the hill. Sergeant Reems was still running up the hill twenty paces behind when he saw what happened. Smiling from ear to ear, he continued to disarm the MILES tones from the aggressors' vests and said to them, "You two are confirmed kills. Get back to base and report for your next set of orders." Sergeant Reems continued up the hill to catch Dan and Karol.

As they were running up the hill, Dan said to Karol, "Grant was right, looks like the aggressors were watching us and waiting for us to move to lower ground so they could set up an ambush. They didn't expect us to take the high ground right away and had no choice but to give up their positions and engage."

Dan and Karol continued up the hill and made it to

within one hundred feet of the main aggressor's stronghold at the top of the hill. That's where they heard the loud blasts of automatic gunfire. Still huffing and puffing, Dan nodded at Karol to take aim and begin firing. They both emptied their magazines into the aggressors' location and the sound of MILES equipment went off.

Karol, out of breath said, "I think we shocked the hell out of them! Let's get back to Grant and Eden. The quicker we get back to their location, the sooner we can regroup and advance to the blockhouse."

Dan could see that Karol had tactical knowledge and she did well in the firefight. She would definitely be useful in a real situation. The two retraced their footsteps down the hill. When within a few feet from Nick and Naomi, Karol yelled, "Sutter and Specter here, area clear!"

Mike yelled, "Great job, you two—we heard the MILES gear go off just a few minutes after you left. We thought for sure you two were waxed!"

Dan composed himself once he got back to the group and said, "We don't have a moment to lose. I'm sure they're going to send in more aggressors after us, so let's come up with a plan to get to the blockhouse."

Mike and Dan decided to stay on the ridgeline for as long as they could before moving down to lower ground just in case some aggressors where taking up the rear. About two miles from the blockhouse, they moved down to lower ground finding a small running creek with large boulders. They used these boulders for cover as they made their way to the blockhouse. The boulders were wet and slippery, and they had to take their time traversing the creek. Nick and Naomi took up the rear, and as they were making their way along the creek, Nick said, "I'm impressed. You didn't clam up and do nothing."

"What did you expect me to do? Sit there and watch as

you got shot? I come from a military family; my Dad taught me a lot, especially about taking care of your buddy. I just tried to take care of you so you wouldn't get your little ass shot up!"

The trek to the blockhouse along the creek bed took longer than anticipated because of the rugged terrain, but it kept them safe from the aggressors. Just before 11:00 AM, Mike assembled the team 150 feet from the blockhouse, still hidden under cover. Karol was the first to speak.

"Hold up a second, I have an idea. The aggressors don't know our capabilities. One thing about American military forces in general is they are all too predictable. We need an element of surprise. Lombard, come here for a second." Karol looked at Naomi and said, "Take off your blouse."

"What do you mean? Have you gone crazy? I'm not taking off anything."

"Just do as you're told and take off your blouse. I'll give it back to you when we're done. We've got to shock the hell out of that flyboy."

Naomi reluctantly took off her blouse, handed it to Karol, and thought, *She's really starting to get on my nerves.*

Dan and Mike could see where this was heading and let them proceed. Next, Karol said, "Now take off your tee shirt." Naomi was now crouched down wearing only her bra. Karol pulled out her knife and poked a hole in the tee shirt then ripped it a few times to make it look torn and tattered. She then reached down and picked up some mud and smeared it across Naomi's face and arms to give the impression she'd fallen.

"Put this thing back on," Karol said. "The rest of the team will take up positions on either side of the blockhouse. When we're in place, I want you to move toward the blockhouse and stop ten feet from the flyboy. Keep your distance then ask the security questions. If it's a trap, we can engage from the flanks. He'll never know what hit him."

Dan said, "Brilliant, why didn't I think of it. Men will instinctively come to Naomi's rescue if she's in trouble.

Mike said, "I'll take Eden to the right. Specter, you and Sutter take the left. Speeder, cover Lombard from the front. Give us about five minutes then, Lombard, you move in. Does everyone understand?"

"Let's move out people," said Dan.

The airman was pacing back and forth in front of the blockhouse. He didn't notice the team moving to the flanks. After a few minutes, Naomi came out from under cover and approached. The airman stopped and looked at Naomi. She walked to within ten feet of the airman and stopped. The flyer looked astounded, just as Karol had predicted. He seemed surprised to the see Naomi cut and scratched. Naomi smiled and started speaking in Serbo-Croatian, "Excuse me, but could you tell me where the nearest farmhouse is located?" The airman stood and stared for a few seconds then looked to his right and left, then reached behind his back, and tried to pull out his pistol. Before he could raise his weapon at Naomi, a burst of automatic gunfire engulfed the area. Naomi jumped back and headed for cover. Sergeant Mc Cullun and Sergeant Reems came from behind Naomi and shouted, "Cease fire, Cease fire!"

Mc Cullun said, "What the hell happened here? Everyone come out!"

The sounds of clapping were heard from behind the blockhouse. Hal Mattingly and Ms. Sara came into view showing their signs of satisfaction.

"Well done, well done. We've got everything on tape. We'll debrief later on what just occurred. Mattingly walked up to the airman and said, "I don't think there would have been much left of you to rescue had this been an actual rescue mission. You just had 120 rounds pumped into you at close range."

The airman replied, "She didn't give me the right code and spoke in some Russian language I'd never heard before."

Karol winked at Dan, "I told you he would be predictable."

"All right, everyone, let's break for lunch," said Mc Cullun. Everyone sat down on the floor of the blockhouse and ate their lunches of a peanut butter and jelly sandwich, fruit, and a drink. Everyone ate not realizing they had built up such an appetite. After lunch, Mc Cullun, Reems, Mattingly, and Ms. Sara got up and walked out of the blockhouse.

Mattingly said to everyone on his way out, "Ms. Sara and I'll be back in a few minutes. We've got to check on the next phase of the training. Stay here and rest a few more minutes until we get back."

Dan said, "I'm tired. I think I'll lay down for some rest."

Mike and Karen did the same while Nick sat on floor and closed his eyes. Naomi had her blouse back on and closed her eyes while sitting against the side of the blockhouse. A few minutes passed in silence when all hell broke loose.

"Get down!"

"Don't say a fucking word!"

"Get your heads on to the floor!"

Several aggressors stormed the blockhouse, guns drawn, all wearing black ski masks.

"Get these sacks over your heads!" said one of the aggressors as he poked Mike in the back of the head and placed a set of flex cuffs on his hands. Another said, "You fucking bitches think you're so smart. We've got something special just for you!"

Another aggressor took Naomi and Karen, placed hoods over their heads, handcuffed them, and then walked them away. "Where's the short bitch?" one aggressor asked. "There were three bitches here, now I only see two."

"We've got the bitch and the other guy in the back of the truck. We'll beat the crap out of them later."

Chapter 13
THE CLASSROOM

At five o'clock the next morning, Dan and Karol were jogging around the track at the base fitness center. It was still dark outside. The exercise felt good to Karol as she made her way around the track. Dan was a lap and a half ahead of her, but she didn't mind. Yesterday had been a strenuous day and most of the team, including her, slept on the bus during the drive back to Bolling. The field exercise was nothing compared to the real thing. Both of the other women made mistakes during crucial moments in a life-or-death situation. This was expected since neither had experience in combat situations. The debriefing session that morning would help clear up a lot of things. If it had been her way, she would have had at least two months of intense training for the other women before turning them loose in the field, but she had no choice. The men would have to look out for them and make sure they didn't spend much time by themselves. Dan caught up with Karol around the track and slowed his pace to keep up with her.

"Good morning, how are you feeling after all the running we did yesterday?"

"I'm a little sore but other than that, I think I'll live. I've been thinking about the exercise yesterday. Do you think Karen and Naomi will be able to handle the stress of a real mission?"

Dan uttered as he took deep breaths, "I think the women performed as expected, but we'll know more once we see the tapes and have the chance to debrief. You've got to remember that most of the time the team will be together as a group or in pairs.

At 8:00 AM, the team entered the DIAC classroom. The room was already semi darkened, ready for video viewing. There was a large projection screen pulled down from the center of the room, and Hal Mattingly was waiting patiently along with Ms. Sara by his side.

"Please take a seat everyone. We've got a lot of information to pass on to you today. This day and especially the morning session will go by quickly, despite the amount of information. Dan, you and Karol please come forward and help with the debriefing."

Dan and Karol made their way to the front of the classroom and took seats off to the side. Mattingly continued to stand with a laser pointer in one hand and a remote control device in the other. "Let me begin by saying that I did not create the scenarios you are about to see. These scenarios were masterminded by Dan and Karol. They wanted to see how each of you would react under an unexpected condition in a tactical situation."

Nick spoke up first, "They did a good job of that, I must say."

Mattingly went on, "They will help with the briefing because they played active rolls in the exercise. Let's begin."

Dan spoke up first, "Overall, I think the group session went well. The aggressors were caught off guard. There-

The Balkan Network

fore, I'm pleased that we worked together as a team. Sutter's idea to surprise the airman using Lombard as bait was very effective."

Karol interrupted, "I did this to show you that U.S. military forces in general are very predictable. Even the airman, presumably a member of our highly trained U.S. Special Forces, was caught off guard, but he reacted just as I expected. I want you to realize that other military forces throughout the world are not as predictable as us. They react without emotion to any given situation. Most U.S. military personnel think emotionally. This was a key concept to the scenarios we developed, to test your predictability."

Mattingly started the DVD player and showed the first scenario.

"I've reviewed the tapes, and, Lombard, your instructions were to go up to the airman and say, 'Good morning, could you tell me where the nearest farmhouse is located?' You said, 'Excuse me' instead of 'Good morning.' Most Eastern Europeans are not as polite in speaking and would never say, 'Excuse me.' The airman was caught off guard and reacted the way he did because you spoke in Serbo-Croatian, not because of what you said. It wasn't until after I saw the tapes and had it translated that I saw the error. If it makes you feel any better, had you spoken in English, the airman would have reacted in the same manner because you gave the wrong brevity code. You said, 'Excuse me' instead of 'Good morning.' Remember that the next time you're in a similar situation."

Naomi nodded her head in acknowledgment.

Dan spoke next, "We needed a way of separating the group. Everyone did such a great job of staying together that we had to come up with this scenario. As it turned out, it worked better than expected. We had the aggressors storm the blockhouse and put the hoods on everyone so you couldn't see Sutter and me separate and leave the blockhouse. We also wanted you to be exposed to a captive situation. If you should be captured, you can expect similar treatment, probably much worse. We separated you and placed each of you in solitary confinement. You can expect this as well if you should be captured as a team or pair. This allowed time for Sutter and me to get down the hill and into the cinder block house in preparation for the next exercises. Grant, let's start with you."

The DVD started with Mike running down the hill, and then Dan said, "I want each of you to take a look at Grant and see what he did. You all did the same things at first. Your objective was to get to the cinder block building without getting shot."

As the DVD rolled, everyone could see that Mike used the storm drains to gain access to the building. Naomi spoke up, "I'm glad I did something right."

Dan continued, "Grant, your Marine Corps. training came in handy during the exercise. We made it difficult for you by placing the captive in the furthest room in the building. You made your way and cleared each room professionally. When you finally reached Sutter in the room upstairs, we tried to surprise you with the wounded aggressor. You didn't fall for that one. You put two slugs in her back. I think Ms. Sara was just as surprised as we were. You placed the safety of your teammate before anything else, even ethics. If this had been conventional warfare, the Geneva Convention would protect the wounded soldier. However, this is not conventional warfare. Shoot first and ask questions later. Just to let you know, the Israelis found this out the hard way. After several losses, the Israelis changed their tactics. To this day, standard operating procedure in this situation is for the Israeli Defense Force

The Balkan Network

to put two rounds into the enemy's heads, to make sure they're dead, then start asking questions."

"Now let's move on to Eden," said Mattingly.

Karol resumed the debriefing. "Overall, we were impressed with your performance, especially for someone with no tactical or combat experience. I tried to surprise you with my appearance, and it turned out you hesitated for just a fraction of a second. I told Specter you'd do that, and he was hiding behind the door waiting to make his move."

Mattingly said, "Always check the sides before you enter a room. Once you clear the room, then you can take care of your objective. Had you checked the areas behind the door, you would have seen Dan and me standing there. You had the automatic weapon. You could have killed both of us with one burst."

Karol spoke up, "Lombard, you found the secret entrance to the cinder block building using the underground storm drains. Once you saw Dan hanging from the ceiling, you knew he was in trouble. Secure the area first then secure your objective. Remember, you're authorized to use deadly force to protect you and your team members. I was waiting for you to do something, anything. I got tired of waiting, so I just fired my AK-74 and killed you."

"Last but not least we have Speeder. I knew there was a reason I gave you that name," said Dan. "I must say, you were resourceful stealing the truck. You did everything right except you turned your back to the window. Never leave an opening uncovered. You never know who's coming or going. The idea of rappelling down the building was not mine. Hal thought we needed the extra training, so the aggressors had Grant and I rappel down the side of the building. Seeing you with your back turned to us was just icing on the cake. If you're ever in a situation where you have several openings and you're by yourself, make sure you clear all areas. All you had to do was turn your body toward the window as you untied the cuffs from Lombard."

Mattingly spoke next. "I think we all learned something here. What I'd like to do is play all the tapes from yesterday's activities and let you watch. If you would like me to stop the tape just let me know, otherwise I'll just let it run."

The team watched the tapes and everyone saw something they hadn't seen before. It was well after twelve o'clock when they finally had a break. Mattingly said, "After lunch I want everyone back here—we have something special for you ladies."

Chapter 14
THE SEAMSTRESS?

After lunch, the team reassembled in the classroom. To everyone's surprise it looked like a thrift store. Several racks of women's clothes were sitting on hangers next to the walls. Boxes of shoes, hats, gloves, and other accessories were strewn about the room and on the tables. Two Army soldiers unloaded boxes of men's clothing, suitcases, duffle bags, hats, shoes, and boots. Hal Mattingly and Ms. Sara were arranging the clothes in different sections and sizes.

Mattingly said, "I trust each of you had a good lunch? I apologize for the mess, but we just got this shipment in from Langley. Before we get started, I'd like to formally introduce you to my personal assistant, Ms. Sara. You've seen her before, but I'd like you to get to know her better, because in addition to her other skills, she's also a seamstress. She'll be making final adjustments to the clothing and accessories you'll be wearing overseas. Please do what she asks."

Dan looked at Ms. Sara and could see that she was arranging the garments according to size and type. By the way she expertly selected the garments, Dan deduced that she was in no way a seamstress, though it was probably one of her many skills. He remembered that Josef said the DIA would arrange for a specialist to help with the clothing. There are only a few people in the country that specialize in this sort of thing, and these individuals usually come from the intelligence community. Furthermore, Dan noticed Ms. Sara still wearing the lapel pin—it looked like a miniature version of the George Cross, but he brushed the thought off and continued with the training.

Ms. Sara grumbled something to herself then motioned to Karen to come forward. Ms. Sara picked out several blouses and skirts with bras and underwear to go with the outfits. Next, she picked out shoes, purses, handbags, and belts to match. Most of the clothes not too dressy or formal. Then she handed Karen casual clothes, things she could wear going to the market or shopping for groceries. Last came her outdoor clothing, something she might wear going on a picnic or a camping trip: boots, heavy socks, and a jacket. Finally, she said, "Give me your dog tags." Karen took the tags from around her neck and gave them to Ms. Sara. She made a small slit next to the buckle of one of the belts, slipped the dog tag inside the belt leather, and said, "This will work out just fine." She gave the belt and dog tags back to Karen.

Very clever, thought Dan.

Ms. Sara did the same for all the women, and as expected, Naomi had the most comments on the clothing.

"I would never pick any of this stuff if it were up to me."

Ms. Sara then gave each woman a different bag or suitcase to carry their garments in and said in her British accent, "You will pack your clothing in these bags that I selected for you. Please do not change or exchange the bags. From now on, do not shave your underarms, legs, or pubic areas. Do not use any makeup, moisturizer, hand creams, lotions, or perfume. When you take a shower, use a natural soap to wash your hair and body. Don't use anything else. Be as natural as you can. I need to ask all you women an important question, so please be honest with me. Do any of you have any small 'tramp stamps' that were missed during your medical examinations?"

All the women shook their heads, then Ms. Sara said, "Good, because if you did, I would have to take a closer look and see if we could surgically remove them. If they were too big and couldn't be surgically removed, then you'd be disqualified from the team." All the women looked at her in disbelief. Ms. Sara was definitely more than Mattingly's personal assistant and seamstress.

"Now for you men. Please come forward."

Ms. Sara handed each of the men similar clothing and different bags and said, "I want you men to stop shaving effective tomorrow. Don't pluck your eyebrows or anything like that either. I want you to use only a mild soap to wash your hair and body as well and remember no cologne or aftershave. Do you understand?"

All the men nodded their heads in acknowledgment and Dan recalled the story Josef told him about the captured OSS operative that used American shaving cream and aftershave lotion and repeated it to the team. Ms. Sara passed out accessories to all the men: hats, belts, shoes, and wallets.

Mattingly added, "From now on do not wear anything but the clothes Ms. Sara has given you unless told otherwise. When you get back to quarters tonight, I want each of you to place everything you own in a box and leave it in the room when you check out. That includes all your personal items, ladies, like makeup, body lotions, and shampoos. Same goes for you men."

Ms. Sara spoke up and addressed the women, "I want each of you to keep a tee shirt and a pair of sweatpants to wear tonight. Everything else, box away."

The entire team placed all their newly acquired clothing and accessories as Ms. Sara gathered the last of their personal clothing and wheeled it out the classroom.

Mattingly added, "Is there anything you ladies might need that we're forgetting?"

Of course, Naomi spoke up immediately and said, "What about nail polish? You didn't say anything about that."

Ms. Sara turned beet-red and it seemed as though steam would come from her ears as she muttered to herself.

"I think where we're going we don't need to worry about standing appointments. Get your crap together like Ms. Sara told you," Karol said sternly.

Mattingly continued, "If no one has any more questions or comments, this concludes your last block of academic training. Now we move on to the planning and preparation phase. Dan, would you come up and brief your team for tomorrow's activities?"

Dan came to the front of the class and began. "Your first assignment is to get your personal gear ready for tomorrow. That means having your field bag with your equipment and the bags you were just issued today packed and ready for deployment tomorrow night. Each of us will wear our respective service uniforms to travel aboard the aircraft. You will only need one service uniform. The other sets you can leave in your rooms with the rest of your personal clothing when you check out."

Naomi spoke up, "You mean we're leaving for Yugoslavia tomorrow?"

Dan replied, "As we have said all along, we're under a time constraint. The sooner we get in place, the sooner we

The Balkan Network

can start the air campaign. Our bus leaves the Billeting Office tomorrow at 1500 hours. From there, we'll travel across the Potomac to Andrew Air Force Base. We'll fly nonstop to Aviano Air Base, Italy. We'll have the whole plane to ourselves. The rest of our gear and equipment will meet up with us once we get to Zagreb. Bring only your field bag and the suitcases Ms. Sara gave you. I suggest everyone get a good night's sleep. I'll be by tonight to check everyone's gear and clothing."

Mattingly said, "Tonight you can contact any family or loved ones. This will be your last chance to make contact with them before you leave. Please do not mention anything about where you are going. Just say that you're going TDY overseas and you will be out of contact for several weeks. Tell them at this point you don't know the exact location of your assignment but you will be in touch with them at a later date to give them an update on your situation. Do not say anything other than that."

"All right people, with that said, you're all dismissed. Don't forget, I'll be by each of your rooms tonight," said Dan.

As everyone left the room and was out of earshot, Mattingly walked up to Dan and said, "By the way, for obvious reasons you are not allowed to contact your parents at this time. I'll let you know when you can; however, contact anyone else you care about."

"I understand, but there is no one else I need to contact. Good night, sir. I'll see you tomorrow at 1500 hours."

Chapter 15
FINAL PREPARATION

Everyone had a quiet dinner before returning to their rooms to prepare for the flight. Hardly anyone spoke a word. The only exception was Naomi.

"Some of the clothes Ms. Sara picked out for me look like something an old lady would wear and makes me look a hundred pounds heavier."

Karol calmly leaned across the dinner table and said, "Live with it, honey, and stop complaining. You got more important things to worry about."

Later that evening, Dan and Karol went to the VAQ and checked everyone's gear to make sure their equipment was packed correctly for the flight. The team did a good job getting packed and ready. Even Naomi listened and boxed her personal items and clothing to be left behind. Karol looked through all the women's bags checking for contraband. The only thing she noticed was the Serbian contraceptives prescribed by Dr. Reed.

After Dan and Karol left the VOQ for the night, Mike knocked on Karen's door. "It's me. Can I come in?"

Karen opened the door and allowed him to come in.

The Balkan Network

This was the first time Mike had come to her room since they'd been at Bolling, and it seemed strange that he came now, but she was glad to see him. Up to this point, it was all training and preparation, but in a few hours they'd be leaving for Yugoslavia to do the real thing.

Mike stepped into Karen's room, "I just wanted to see how you're doing tonight. Is everything okay?"

"Come on in, I need to talk to you."

"I came here to have a few words with you also, away from the others."

"Can I offer you a soft drink or something? I think I still have a few in the refrigerator."

"No thanks, I'm fine. The reason I came here tonight is because I wanted to tell you personally that I thought you did an excellent job at the exercise yesterday. I don't think you need to worry about anything on this mission."

"Thanks for the nice words. You know, I'm not afraid of *going* on the mission. I think I'm more afraid of screwing up or letting the team down in some way. I'm afraid I might slip and say the wrong thing at the wrong time— maybe a word or phrase out of place. Naomi's Serbo-Croatian is perfect. She never misses a cue. She doesn't even have an accent. I tried to twist and turn her around during casual conversations, but she never got confused or said the wrong word at any time. I don't know if I can do the same thing."

"I didn't notice anything when you two were conversing, but again, I'm not the language expert. I think you'll do fine on this mission. Don't forget, we'll be together almost the whole time."

Karen was dressed only in a pair of sweatpants and a tee shirt, like Ms. Sara instructed, and Mike couldn't help notice her nipples under her shirt. She had obviously packed away her American made underwear. Her red hair was down instead of pulled back like she normally wore it. Karen sat down on the edge of the bed. "I know we've been told that everything will be okay and we'll be safe, but you never know what could happen in the fog of war. Please tell me you'll look after me?"

"Of course I will. We'll both come back."

As he said this, Mike noticed Karen trembling.

"What's wrong? Is there something I can do for you?"

"Yes, could you please stay with me tonight?"

Just a few doors down the hall, Naomi was getting off the phone talking with her father. He was proud of his daughter and told her to be careful. Nick finished talking with his grandmother and he promised her that he would be careful and for her not to worry. As he hung up the phone, Nick sat in his chair and stared out the window for a few minutes before his telephone rang again.

"Are you still up?" asked Naomi.

"I can't sleep. I just got off the phone talking with my grandmother, and she thinks I'm going to Germany. I had to lie to her and tell her that because she kept asking me where I was going. What are you doing right now?"

"I'm going to have a hard time falling asleep just thinking about the mission."

"I've got the best cure for insomnia." Nick walked over to the refrigerator and pulled out six-pack of beer. "I've got a cold six-pack in my room. I've been saving it for just such an occasion, except I was planning on drinking it by myself. Would you like to join me?"

"Give me thirty seconds, and I'll be at your door."

Dan was back in his room cleaning his AK-74 when he heard a knock on his door.

"Come on in, Karol, it's unlocked."

"How did you know it was me?"

"Who else would come to my room at ten o'clock at

The Balkan Network

night the last day before we head out on a dangerous secret mission?"

Karol had on sweatpants and a tee shirt with no underwear, just as instructed. Dan, still looking down at his assault rifle, said to Karol, "Are you packed for tomorrow? You know, I didn't check your gear. I hope everything is in order?"

"What if I told you it wasn't?" What if I told you that I want you to come over and help me do just that?"

Dan stopped cleaning his weapon and looked up at Karol. She looked attractive despite wearing sweats. Her brown hair was down, and a few strands hung in front of her eyes. Her eyes were red and bloodshot and looked as if she had been crying.

"I made a long-distance call to Hawaii to tell Tom I was going TDY overseas."

"And what happened?"

"Another woman answered the phone, so I hung up."

"I'm sorry to hear that. Is there anything I can do to make this easier?"

"Well, you know, Major, I *could* use some help with my gear."

Dan got up from the chair and walked over to Karol still holding his rifle. "I'll have to go inside your room and check your bags to make sure you don't have any contraband."

"Yes, I know that."

Karol turned, walked out of the room, and proceeded down the hall to her room. Dan put down his rifle, closed and locked his door, then followed. This time he wasn't going to hold anything back. As they approached Karol's room, she left the door slightly ajar for him to come in. Once inside, Dan closed the door behind. Neither said a word. They just stared at each other then Karol wrapped her arms around him and said, "I need you to stay with me tonight."

"This could get complicated."

"Yes, I know the consequences; I could jeopardize our mission, the team, and my career. But I need this. Besides, as long as I don't get pregnant, everything will be okay."

He didn't resist and slowly worked his hands under her shirt and grabbed hold of her breasts. Karol let out a slight moan and said, "Let me help you."

Chapter 16
THE FLIGHT TO AVIANO

At 8:30 in the morning, the phone rang, waking Karol up from a deep sleep. She rolled over and answered the phone. "Hello, this is Karol."

Mattingly was on the other end. "Karol, I'm trying to reach Dan. Have you seen him this morning?"

"Just a minute." She covered the phone receiver and collected her thoughts on how she was going to proceed. Dan was still asleep next to her. He had made love to her all-night long. "No, I haven't seen him all morning. I could go down the hall and check his room."

"No, that won't be necessary. If you see him, tell him to call me on my cell phone, immediately."

"Sure, no problem. I'll let him know if I see him. By the way, is it something I can relay to him?"

"No, I need to talk to him about a personal matter. Have a good morning, Karol, and I'll see you on the flight line."

Karol hung up the phone and rolled Dan over. "Get up! That was Hal. He wants you to call him immediately. He's been trying to reach you all morning. He didn't say what it's about—only that it's personal. Do you think he knows you slept with me?"

Dan rubbed his eyes to wake up. "I don't think so. The satellites can't track us to that degree."

Dan took Karol's phone. He wondered how he was going to explain himself out of this one. Then he called Mattingly from her room phone.

"Good morning, Hal, this is Dan."

"Dan, I called your room and your cell phone but there was no answer, so I asked the operator to connect me to Karol's room. I was hoping she knew where you were. Anyway, I need to speak to you. Is it okay to talk?"

"Yeah, it's okay. Sorry I missed your call. I was probably in the shower and didn't hear any of the phones ring. I just happen to come by Karol's room to see if she needed help packing her things. I'm calling from her room. She said it was urgent."

"I'm sorry to tell you this, but I just received word that Josef passed away last night. He died peacefully in his sleep."

Dan didn't say anything for a few seconds. "It's not surprising. He wasn't in the best of health. I could tell he'd been ill for some time."

"Dan, I want you to know that Josef thought highly of you. He was hoping to see you off today and be there to meet you when you got back. You know, this was his mission. He planned everything from the moment I asked for his assistance."

Mattingly collected his thoughts then said, "Now that Josef's passed away, there's something you need to know about him. His story is largely untold, mainly because it involved two opposing political leaders in Yugoslavia during World War II: Josef Tito and Draza Mihailovich."

"Go ahead, I'm listening."

The Balkan Network

"Do you recall anything Josef said to you about the Halyard or Alum Missions while you were his student back at Berkeley?"

"No, he never mentioned it during his lectures, but he did say something to me aboard the train. In fact, he gave me a dagger that belonged to Mihailovich. It's packed away with my personal belongings."

"The Halyard Operation was one of the largest rescue operations behind enemy lines in the history of warfare. The OSS sent a team of operatives to Pranjani to coordinate the rescue of 516 Allied airmen held captive inside Nazi-occupied Serbia. Most of the airmen were shot down returning from Ploesti. Josef was the OSS field commander for that operation. He coordinated the overall operation along with Mihailovich and several other OSS agents to successfully rescue all 516 of the airmen."

"Then he really was the last person alive that knew anything about setting up covert operations inside Yugoslavia."

"Indeed he was. He was the last American to leave Serbia in December of 1944. Now you know the real reason why I asked an aging university professor to assist me with this operation. I thought you should know."

Dan could tell by his voice that Mattingly seemed deeply moved by Josef's death.

"Anyway, Dan, I know you've got a lot to do this morning. I just wanted to get the word out to you as soon as possible. I'll be arriving late for the flight tonight. I need to follow up on work Josef did before we leave and make sure nothing was left undone. I'll see you aboard the aircraft."

"Thanks for letting me know, sir." Dan hung up the phone and thought about Josef. On this mission, Dan was asked to look after just five other operatives and perhaps help rescue one or two NATO airmen, but Josef rescued 516 and was in charge of dozens of operatives.

"What was that all about?" Karol asked.

"Luckily, it wasn't about us. It was about my college professor; he's the one that's been organizing this mission with Hal and me from the very beginning. He passed away last night. He was eighty-five."

"I'm so sorry to hear that. Is there anything I can do?"

"You're part of the team now and the only other officer. This is as good a time as any to give you details of how the three of us met."

Dan told Karol about Kostinic and his undergraduate studies at Berkeley and how they met again aboard the Amtrak Coast Starlight. He also told Karol the story about Hal Mattingly's fiancée and her brutal death.

"There's more. Professor Kostinic told me that Penelope Walsh left behind a young child by the name of Sarah. It could be a coincidence, but there might be some connection between her and Mattingly's personal assistant, the mysterious Ms. Sara. We don't even know her last name. Hal never mentioned it to us."

"What makes you think there is a connection?"

"She's about the right age, and she's seems to always be with him. Furthermore, I didn't examine it closely, but Ms. Sara wears a lapel pin in the shape of the George Cross. There's only been about four women awarded that decoration, and most of those were British secret agents during World War II."

"It's possible, Dan—Ms. Sara does seem more than a personal assistant and seamstress—and you're right, we don't know her last name—but what's the connection between her and Mattingly?"

"I honestly don't know. I haven't figured that out yet. Anyway, it's not that important as far as the mission is concerned. I just happen to notice it. There's a lot more I need to tell you, but we can do that later. In the meantime, let's get everyone up and get some breakfast. I'm absolutely starving."

At three in the afternoon, the team assembled in front of the VOQ. As Dan instructed, they checked out of their rooms and left their personal items behind in a box. Dan made sure the dagger given to him by Kostinic was left in a safe location with his personal belongings. A military bus was waiting to take the team to Andrews in front of the VOQ. Dan was dressed in his Air Force blues with a brown leather flight jacket. Naomi was dressed in her Air Force service uniform, and she looked even more attractive than on the first day. Karol had on her black and white dress uniform with her white hat. Mike was dressed in his green Marine Corps. service uniform. Karen and Nick had their Army service greens on with their dark olive-green overcoats. Everyone looked neat and professional, and on initial glance, no one would ever suspect they were departing for a highly clandestine assignment behind enemy lines. Dan called the team together for a few final words.

"I just got off the phone with Hal. He'll be flying with us to Aviano. When we get to Andrews, there'll be a mobility processing line there to do our final out-processing. We'll be treated just like any other duty personnel leaving on government aircraft deploying overseas. Don't expect any special treatment from AMC. We're getting to the terminal with plenty of time to mingle around and do nothing. The KC-10 will be configured with twenty airline type seats and a DV comfort pallet positioned just aft of the seating area. I made the request for that configuration personally so we'd be comfortable on the trip. Except for the working crew, the entire aircraft will be ours. Hal will meet us at the aircraft just before scheduled departure time. Okay, that's all I have to say. Let's go."

The team arrived at the Andrews Air Force Base passenger terminal. As predicted, the mobility processing line processed all team members. Each female took a pregnancy stick and signed a disclosure saying they were being deployed to a combat zone and that pregnancy during combat operations was grounds for court martial.

As she was taking her pregnancy test Karol thought to herself, *Damn, I forgot about those stupid sticks.* Thankfully, her stick came out negative.

Just as Dan requested, the KC-10 was large and spacious. Behind the seats was a smoke screen to separate cargo from the passenger compartment; most of the cargo space was taken up by their equipment and supplies for their mission. The KC-10 boom operator, who also doubles as loadmaster, was completing his preflight checks and making sure the cargo was secured and properly documented. When the team boarded the aircraft, everyone took seats spaced throughout the cabin. At 6:20 P.M., a blue Air Force staff car with three stars in the window and a black civilian SUV approached the aircraft. Dan and Mike stayed at the top of the stairs looking down on the tarmac. As the vehicles stopped in front of the aircraft, Dan saw Undersecretary Mattingly arrive with full DV honors. Lieutenant General James Hamilton got out from his staff car and waited for Mattingly to exit his SUV. Dan noticed Ms. Sara driving the vehicle to the flight line. As the SUV came to a stop, Mattingly got out from the passenger's side and General Hamilton walked up to him and saluted. Mattingly returned his salute then picked up his briefcase and walked to the stairs of the waiting aircraft while Ms. Sara carried his bags up the stairs.

The boom operator motioned Mattingly to the front of

the aircraft and said, "You can take any one of these seats, sir." Ms. Sara gave Mattingly's luggage to the boom operator to secure for the flight. Mattingly said good-bye to her and gave her a hug. She looked at the team with red, swollen eyes, and said *Merde*—an SOE French Section, time-honored salute of farewell. Karol, Naomi and Karen, the French speakers, gave Ms. Sara a strange look upon hearing her remark, not fully understanding the significance. Next, she turned to Dan and said, "Please look after everyone, Major. I'm counting on you to bring everyone back safely." then departed the aircraft.

Dan and Mike returned to their seats as the boom operator started his safety briefing. Dan sat next to Karol, and Mike sat next to Karen. Naomi and Nick were seated in the back row, already sound asleep. Once the briefing was completed, the boom operator closed the door of the aircraft and began departure procedures. A short time later, the KC-10 was airborne and headed for the base in Italy.

Once the aircraft reached cruise altitude, Mattingly came over to Dan and Karol and said, "Get the rest of the team assembled. I need to speak to everyone."

Mattingly made a conference area on the seats between Dan and Karol and the rest of the team members gathered around. This was a Top Secret mission, and the Air Force crew was instructed not to ask any questions or listen to any conversations made by the team. Mattingly opened his brief case and took out maps of Yugoslavia.

"The aircraft is quiet and comfortable, Dan, just like you mentioned. We can get a lot of work done on the flight. The first thing I need to say is that I will not be going on to Zagreb with you. Once we get to Aviano, I have some logistical items to work out, so you'll be on your own from that point. This next phase of our mission is to get the team placed inside Croatia. We will stay overnight at Aviano and do some last-minute checks of our equipment. From there, you will be flown to Zagreb International Airport by C-17 transport, which is a joint military and civilian airfield."

The boom operator handed out snacks and soft drinks to the team while Mattingly continued his briefing.

"Your equipment will be loaded onboard three mid-sized Yugoslav utility trucks by Croatian Ministry of Defense personnel and then driven off the compound by the team. Each couple will have a truck. Dan, you and Karol will have the first one. Mike and Karen will take the second. Naomi and Nick will take the third. While working inside Croatia, you've been given the cover of agriculture equipment and supplies representatives from the European Union."

Mattingly handed out six yellow envelopes. "These are your credentials, ID cards, and cover stories. Make sure you keep them in a safe place. You will not show or display these credentials unless you are stopped or questioned by Croatian police or military personnel."

All six of the team members opened their envelopes and examined their contents.

Mattingly continued, "All three trucks will supposedly have agriculture equipment and supplies but of course will be carrying your equipment for the mission. You will drive on Highway E70 toward Eastern Croatia, or the Slavonian region, as it is known. Once you get your trucks on the road, the next phase of the operation is to set up the Forward Operating Base (FOB) in Croatia. We've secured an abandoned farm warehouse located outside the town of Bapska, located a few kilometers away from the Serbian border. This warehouse is believed to have been used last by the United Nations Peacekeeping Forces monitoring the

The Balkan Network

cease-fire. Here is the location and directions to the warehouse."

Mattingly gave each driver directions to the warehouse.

"Eastern Croatia is still pretty much destroyed from the 1991 war, so we chose the rural areas instead of the urban areas simply because there are a few large buildings still standing. All three trucks will meet at this location and help set up the FOB." He pointed to a position on the map and said, "This is where we'll establish the Croatian FOB."

Naomi read the writing on the map and translated it out loud. "It's called Bapska Vineyards. It's an abandoned warehouse vineyard."

"Excellent. The team will stay at this location until we move into Serbia. Here are maps of the area. I want you to go over these maps and study the roads since you'll be driving the trucks. I know this seems rushed, but remember, this is part of your training now. Once you're inside Croatia, you'll be using the cell phones to communicate with one another so we can get practice using the devices. If anyone has any questions, I'm here to answer as best I can. In the meantime, I would suggest you use this time to study and prepare for the operation.

"I've got some questions," said Karol. "How long of a drive is it from Zagreb to Bapska?"

"That's a good question. As near as we can tell, E70 is an excellent road. It's the main thoroughfare from Zagreb to Eastern Slavonia and on into Serbia and is well traveled. Fuel along this route is not a problem, especially since Slavonia was a large oil-producing region—at least until 1991. Traveling an average speed of 120 kilometers per hour should take you approximately six to eight hours depending on traffic."

"The reason I asked, sir, is I wanted to know if we

should stop along the way or would you prefer us to go on through?"

"You can make stops along the way, but we'd prefer you to go through as much as is practical. The only good stop along the way is in the town of Slovanski Brod. There was shelling, bombing, and sniper fire during the Croatian War, but much of the city has been restored to its original luster. It's a good place to get a meal or buy some clothing."

Naomi interjected, "We may need to purchase some additional clothing or get a haircut once we get inside Croatia and see what the locals are wearing."

"Point well-taken; why don't we plan a relief stop in Slovanski Prod. Dan, you can coordinate the stop once the team gets on the road. Don't forget, by that time, you'll be using your cell phones extensively to communicate."

The team broke up and began going over their maps and routes and discussing the details of the trip to Slavonia. A few hours into the flight, the boom operator passed out box lunches and snacks, and then the team slept.

Chapter 17
AVIANO AB, ITALY

The overnight flight aboard the KC-10 landed at Aviano at 9:30 AM. The air base was overflowing with aircraft and personnel in anticipation of Operation Allied Force and the services were taxed to the limit. Even with a distinguished visitor on board, they had to wait an hour for a bus to come out to the aircraft and offload the team. The team billeted in a temporary tent city located near the flight line. The women shared a tent together, and the men shared another. The exception was Undersecretary Mattingly who occupied the only DV quarters on the base. After the KC-10 was downloaded and quarters were secured the team met at the 940th Air Expeditionary Wing Headquarters, Intelligence Squadron. This was the only secure location on the base and enabled them to continue briefing the classified portions of the mission. Air Force intelligence officers briefed them on the latest tactical threats in the area and had all the team members fill out an updated ISOPREP card to be kept on file at Aviano. After everyone received intelligence updates, Mattingly assembled them in an isolated room to begin his DIA briefing.

"Once we have our FOB established at the Bapska winery, we want you to find the safest way into Serbia. Dan, you'll have to coordinate this activity. I wish I could give you more information on how to do this, but unfortunately, we don't have the assets in place to begin. That's why we need you there."

"I understand, sir, we'll make it happen," said Dan as he looked everyone over.

"We have less than fifteen days to set up the Serbian location. When the team is settled inside Serbia, we can begin briefing our aircrews on escape, evasion and safe passage and prepare a timeline for the first airstrikes over Belgrade. A key factor in the safe passage of our airmen is to get them as close to Eastern Croatia as we can. From there we can mount a successful rescue operation. With all this going on, we also need information on the Serb forces moving into Eastern Croatia. We believe they're paramilitary, but we'll have to make sure so we don't come across any during a rescue operation."

Karol said, "It's a sure bet the Serbs know this area will be our safe passage route and could be positioning paramilitary forces along the border to disrupt rescue operations."

Mattingly rummaged through some notes and memos in his folder and said, "The Croatian police have been on patrol looking for these forces, but up to this point in time they have not been successful in apprehending them. One reason is the Croatian police are stretched to the limit. Most of their police force was wiped out during the last war. If you come across any of these paramilitary forces, you need to report back to us on their locations. We, in turn, will pass that information on to the Croatians who will take over from there. That's all I have for now."

Dan spoke up, "Specifically, what dangers are we going

to be exposed to once inside Serbia and before the air war begins?"

"Your team will be traveling incognito and traveling as couples and farmers. The Serb-Croatian border is open, especially to commerce, agriculture, and anything in connection with food production. You should have no trouble crossing the border traveling as working farmers. The only danger is getting caught or exposed by Croat-Serb sympathizers working inside Croatia or stumbling upon Serb paramilitary forces inside Serbia."

Mattingly finished briefing the team and dismissed everyone back to their quarters to get some rest. Dan stayed behind to go over the equipment and supplies that had come on board the KC-10. Mattingly brought Dan to the aerial port squadron located adjacent to the flight line. Inside the aerial port, he directed Dan to the pallets of cargo waiting to be loaded onboard the C-17 for the next day's flight. Mattingly reviewed the manifest with Dan. One of the pallets had six off-road motorcycles and one Honda Rancher ATV. Another pallet had farming equipment and supplies. One pallet had poultry feed and corn seeds. There was a pallet with computers and communications equipment, extra ammunition and plastic explosives, timers and detonators. Another had clothing, household items, and camping equipment. Mattingly then told Dan that more supplies will meet with the team at Zagreb.

"Dan, starting tomorrow, ensure everyone has their cell phones charged and ready for use. I want everyone communicating with these devices. For now, get back to your quarters and get mentally ready for the mission. You will still be under DOD command authority until the air war begins. I will be monitoring your positions throughout the mission. You have my number, so you can call me directly. I won't see you tomorrow because I have more work to do here before I leave for Washington."

Mattingly then reached out and shook Dan's hand, "It's been a pleasure, Dan. I know everything's going to work out. You've been trained by the best. Josef would have been proud of you. Be safe."

Dan shook Mattingly's hand, "Thank you, sir, I'll see you back in Washington."

Chapter 18
ZAGREB, CROATIA

The USAF C-17 landed at Zagreb International Airport at 8:30 the next morning. By now, Dan, Mike, and Nick had three-day stubble on their faces and had not showered since leaving Bolling AFB. The women had not showered or shaved their legs or underarms since leaving Washington and were beginning to look very natural. Everyone was wearing their Croatian clothes and carrying their suitcase and field equipment bags. At first glance, it looked as if they were just ordinary villagers getting ready to work in the fields. The Air Force C-17, when diplomatically cleared, is a sovereign instrumentality of the U.S. Government and was immune from searches, seizures, and inspections—including customs and immigration—by foreign officials. When the C-17 landed, Dan met the local Ministry of Defense representative and gave him a courtesy copy of the passenger and cargo manifest. This was all that was needed for the team to pass into Croatia. The C-17 Loadmaster downloaded the cargo from the aircraft and then loaded it onto the three utility trucks waiting on the tarmac. The whole process took fewer than two hours and the team headed off the airport compound. Each pair was driving an EU truck. Dan drove the first one with Karol riding shotgun. Mike drove the second with Karen riding in the front seat and finally Nick and Naomi were in the third. There was some question about who would be driving the last vehicle—Nick or Naomi—but Nick lost the argument because Naomi's Serbo-Croatian was better. She took the driver's seat where she could communicate better. With relative simplicity, the team was off and heading eastward on Highway E70 just as Hal had described. The highway was in excellent condition, with warning signs clearly marked in three languages.

The first leg of the trip went smoothly. Once everyone arrived at Slovanski Brod, they parked their EU trucks at a rest stop and asked directions to the nearest department store. It didn't take Naomi long to find the right store and purchase additional clothing needed for the mission. Everything was within walking distance of the rest stop. All three women took time to notice the latest Croatian hairstyles and had their hair cut accordingly in shorter bobs to look like local villagers. The three men stayed behind and guarded the trucks. After a two-hour break, the team was back on the road headed for the Bapska winery.

As they made their way into Eastern Slavonia, the landscape changed into flat farmland. Most of the fields were fallow, and many were overgrown with weeds and shrubs obviously still recovering from the war in 1991. Many of the fields were marked in pictorial format with skull and crossbones making it obvious to anyone, even small children, that there were dangers in the fields. It would be several years before the Croatian government could clear these fields for agricultural use. All along their

The Balkan Network

route toward Bapska, there were still signs of military activity. Many of the small bridges across the Sava River were bombed out or partially destroyed and most buildings and warehouse were abandoned with windows broken or riddled with bullet holes. The people in the area were glad the war was over and were looking forward to peace, independence, and prosperity. Even the toll collectors along the highway seemed eager to move forward. The team did not experience any delays or questioning. Just outside the town of Vinkovci, the team made a northeast turn toward the city of Vukovar and paralleled the Danube River for several miles. Here the damage was much greater than in any other part of Croatia the team had witnessed so far. Tanks or land mines had destroyed many of the vineyards and farms. Finally, outside Sorrengrad, Dan turned off the main road toward the south and made his way to the abandoned warehouse. The building was a wine processing facility rather than a warehouse. It was located two miles off the main highway on a gravel road. Several large trees surrounded the facility and offered cover from the main road. Judging from the size of the operation, this was once a profitable and private vineyard before the war.

Karol looked at Dan while he was driving and said, "That's it, over there in the trees. I'll open the gate."

Dan drove the truck into the vineyard. The trip had taken much of the day, and it was after 5:00 PM. A few minutes later, Mike and Naomi drove the other two trucks into the compound. Dan motioned them to stop and get out of the trucks. Even though the DIA reported this area secure, Dan took out his metal detector and gave a quick sweep. Just as expected, the vineyards and fields were loaded with mines, a major reason the vineyard was long ago abandoned. Dan determined the warehouse and all the working areas immediately surrounding the warehouse were clear. Dan took out his AK-74 and motioned for Mike and Nick to do the same.

"Let's make a quick security check of the area to make sure no one is hiding inside the buildings before we unload the trucks. Karol, you take Naomi and Karen and cover us."

Karol took out her AK-74 and motioned the other women to do the same. They took up positions alongside the trucks as the men moved around the outside of the warehouse.

The men quickly moved through the area and found it secure. Karol could see that Dan was doing a training session with the men and thought, *He's using our time wisely.*

Dan waved his hand to the rest of the team and said, "Let's get the trucks inside."

The team moved inside the building and began unloading their equipment. Dan told Nick and Naomi to check the upstairs.

The Bapska Vineyard had been a working vineyard complete with fermenting barrels and crushing machines. Most of the oak barrels were destroyed to use as firewood. The main building was large, could accommodate the three trucks easily, and had several rooms that could be offices. There was an upstairs area as well. When Naomi and Nick made the sweep of the upstairs, they found a small apartment complete with kitchen, bathroom, and several small bedrooms. Just as Hal mentioned, the place looked as if it could have been used by United Nations Peacekeeping officers before relinquishing control to the Croatians in 1998. Graffiti was marked on the walls in several languages. Electrical power had been cut off to the compound, and as darkness fell, the team had to rely on flashlights and lanterns to move around.

The Balkan Network

"Let's keep the lights and noise down to a minimum. It's too late to finish unloading the trucks. We'll have to wait till daylight to continue. Our priority at this point is to set up some sleeping areas and begin working at the crack of dawn," said Dan.

Karol spoke up, "I think it's a good idea for the women to sleep upstairs and the men can stay downstairs and keep watch. We don't want surprises in the middle of the night by unwelcome intruders."

"I agree," said Dan. "Nick, what did you find upstairs?"

"Three or four rooms used as sleeping quarters at some time. There's no beds or mattresses but plenty of space to crash in each room."

"We'll have to break out the camping gear. We'll use sleeping bags tonight. Nick, you take the women upstairs and help them unpack. Mike and I will stay down here and set up a sleeping area for us."

Karen couldn't help but notice Naomi giving Dan a cold stare as he asked Nick to help the women.

Nick helped the women with their camping gear and Dan and Mike unloaded sleeping bags and air mattresses from the trucks. Because everyone on the team was in the military and had, at one point in their careers, been exposed to field conditions, no one voiced any complaints. Surprisingly, even Naomi didn't complain. Everyone was exhausted, and the main objective for the night was getting sleep.

As everyone went down for the night, Dan stayed up and reflected. So far, Phase Two of the mission had gone off as planned and without a hitch. Everything went just as Josef had predicted. The next day would tell just how secure this area was. The Serbian border was less than five miles to the north across the Danube River and three miles to the south of their position, almost surrounded by the enemy. Dan walked to the back of the warehouse, turned on his cell phone and pressed Hal Mattingly's preselected number. The phone rang and sounded just like any other telephone. After two rings, the phone answered and a voice said, "This is Finder?"

Dan was surprised by the clarity of the transmission. "It's Specter. We made it to the FOB and have secured the location. Everyone is safe and getting some well-deserved sleep."

"All the satellite tracking systems are working, and we've been monitoring your movements all day. We have you in radar contact at the Bapska location. It also appears at this point there is no one else in the immediate vicinity. The JSTARS has been orbiting over Bosnia monitoring your situation. You should be safe for the night. If the JSTARS detects movement in your area, they'll contact you directly."

Dan was surprised to hear this piece of information. He didn't realize the JSTARS had the capability to track individuals without interrogation equipment. "Sir, it appears electrical power is cut off in the structure. Tomorrow, when we have daylight, we'll finish unloading the trucks and establish power to the building. Do you have any suggestions where we could start looking?"

"The power was probably cut off by the UN as they redeployed. I'll check on that and get back with you by tomorrow. It's 2000 hours GMT right now. I'll call you back at 0500 hours—that would be 0700 in Croatia. Let's synchronize our clocks to use GMT from now one. Everything we do will be coordinated on GMT. By the way, good work on getting your team in. Were there any problems on the way?"

"No sir, everything went just as you and Josef predicted."

"Great, I'll check on the electrical power and get back with you by morning. Until then, stay alert."

"Good night, sir."

Chapter 19
FORWARD OPERATING BASE

At dawn, Karen was the first one up. It was cold, so she put on her jacket as she got out of her down sleeping bag. The women slept on the floor in one of the upstairs bedrooms on top of air mattresses. Despite being the middle of March, the air was still cold and damp and made sleeping uncomfortable on the wooden floor. Karen walked down the hall to the kitchen. Inside, she saw a small table and four chairs. Next to the table was a window overlooking the countryside. She thought to herself how beautiful a setting this place was at one time—the kitchen had cupboards and drawers with a few utensils. As she rummaged through the cabinets, she found two large cups, two spoons, a fork, knife, and three plates. She went over to the sink and turned on the faucet. To her surprise, water started flowing and with good pressure. The only question: was it safe to drink? Before she could investigate further, she heard footsteps coming up the stairs. Dan walked into the kitchen, "Good morning, Karen. I didn't think anyone was up yet."

"It looks like the water faucet works up here, sir."

The Balkan Network

"Yes, I know I've already used the bathroom. At least that's one thing we don't have to worry about; however, the water source could be contaminated. Until we can check it out, we'd better boil it first. I've got my stove on downstairs boiling some water right now. Would you like some coffee or tea?"

"Tea would be great."

"While you ladies were out shopping yesterday, I picked up some instant coffee, tea, sugar, and a few more bottles of water in case we encountered a situation like this. When we finish unloading the trucks and setting up the base, we need to go into town and buy some supplies. I'll be right back." Dan headed down the stairs and came back with two cups of boiling liquid.

"How do you take your tea?"

"Just black will be fine."

Dan gave Karen the cup of tea, and the two of them sat at the small table.

"Is it alright if I go into town and do the shopping? There's a few things I think we could use here, especially if we're going to be here for a few days. Besides, I need to find out which dialect they're using in this part of the country."

"Of course, as long as you take Mike with you."

"Speaking of Mike, there's something I want you to know about us. The last night before we left Bolling, Mike spent the night with me. Don't worry, nothing happened between us. I asked him to stay with me. He was quite the gentleman. He just turned off the lights and climbed into bed with me. I was feeling a little worried about the mission. I hope you're not upset with us?"

"It's quite alright. Remember, we'll be working incognito and traveling as couples. It would look suspicious if we looked like we hated each other. The exception is Nick and

Naomi. For some reason, they don't seem to be getting along as well as I hoped."

"You know the reason why, don't you? I've been watching Naomi these past few days. I think she's attracted to you. I've seen the way she looks at you, and I see the way she looks at Karol. I'm a woman, remember, we see things differently than men."

"I'm hoping Nick and Naomi get along better after all, when we're inside Serbia, neither of us will be with them."

"While we're on the subject of Naomi, there's something you should know. My biggest fear on this mission wasn't the actual mission but the fear of making a mistake. That's why I asked Mike to stay with me. More to the point, I'm worried about saying the wrong thing at the wrong time. Naomi seemed natural yesterday. In fact, she did most of the talking. Karol and I just watched as Naomi asked for directions and spoke with complete confidence—she never faulted."

"There's a simple explanation for this. We're still in friendly territory. She's just more comfortable speaking in Croatian than the rest of us. Anyway, don't underestimate your skills. You're a highly trained language expert. Why don't you get the other women up, and I'll get the men going. We have a lot of work to do today."

When everyone was awake, the team started to unload the trucks. The motorcycles and ATV came out first then the grain and feed and all the remaining equipment. At 0500Z, Dan's cell phone rang.

"Hello, this is Specter."

"Good morning, Dan," replied Mattingly. "We're on secure voice. We can talk freely. Put us on speaker so everyone can hear."

Dan motioned everyone to stop working and gather around.

The Balkan Network

"Can everyone hear me?" he asked.

"Yes, sir, we can hear you fine" said, Karol.

"Great, first of all, I want to congratulate everyone for doing an excellent job so far, but we still have a long way to go. The first thing is the power supply. Just as I suspected, the UN removed electrical power as they withdrew. You can reconnect it outside. It's a simple connection, but it's 220 volts. You'll have to use the converter adaptors on all your equipment. As soon as you get the power installed, connect your converters and let me know how they work. If there's a problem, I need to know so I can get replacements. Have any of you checked the water pressure?"

Dan interrupted, "Yes, sir, we've got good pressure, but we're not sure if it's contaminated."

"The UN tells me the water is potable and comes from a well. You will need electrical power to operate the well, so don't drink any of the water until power's restored."

"We're one step ahead of you, sir," said Karen. "We've boiled the water here or drank from bottles."

Okay, sounds great. Once you get power and water and all the AC adaptors checkout, you're cleared to start up operations from Bapska. Now listen very carefully. Your next assignment will be to get into Serbia. Dan, you and I have already discussed this issue, so please bring your team up to date. To accomplish this, we need you to modify one of the trucks. Use the flatbed with the removable sides. Once the modifications are complete, let me know, and I'll give you the timetable to move into Serbia. Let's plan another call tonight before you turn in at 2000Z. Until then, good luck, ladies and gentlemen."

Dan hung up the phone and turned it off to conserve battery power. "Karol, take the women with you upstairs and cover the compound from the second-floor window. Mike, grab the tool kit. Nick, get your AK and come with us outside. Let's get the power connected so we can at least take a shower."

It didn't take long to find the power connectors and reconnect the 220 line back to the warehouse. The whole process took less than an hour. All the overhead lights worked in the main warehouse and power to the upstairs apartment was fully restored. The stove was a six-burner electric 220 model made in the UK and worked surprisingly well. The 220 water heater also worked well despite not being used for some time. All the AC power adaptors worked and recharged the cell phone and laptop batteries. Everything was proceeding according to plan. Next, Dan and Nick removed the floorboards from the bottom of one of the trucks. Each floorboard had a space about ten inches wide by eight feet long—plenty of room to store their equipment and weapons. Dan then briefed the team on how they were going to enter Serbia.

"Up to now, the mission has been fairly safe, that is, we've not been in enemy territory however the next phase of the operation is extremely dangerous. We need to establish three operating bases *inside* Serbia. To do this we must cross the border."

Everyone gathered around the small kitchen table while Dan briefed.

"As Hal mentioned earlier this morning, we've already come up with the basic insertion plan. First: we load our weapons and equipment on the truck. Next: we drive across the border. Finally: we set up a location inside Serbia. We've chosen the town of Sid located not more than eight miles from our current location."

Dan spread the map across the table.

"We need to be in this area before the start of the air campaign and before the Serbs seal the border off. Once hostilities begin and we start sending aircraft into Serbia,

The Balkan Network

we can expect the Serbs to throw up everything they have to try to shoot them down. Should one of our aircraft go down, we're already in position to contact the downed airmen before hostile forces do. It's that simple. We'll use motorcycles and the ATV to get around once we're inside Serbia."

Karol moved closer to the map and addressed the team.

"Let's talk about getting across the border. The Serbs and Croatians have not sealed off the borders. They're letting people come and go, especially those in connection with the agricultural industry. If we look like farmers, dress like farmers, work like farmers, and smell like farmers, then we'll be treated like farmers. There should be no reason we'd be stopped or questioned at the border."

Dan added, "On the other hand, if we look like and act like U.S. Special Forces, then we're going to be treated as U.S. Special Forces. By the way, it's a sure bet the Serbs are keeping a sharp look out for U.S. Special Forces, especially American GIs that don't speak Serbo-Croatian. Karol and I have already agreed to take two of the EU trucks across the border. The rest of you will stay here until we get back."

Mike immediately raised his concern.

"With all due respect, sir, let me go with you. You may need me. I can get that truck into Serbia better than any of us."

"We can't take that chance, Mike. I know you speak the language just as well as I do, but we feel it's best for a couple to cross instead of a threesome. Besides, we may need you back here in case the team gets into trouble."

"You're right, sir. I'm sorry."

"Don't be to sorry. I'd rather have you volunteer for something than sit back and do nothing."

Dan continued, "When I talk to Hal later tonight, he'll coordinate a shipment of live hogs and chickens to be delivered to our location. We'll load the hogs and chickens on the trucks then drive across the border. The flatbed is open and anyone can see inside the truck. I guarantee no one is going to stop us and search the bottom on the flatbed especially after the hogs have defecated on the truck all day long. The only weapons and equipment we need to bring across the border are the motorcycles, ATV, AKs, pistols, night vision goggles, and ammo. No one will, of course, be able to see these because they'll be hidden under the floorboards."

Karol said, "As far as the motorcycles and ATV, I don't think there is a hog farmer anywhere in Europe who doesn't use one. It'll look perfectly natural. Once we get the first load into Serbia, Dan and I will ride the motorcycle back to Bapska, which should be no more than a ten-minute ride."

Dan said, "Look, I know each of you may have some concerns about Karol and me going across the border alone, but trust us. We've thought this through. Karol and I speak the language, and we'll look and smell just like hog farmers."

Dan refolded the map and began clearing off the table. "We've worked hard all day, and I'm sure everyone has worked up an appetite, so let's have a celebration. Karen, you've been waiting for this. Take Mike into Ilok, or what's left of it, and get us some supplies. Some cold beer and wine would work too, but please no whiskey. You two are already dirty and looked liked you've been working in the fields. You can clean up and shower when you get back. Just be back here for dinner. Take your cell phones in case we have to contact you."

The Balkan Network

Karen grabbed Mike's hand and said, "Get a bike ready. I'll ride with you."

Mike wheeled one of the bikes out of the warehouse and started it. Karen came running out with two helmets and a bag for groceries, then the two sped off the compound. The rest of the team continued their chores, unloading boxes and putting away equipment.

The road to Ilok was just a short ride from the compound. The road was well maintained despite the damage during the Siege of Vukovar. The road paralleled the south bank of the Danube River, and as Mike and Karen made their way into Ilok, the late afternoon sun was breaking out from the low overcast. It started to shine along the Danube, and it was peaceful watching the small fishing boats and freight barges float peacefully along the lazy river. Just to the other side of the river, not more than two kilometers away, was Serbia. In a few short weeks, there would be an air armada of over one thousand aircraft raining down bombs, death, and destruction on this peaceful setting. As they made their way closer to Ilok, she held onto him harder and with more affection.

Ilok is the most eastern town in Croatia. It lies just on the border between Serbia and Croatia, along the banks of the Danube. Mortars shelled the city from across the river during the 1991 war; however, the city was spared total destruction, unlike Vukovar. The only bridge that crossed the Danube into Serbia was still standing and was a major crossing point. As the couple made their way into the city, they could see small shops, taverns, and restaurants all open and functioning. Life was returning to normal after years of fighting and bloodshed. Near the center of the city, Mike slowed down to see an outdoor farmers market located near the city center. As he slowed down, Karen said, "Everything we need is right here. Park the bike, and we'll walk the rest of the way."

Mike parked the bike in a parking place near the market. There were few cars in the city. Most of the city dwellers were on foot, but a few had motorcycles, scooters, or bicycles. Located near the front of the marketplace, Mike noticed a small beer garden with long, Bavarian-style tables to enjoy the local brews. Mike began speaking in Croatian and said to Karen, "Let's make this our first stop. I think a cold beer is in order."

"I think that's an excellent idea; besides, I want to find out what dialect they're speaking here. Keep speaking to me in Croatian."

Mike and Karen ordered two local lagers and found space at one of the long tables. They sat and enjoyed their first Yugoslavian drink together. The weather was beautiful. The sun was actually shining and the warmth felt good, especially after a cold night on a musty wooden floor. People in the marketplace seemed friendly and nice. The long tables in the beer garden were crowded with many shoppers also enjoying the moment. Remembering their rules of engagement, Karen and Mike had to keep to themselves so as not to start a conversation with one of the locals. Karen reached over and grabbed Mike's hand and said, "Try to look like you actually like me. If we act like we're in love, then no one will bother us"

The couple moved closer and spoke in Serbo-Croatian. The first beer went down fast, and it was time to get another. As Mike was getting up to order another round, he noticed a group of four young men, probably in their mid-twenties, at the far end of the beer garden. The men seemed out of place because they were too young and didn't look like farmers or local villagers. They were dressed in paramilitary-style clothing. Mike leaned down

The Balkan Network

like he was going to kiss Karen on the check then whispered into her ear.

"Don't look now, but there are four men at the other end of the garden. They look out of place. They're too young to be police and too old be hoodlums." Then he kissed her gently on the check and said, "I'll get us another round and keep an eye on them from a distance."

As Mike was getting two more beers, Karen sat back in her chair and got a quick glimpse at the men across the market. Mike was right—they were too young to be Croatian police but not too young to be in the military or insurgency. As she was stroking the red hair from her face, she noticed one of the men staring at her intensely. The others were making remarks to each other, and it was obvious they were checking out everyone in the marketplace, especially young women. Mike came back with the beers and Karen leaned closer to his ear and said, "They've been watching me. I think one of them in particular might be looking at me."

Mike looked up at them and immediately they walked away.

"I think they're just young men with nothing better to do on a beautiful day. I'll keep an eye on them should they reappear. I think they know you're with me."

Mike and Karen went about enjoying their beer and talking about the items they needed to buy for the team. If they were going to have a celebration tonight, then they had to buy some things that everyone would enjoy. There were stalls selling prsut, cold cut meats, fish, cheeses, bread, fruit, vegetables, and wines. They could buy everything they needed to last them for several days. As they finished their beers, Mike said, "I need to find a restroom before we make our way through the marketplace. The beer went right through me."

"Let me know where it's at. I'll do the same when you get back."

She watched as Mike made his way around the back of the beer booth and disappeared. Karen closed her eyes and was enjoying the sunlight on her face when she felt a bump on the chair next to her. The young man who was looking at her earlier was now sitting next to her with a cigarette dangling from his lip. He was about twenty-five with long brown hair, blue eyes, and tattoos all over his arms. He hadn't shaved in several days and the stubble on his face made him look a few years older than he was. He seemed nervous and finally spoke.

"I see your glass is empty, can I buy you another one?"

Karen was in shock, he spoke in a Serbian dialect, not Croatian, and on closer observation she saw he had scars on his hands and face, probably from fighting or some type of combat. She didn't know what to say so she said the first thing that came to her mouth. Remembering her training exercise back at Quantico, she said in Serbo-Croatian, "Did your friends put you up to this? Well, you can go back and tell all your buddies to go fuck themselves!"

The young man blew cigarette smoke in her face. He put his cigarette out on the table and said, "Croat bitch! We should have butchered you when we had the chance!" Then he got up and walked away.

Karen, still in shock at what she just heard and witnessed, closed her eyes and pretended she was somewhere else. It wasn't until she heard a soft voice that she came to her senses.

"Chetniks! Serbian insurgents! What did you say to him?" a woman said to Karen as she opened her eyes. Karen noticed the older woman that was sitting just a few seats away from her when Mike and she first arrived.

"They come here from across the border. They come

The Balkan Network

and go as they please. This was once their land and their property. They feel it is still their country, but they chose to go back to Serbia and live. Those four men are very dangerous. Keep away from them. The police have been looking for them for days."

Just then, Mike came back from the bathroom. He could see Karen talking with the older women and said in Croatian, "What's wrong?"

"Nothing, this kind woman was just telling me to be careful, that's all."

"Come on, honey, we have a lot of shopping to do."

Mike and Karen got up from the beer garden and started shopping in the marketplace. It turned out to be a beautiful late afternoon day. As they browsed the various stalls and booths looking for food, the afternoon turned to dusk. As they were doing their shopping, Karen told Mike what happened while he was using the restroom. Mike was wondering if he should have brought his pistol—at least he would have some protection in case something did happen. They bought all the items they needed and loaded them into the shopping bag Karen brought along. They had bought so much beer, wine, cheese, and meat that the bag would not hold anything more.

Mike said, "Wait here, and I'll go get the bike and be right back. Don't worry, I'll only be gone a few minutes, besides, you're out in the open and no one will do anything."

Mike turned and ran to his parked motorcycle. Karen was starting to get nervous so she reached into her pocket and pulled out her cell phone. As she was making the call to Karol, a hand came out of nowhere and slapped the cell phone to the ground. The four young men were standing next to her. They had probably followed them through the marketplace.

The young one that came up to Karen earlier said, "Who were you trying to call?" He reached down, picked up Karen's cell phone, and held it up to his ear. The young man could hear a female voice on the other end, speaking in Croatian saying, "Hello, is everything okay? Hello, should I send for backup?"

In a flash, the younger man threw the phone down on the ground and said, "She must be a cop! There's another bitch on the other end of the line asking for backup. Quick, get her in the van before the rest of them show up!"

Two men grabbed Karen from behind and held her arms back so she couldn't move. One of the men ran off around the corner, and the third pulled out an AK-47 and started shouting to everyone in the area to get away. A small van pulled around the corner and the man holding the AK-47 opened the side door and pushed Karen and the two other men inside. The van sped away.

At the same time, Mike was coming around the corner on his motorcycle. He had only been gone two or three minutes, but Karen was nowhere in sight. He looked on the ground where he had left her and saw the bag of groceries and her cell phone. He went up to the first person he saw on the street.

"Did you see anything? There was a woman with me—a redhead—has anyone seen her?" People just shook their heads. Finally, Mike saw the older woman who was talking to Karen back at the beer gardens. "Can you help me? My wife, she's gone, have you seen her?"

"Chetniks! Serbian, paramilitary terrorists. They took her away in a white van. I told her to stay away from them. She did not listen. You must try to find her before they take her across the border; otherwise, you will never see your woman again."

Inside the van, Karen tossed around like a rag doll.

The Balkan Network

There were no seats in the back, just an empty floor. The driver was speeding through the streets of Ilok while the other three were in the back with Karen. One had his AK-47 pointed at Karen.

"Where are you taking me? I haven't done anything to you!"

"Shut up, bitch!" shouted the one holding the AK-47. "We know all about you people pretending to be citizens, but in reality, you're undercover cops trying to hunt us down!"

"That's a lie I would do no such thing! I'm just an ordinary pig farmer!"

At that moment, the young man that first approached Karen slapped her across the face. "Shut up, bitch. I think you're right. We're all going to get fucked tonight, especially you!"

Mike was now frantic. He could not believe this was happening. They were supposed to go into town and get food and supplies for a celebration. His cell phone started to ring and snapped him into consciousness.

Dan was on the line, "Grant, what the hell's going on there? Sutter got a call from Eden and all we could hear was shouting!"

"They took her, sir. Insurgents—possibly Chetniks, a woman said—probably three to four men. I'm sorry, sir, I was only away from her for just a couple of minutes to get the motorcycle."

"I need you to remain calm and listen to me carefully. Stay where you are and keep a clear head. Pretend you're still looking around for her but don't cause too much attention. There could be others waiting to set up an ambush. Don't worry about Eden, we'll get her back. I'll call you when I need you. Do you understand?"

"Yes, sir."

Dan hung up the phone. Karol was beside him. "What did you find out?"

"He said they were paramilitary insurgents. They took her away. They could possibly be Chetniks. Get the computers on—we've got to find her."

Naomi already had her laptop on and running then said, "She's close by, maybe four or five kilometers at the most.

"Let me have a look," said Dan as he looked over Naomi's shoulder and saw the GPS icon displaying Karen's location.

"Naomi, you and Nick stay here. Lock onto my position in relation to Karen's. Karol, you and I'll go after her. Everyone go hot-mic on your cell phones. I'll need instant communications and locations at all times."

Dan and Karol grabbed their AK-74s. Dan went over to one of the equipment boxes and opened it up, taking out two Makarov pistols with silencers. He handed one to Karol along with two sets of night vision goggles. "Let's go."

Dan and Karol hopped on a motorcycle and sped out of the warehouse. Along the way, Karol had her cell phone on and connected to her helmet headset, enabling her to communicate hands free.

"Radio check, how do you hear me?" said Dan.

"This is Sutter, I can hear you loud and clear."

"Lombard, can you hear me?" asked Dan.

"Yes, sir, I can hear you just fine. I have you interfaced with Eden's GPS coordinates. She appears to be moving toward you. She's less than two kilometers away now. Continue down the main road another hundred meters to the left by the river. You should see an access road."

Karol said, "Here it is, just up ahead."

The Balkan Network

Naomi added, "Take the access road. She's somewhere close to the river."

Dan was riding at speeds in excess of ninety miles per hour with Karol hanging on for dear life. The main road he was traveling on made its way closer to the outskirts of town. There were buildings and structures off the road to the right and left. Dan decided to continue on the main road and double back on foot just in case any of the insurgents heard the sounds of the motorcycle. Dan saw the remnants of a bombed-out building to the right and decided that this was close enough. He pulled off the main road and parked the bike behind the building and turned to Karol.

"You stay here until I call for you. I'm going to make my way back to Karen's location. Give me updates on her location as I make my way."

"No way, Flyboy, I'm going with you! Remember, we stay together at all times. We've already lost Karen, and we're not going to lose anyone else on this mission, and we're bringing everyone back home alive."

Dan looked down at Karol, "You're right, I can't afford to lose anyone else. Follow me. When we get closer to Karen's location, cover me as I approach."

"Got it. I'll be right behind you."

* * *

LATE AFTERNOON TURNED TO SUNSET. Dan and Karol crouched off into the darkness along the side of the access road trying to keep from being seen. A few feet down on the access road, Dan saw an abandoned pumping station along the edge of the river. It was a small brick building with a single entrance and no windows. As the two made their way toward the pumping station, Dan could see a white utility van parked out front. "There could be three or four insurgents. I don't see anyone in or near the van. They could all be inside or there could be one or two left outside to stand guard." He put on his night vision goggles and handed a set to Karol. "Can you see anything with the goggles on?"

"I don't see anyone, but someone could be hiding down by the water in the trees."

"It's a chance we've got to take. Karen's in jeopardy. I'm going to make my way to the door. Cover me and shoot at anything you see that moves toward that structure."

"You got it," said Karol scanning the area as Dan made his way to the front of the structure.

Dan approached the opening and heard voices—one was a female's muffled voice. The inside of the structure was almost completely dark, with only dim light coming from the ventilation slits along the building's sides. Through his goggles, Dan could make out figures of three men standing with their backs to the entrance. *A costly mistake*, he thought. Karen was still alive. Two of the insurgents were holding her down. One was on each side, holding her legs spread as she was kicking and fighting back. The other insurgent was in front of Karen with his pants down around his ankles. He was saying something to Karen and slapping her across the face. She seemed to scream out in agony with each blow but her cries went nowhere because of the duct tape over her mouth. She had both hands bound behind her back, and her shirt and bra were torn off exposing her breasts and stomach. The man standing in front of her had a cigarette dangling from his lip. He was starting to say something to Karen when Dan made an instant decision. He was now less than ten feet away and still unnoticed by the three men. He took careful aim, held his breath, then fired off three shots from his pistol. All three men crumbled to the ground. Karen immediately stopped kicking. Dan could see her head and face covered in blood and brain matter. For a moment, he was sickened at the thought of having hit Karen from a stray bullet. Dan put his weapon down, took off his goggles, and crawled to the bodies. Karen's eyes were still open, tears running down her face. She was breathing, and most importantly, *alive*. Dan removed the tape from her mouth, put his arms around her, and said, "It's okay, it's all over, Karol and I are here. You'll be all right now?"

Karen nodded, "Thank God you're here. How did you ever find me?"

"I'll tell you later, but I've got to get you out of here. Are there any more?"

"There's one more, the driver. They left him outside to stand guard. I'm surprised you didn't run into him."

"Is everything okay?" was the message Dan heard in his earpiece.

Immediately he talked into his microphone. "Area clear. I got her. She's okay. We're coming out now. Clear the area so we can get the hell out of here."

Dan and Karen came out from the structure and made their way to Karol. As they were about to start running, the other insurgent emerged from the bushes with an AK-47 slung over his shoulder. He was zipping up his fly when Dan heard the unmistakable sound of a Makarov with silencer. The man fell to the ground still holding his fly.

Karol popped up a few feet ahead and said, "I'm over here!"

Dan and Karen raced toward her. Dan removed his jacket, placed it around Karen, and said to Karol. "Get her on the motorcycle and get the hell out of here. I'll have Mike come and get me." Dan patted each of the women on the back and said, "Now go!" He reached for his cell phone and called Mike.

He answered on the first ring and said in Croatian, "Hello, Grant here."

"Everything's okay, Sutter has Eden. They're on their way back to the warehouse. I need you to pick me up. I'm just off the main road heading out of town by a dirt access road."

"Thank God, she's all right. I'll be there in a second."

Dan switched back to hot-mic on his cell phone and listened.

"We're on the bike heading to the compound," said Karol, transmitting over hot-mic. Eden's a little shook up but otherwise okay. Most of the blood on her face was from the abductors. We should be at the compound in less than ten minutes."

"Good work. I'll see you then. Let's all meet in the kitchen," interrupted Dan.

He sat back on the tall grass just off the road. It appeared the rescue operation, for the time being, went unnoticed. There were cars and other vehicular traffic traveling on the road out of town, with no sirens. He had just killed three men, the first casualties of his mission. He had never killed another human before, so he sat in silence thinking about the men. Hal and Josef warned him this mission would be potentially dangerous. Dan tried to piece together why this happened. If they were Serbian insurgents, then who could have possibly known they were here? More importantly, who tipped them off?

Dan's thoughts were interrupted as he heard the sound of an approaching motorcycle. He ducked behind some bushes then spoke into his cell phone, "Grant, is that you approaching the access road?"

"I'll lower my gears to let you know it's me."

Dan heard the sound of a motorcycle lowering its gears as it slowed down. "Okay, I confirm it's you, Grant. I'm just off the main road to the right. You'll see a dirt access road near the river. I'll be waiting for you."

Mike turned off the main road and headed toward the direction Dan had mentioned. As Mike was slowing down, Dan came out from the bushes and hopped on the back of the motorcycle. Dan patted Mike on the shoulder and yelled in Croatian, "Head back to the compound as quick as you can without speeding. We don't want to create too much attention in case someone notices."

Back at the Bapska vineyard, Dan, Mike, Naomi, and Nick sat around the upstairs kitchen table. Karol was in the bathroom helping Karen take a bath. Everyone was silent. Finally, Dan broke the silence.

"It looks like it was just bad luck and bad timing. I don't think the insurgents were looking for us in particular. Our circuit's too secure, but nonetheless, from now on we need to keep on our toes."

Karol walked into the kitchen from the bathroom and Mike immediately said, "How is she ma'am?"

"She's a little shook up with a few bruises and a fat lip, but other than that, she's fine. Luckily, she wasn't raped. Her abductors were drunk, horny, and all four reeked of beer. She's asked for you, Mike. I told her I'd send you right in."

Mike got up from the kitchen table and hurriedly went to the bathroom knocking over his chair as he left the kitchen. Karen was coming out of the bathroom when Mike met her in the hallway. He immediately put his arms around her. "I'm sorry for all this. It's my fault. I should have never left you, not even for a second." The two walked back to the kitchen, no one noticing their sign of open affection in the hallway.

Dan said, "I'd like everyone to gather around so we can debrief this together. It appears this was all nothing more than bad luck. Mike, I understand how you must feel. You had to leave Karen for a few minutes to retrieve the motorcycle. I don't think the insurgents were setting up an ambush. It's a matter of being in the wrong place at the wrong time. I had information all along that there was the possibility of insurgents being in this area. I'm glad Karen wasn't seriously injured, but nonetheless, she did go through enough turmoil."

Karol interrupted, "We had no choice. We had to do what we had to do. Dan, you didn't notice the other guy coming from the riverbank. I spotted him using the night goggles almost the moment you entered the structure. He was probably smoking a cigarette by the water and decided it was time to come back and check on his buddies. If I hadn't taken the shot when I did, he would've stumbled right into you and Karen."

"Thank you, Karol. I want everyone to take notice of what she just said. If she didn't take action when she did, without hesitation, then both Karen and I would have been killed. Don't think with emotion. Remember your training back at Quantico. We're all authorized to use deadly force to protect one another according to our rules of engagement. These men were terrorists causing nothing but trouble." Dan continued. "I'm happy our equipment worked just as Hal said it would. We had Karen's exact location in a matter of seconds after we got word she was in trouble. As soon as Naomi went to GPS tracking mode on her laptop, it immediately tasked the satellites to activate Karen's locator beacon. Karen did the right thing as soon as she felt she was in trouble: she immediately made contact with us using her cell phone."

Dan looked up at Naomi, "You had your laptop on and

were tracking our movements in real time. Nick, if you hadn't prepped the motorcycles earlier in the day we wouldn't have reached Karen in time. Mike, you stayed where I told you to in case I needed you. You picked me up in no time because you were just a short distance away. This is what happens when we all work together as a team. Thanks, everyone."

Karen finally spoke up, "No, sir, I want to thank you and Karol. You two saved my life."

"I know each of you would do the same for me and anyone else on the team."

Karol looked at Karen, "Is there anything else you can tell us about your abductors?"

"Their dialect was definitely Serbian. When I was in the van, two of the men had Krajina flags tattooed on their arms in Cyrillic. The guy that was about to rape me had one tattooed on his stomach. I would say they were definitely Serbian paramilitary. True Croatians wouldn't take time or have a reason to tattoo something in Cyrillic. They also mentioned getting across the border using the bridge at Ilok. Other than that, I don't remember anything important."

Karol said to Dan, "Well, I guess that answers one of our first concerns. It looks like we know the forces coming across the border are not regular Serb military. There is one other scenario we must consider. When these insurgents come up missing it could signal regular JNA forces that our team is in place. In other words, these four men could have been used as bait."

"That's a real possibility, Karol. We'll have to keep a close eye on future insurgent activity here in Croatia. Hopefully, when I send in the report, the Croatian police will take over," said Dan.

Nick broke his silence and said to Karen, "Whatever

happened to the food you were supposed to get us? I don't know about the rest of you, but I'm absolutely starving."

"Wait a second, young fellow, I'll be right back," Mike said, and he disappeared downstairs to the warehouse. A few minutes later, Mike reappeared in the kitchen with Karen's grocery bag.

"Along with Karen's cell phone, I managed to salvage her goodie bag. I think we could all use one of these." Mike pulled out the beer and wine first.

"Did anyone remember the wine opener?" asked Naomi.

"Heck with the wine opener, what about the bottle opener?" said Nick.

"Everyone help yourself to what's left," said Dan. "After a rough day, I would say that everyone needs a break."

Mike put his arms around Karen and kissed her affectionately on the lips, not worrying if the other team members noticed. Just then, Dan's cell phone rang. With all the commotion and excitement, Dan lost track of the time—it was 2000Z.

Dan briefed Mattingly on the abduction. Mattingly agreed with him that the Prospector circuit was too secure, and it was just bad luck; however, there would probably be some police activity since they left four bodies along the river. Dan also informed Mattingly that he and Nick completed the modifications to the floorboards in the truck and they were ready for the shipment of goods from Zagreb.

Mattingly said, I'll forward the report on to our Croatian contacts."

Mattingly continued and changed the subject. "It'll take two days to coordinate and have the shipment of goods delivered to your location. In the meantime, I want

The Balkan Network

you to check out the roads heading south into Serbia from Ilok, Sarengrad, and Tovarnik. We need to know how bad the land mine situation is around those areas, as well as general border activity. This will determine which route you take into Serbia. Call me back tomorrow night this same time. Good work, Dan, keep it up."

Dan ended the call and went back to the celebration in the kitchen. He filled himself with bread, meat, cheese, and the beer Karen had bought. He didn't know how good the food in Croatia could be. Either that or he was just very hungry. After a couple of beers, he said to the group, "Mike, I want you and Karen to take the bedroom next door. Nick and Naomi can share the room that the women slept in last night. Karol and I will set up a new sleeping area in the other bedroom upstairs. This is a good time to start pairing up. We might as well get use to sharing space because we'll all be doing it inside Serbia. Does everyone understand?"

"Yes, sir," was the unanimous response from the group —except for Naomi. She gave Dan another cold stare and nodded her head in acknowledgment.

"Okay, I want everyone to try and get some sleep. Tomorrow we're going minesweeping."

Mike hurried Karen to the bedroom. Nick went downstairs to move his gear to the upstairs bedroom. Naomi volunteered to stay in the kitchen and clean up. Dan and Karol started working on the other bedroom down the hall that was empty. Once the kitchen was cleaned up and everything put away, Naomi turned out the lights in the kitchen and went to her bedroom to help Nick.

Dan moved his and Karol's sleeping bag and mattresses to the other bedroom upstairs while Karol swept and cleaned the floor. Their bedroom was the smallest of all the rooms but would make do because they wouldn't be there long. In a few days, they would move to the Serbian location.

After finishing the floor, Karol said, "Do you mind if I take a bath? I haven't showered for four days, and I think I'm overdue."

"Not at all. Remember, don't shave your legs. Make sure there's enough hot water for the rest of us."

"Somehow I knew you were going to say that," she said as she grabbed her towel and went down the hall to the bathroom.

Dan rolled out his sleeping bag on the air mattress then heard a light knock on the door. "Can I come in?" Naomi asked in a light Serbo-Croatian voice.

Dan replied in English, "Come on in, the door's open. There's no one here except for me."

Naomi, still speaking in Croatian, said, "I'm not happy with the sleeping arrangements. To put it bluntly, why can't Karol share the room with Nick?"

Dan paused for a moment because he was not expecting to hear this. Slowly, he turned to her and switched to Serbo-Croatian, "I didn't ask you to sleep with him. I just wanted you two to share the same space, that's all."

"Well, you know how things have a way of working out—one thing leads to another. Who knows what could happen in a combat situation cohabitating."

Dan stood up and placed his hands on her shoulders like a father taking to his daughter. "Is *that* why you came here? What's really on your mind?"

Naomi continued in Croatian, "I don't get along with Nick. He hasn't done anything to me. It's just that he's too young and short and our personalities clash. I'm much more comfortable being around you. Can we switch partners?"

The Balkan Network

Dan remembered his conversation with Karen that morning about Naomi. "I feel your concern, truly I do, but you have to remember, we're all in the military and this is a real mission. I just killed three men today, and Karol killed another. Doesn't that mean anything to you?"

"Yah, it's all the more reason why you need to be paired with *me* instead of *her*. Karol can babysit Nick now. I can be your courier, organizer, and right-hand man. Overall, you'd be better off with me tonight and throughout the mission."

"Karol and I are commissioned officers. She's a lieutenant commander in the Navy. I'm a major in the Air Force. I think better discretion and judgment is more appropriate here."

Naomi stared at him thinking about what he said then let out a huge sigh, "I suppose you're right. But if you should change your mind tonight, you know where to find me." Then she turned and looked at the door, "Assuming *she* left me some hot water, is it all right if I take a bath when Commander Koskov is finished?"

"Of course you can. There should be plenty of hot water because I reminded her not to shave her legs. The same goes for you too. I want you to look natural."

She snickered back at him, "I'll remember to do that. Good night, Major." With that, she turned and went down the hall to the bathroom.

Dan's mind was spinning. Not only was he trying to run a mission, but he was also refereeing emotions between himself and his team members. He thought she could be demonstrating a more dominant role on the mission. *Is she telling me she's up for the job?*

Karol interrupted Dan's thoughts as she walked in holding her dirty clothes. She had nothing on except a towel wrapped around her body, and her hair was still damp. She just passed Naomi in the hallway.

"What's with *her*? She just gave me a dirty look."

"I hope there's not going to be a problem between you two."

"What do you mean by that?"

"She just left here. She told me she wanted to switch partners with you."

"And, what did you tell her?"

"I said, I'm in charge here and I make all the decisions and we're not switching partners."

"Well, that explains *the look*. Now that she understands this, let me show you something." Karol dropped the towel wrapped around her waist and came toward Dan. She put her arms around him and kissed him on the lips. Dan put his arms around her to embrace her warm, moist body. They had not slept together since the last night at Bolling. Suddenly, Dan pushed her back. "Not tonight, we've got a job to do—and we just killed four men."

Chapter 20
OSIJEK, CROATIA

Chief Inspector Sergi Boraviko of the Croatian Interior Ministry of Police (MUP) got the call early that morning from local police headquarters in Ilok. Chief Branko Valpovo of the Croatian Police (CP) was on the phone with Sergi.

"A local fisherman found the bodies of four men outside Ilok. Each victim had a single gunshot wound to the head—a professional job by a skilled marksman. One body was found on an access road near the river. The other three bodies were found in an abandoned pumping station a few meters away. The victim along the access road was armed with an AK-47 and several small pistols. The other three victims were unarmed. We also found a woman's bra and shreds of a woman blouse near the three male victims inside the structure. It could have been a rape, or it could have been staged to appear as if it were a rape. Either way, we believe this is an MUP problem since all the victims are Serbian."

Boraviko replied, "I know the location well; it was used extensively during the war. We used the station to guard against Serbian gunboats patrolling the river. It was taken out by Serbian artillery fire. Later it was used by the Serbs in the siege of Vukovar. Please secure the area. Do not remove anything at the crime scene until I get there."

"I already have four of my best men guarding the area."

"Good, I'm on my way. I should be there within the hour." Boraviko hung up the phone and dialed a number on his personal cell phone. A voice answered, "Good morning, Sergi, how can I help you?"

"I believe we could have some trouble along the border. Croatian police in Ilok reported the murder of four men, possibly Serbian insurgents. Looks like a real professional job."

"Let me know what you find out. I haven't heard anything, but it's still early in the mission."

"I understand," said Boraviko. He ended the conversation with Yuri Pavol and left his office for Ilok.

Sergi Boraviko was an attractive man in his mid-thirties with short black hair, blue eyes, and a handlebar mustache. He was medium build, five foot ten and wore a black leather jacket. In May of 1991 during the War of Independence, Boraviko was a regular Croatian police officer stationed in Osijek. Two of his fellow Croatian police officers were taken prisoner near Borovo-Selo by Serbian paramilitary forces commanded by radical party leader Vecili Vorchek. A detachment of Croatian police was sent to rescue them. The rescue team arrived in a school bus on the outskirts of town, but their arrival was tipped off by Croat-Serb sympathizers and ambushed by Serb paramilitary forces. The team suffered heavy casualties. There were twelve fatalities and another twenty critically injured. Boraviko was one of only two men who survived the ordeal unscathed. He witnessed the mutilation of his dead comrades by Serb paramilitary forces and the bodies displayed near Borovo-Selo. After the massacre, Boraviko went on to serve with the Croatian National Guard in the War of Independence. During the war, Boraviko lost his wife and son, both killed by Serb shelling during the eighty-seven-day siege of Vukovar. After the war, Boraviko returned to police service, this time with the MUP and was promoted to Chief Inspector. One of his main responsibilities at MUP was to find and capture Serbian paramilitary forces who committed atrocities and crimes against humanity during the war.

* * *

BACK AT BAPSKA vineyard at 9:00 AM, the team was awakened by the smell of sausage and eggs being cooked by Karen and Mike. Naomi and Nick rolled out from the bedroom, still sleepy-eyed but well rested. Dan and Karol were the last out of bed because, just as Naomi predicted, the reality of killing did not set in until later in the night. They tossed and turned all night. After breakfast, Dan displayed maps on his laptop computer and briefed the team on the day's activities.

"Today our objective is to move along the farm roads heading out from Ilok and Sarengrad toward the Serbian border. This area is heavily mined and sparsely populated. Croatian forces planted most of the mines to slow the advance of Serbian heavy armor moving into Croatia and they've been slow to remove them. It could be years if not decades before all the mines are cleared."

Dan pointed to the areas alongside the main roads. "This is the area we're concerned with the most. There is no official border along the Croatian-Serbian frontier, and it's all flat terrain. The official border could be in the middle of a wheat field or vineyard. The only way to tell where the official border lies is to find the land mines. The Serbs have done an excellent job clearing the mines in their sovereignty, so we won't have to deal with that threat. We just have to find the mines on the Croatian side. We'll use the metal detectors to find their locations then mark the locations with the flags."

Dan held the metal detector in his hand and continued, "Most of the mines in this area are antitank and not antipersonnel, which means they're large. All we're looking for is an area clear enough to drive a motorcycle, ATV, or small utility truck through. Once we find a clear area through the minefields, it will become our emergency escape route back into Croatia from Serbia. As an added objective, Hal wants us to reconnoiter the general border area. Border police, not the military, patrol the main roads leading into Serbia."

Dan thought about his briefings from Josef back on board the train.

"Most people living along the border are trying to get their lives back to normal after the last war. They're tired of killing and bloodshed. All they want is food on their dinner plates. We believe anything connected with food production or agriculture on both sides of the border is a top priority. I've been told the local border police on both sides will do anything to keep the industry going, including unimpeded access across the border. We just need to make sure that's still the case before Karol and I try crossing the border with a truckload of automatic weapons. "Finally, Serbian mobile SAMs could be placed anywhere in this area along the border. This is the area our aircraft will enter and egress out of the country, and the Serbs know it. We need to record their locations and report back to NATO. We'll split up into three groups. Mike, you and

The Balkan Network

Karen take the road leading from Sotin to Tovarnik and cover the area off the main road. Nick, you and Naomi take the area around Bapska vineyard and the roads leading out of Ilok. Karol and I will cover the farm road heading out of Sarengrad toward the Serbian border. This area is our best location for crossing into Serbia because it's right in the middle of an overgrown orchard and allows for cover in the trees."

Dan pointed to the location on the map. "We'll meet at this location later tonight. Each of us will take a motorcycle so we can practice riding. Take all your weapons but stow them inside the backpacks. We don't want another encounter like we had yesterday. This whole area is less than ten miles square, so no one will be separated by more than a few kliks. It shouldn't take us more than six hours to sweep the area. Use the metal detector first, then walk, mark, and input the coordinates into your GPS."

The team broke up and covered the areas just as Dan directed. Mike and Karen found their area mined heavily with antitank mines along the road; however, the roads themselves were clear. Dan and Karol found their area heavily mined also but found a clearing in the overgrown orchard. Nick and Naomi found the Bapska vineyard area mined with antitank mines as well. They did find an area south of the vineyard sloping up the hills to be free of mines. The only drawback was that the area was in plain view from all approaches and would only be usable at night or dusk. The team used their communication devices to keep in touch with one another's exact location during the day, and no one experienced any problems with the equipment.

* * *

NOT FAR FROM the team's location on the banks of the Danube, Chief Inspector Sergi Boraviko, along with Police Chief Branko Valpovo, looked over the bloody crime scene.

Valpovo said, "The killer entered the pumping station through the opening and fired his weapon from there. Three spent cartridges were left on the ground where the killer felled his victims. Blood and brain matter is still splattered against the back wall, suggesting the he fired with the victim's back facing him."

Boraviko looked at the victims and nodded his head in agreement. "You're right about the killer—an absolute professional, cold, ruthless, highly organized—yet he doesn't just kill on sight, there was a reason. He obviously knew the three men were here and entered unnoticed through the opening."

Boraviko looked around inside the structure. "It must have been dark in here last night. To be this accurate, the killer must have had a laser sight or night vision hardware, otherwise it would have been a difficult shot."

Boraviko bent over and looked at the bra and shredded blouse. "These are all locally manufactured. They belong to a young woman, slender in build—she could be a local."

Boraviko placed the bra and blouse in a plastic bag then picked up one of the spent casings and examined it closer. "These are 9.3 mm rounds, virtually impossible to trace. Show me the victim outside."

Valpovo showed Sergi the victim outside near the front of the station, "This man was caught by surprise—his rifle is still slung over his shoulder, and he's still holding his fly. We found one shell casing up the road in the bushes, another 9.3 mm. The shooter fired from that location."

"Four shell casings, four dead bodies. There could be more than one shooter, or it could be a team working together," Boraviko said thinking out loud. "Collect the casings, and I'll have them analyzed back at MUP headquarters. Photograph the entire area then remove the bodies. I'll take over from here."

Boraviko turned and looked toward the access road heading up to the main road. He thought to himself for a moment then looked back at Valpovo and asked one final question, "By the way, chief, have you noticed any unusual activity in the minefields lately?"

Chapter 21
BAPSKA VINEYARDS, CROATIA

The sun was setting, and the team met at Karol and Dan's location near the fruit orchard. Dan looked at Mike and asked, "What do you think of this location?"

"I think this will work. There's plenty of cover with the trees, and we can easily get back into Croatia without being seen."

"Good, from now on let's call this location 'touchdown.' I'll give each location a code-name so we don't compromise the exact location when we're conversing. Let's get back to the vineyard before it gets dark."

It was around 6:00 PM when the team split up for the return ride to Bapska. Mike and Karen went first so they could start dinner. Karol's stomach wasn't feeling so good, so she and Nick left together. Dan stayed back with Naomi and gathered all the remaining metal detectors and flags. As Naomi was walking back to her motorcycle, she made a step on the soft earth and heard the sound of a light *click*. She froze dead in her tracks and cried out for help.

"Dan, help me, I think I heard something!"

The Balkan Network

Dan looked up from his tasks to see Naomi standing lightly on one foot and trembling like a leaf.

"Shit! Don't move another inch' I'll be right there!" Dan made his way back to Naomi's location, carefully placing his footsteps on the marked areas that were safe. Naomi was standing still with her weight on her right foot. Dan put on a head flashlight freeing up both hands, then took out his knife.

"It's probably a very small antipersonnel mine, probably improvised. Listen to me, remain calm and do exactly as I say. I can disarm just about any antipersonnel mine."

Dan inserted his knife into the soft soil and probed around to get a location of the device but was surprised how large it was. He pulled his knife out of the soil and inserted it again in another location. Again the device appeared larger than an antipersonnel mine.

"Stay still. I'm going back for the metal detector. As long as you don't move, you'll be safe."

"Dan, please hurry, I don't know how much longer I can hold my position."

"You can do it. Breathe slowly. I'll be back in twenty seconds." Dan raced back to the motorcycles and his backpack and pulled out the small metal detector he'd been using and rushed back to Naomi's location. He turned on the device and scanned the area. As expected, he detected a large metal device, probably a propane tank with explosive material.

"Someone must have mistaken the tank for a well." He inserted his knife again into the soil and determined the device was at least two to three feet in diameter. There was enough explosive firepower to take out an entire city block.

"This is the biggest antitank mine I've ever seen. It's more likely some sort of an improvised explosive device (IED). It could be why we missed it on the initial sweep.

Antitank mines work on pressure sensitivity instead of a detonation switch like the antipersonnel mines. This thing should have gone off as soon as you stepped on it. Don't move!"

"What the hell do you think I'm trying to do?" Naomi cried out, tears rolling down her cheeks and her voice trembling. "Isn't there anything you can do?"

"I don't know. I'll have to call Washington to see if someone can give me some advice on this type of explosive." Dan pulled out his cell phone and called Nick. He was riding double on his motorcycle with Karol. "Speeder this is Specter. Lombard is standing on top of a mine out here in the orchard. What's your location?"

"We're almost to the vineyard. I can drop Sutter off and get back to you within five minutes."

"No, that won't help. Continue back to the vineyard with Sutter. She's not feeling very well, probably something she ate. When you get back, stay there and wait for my orders. If this thing should go off, I don't want it to take out the rest of the team."

"Yes, sir, I'll be standing by in case you need me. I'll tell the others."

"Thanks," and he ended the call. Next, he called Mattingly's number. He answered almost immediately.

"This is Finder, can I help you?"

"Sir, Lombard is standing on top of an antitank mine. I'm with her right now. I think it could be

some sort of a homemade device. Can you patch us through to anyone that knows something about IEDs?"

"Hold on, I'll be back with you in a second."

Dan looked at Naomi. Tears were still running down her cheeks. Dan wanted to hold her and comfort her but he couldn't take the chance on the pressure sensitivity switch.

The Balkan Network

"I'll get you out of this, you have to trust me."

Mattingly came back on the line, "We're on secure communications. I've got Sergeant Hunnington on the line with me. He's from the Army Munitions Training Center at Fort Sill. No one knows more about these types of IEDs than he does. Sergeant Hunnington, go ahead."

"Could you give me a brief description of the device, sir?"

"The device appears to be about two to three feet in diameter and circular and set approximately six to eight inches below the surface. There's a female about 110-115 pounds standing on the device. As near as I can tell there are no wires or switches connected to the device which rules out remote detonation."

Hunnington replied, "The pressure sensitivity switch could be rusted or corroded and that's why the device has not gone off. Here's what I want you to do. Find something to place on the device that weighs the approximate weight of the person standing on it. Place the weight on the device and slowly have her release the weight off the device at the same time you put the weight on. Try to keep the weight even. Once you're clear, run like hell! All we're trying to do is buy some time with the sensitivity switch."

Dan said to Mattingly, who was still monitoring the call, "If you don't hear back from me within the hour, one of the team members will contact you. I've already let them know our situation. They're standing by for my orders."

"You two will be all right, just take your time."

Dan secured the call and looked around the area to find something that weighed roughly the same weight as Naomi. The only thing he saw was Naomi's motorcycle. He'd have to put the rear end of the bike on the mine because if he used the whole weight of the bike it would be too much.

"Hang on just a little bit longer. I'm going to get one of the bikes and place the rear tire on the mine. As soon as I put weight on the mine, I want you to take your foot off the mine slowly. When I tell you to roll, I want you to fall down to the ground and roll as fast as you can away from the mine. If it should go off, the blast trajectory will be upwards and away from you."

Naomi still crying said, "Wha ... what about you?"

"As soon as you're clear, I'll roll with you." Dan placed his hand on the side of her cheek. "Naomi, whatever happens, I want you to know that you're one of the most remarkable women I've ever met."

Naomi continued to sob, "I'm so scared, Dan. Please don't let me die like this."

Dan got Naomi's motorcycle and came back. Slowly he moved the bike toward the front edge of the mine. "I'll tell you when to start relieving the pressure on your foot." Dan moved the rear end of the bike onto the mine and nothing happened. Next he nodded his head at Naomi and said, "Go slowly as I roll the bike further back."

Naomi started to relieve the pressure on her foot and, at the same time, Dan rolled the rear end of the bike further onto the mine. Again, nothing happened. They repeated this motion several times inch by inch, Naomi closer to safety with each inch. Finally, her foot was completely off the mine and the rear of the bike was about halfway on the mine. Dan yelled, "Roll like hell!"

Naomi fell to the ground and started to roll as she felt the weight of Dan's body coming down on her. He grabbed her, put his arms around her and together they both rolled away from the mine. They didn't stop rolling until they were several feet from the mine. Dan was on top

The Balkan Network

of Naomi embracing her. Naomi still had tears running down her cheeks mixed with dirt. They looked at each other briefly then began kissing each other passionately on the lips. He put his hands around her face and continued to kiss her face, lips, and neck. Naomi sobbing, finally said, "You did it!"

Dan stared into Naomi's eyes and said, "I can't believe we just pulled that off. We'd better get the hell out of here before that thing explodes." Dan got Naomi to her feet and together they started running away from the mine. They were approximately 100 yards away when they heard and felt the explosion. The concussion from the explosion knocked them both to the ground.

Back at the vineyard, the team heard the explosion and felt the shock waves inside the building. They were all seated around the kitchen table. Karol stood up, stunned. Mike stood up and went over to her, "Ma'am, I'm sure they're both all right."

Karol picked up her cell phone and called Dan. There was no answer. Mike pulled out his cell phone and called Dan—again, there was no answer. "Let me try mine," said Karen. She called Dan and again no luck. Mike tried Naomi's cell phone and again the same results. There was total silence in the kitchen for several minutes, then Nick stood up and said, "I don't care what the Major said, I'm going looking for them."

"I'll go with you," said Mike. "You two can stay here. If they're both dead, it's the end of our mission anyway."

Karol nodded her head agreeing.

Nick was already downstairs starting his bike. Mike was right on his tail. They retraced their way back to the general location of Dan and Naomi. It took them less than ten minutes to reach the crater. Strands of metal, pieces of rubber, and debris were scattered everywhere, but there was no sign of human remains. Nick took out his flashlight and began scanning the area away from the crater. Finally, he started yelling in English, "Lombard. Specter! Can you hear us?" Mike started walking in a different direction away from the crater being careful to step in the areas that were clear of mines when he noticed the soles of two pairs of boots lying face down in the soft earth.

"Nick, get over here, I think I've found something!"

Nick ran over to Mike's location, being careful of his footsteps in the darkness as well. Thoughts were going through Nick's mind of the possibility that Dan and Naomi had been blown to pieces. Nick could see Mike standing a few feet ahead pointing his flashlight down into the darkness. The two men stopped in their tracks and brought their flashlights on the boots ahead.

Nick, breathing heavy and sweating, looked at Mike, "You go ahead. I don't want to see what's left of them."

Mike nodded his head, "Alright then, stay here and don't move. I don't want you to step on a mine as well."

Slowly, Mike walked closer to the pair of boots sticking up from the earth. As he got closer, he could see the outlines of two figures, both male and female with their heads down facing the ground. As Mike inched his way closer he shined his flashlight on the figures and could see Dan and Naomi laying face down covered with dirt and debris.

"Nick, get over here, I found them. I think they're all right!"

Nick approached Mike as he was turning Dan over on his back.

"Can you find me some water? I think they're both unconscious."

Nick handed his bottle of water to Mike. Mike splashed some water on Dan's face, and he slowly came to.

The Balkan Network

Dan shook his head and said, "Where am I?"

"You're okay, buddy."

Nick rolled Naomi over on her back then splashed some water on her face and she came to as well. "Naomi, can you hear me? It's Nick."

"Where's Dan? Is Dan all right?"

Nick thought that was a strange question coming from someone who just stepped on a mine.

Mike took out his cell phone and called Karen. She answered on the first ring.

"We found them! They'll be okay! They were both knocked unconscious. Bring the ATV."

Back at the vineyard, Karen got off the phone with Mike. "They found them, ma'am. They're on their way back, everyone's okay.

Karol replied, "Take the ATV, I'll wait here."

Chapter 22
INSERTION

Dan and Karol were up early the next morning in their small bedroom. Neither slept well. Dan's head was still throbbing from the shock waves, and Karol couldn't sleep because she was vomiting all night. Dan was on the phone talking with Mattingly giving him a briefing on the previous day's events. Karol sat on the floor next to him, wrapped in her sleeping bag, listening to their conversations as she was starting to do consistently now.

Mattingly said over the phone, "Thanks for the update. I'll inform our Croatian sources about the mine. I'm glad everyone's all right. Now we've got to move forward with the next phase of the operation. The air campaign is just a few days away, and we need to set up the Serbian location. Today you will receive the shipment of goods I told you about. A truck with letters EU on the side will be arriving at your location around noon local time. The truck is a shipment of live hogs and chickens. You and Karol will take the shipment across the border and establish the Sid location. You'll have to unload the hogs and chickens first so you can load the weapons in the floorboards. Then you

The Balkan Network

need to reload the livestock, with the motorcycle and ATV. You have to do your best with the animals."

"I'll make it work", said Dan.

The next thing I need to do is introduce you to a new communications device called webcasting. It's voice-over Internet protocol—completely secure. At 0900Z I want you to log on to your computer and download the small chat software that will appear on your screen. Then, follow the onscreen instructions once the software is downloaded. Assemble the entire team around the computer screen, and I'll commence the briefing. This is new technology, but once you get used to it, you'll wonder how you ever lived without it. Do you have any questions?"

"No, sir, I think that about does it from here."

"Okay, Dan, I'll talk with you again on the Internet at 0900Z. By the way, how is Naomi doing?"

"She has a headache just like I do, but surprisingly she's handled this stressful situation well."

"Glad to hear that. Keep an eye on her and look for any signs of stress."

Dan secured the call and turned to Karol and said, "According to Mike and Karen, the road from Tovarnik to Sid looks the best. Mike said he counted over twenty-five trucks loaded with agricultural supplies and livestock go right through the border checkpoints without even a flinch from the Serbs. I think it's our best entrance into Serbia."

"Dan, I think you and I should take all the trucks into Serbia by ourselves, not just one, and leave the rest of the team here. We've already had two close encounters with death, and if we get into trouble on the other side, at least the rest of the team will be safe here in Croatia."

"I think you're right. I was going to have Naomi and Nick drive one of the trucks with us but after what happened yesterday, I think it's best we leave them here."

"I'll get the rest of the team up."

* * *

SITTING at his office in Osijek just after 7:00 AM, Inspector Boraviko received another call from Police Chief Branko Valpovo in Ilok.

"Sergi, another mine detonated along the border last night. It appears that it was a large device. The location is somewhere off the main road heading south from Sarengrad near Bapska. There could be insurgent activity in that vicinity. So far no one has checked into the hospital here for injuries, and no deaths reported. A lot of twisted metal left behind, perhaps from a motorcycle. I thought you'd like to know."

"Thanks for the information, Chief. I know this area as well. We mined it heavily during the war to take out Serbian tanks as they retreated across the border. I'll check the area out myself."

On hearing this piece of information, Sergi made a local call on his cell phone again, and Yuri Pavol answered on the first ring.

"Yes, inspector."

"I just received word that a large explosive device was detonated near the Bapska vineyard. Have you heard any news about the homicides from your sources?"

Yuri replied, "I have confirmation that there was an abduction of one of the cell members, a female, and she was rescued by other members of the circuit. I also have confirmation that a female was involved with the detonation of the explosive near Bapska. So far, there were no injuries or fatalities from this explosion. For the time being, we can proceed with our plan. They should be out of the Bapska location within the next few days."

"Everything makes sense to me now. I've learned the four shell casings found at the crime scene were fired from a Russian-made Makarov pistol."

"Be patient, Sergi, we only have a few days left of Phase Two of the operation. Concentrate you efforts on finding more insurgents coming across the border. We don't want any more surprises."

Chapter 23
CROSSING THE BORDER

Back at Bapska, the team was getting ready for the day's activities. Naomi slept surprisingly well that night and seemed glad Nick was in the room with her. Karen and Mike stayed up late getting the trucks and weapons ready for travel across the border. A few minutes before 0900Z, Karol logged on her computer and downloaded the chat software. Five minutes later, a screen appeared on the laptop monitor that read, "Defense Intelligence Agency Briefing." Karol called everyone to the kitchen table.

"I think we're ready for the webcast. Everyone gather around so we can hear the briefing."

At exactly 0900Z, a voice came over the laptop, "Can everyone hear me? This is Hal. I want everyone to talk directly into the speakers and give me a voice check.

One by one, each member of the team gave a voice check. Everyone's voice sounded clear over the Internet connection. Hal continued.

"We've secured a countryside location outside the town of Sid. The owners of the farm agreed to let us use the property in exchange for legal immigration into the United

The Balkan Network

States. At this moment, they're en route to an undisclosed location somewhere in the States. Dan, you and Karol will take their place running the farm. The local neighboring farmers have already been told the residences are leaving on an extended holiday to Hungary and that relatives will be taking over the farm during their absence. There should be no surprises from the local residences when you and Karol show up later today. The bad news is, of course, you and Karol will have to assume the duties and responsibilities as farmers."

As the team was looking at the laptop, a map of the surrounding area appeared.

"This is one of the beauties I like about this voice-over Internet system. It allows me to put up displays on the screen that you can view with me. Here is a map showing the roads leading into Serbia from Croatia. Dan, have you decided on a road to use to enter Serbia?"

"Yes, sir, we believe road numbered E-20 from Tovarnik to Sid looks the best. It's a little out of our way from our present location, but the entire distance is still less than fifteen miles."

"Good, it should take you no more than an hour to drive from your present location to the farmhouse outside Sid. Here is the location of the farmhouse on the map." Hal highlighted the area. "Once you get to the farmhouse, unload the animals and store the equipment. You should have no trouble doing that. The farmhouse is fully operational. Leave the truck and ATV there and take the motorcycle back to the Bapska using this road." Mattingly pointed to one of the roads leading up to Croatia along the Fruska Gora hills.

"We already know of this road," said Karol.

"Good, the reason I want you to take this road is we want you to record SAM sites along the way. It appears from our satellites the Serbs have repositioned several batteries along this highway; however, we can't tell whether they're SA-3 or SA-5 or SA-6. This is important because this area is also the area where NATO aircraft will enter and egress out of Serbia. You don't need to be too detailed or technical because these are mobile sites and can be moved quickly. We just need to know their make and model and approximate number."

Dan said, "This should be easy to do since Karol and I will be riding double on the motorcycle. We can ride off-road and use some of the farm roads. If we're stopped by the JNA, we can tell them we're farmers trying to get back to our fields."

Hal interrupted, "You should be able to do all of this before nightfall. I want you to contact me as soon as you get back so we can debrief and send the report on to Naples. Dan, once you have the weapons in place and you're back in Croatia, we'll start moving the rest of the team into Serbia. I'll set up the next webcast so we can cover that phase. For now, this should be enough to get you through tomorrow. Call me as soon as the shipment of livestock arrives. I'll give you a timetable at that point. We can secure the webcast call for now. Good day everyone, keep up the good work," then the computer screen went blank.

"Okay, everyone, you heard if for yourselves. We're all going to be farmers now," said Dan. "Let's get ready for that shipment of hogs and chickens."

As planned, a truck with the letters EU marked on the side pulled into the compound around noon. Dan met the driver and spoke to him in Croatian. He was just an ordinary delivery driver making his rounds to the Slavonian region. He told Dan that he makes several deliveries each week to farmers in this area but never to the areas with

The Balkan Network

minefields. Dan told the driver to pull the truck into the warehouse and unload the hogs. The chickens were in cages so they were left outside until ready to load back onto his truck. Dan instructed all team members, except Karol, to stay inside and upstairs. Karol helped unload the chickens while Dan and the driver did their best to unload the hogs without making too much of a mess. The whole delivery took less than two hours. After that, the driver was anxious to get back to Zagreb so he left just as soon as his delivery was complete. When the truck and driver were safely out of sight, the rest of the team came down from upstairs and immediately began helping Dan and Karol finish loading their truck with the hogs and chickens. They left a few cages of chickens behind for another trip across the border.

Dan and Karol changed into their farmers' clothes and went over their route to the border. Their cover story would be that they were delivering the animals for slaughter. Any hungry border guard or soldier would never question them any further because it could be their next meal. Dan called everyone together in the kitchen for a meeting.

"As Hal mentioned, it should take us no more than one hour to cross the border. Once Karol and I are safely across, I'll give you a call to confirm. You can monitor our GPS positions on the laptop. It should be another twenty-minute drive to reach the Sid farmhouse. All we have to go by to recognize the farmhouse is the pictures Hal showed us on the webcast. It'll take time to offload the animals and equipment. I anticipate no more than a couple of hours for that task. Once we've done that, we'll ride back. The distance is less than twenty kilometers from the farmhouse back to this location; however, we will probably take more time looking for the SAMs. I don't foresee any problems, but if we get caught or detained, contact Hal and get instructions from him. My guess is the JNA are used to farmers seeing SAMs on their properties so this should be routine."

Dan and Karol got inside the truck and Karen handed them a cloth napkin with extra food for the trip. "I've made you some sandwiches with local bread and meat. I made them look natural and rural. Remember, there are no fast-food restaurants along the way should you get hungry."

Karol took the napkin and placed it between her and Dan on the front seat. "I'm already getting hungry with the smell. Thank you, Karen, we may need it later this afternoon."

Mike came up to the driver's window, "I wish I was going with you, sir. I'll be standing by here monitoring your location at all times."

Dan replied, "I want you to look after everyone during my absence. Stay inside the warehouse as much as practical. With that mine going off yesterday, you could have some visitors. If you need supplies, send Naomi and Nick to Sarengrad rather than Ilok. It's further away from the Serbian border. We don't want any more surprises in town."

Karen added, "Good luck to you both. We'll be waiting for you tonight with a big dinner."

"We'll need it. My favorite is vegetables and chicken," replied Karol.

Dan checked his equipment and supplies one last time making sure his belt buckle and dog tags slipped inside the leather next to the buckle was in place. Karol did the same. This was the only thing on them that identified Dan and Karol as U.S. military personnel.

Dan drove the EU truck on the main road paralleling the Danube up toward Sarengrad and Sotin. Once on the outskirts of Sotin, he took the road to the southwest heading toward Tovarnik. The weather conditions that afternoon deteriorated as the day progressed. The overcasts skies eventually turned to heavy rain. It was well after 2:00 PM when Dan and Karol arrived at the border crossing at Tovarnik. There was a small backup, but other than that, traffic was proceeding across the border normally. Their truck pulled up to the Croatian side of the border and the guards were inside their guardhouse, motioning vehicles to cross. They obviously were concerned more about not getting wet than anything else. As Dan pulled the truck to the Serbian side, border guards made a look into the back of the flatbed and saw the hogs and chickens. One of the guards approached Dan on the driver-side window and spoke in Serb-Croatian with a Croatian dialect.

"Are they for Prsut or bacon?"

Dan replied, "I think they're for a little of both."

Karol looked at the young border guard and said, "They're scheduled for slaughter this afternoon along with the hens." The guard smiled then waved them through.

As Dan and Josef expected, the crossing was uneventful. An added benefit Josef probably remembered was that the Serbs knew pig farmers were not Muslims. The truck traveled along the highway leading to Sid, and for the first time Dan and Karol were inside enemy territory as combatants. Karol took note of the surrounding areas but the visibility was limited because of the rainfall and overcast. She could see antiaircraft batteries positioned in the distance. To the right of the road facing northeast, Dan could make out a few older fixed SA-2 sites position in some of the fields in the distance. The Serbs didn't seem too concerned about concealing their locations because they could be seen from the main highway. It also looked like vegetation was encroaching upon the sites and had not been cleared or mowed for several months. He wondered if they could be decoys.

Karol picked up her cell phone and called Mike.

"We crossed the border with no problems. There seems to be several utility vehicles on the road just like the one we're driving with similar payloads. The countryside is mainly farmlands, dairy cattle and a few sheep. Can you give us directions to the Sid location?"

Mike had his laptop on, and Karen was viewing the location on the screen. One of the advantages of this system was that it did not leave a paper trail. The team members could access any amount of detailed, classified information on the DOD Internet site, and when they were finished, they simply turned off the computer. None of the information was stored on the hard drive.

Mike replied, "We have your position established on the map display. The system works like a charm. The farmhouse is located past the town of Sid. Looks like you need to go three miles past town then make a left turn off the main highway heading north-northeast. I'll let you know when you approach the turnoff."

"I'll stay in contact with you. The cell phone reception is great. It sounds like you're in the backseat," said Karol.

Dan continued to drive the truck as he noticed everyone on the highway had cell phones up to their ears. Josef and Hal did their homework well. Communicating by cell phone was perfectly natural in the countryside. As they came to the town of Sid, Karol relayed their position back to Mike. "We're now approaching the outskirts of town. Nothing looks out of the ordinary."

Mike replied, "Keep going past the city limits. Let me know when you're heading east outside of town."

The Balkan Network

Dan glanced at Karol, "So far, so good. How much further?"

"Keep going past the town. Mike says the location is outside town."

Dan was surprised to hear this. He thought the location was on the western side of the city, closer to the Croatian border. The distance to the next town along the highway was less than seven miles. A sign ahead written in both Serbian Latin and Serbian Cyrillic said the town of Kukujevci was ahead eighteen kilometers.

Mike came on the phone again with Karol, "The turnoff is just ahead, less than a mile. Look for an unpaved road off to the left. Take that road and go about three miles. The farmhouse is located on the right side."

Karol relayed the directions to Dan who was not monitoring the cell phone transmissions as he was busy looking at the countryside taking note of military facilities. He followed Karol's directions, and in less than fifteen minutes, the truck pulled up to the gate of a farmhouse located along a small creek.

"This is it," said Karol. "It's perfect. I'll get out and open the gate."

Karol jumped out of the truck and opened the gate. As soon as Dan drove the truck through the gate, Karol closed and secured it, then climbed back on board the truck. The farmhouse was set in a beautiful location bordering the Fruska Gora hills. There were fields all around the farmhouse. The main house was a small two-story rock building about 1800 square feet. There were several large trees around the house giving cover from the road. Next to the farmhouse was a livestock barn big enough for the truck. The barn was designed for slaughtering pigs. There were already three or four hungry hogs making noise as they approached the barn.

"We'll drive the truck inside the barn and release the animals into the pens," said Dan.

"Grant, are you still on the line?" said Karol.

"Yes, ma'am, we have you on the computer as well. In fact, you're just fifteen miles due south of our Bapska location, just across the border."

"The farmhouse is secure. Specter and I will be off headset for a while until we unload the animals and equipment. Get a current uplink from the JSTARS and monitor our location. If you notice anyone approaching, let us know immediately; otherwise, we'll see you back at the vineyard tonight."

Chapter 24
THREAT ANALYSIS

Dan and Karol spent the next hour unloading, feeding the animals, and storing the equipment. They decided to leave the ATV and truck inside the barn. They hid the AK-74s and extra rounds inside grain sacks that were in the barn. If the Serbs searched this location, it would take hours to go through every sack. With the Serbian location secure, they offloaded the motorcycle and got ready for the trip back to Croatia using the road through Fruska Gora. Dan decided to ride cross-country through the farmlands, following the small creek which would meet up with the road coming from Kuzmin. They locked the farmhouse and got on the motorcycle, wearing their black helmets.

A light rain was still falling. Dan started the bike and headed out the gate of the farmhouse. Along the way, they did see mobile SA-6 sites. The crews were not visible from the roads, probably inside tents or their vehicles getting away from the rain. Dan estimated that four sites were along the small river. As they reached the main road, they headed northwest toward Croatia and Ilok. From the road, looking up to the hilltop ridge to the heavily wooded area of Fruska Gora, Dan could make out more SAMs. He counted six SA-6 sites. These were the latest Soviet models, the so-called "3 Fingers of Death" model. Rain started to pour down on them as they rode back to Ilok. Traffic was light on the road, and even after stopping to record the SAM sites, they made it back to the border by 5:00 PM. Serbian border guards were staffing the station. As they come to the crossing, Dan stopped his bike and turned off the engine. He and Karol took off their helmets.

"What brings you to Croatia?" said one of the border guards.

Dan replied in Serbo-Croatian, "We dropped off a fresh supply of hogs ready for slaughter. The farmer is still unloading them from the truck. Because of the rain, it's taking longer than expected, so he let us use his motorcycle to ride back home before it gets dark."

"And the woman, who is she?"

"She's my wife and my partner. If it wasn't for her, we wouldn't have any hogs fat for slaughter. Her job is feeding the animals."

"Then we can't afford to delay her, carry on."

Dan started the engine and drove across the border.

Safely back at Bapska, the team monitored the webcast with Mattingly. Dan gave Hal a debriefing on their trip into Serbia and detailed the location of SAMs in Serbia. He told him that most of the Triple-A sites were concealed within the clumps of trees scattered throughout the countryside. The SAMs were hidden in the same way but were more difficult to see from the road. The Serbs did an excellent job of concealing both the Triple-A and SA-6 sites within the wooded areas of the Fuska Gora hills.

"I'll transmit the information to Naples as soon as I get off the phone. This is very important information because our information led us to believe this area did not contain as many SAMs as you described."

"If that's the case, sir, remember what we discussed back on the train. Langley will be waiting for the report as well. I think this is one of those instances where we should hold off transmitting to CIA as long as we can, especially since I have to make another trip across the border using the same entrance and exit point."

"Point well-taken, Dan—anyway, it's time for the team to split up and move into Serbia. The air campaign is getting closer every day. Dan, I want you and Karol to set up permanently at the Sid location starting tomorrow. Mike and Karen will move into Novi Sad, and Naomi and Nick will move south of the Sava River to the town of Varna. Karen, Mike, Naomi, and Nick, the four of you will stay in safe houses we've secured. They're both guest-houses, and you'll be the only occupants in the inns. You can move about freely. This will help conceal your identity. Since you're disguised as local Serbs, at the safe houses you won't have to register with the local police."

Mattingly pointed to the locations on a map on the computer screen and said, "Mike and Karen, I'd like you to survey any SAMs near Novi Sad. There's one more important thing we need Mike and Karen to do. Just to the north along the road leading into Novi Sad, our satellites picked up three heavily armored, mechanized divisions sitting in the open near the town of Glozan. We'd like them to get visual confirmation on the division and let us know how many and what type of SAMs are protecting the area. It seems odd to U.S. intelligence that the Serbs are placing this large of a division so close to the Croatian border knowing they'd be targets in an air strike. Naomi, once you and Nick established yourselves at the Varna location, we'd like you to search for any SAM sites in your area."

"I'll have the team get on it right away," said Dan.

Mattingly continued, "Nick and Naomi will be the last to leave the vineyard. I need you two to set up an additional satellite dish so we can have a repeater for transmission once the team's inside Serbia. The repeater dish will make it possible for anyone to communicate via cell phones in all modes anywhere and anytime."

Dan logged off the DOD Internet site and briefed the team further.

"Karol and I will take the second truck across the border to the Sid farmhouse. That leaves four bikes and one EU truck left over, which we'll use in an emergency egress situation. The four of you will make the trip across the border on motorcycles. Use the crossing at Ilok that Karol and I used last night. It seems to be the most unattended checkpoint. Once we cross, everyone will meet at the Sid location. There, we'll distribute your equipment and weapons. Karol needs to reprogram all cell phones and change out the SIM cards so your phones will look like they're making local calls from the 381 country code of Serbia."

Chapter 25
THE ENCOUNTER

The next morning, Karen was up with Mike, packing their backpacks for the motorcycle trip across the border. Mike rolled up their sleeping bags and said, "I hope Dan and Karol get across the border with everything; if not, it'll be a quick end to our mission."

"They didn't have any problems the last time so I would expect the same this time," replied Karen.

Dan and Karol, dressed in their farm clothes, came down from upstairs, and started loading the second truck. They removed the floorboards that Nick modified to conceal their equipment and supplies. The laptops and communications gear took up most of the room rather than the weapons. They replaced the floorboards and started loading the sacks of grain and feed that were stored in the warehouse. Inside each of the sacks was more equipment and supplies. Finally, they loaded the last of the chicken pens onto the truck and were ready to go. Mike and Karen came down with Nick and Naomi to say good-bye.

"This is a critical segment of our mission. Should one

of the elements be caught or captured inside Serbia, it means our circuit will be compromised and we'll have to extract the rest of the team. This means our airmen will have a more difficult time being rescued or the air campaign may be postponed until a new team is inserted. Everyone be on your toes. Karol and I should be across the border in less than an hour. Mike, you and Karen follow one hour later. It should take you less time since you'll be able to ride faster than us. Let's plan on meeting at the Sid location at 1130 hours. Naomi, you and Nick follow once you've setup the satellite dish, and rendezvousing with us at the Sid location at 1300 hours. Should you get held up, call Karol. Does anyone have any questions?" Dan paused for a moment, then said, "Good, let's get going."

* * *

DAN AND KAROL drove off the vineyard compound at exactly 9:00 AM. Mike and Karen followed with their bikes one hour later. Naomi and Nick stayed behind at the vineyard to sweep up and set up the dish. Nick unpacked the dish from the box and carried it up to the rooftop to install. Naomi stayed downstairs and began combing the outside area, cleaning up signs of their existence. She shouted up to Nick on the roof, "I'll take one final look around the compound and clean up."

"Okay, I'll be up here if you need me. I should be done with the dish in twenty minutes."

Naomi began walking around the vineyard. The morning sun was trying to come out from the low overcast covering the countryside. She walked out to the main road to make sure the land mine warning sign was still in place. She cringed thinking about the one she stepped on the other night. As she was making her way to the main road, she noticed an unoccupied white sedan parked outside the gate. She reached for her cell phone to call Nick but remembered she left it with her gear back at the warehouse. She looked out toward the road and didn't notice anyone in either direction. She turned and started to walk quickly back to the warehouse when she heard a voice say in Serbo-Croatian, "Good morning, young lady."

Naomi froze in her tracks. She turned around and saw Chief Inspector Sergi Boraviko standing alongside the road. He was less than ten feet away. She couldn't run without causing suspicion.

"What's a nice girl like you doing in a place like this?" he said.

Naomi was speechless.

"Didn't you read the signs warning about undiscovered mines?" asked Boraviko.

Naomi came to her senses and replied in Serbo-Croatian, "Yes, I did notice them, that's why I'm here. Is there something I can help you with, kind sir?"

"Why yes there is, miss," as he held up his MUP badge. "My name is Inspector Boraviko. I'm with the Interior Ministry of Police. What is your name, young lady?"

Naomi replied again in Serbo-Croatian, "My name is Naomi Markof. I'm also with the Interior Ministry, except I'm here on behalf of the European Union. It seems our government and the EU are deeply concerned about getting the agricultural industry up and running again in Eastern Slavonia. I was just looking over this lovely vineyard to see how we can get the wine production going again."

"This vineyard hasn't been used for years. United Nations forces used it last monitoring the cease-fire. Do I detect a slight French accent in your dialect?"

"Your observation is correct inspector. I've been living

in Brussels for the past four years working for the EU. I can't help it if the French rubbed off on me."

"Are you here alone, miss?"

"No, sir, I'm not. My assistant and guide is here with me. He's back at the little farmhouse. We rode our motorcycles here from Zagreb, and one of the bikes has a flat tire. He's fixing the tire now."

"What's his name?"

"You have a lot of questions, Inspector, did we do something wrong?"

"Of course not, it's just my job and my nature to be inquisitive."

"Nikola Belleu is his name. He's also from the Interior Ministry, except he's not the educated type. In fact, he doesn't speak much, not to me or to anyone else for that matter. He's here with me to keep me out of trouble and to make sure I don't step on any mines."

Naomi caught herself because she almost said *again*.

Sergi could not help but be intrigued by the woman he faced. She was young, intelligent, and naturally beautiful even though she was not wearing makeup and dressed in peasant clothing. Her Serbo-Croatian was perfect. He just mentioned the French accent to get her reaction. There was something about this young woman, but he couldn't place it. She was obviously well educated and probably spoke a number of languages. He decided to take a chance on her identity. He spoke in German.

"There's been some trouble outside Ilok, a quadruple homicide. Four young men murdered a few nights ago. We believe there was a rape victim as well. Have you noticed anyone or anything suspicious in your travels?"

Naomi paused for just a second because she understood everything Boraviko said and replied in Serbo-Croatian. "Very clever, Mr. Inspector," then switched to

The Balkan Network

German. "If you wanted to know if I spoke German, you should have asked!"

Sergi, now caught off guard, was at a loss for words. Her beauty and intellect were stunning. "I guess you're right. I should have just asked you."

As Naomi was about to say something, a cell phone rang in Boraviko's pocket. "Excuse me miss, I have to take this call." He began talking and then said to her, "I must leave you now. I have urgent matters to attend to. A police officer's work is never done, and he is always on call. Please be careful, young lady, and tell your assistant the same."

Naomi replied back, this time in Serbo-Croatian, "Yes, Inspector, I best be getting back to him. He might be wondering where I'm at." She turned and quickly walked back to the warehouse. Boraviko still talking on his cell phone walked back to his car.

Naomi, now trembling from the encounter, picked up her pace as she saw Boraviko's car drive away briskly kicking up a trail of dust. She began running back to the warehouse.

"Nick! Nick! Get the hell down here right away! We've got to get our asses out of here!"

Nick was coming down from the roof when he heard Naomi's screams.

"What's wrong? Did you step on another mine?"

"This is no time to be funny, you little shithead! I just ran into a Croatian Federal cop out front. I think he's gone now, but I'm not sure. He could be setting up a trap. He seemed clever enough. We've got to get out of here before he brings in reinforcements or holds us up."

"I'm sorry, Naomi—it's just that you ran here screaming like a madwoman I thought something was terribly wrong. What did you say to him?"

"I used the cover story. I think he bought it, but I don't

know for how long. I told him you were with me and you were fixing one of the motorcycles and we had to get going. I'm sure he'll be back or at the least will be snooping around here again."

"You're right, we'd better get going. Did you sweep the place down?"

"I did it as best as I could in the short amount of time but didn't have time to burn. If they should come back it will look like someone was here, but hopefully they won't be able to trace anything back to us. There's one more thing. The cop said there had been a homicide in town and asked if I saw anything suspicious."

"What did you tell him?"

"I wasn't going to tell him Dan popped three of them in the head! I didn't say a word! I just stood there. Luckily, his phone rang, and he had to take the call. It was obviously urgent because he left."

"Get the backpacks. The sooner we get out of here, the better."

Nick and Naomi closed up the warehouse. They made one final sweep around the warehouse and apartment, making sure nothing was left behind that would indicate a team of covert operatives stayed there. They got on their motorcycles and headed out of the compound toward the Serbian border.

Chapter 26
ENEMY TERRITORY

At exactly 12:30 P.M. the entire team began to meet at the Sid location. No one had any trouble crossing the border. Mike and Karen made better time than expected and arrived at the Sid farmhouse just a few minutes after Dan and Karol. Nick and Naomi followed and arrived around 1:30 P.M. Naomi told Dan about the encounter she had with inspector Boraviko and mentioned to him the police knew about the murders in Ilok.

"I knew it would be a matter of time before the local authorities fanned out across the countryside looking for anything suspicious. I think luck was on our side today when the inspector got the call. There is a possibility the Bapska vineyard is compromised. At this point, we don't need the warehouse anymore. We may need to use the vineyard on our escape route. For now, let's consider it a last resort."

Dan called everyone together around the kitchen table of the farmhouse. The Sid farmhouse location was much better than the warehouse back in Bapska. The farmhouse was a working farm, fully furnished and functional. In addition to the large wooden table, there were several chairs, an electric stove, oven, refrigerator, and even a microwave. Dan used his laptop and began briefing the team.

"As of now, according to international law, we're all classified enemy combatants. We're foreigners who just crossed a border and brought in military weapons and equipment. The air campaign is just a few days away. Except for the deadly force we used to rescue Karen, we've been in a training mode. Now it's the real thing. Up to this point, we've been vague in telling you what our specific mission requirements will be here in Serbia. There was a reason for not telling you and the encounter with the police officer today was a good example. Naomi, had you been detained for questioning, they wouldn't have got much out of you that would comprise our mission. Today, I'll be giving each of you your specific assignments and responsibilities. The first order is chain of command. Effective immediately, I assume operational command of the mission from this point on. Karol will be my assistant. All tasking and orders come through me or Karol. Karol and I will make up one element. Mike and Karen will be in another. Karen, you'll be in charge of your element. Nick and Naomi will be in another, and Naomi you'll be in charge of that element. There's a reason why we split you up like this and the best way to explain this is to describe our location on a map."

Dan pulled out one of the basic Rand McNally maps he had been using on the road and spread it over the table.

"Our area of responsibility is known as the Vojvodina area of Serbia. This is the area our NATO fighters and bombers will enter and egress during the air war. As you can see from the map, our location is divided by two large rivers, the Danube and Sava Rivers. If one of our airmen

The Balkan Network

parachutes down, they will most likely land somewhere between one of these two rivers. It will take SARs several hours before they can mount a rescue operation and pick up the airman. Meanwhile, the downed airman has to evade enemy aggressors and hide until he can be rescued. The Serbs know this and will concentrate defensive forces between the two rivers. Our job, should we get tasking from NATO headquarters, will be to make contact with the pilot and help him evade capture until SAR forces can pick him up. Each night during the air war, we wait in the cover of darkness and keep a lookout for NATO aircraft being shot down. We will monitor tactical frequencies, UHF Guard, and the JSTARS and AWACS frequencies. If a NATO aircraft should go down, we'll be directed to the last known position of the airman. Our existence and our locations are extremely confidential. SARs don't even know our locations. Mike and Karen, you'll cover the area north of the Danube. Karol and I will cover the area south of it and north of the Sara River. Naomi, you and Nick will take the area south of the Sara River. This is the reason why Hal wanted you to take the locations in the towns we talked about yesterday. Once you move to your respective locations, you'll be isolated and cut off from the rest of the team. For Mike and Karen, there is a high probability that NATO forces will take out the bridges at Novi Sad on the first night of the attack. There will be no way for you to cross the Danube without going all the way to Belgrade—unless you swim. Likewise, Karol and I will not be able to get to you for the same reason. Naomi and Nick have a better chance of crossing the Sava River because there is no reason NATO should take out the bridge at Sabac. However, NATO pilots could target the bridge as a possible 'target of opportunity.' Your orders from now on, are simple. You will set up your locations and wait for further tasking. I will contact you and let you know where we want you to hide out for the night. We'll probably have a day or two before the air campaign starts. In the meantime, we'd like you to reconnoiter your respective areas. Look for areas of concealment, unmarked roads, and other areas that you can use to help evade. Mike, you and Karen already have been tasked to check out the armored division outside Novi Sad. Karol and I have a lot of work to do in the Fruska Gora hills looking for more SAMs. Now I want to go over your equipment. Karol, will you please take over from here?"

Karol said, "I've reprogrammed everyone's cell phones with a new SIM card and local area codes. Next, I want each of you to memorize this phone number." She wrote the number down on a piece of paper. "Let me know when you have it engrained in your memory." Everyone on the team took a few moments and then nodded their heads. "This is the direct telephone line to the JSTARS. It will get you to the onboard mission commander aboard the aircraft. The JSTARS will have access to our exact GPS locations from our transmitters implanted in our heads. Your cell phones have the capability to monitor and transmit on several frequencies and wavelengths. You will get instructions that are more detailed on those frequencies when you read your daily Special Crewmember Instructions (SPINS). Dan will go over that in more detail later. The AK-74s, personal gear and extra rounds made it across the border and are here. Make sure you check your equipment before you leave. Next, we have the clothing you need to wear when the air campaign starts. You will be disguised as local farmers working in the fields so you will wear your work clothes issued by Ms. Sara. This set will get you through the first few nights of the air campaign; after that, you may have to launder them—or better yet, buy something similar at a local store. Next is your military clothing."

She handed out specially made lightweight, night-camouflage jackets for each individual. "These jackets were specially made for our team back at Bolling. They'll be worn as outer garments over your local clothing and help camouflage you at night. If you look closely inside the camouflage markings, you can make out the U.S Navy symbol and a brown subdued oak leaf of an O-4. This is my jacket. Each of you will have a jacket with similar markings and rank for your respective services. Under the Geneva Convention, armed combatants must wear a specific uniform with rank to be protected by the convention. Should you be captured, this jacket, along with your dog tags, covers you under the Geneva Convention. They can't shoot you on the spot for spying. If you forget or lose your jacket and are subsequently captured, you will not be protected, so take good care of these garments."

"Now, I'd like to cover more specific duties and responsibilities," said Dan. "You will be working mostly during the night time. The first combat aircraft will launch from Aviano around 2300Z and be over Serbia by midnight local time. We want you in place around that time, each day during the air campaign. You'll hide out until called upon. I know this sounds dirty and unglamorous, but it's the job we've been tasked to do, which means it will probably be hours of sheer boredom, followed by moments of stark terror. During the day, we expect you to sleep back at your safe houses. Sometime before 1700Z log onto your laptops and get on the DOD Web site we gave you. Look for the link that says "Daily SPINS.' Click on that link and read the SPINS. These are very important instructions because it gives our pilots specific instructions about each mission including SAR and safe passage information. Each

Zulu day will have a set of authentication codes. There will be code words for the day and code words for the color of the day. Pay particular attention to the code word for friendly forces. It could change daily or it could stay the same everyday, a lot depends if friendly forces are compromised. If you make contact with a downed pilot, they're going to be scared. Being shot down over enemy territory is a fighter pilot's worst nightmare. They might even fire at you—so use the code word. As of today, the code word for friendly forces is *Dodger*. Be prepared to authenticate using any code. Let me give you an example. As you approach the downed airman either whisper or call him on his frequency and say something like this, 'Flyboy, this is Dodger.' He'll know you're friendly, but he may ask you to authenticate further. Be prepared to respond because we don't want him to shoot at you. I think I've covered everything I wanted to talk about for now. Does anyone have any questions?"

Mike spoke up immediately, "In looking at your map, it appears we're in a relatively small area. What happens if an airman is shot down and lands outside our areas?"

Dan answered, "That's a good question. As I mentioned, our team's location is extremely confidential, and we are isolated to a specific geographical area. If an airman is shot down and parachutes outside our area, there could be another circuit operating in another area—we honestly don't know. That information would be extremely confidential, even from us to enhance security of the circuits. My guess is that part of the NATO air egress plan is to get the pilots as close to the Croatian or Bosnian borders as they can so friendly forces can assist them. During Desert Storm when I was flying C-130s, our instructions if we were shot at were to try to fly the aircraft as close to the Saudi Arabian border as we could or as close to the Persian Gulf as we could so rescue forces could pick us up. The same may hold true for the Balkan. The pilots may be ordered to try to fly their crippled aircraft as close to the Bosnian or Croatian borders as they can. All I'm saying is it's a closely guarded secret if there are any other friendly forces inside Serbia."

Now it was Karen's turn to speak up and ask questions. "What's our escape plan?"

"Good question. We stay in our location until the end of the air campaign or until we are instructed to use one of the escape routes. Each element has a specific escape plan. Let me go over this on the map because it's much easier. Mike, for you and Karen, your escape plan is to get to the Croatian border near the town of Backa Palanka. From there, SAR forces will pick you up. Naomi and Nick, you'll be farther south but closer to SAR forces in Tuzla, Bosnia. Get as close as you can to the Drina River. There SAR will pick you up. For Karol and me, our escape plan is to get across the Croatian border near the cleared mine area we discovered the other day. Finally, our emergency egress route is by the Fruska Gora hills to the Bapska winery. We must walk across the border at this location."

Dan pointed to a position on the map. There was a road leading toward Ilok cutting through the Fruska Gora hills. "Take this road. This is the same road Karol and I used yesterday to get back into Croatia. Before you cross the border there is an abandoned vineyard with several overgrown grapevines. This vineyard leads to the clearing Naomi and Nick found through the minefields and leads straight to the Bapska winery. The only drawback to this route is that it's exposed from all sides and you'll be visible. Your best bet would be to use this escape route at night or at dusk. We'll call this escape route the *goalpost*."

Karol spoke up and addressed the team, "Believe me,

when the time comes and we have to egress, they'll get us out."

"Okay, I think we have the general plan. What I want everyone to do now is get packed, say your last good-byes, and move out. I have to contact Hal tonight and let him know the team is in place and ready for the air strikes. Contact me as soon as you get to your safe houses tonight. Karol and I will stay here and monitor your locations with the GPS tracking system. Call if you need anything. Good luck, everyone."

The team broke up from the meeting. Karol helped everyone check their communications gear and computers to make sure everything was working. Nick worked on the motorcycles to make sure they were ready to go. Mike was busy loading rounds of ammunition into the magazines. Karen was counting all the money and distributing the cash to each element. Naomi was loading her backpack when Dan approached her. He could tell there was something on her mind because she kept unusually quiet during the briefing.

"I'm glad the Croatian police didn't detain you for questioning. You were smart and clever and used the cover story as we talked about. Did something else happen that you're not telling me?"

Nick finished working on the motorcycles and said, "I'll give you two a moment. I've got to get something to eat," and he left the barn.

Naomi gazed at Dan with a concerned look, "He said I had a French accent and he spoke to me in German. Why he did that I don't know, but I pretended I didn't fully understand him. He said he was looking for a murder suspect of four individuals and a possible rape victim. They're on to you Dan. What happens if they come after you?"

"Sounds like a very clever man. He's not your ordinary detective. Anyway, I had to do what I had to do to get Karen out of trouble. If the Croatians are after me, they'll just have to catch me and bring me to justice. The U.S. and Croatian Government will have to take over from there."

"There's one more thing, about the other night in the minefield. I'm sorry for acting the way I did. I stepped over the line. I was acting like a schoolgirl."

"It's all right, apology accepted. Under the circumstances, I think you were just happy to be alive. Don't forget, I was the one that had my hands all over you. I should be the one apologizing."

"By the way, Dan, since we'll be breaking up as a group this afternoon, will we ever see each other again?"

"I can't talk about the details, but yes, when we've completed our mission we'll all meet at Tuzla Air Base in Bosnia-Herzegovina; from there, we'll fly back to Aviano."

"Good, I just didn't know if I should say my final goodbye now—but just the same, be careful, sir."

"The same goes for you too. Be careful and look after Nick."

Dan put his arms around Naomi and thought about kissing her again on the lips but instead slowly kissed her on the forehead. *She's a beauty*, he thought to himself.

Mike and Karen rode north across the Danube toward Novi Sad while Naomi and Nick headed south, across the Sava river to Sabo and Varna. Since the four operatives were traveling on motorcycles, they had to store all their equipment either in their backpacks or in limited storage space on the bikes. Dan and Karol stayed at the farmhouse and monitored the team's locations with their laptops.

"So far it looks like everything is going as planned," said Karol. "I had a chance to get deeper into the DIA Web site last night. Did you know I can download ring tones to our cell phones that will sound like frogs or birds from the local area? It could come in handy when were out in the dark."

"You're a real computer genius. You can start with mine. This area is predominately wetlands. Give me the one that sounds like a frog."

"I should have the download complete within the hour."

"While you're doing that, I'm going upstairs to try to get the television working. I don't think they have satellite access here, so it'll probably be a local feed. We should start watching the local news. It could give us some indication as to when the air war will begin."

Mike was riding north on E75 going toward Novi Sad through the thickly wooded areas of the Fruska Gora hills. All along the side of the road, he could make out the marks from some kind of tracked vehicle. He couldn't tell for sure because he didn't want to stop the bike and take a closer look, but he was sure they were tracks from a mobile SA-6. The tracks headed toward the monasteries of Novo-Hopavo and Staro-Hopovo. In addition, he saw many JNA forces setting up encampments in the wooded areas at the higher elevations. Mike called back to Karen using the walkie-talkie mode of the cell phone. She was riding just a few feet behind.

"Can you see what I see?"

"I was about to call you. Do you think they could be missile crews?"

"I think they are. You couldn't ask for a better location for a missile site. It's the only high terrain within hundreds of miles overlooking a strategic city and in an area were NATO aircraft will no doubt fly over."

"Should I call Dan and let him know?"

The Balkan Network

"Why don't you do it now so he can get a GPS fix on the locations?"

Karen called Dan's cell phone and he answered on the first ring.

"This is Specter, what's up?"

"Sir, can you get a fix on my location? Just to the right, alongside the road, we think there's several SA-6 sites hidden near the monasteries of Novo-Hopavo and Staro-Hopovo."

"Okay, just a minute while I get Sutter on the computer."

Dan went downstairs from the bedroom where he was watching television. Karol was still working on the computer in the kitchen and monitoring the movements of the team.

"Get a fix on Mike and Karen's location. She thinks they've spotted more missile sites."

Karol put the curser on Karen's icon and got GPS coordinates for her location.

Dan talked into his cell phone back to Karen, "Okay, we got your location. We're watching you move to the north. We suspected there could be SAMs in that area of the mountains. We'll have to check it out at a later time, but thanks for giving us the heads up. Call me when you get to your safe house and give me an update on the armored division."

"Yes, sir, over and out."

Dan turned to Karol, "Just as we suspected all along. The Serbs could be hiding SAMs near the monasteries. Tomorrow morning you and I need to go on a picnic."

Chapter 27
DECEPTION

At 10:00 P.M. Naomi called Dan. "We're here. I found the safe house not far from the town of Varna. It's a small little guesthouse off the main road—perfect location. The owners said we could live in the upstairs room for as long as we wanted. She didn't ask any questions when I told her I would pay cash in advance for a month and showed her my Serbian agriculture inspector credentials. I think they needed the money because they took it and left in a hurry—hopefully never to come back."

"Good work. You and Speeder are in the safest location. Tomorrow I want you two to take a bike and reconnoiter the area. Let me know what you find out."

"It's mostly flat farmlands around here, sir, a few sheep ranches and dairy cattle. It's going to be hard finding some trees or other kinds of hiding places, but we'll do our best."

"Call me back tomorrow."

Later that night Dan got a call from Karen.

"We had a hard time finding the safe house, but we finally found it. It's officially called Hotel Jet, just outside

The Balkan Network

Novi Sad heading toward Temerin." Mike came on the line.

"Are you sure we're on secure communications?"

"Yah, Grant, what can you tell us?"

"We found the armored division, and it's just like you said—very large, probably two or three divisions protected by several older SA-2 SAM sites. There's something else odd about the setup. There's a huge fifteen-foot fence surrounding the area."

"What's so strange about that?"

"It's the fence itself. This isn't just an ordinary fence. It looks like a prison fence with concertina wire on top, surrounded by guard towers on all four corners. It looks like it's installed permanently."

"You're right, it does seem strange, and why would they want to put a permanent fence around a mobile armored division?"

"Possibly to keep people from coming in or from going out?"

"And if you don't want people going in or going out, there must be a reason." Dan pondered for a moment then said, "Maybe the division is not a division at all, but made to look as if it *were* a division. I'll pass this information to Finder. In the meantime, I want you to continue to scout the local areas. Call me tomorrow night."

Dan secured his phone and turned to Karol who was monitoring the call, "What do you make of that?"

"I think you're on to something, Dan. It could be the fence is designed to keep people from looking in. I can't imagine any military commander wanting a permanent fence around his prized armor knowing that an aerial bombardment is hours away."

"It's a trap! A decoy! During World War II before D-

Day, the Allies used wooden and rubber decoys, throwing the Germans off as to where the invasion would take place. The Serbs are doing the same thing now. The Serbs placed fences around their decoys to keep people from looking in."

Dan picked up his phone and called Mattingly. He answered on the second ring.

"This is Finder."

"The team in place, sir, everything is set to go."

"Anything unusual to report?"

"I'm sending an update via data link. Sutter is sending it off to you now. There's something strange about the armored division at Novi Sad. I have visual confirmation the whole thing is a trick, a decoy perhaps, made to look like real armor. The Serbs could be trying to lure our fighters into bombing the area and then fire their missiles hidden in the Fruska Gora hills."

"What information leads you to that conclusion?"

"There's a fifteen foot, barbed wire fence surrounding the area with guard towers. Remember D-Day and the faked Allied landings at Calais? It's the same trick all over again. I'm sure if Josef were still alive, he'd verify my predictions."

"I'll pass it on to Naples right away. NATO may have to target the site anyway. Dan, listen very carefully. I have just received word the air campaign is set for March twenty-third. That gives you two more days to get ready. Once the air war starts, you'll receive all your orders from NATO via cell phone or from the JSTARS. You've done an excellent job so far. Keep up the good work. I'll be monitoring your situation from Washington."

Dan secured the phone and looked at Karol, "It's on for the twenty-third."

"You look tired. It's been a long day. What do you say we call it a night? I think it's time you and I catch up."

"You're right, let's try the bed upstairs."

Chapter 28
BELGRADE

Belic logged off his personal computer just after midnight local time in his kitchen apartment. He sent the last of his target information to CIA Headquarters back in Langley. One of the targets marked "High Value" was a building in downtown Belgrade, said to be a secret meeting site for Serbian high-ranking military officers but in reality was nothing more than the Chinese Embassy. He also received the information he'd been waiting for. Operation Allied Force was set to begin on the night of March 23, 1999. He went to his bedroom and made a call to Vecili Vorchek.

Belic replied, "I have good news for you, Comrade. The NATO air attack will start on the evening of March twenty-third. It'll commence with an air armada, quickly establishing air superiority. Expect a massive aerial bombardment."

"Thank you, old friend, we're ready on our end. Let me know when you get the location of the invaders. We'll be waiting for them again. Four of my Young Tigers were killed inside Croatia. A single shot to the head, standard operating procedure for U. S. Special Forces. That's the signal we've been waiting for. I want their heads on a platter!"

"I won't let you down. I should have the information within twenty-four hours." Belic, distraught, hung up the cell phone and walked back to the kitchen. He poured himself a tall glass of Scotch and drank it down in one gulp. Then poured himself another.

* * *

BACK AT THE KUKUJEVCI FARM, Dan woke up at five in the morning. It was still dark outside, but he had to continue operating the farm for a few days longer. He and Karol slept soundly that night. It had been the first time since they left Bolling that they slept in a real bed with real sheets, pillows, and blankets. The chickens were already up, and the roosters were crowing as Dan made his way to the barn. He fed the chickens and hogs then checked on the motorcycle and ATV. As he walked back to the farmhouse, Karol was just getting up. He could hear her in the bathroom, and it sounded like she was throwing up. As she came out of the bathroom, she still had on her long sleeping gown, which looked more like a large tee shirt.

"Good morning, Dan. I slept like a baby last night—that's the first time since Bolling—how about you?"

"Same here—it's nice to get a good night's sleep once in a while. Are you feeling okay? I heard you in the bathroom, and it sounded like you were sick."

"I'm fine. I don't think I'm used to the food, that's all."

"I fed the animals. Later, I'll take the hogs to the farm down the road and let them loose. I'm sure the farmer won't mind having five hogs mysteriously appear on his property. The chickens I can deal with. In fact, we could always have a few for dinner."

"I hope you know how to slaughter them."

"It can't be that difficult. I've seen it done before, but I've never had to do it personally. You forget, my family used to travel in these parts of Serbia and some of the best meals we had were fresh off the farms. Speaking of which, today I'd like to take a ride over to Fruska Gora. Mike said there could be more SAMs hidden near the monasteries. My father and I visited some of these monasteries on our travels. I mostly remember how isolated they were. The monks were very reclusive and didn't talk much; they just prayed and worked all day long like slaves. On the way back, I'd like to reconnoiter the road situation. A lot of the roads around here are farm roads and unmarked on the map. I'm sure the JNA will have the same troubles finding their way around, especially at night."

"We need to buy some groceries today. I can't live on chicken and eggs every day."

"I think we'll do that in Ruma instead of Sid. We can stop there on our way down from the monasteries."

* * *

TWENTY KILOMETERS south of Dan and Karol's location, outside the town of Varna, Naomi was waking up to the sounds of tracked vehicles moving along the road outside her motel bedroom. The sound was unmistakable. She had heard those sounds before and was convinced without looking out the window it was the sound of mobile SAMs or Triple-A vehicles moving southwest along the highway headed for the Bosnian Border. Nick was sound asleep in the twin bed next to her. She got out of bed and shook him awake.

"Nick, get up! I think there's something going on outside."

The Balkan Network

Nick sprung out of bed as he heard the last of the vehicles rumble past the guesthouse. He peeked out of the window curtain, "Looks like mobile SA-6s heading out of town. Do we have a map anywhere?"

Naomi took out a road map she had picked up back in Sremska Mitrovica as they crossed the Sava River. There was not much detail to the map, but it gave general information on the local area. Naomi said, "This is all I have for now without downloading from the Internet."

They spread the map out on the small nightstand in their room and noticed the road headed toward the Bosnian Border and the town of Zaviaka. Just beyond the town was a small mountain range.

"I bet they're heading here," as he pointed to the small range of mountains. "There's probably wooded areas in the hills—perfect cover for the SAMs. They must be aware the air war will start any day now. Is there a TV we can watch here in the inn?"

"I'm sure there's one downstairs."

"Let's get dressed and go down for breakfast. I'm sure everyone in Serbia will be watching the news."

* * *

THE PROSPECTOR CIRCUIT spent the rest of the day reconnoitering the local geography of their respective areas. As predicted, many of the roads were not on the map. It turned out the entire area of Vojvodina was laced with intersecting roads, trails, and highways that were unmarked on any maps. Many of the roads were accessible only by off-road vehicle. Dan and Karol visited several monasteries and most were closed to the public. Dan suspected that JNA forces had taken over these facilities. All he could do was annotate the locations and avoid the areas once the air war started. At the end of the day, all team members checked in with Dan and debriefed the day's activities. Dan gave them their orders for the following day by conference call.

"Tomorrow I want everyone to log onto your computers and read the daily SPINS for March 23, 1999. There is a lot of information in these SPINS, and it changes daily. During Desert Storm, I found the best way to review the SPINS was in a team format; that way if you missed something, your teammate will pick it up. Log onto your laptops and review the SPINS together. When I'm done briefing, Karol and I we'll review the SPINS together. Please pay attention to the code word of the day, color of the day, and any changes to the code word for friendly forces. Up to this point, it's still *Dodger*. This code word was compliments of one of our own team members. Karen picked it out for us back at Bolling when we were planning covert communications. She chose the word Dodger because of the way most Americans pronounce the word. It would be unmistakable to any U.S. serviceman. The other update is the JSTARS. They'll be on-station orbiting over Bosnia. They'll be monitoring us constantly. Should there be a sudden change in mission requirements, we can expect a call from the JSTARS. Their call sign will be *WIZARD 86*. Don't get this confused with the NATO AWACS call sign: *MAGIC 41*. That's about all I have for today." Dan looked at Karol and said, "Karol is the expert on covert communications. If anyone should have any trouble with your equipment, she's the one to talk to. You can always call her direct."

Dan continued, "I would suggest everyone get a good meal and rest tonight because starting tomorrow our sleep cycles will be reversed. Karol, is there anything you want to add?"

Karol said, "Stay low and out of the limelight. As the air war approaches, the JNA are going to be on a heightened state of alert. We may not have the freedom of movement as we once had a few days ago. We'll also need more security on our locations too. From now on, we'll assign code words for our locations. Let's keep it simple and use the city of San Francisco as a reference point since I grew up there. My location here near Sid will be called *Chinatown*. Mike, you and Karen's location is *North Beach*, and Naomi and Nick will be in the *Tenderloin*."

"What about our escape routes? Should we assign code words for them as well?" asked Naomi.

"I think that's an excellent idea," said Karol. "I'll mark up a map of the escape routes and post them on the Web site; you can review those code words when you review the SPINS."

Dan secured the conference call with the team as Karol established sat-com secure uplink on her computer and prepared to review the SPINS with Dan. As she opened the first page of the SPINS, they both noticed in bold red print: Updated March 22, 1999 2100Z Friendly Forces Established in AOR.

Chapter 29
PREPARING FOR ATTACK

Mike and Karen slept in because they had stayed up late the night before having a good dinner at a local restaurant outside Novi Sad. Tensions were high in the city as everyone in Serbia was anticipating an aerial attack to begin any time. Many people were stockpiling food and water. Few people, however, left the city. It was just after 3:00 PM when Karen logged onto her laptop to review the SPINS. Mike sat down next to her and viewed the pages with her.

Karen said, "Looks like there's nothing new on the SPINS; radio frequencies are the same and call signs have not changed. The weather report does not look good for tonight. They're calling for overcast skies with a possibility of light rain."

"I've got the motorcycles all gassed and ready to go. I was able to buy two additional cans of fuel, and I hid them in the farm fields just outside our holdup area. I'm sure the oil refinery here in Novi Sad will be one of the first targets of opportunity, and the fuel situation could be critical. Either way, we've got enough gas to last us at least a couple

The Balkan Network

of weeks. After that, we'll have to scrounge around for more. I would suggest we leave the motel around ten tonight. This should give us plenty of time to get to the hold-up area."

"I'll buy that. Do you think we'll see any action tonight?"

"It's hard to say, anything is possible. My guess is that if it's anything like the Gulf War, the first wave will be cruise missiles followed by stealth fighters hitting high-value targets. The cruise missiles will come in waves and come in from different directions. The Serbs will launch their SAMs at any incoming targets because they won't know if they're missiles or aircraft. Once the SAM radars go active, the F-16 will take out the sites. That'll clear a path for the F-117s."

"What happens if they don't turn on their radars? How will they know where the sites are located?"

"Then we can expect a call from the JSTARS to get a laser designator on them."

Karen said, "I'll get the gear packed and ready to go. The only thing we can do now is watch TV and see if the local news has anything to report."

Back at Chinatown, Dan and Karol were watching TV. CNN was reporting live from Belgrade and Brussels. The only information was that an attack was imminent.

"Our hold-up location we found is excellent," said Dan. "We have plenty of cover, and it's just along the foothills of the Fruska-Gora range. We'll have a commanding view to the south from our location. We'll leave here around ten. This should give us plenty of time to get there. You'll take the ATV, and I'll ride the bike. All we can do now is wait for the bombs to start falling."

Belgrade, Serbia 1900Z

Milan Belic was having dinner at the Trandafilovic

restaurant in Belgrade. Tensions were extremely high in the streets of Belgrade. Throughout the day, local television stations broadcast live updates on the possibility of an air attack. The Trandafilovic was less crowded than usual this time of night, and there was no one within earshot of Belic when his cell phone rang. Belic answered and heard Vorchek shout into the phone, "Do you have the information I've been waiting for?"

"Calm down, old friend. It's taken me awhile, but I have some useful information. I've received word that U.S. Special Forces have crossed the border near Backa Palanka and are somewhere near Novi Sad. They have transmitted a report to Washington on the location of your armored divisions in the area. It appears they have fallen for the trap."

"Can you give me specific locations and numbers?"

"I'm afraid not. The U.S. military is being very cautious about giving out specific locations of their assets. This is quite different from the past when the CIA divulged everything about the locations of their operatives. I can only tell you there is a team in place north of the Danube River. When I get more information, you will be notified."

Belic hung up his cell phone and returned to his dinner.

Vorchek then called Domonik Slavo. "Move your men out. I want a perimeter barrier set up from Backa Palanka north to the Mali Kanal and eastward toward Novi Sad. Kill anyone you suspect as a foreign invader!"

Chapter 30
OPERATION ALLIED FORCE

Sergi Boraviko was still at his office desk and was getting off the phone with his superiors back in Zagreb. He had just received word that U.S. Special Forces had crossed the border and were inside Serbia in anticipation of the NATO air strikes. All Croatian armed forces, including Interior Ministry of Police personnel, were placed on high alert in case Serbian forces marched across the border. His thoughts went back to the young woman he encountered at the Bapska winery. If only he had not received that call from Yuri Pavol, he would have been able to question her further and determine her real identity. Her language skills and her posture were much too refined to be Croatian—or European for that matter. She was beautiful, yet potentially deadly. He wondered if the U.S. military could deploy such a person.

* * *

A FEW MINUTES AFTER MIDNIGHT, Naomi and Nick were in their positions at the Tenderloin in the wheat fields outside Verna. It had been difficult finding a place to hide in the flat terrain of the area, but Naomi suggested using the irrigation canals and ditches as hiding places. It turned out that these ditches were the best places because they could be concealed without anyone seeing them from higher ground. In the distant east, they could see the reflection of the lights from the city of Belgrade and hear the sounds of air raid sirens followed by the sound of jet engines in the air. A few seconds later, several flashes of light flickered in the distance followed by the muffled tones from explosions. Operation Allied Force had begun.

To the north across the Danube outside Novi Sad, Mike and Karen were hiding in their spot known as 'North Beach.' They too heard and saw explosions. Mike looked at Karen and said, "I think they just hit the oil refinery."

Dan and Karol were in their hiding place in the Fruska Gora National Park. They heard the distant sounds of air raid sirens followed by muffled sounds of explosions. Dan looked a Karol, her face and hair covered with a black ski mask. The only things visible were her two green eyes staring at him, the skin around her eyes darkened with face makeup.

"Probably cruise missiles," said Dan as Karol held onto his arm. Dan switched his cell phone to tactical radio and placed the earpiece inside his ear. He tuned in the required frequency and turned up the volume.

"Go to common network and turn your volume down low," he said to Karol.

On one channel, Dan and Karol were now monitoring transmissions coming from all NATO aircraft within a 200-nautical-mile radius. MIRA 21, an F-117 flight of four had just completed in-flight refueling with a KC-135 tanker and were making their way to downtown Belgrade. For the next two and a half hours, Dan and Karol listened to the sounds of war coming through their earpieces. A Serbian MiG-29 taking off from Batajnica Air Base near Belgrade was shot down by a Royal Dutch Air Force F-16, and the pilot ejected safely. U.S. F-16s shot down two more MiGs near Pancevo. The fate of these MIG pilots could not be determined. To the best of their knowledge, the first night of the air war did not go as planned. The overcast weather was instrumental on the effectiveness of the air strikes. Several aircraft reported they were unable to acquire their targets and returned to base. At 0100Z most of the radio chatter was down to a minimum. All NATO aircraft returned safely to their bases. For the time being, it appeared that *Day One* of Operation Allied Force went off with no downed NATO aircraft. Dan secured his com link, switched his phone to cell phone, and called North Beach. He called Karen, the senior ranking member of her element.

"Eden, this is Specter, what's your situation?"

"We're okay, looks like NATO aircraft dropped a lot of bombs near our vicinity, but no SAMs fired at incoming aircraft."

"That's good news. I've received word that all NATO aircraft returned safely to their bases. Get back to quarters and bed down for the night. I'll call tomorrow with more tasking."

"Thank you, sir, we'll be waiting for your call tomorrow."

Dan hung up the phone then called Naomi.

"Lombard, this is Specter, give me an update on your situation?"

Naomi replied in a shaken voice, "We could hear several aircraft flying overhead, but no missiles went up after them, just heavy antiaircraft artillery with search lights. We could hear the sounds of explosions in the distance."

"It looks like first day of the air war is over. I want you and Speeder to return to quarters and bed down for the night. I'll call you tomorrow."

"Sir?"

Dan could detect fear or concern in her voice. "Yes, what is it?"

"We detected heavy movement of ground forces moving in your general location across the bridge near Sabac. They started in your direction almost the moment we heard the first explosions."

Dan paused in thought. "Thanks for the info. It could be the forces are repositioning across the river in anticipation that one of the bridges will be taken out by NATO aircraft. Did you notice if any of the bridges were targeted?"

"No, sir, everything around here appears to be just as it was last night."

"Let me talk to Speeder."

Nick got on the line, "Yes, sir."

"Get Lombard back to quarters as soon as you can. Look after her. I think she's a little shook-up. This is all new to her. She's not used to combat."

"Yes, sir, we're already on the bikes heading in that direction."

"Good work, I'll check back with you tomorrow with new tasking."

Dan secured the call as Karol looked up at Dan. She was monitoring the transmissions from her cell phone, "We need to get back to the farm. There's still a lot of work we need to do before we can ... what did you call it, bed down for the night?"

"Okay, I know what you're thinking. Yes, I was concerned about Naomi. She's the most fragile. She's not like you."

"I think you're wrong about Naomi, Dan. I think she's got more guts than all of us put together.

Chapter 31
DAY 1 OPERATION ALLIED FORCE

March 24, 1999

Dan and Karol returned to the farmhouse. They stayed up several hours filing their reports to NATO. It was after sunrise before they went to bed and made love before falling asleep. Dan's cell phone went off, waking him and Karol. It was already late in the afternoon. Dan got out of bed, looked at his cell phone, and saw an unfamiliar number on the caller ID. The area code and country code indicated the call was being made from Naples, Italy. Karol got out of bed too, retrieved her cell phone, and put it on monitor mode so she could hear the transmissions. When her com-link was established, Dan nodded his head and said, "Hello, this is Specter?"

"Yes, good afternoon," a voice said with a heavy British accent. "This is Group Captain John Snell, Royal Air Force. I'm calling from AFSOUTH. I will be working with you and your cell from now on. All of your tasking orders will come through the JSTARS or me. My call sign is simply, *Naples*."

"Group Captain Snell, what can I do for you?"

The Balkan Network

Karol listened intently to the conversation.

"For starters, it's not what you can do for me today, but rather what you can do for me over the next several weeks. First, I'll be contacting you every day at this same time to assign your circuit's tasking orders. If, for some reason, I'm unable to contact you, then you'll receive a call from the JSTARS, and they'll assign your tasking orders."

Dan held the phone away from his ear as Snell continued to talk.

"The first day of Operation Allied Force just ended. Luckily, no NATO aircraft were lost last night; however, we can expect losses during the campaign. As you were told, your primary responsibility is to assist in the SARs of downed NATO airmen. Your secondary responsibility is to help minimize the threats so we do not have any downed airmen or as few downed airmen as possible. This means doing threat analysis work after each day's bombing."

"I'm listening, go on," said Dan.

In your area, just to the north of you in the Fruska Gora hills, none of the SAMs went active last night, which means the Serbs didn't turn the radars on for some reason. We have the locations and GPS coordinates of each of the SAM sites, but they are cleverly hidden inside or near the monasteries. I understand you're familiar with the locations of each of these monasteries?"

"Yes, I'm familiar with all of the sites."

"Then you must know that according to international law, because the Serbs have willfully placed military weapons in those sites, we have the right to self-defense—so they become legitimate targets. We believe the Serbs will fire their missiles in tonight's attacks. We can't take them all out in one night so we are targeting the most heavily defended ones to the east, namely Novo-Hopovo and Staro-Hopovo monasteries. Four B-52 bombers loaded with one-thousand- pound standoff cruise missiles are scheduled to hit those sites tonight. We'll be using precision- guided weapons, so we'll keep the collateral damage down to a minimum. We need your eyes on the ground during the attack to provide us with instant feedback. The raid is scheduled for 0100Z tonight. Be in place by then and call Wizard with your updates."

"You do know I sent a report to Washington with the locations of all the SAMs in that area? The Serbs are deploying mostly mobile SA-6s and not stationary SA-5s. They may not be in the same location as they were last night."

"Yes, we received that report, but our sources lead us to believe the sites at Novo- Hopovo and Staro-Hopovo are stationary, probably SA-2s or SA-5s. That's why we're targeting the area."

"What sources? We're supposed to be the ones providing that information."

"I don't know, Major, I'm only following orders. I don't create the target lists."

"Then you realize that it may take full-saturation carpet bombing of the entire Fruska Gora National Park and the monasteries to eliminate the threats."

"It may eventually come down to that, but again the Serbs were the ones that made the decision to place the missiles near the monasteries. We'll try to take them out one by one."

"Okay, is there anything else we need to do?"

"The oil refinery in Novi Sad was partially hit last night. Unfortunately, the weather played a factor. We have it on our target list again tonight. Have your team get visual real-time information on the air strike back to Wizard."

The Balkan Network

"Are you talking about the oil refinery outside Novi Sad along the Danube?"

"That's the only one in the area."

"Then why is AFSOUTH targeting an oil refinery that was shut down well over eight years ago?"

There was silence on the other end, obviously catching Group Captain Snell unprepared with this information.

"Your job is not to question our tasking. We have our reasons for targeting the refinery."

"All right, I'll pass that on to my team; is there anything else?"

"That's it, good luck tonight," and he hung up the phone.

Dan said to Karol, "It doesn't make sense. NATO air staff is already getting wrong information. Hal specifically asked us to check out the Fruska Gora hills and record all the SAMs in the area. At great risk, we got that information and we transmitted that report, hoping NATO would update their targeting plans. Now it seems they're ignoring the latest information and using whatever information they have. The SA-6s are not going to be in the same place."

"Do you think NATO could be getting their information from another circuit?"

"That's a possibility, but I was under the impression that our circuit would be providing the latest information or double-checking the information that goes to the NATO Air Staff in this area. As far as I know, we're the only assets that can provide this information."

"We can't get too involved in TA. Remember that's our secondary job. We need to focus on our primary job of rescuing downed airmen. By the way, Dan, how did you know the oil refinery was shut down?"

Dan reminisced the lengthy conversation with Josef back on the train, "I had an in-depth geography lesson from Professor Kostinic on the way to Washington, remember?"

Karol got out her cell phone, connected it to her laptop, established the secure sat-com link, and logged onto the DOD Web site. She downloaded maps of the Fruska Gora hills, and the area across the Danube near Novi Sad where Mike and Karen would have to get closer to monitor the air strikes.

"We can get as close as a half mile to Novo-Hopovo and Staro-Hopovo tonight. We can hide there," as she pointed to a remote location on the map to Dan. "This will give us a good vantage point to call in the information to the JSTARS."

"I wouldn't get any closer. The Boeing air-launched cruise missiles are accurate, but I'm not sure how accurate once they get closer to their targets. The Serbs will be trying to take them out with their antiaircraft artillery as they streak across the sky at low altitude. If they damage the guidance systems along the way, the ALCMs could come down anywhere including on top of our heads."

Dan looked at his watch. It was 4:00 PM local time, Mike and Karen would be up by now, and he wanted to give them time to review the SPINs to prepare for tonight's mission. "Should I give Mike a call or should I wait awhile?"

"It's the middle of the afternoon. They probably can't sleep anymore than you or me. I'll make the call."

Karol called Karen.

"This is Eden, how are you doing today, ma'am?"

"Just fine, thank you. We have your tasking for tonight. You'll have to get closer to the oil refinery at Novi Sad. Naples wants you to monitor the air strikes tonight and report to the JSTARS with real-time information. I don't know what you can expect. Specter says the pipeline

The Balkan Network

running into the refinery was shut down eight years ago and has not been used since. I've downloaded and posted a map of the area on our Web site. You'll see the location of the refinery on the map. This should help you find a location to acquire the data. Once you've found a place, let us know. We'll be monitoring your GPS location during the attack. Specter and I have our own tasking orders tonight."

"Yes, ma'am, I'm downloading the map as we speak."

"Don't forget to review the SPINs. There's already been a change. They've assigned each of us a unique numeric tactical call sign to use if we need to make contact with a downed airman. This call sign is to be used only to identify friendly forces to a downed airman or to communicate with rescue forces and the JSTARS. We'll still use our regular tactical call signs in day-to-day conversations with each other. I'm Dodger 22. Specter is Dodger 23, and you'll be Dodger 24. You can review more in the SPINs. Be safe tonight."

"Thank you, ma'am, and same goes for you too."

* * *

IN BACKA PALANKA, Serbia, Domonic Slavo and his men were scouring the wheat fields outside the town of Glozan. His latest information reported that U.S. Special Forces were in this vicinity. The abandoned oil refinery was bombed last night by cruise missiles and they could have been instrumental in that attack. However, Slavo could find no signs or footprints that led him to believe these forces were in the area. He had some of his men recruit local villagers living in the outskirts of Novi Sad and Backa Palanka to help search the surrounding areas. Nothing was uncovered that would indicate U.S. Special Forces were in the area: No American-made cigarette butts or chewing gum. He was beginning to wonder if the reports were accurate. He placed a call to Vorchek.

"I've searched the area and have found nothing! JNA forces have found nothing! And the locals have seen nothing that would indicate the presence of commandos! I hope your information is correct."

Vorchek replied, "Increase your search to the local farmhouses. They could be hiding or using the farmhouses as cover. Kill anyone who provides safe haven to the invaders on the grounds of treason. There's been a lot of refugees fleeing Novi Sad to the outlying areas. They could be trying to hide in with the refugees. If you find any of the raiders, kill them on the spot!"

Chapter 32
DAY 2 OPERATION ALLIED FORCE

Just before 10:00 PM at the farmhouse, Karol woke up from her nap and went downstairs to the kitchen. Dan was still asleep upstairs. Their sleep schedules were off because most of their work was done at night. She decided to check the weather forecast and review the SPINS for the day and let Dan sleep for awhile longer. She logged onto her computer and accessed the secure web site. The weather forecast for that evening was much better than the previous night. They were calling for mostly clear skies over Novi Sad and few to broken cloud layers over Belgrade. After spending an hour reviewing the SPINS and classified information, she decided to surf the Web further. There was a lot of information on the DOD Web site and in the past, she did not have time to go into all the sites. Tonight, though, she decided to go deeper into cyberspace. Dan mentioned that NATO could be getting their target information from other sources. She remembered Hal mentioning the Prospector circuit would be operating independently from the other circuits. She didn't know if this was a slip on his part or if there was indeed another circuit in the area. She searched the communications folder and found nothing. Then she went to the radar page and looked at the GPS locations of assets in the area. She zoomed out to include all of Croatia, Bosnia, Serbia and Montenegro. She could see GPS icons of several assets in place. She recognized the locations of Mike and Karen as well as Nick and Naomi and their locations looked normal. Other icons were displayed in eastern Bosnia, near the Serbian border. These assets were too far away from the Fruska Gora to provide any tactical information. Next, she searched down to the south and found several icons in Kosovo. Again, these assets were too far away to provide any useful information to AFSOUTH. She tried a different approach. She went to the com-link page and took note of all the assets that logged onto the Web site by secure satellite cell phone. Everything seemed normal until she noticed a telephone number that was different from the rest of the phone numbers. By the looks of the number, the calls were being made from Belgrade. She remembered there were no assets in place in Belgrade, but she was viewing information on the screen to reflect the contrary. Karol tried to go deeper into the Web site, but Dan's sudden presence stopped her as he came into the kitchen.

"Thanks for letting me sleep longer. Find anything new on the SPINS?"

"There's something I want you to look at."

Karol showed Dan the phone numbers that logged onto the Web site and the one that originated from Belgrade.

"Can you trace that call?"

"It may take awhile because I'll have to access the NSA database, but I think I can do it."

"We don't have time tonight. Let's get ready to move out. We'll work on that tomorrow. I'll take the motorcycle,

The Balkan Network

you can ride the ATV again. We'll hide the ATV in the usual spot and ride double on the bike to the monasteries."

Dan and Karol rode the vehicles on the back roads toward Fruska Gora. Most of the roads were unmarked on any maps. As they made their way to the city of Irig, they turned off and followed a smaller dirt trail that led to a primitive campsite. The campsite was made for hikers and bike riders and had no facilities except a few blackened rocks used as fire rings. Just beyond the campsite was a thicket of heavy brush and lime trees. Hidden by the brush was a dilapidated structure used at one time to house water pumps for the nearby agricultural fields. A small dirt road led to the structure. It had been abandoned and was slowly rotting away. Dan and Karol discovered this site on one of their scouting missions. Karol parked the ATV inside the structure. Dan followed on foot behind her. Inside the structure, covered under a green tarp, were their weapons and other equipment. Dan took out the backpacks and loaded the AK-74s, extra rounds of ammunitions, the Makarov pistols with silencers, night vision goggles, and laser designators into their backpacks. Next, he and Karol took off their jackets and turned them inside out to show the night camouflage pattern and put them back on. Finally, they put on their black ski masks under their motorcycle helmets and then returned to the lone motorcycle. They headed toward the town of Irig riding double. They approached the town well past midnight. A detachment of JNA forces was assembling on the road heading out of town. Dan suspected they were there to guard the road leading up to the Novo-Hopova and Staro-Hopovo monasteries. He turned off the main road and headed down a small embankment out of sight of the JNA forces. The JNA forces were mainly young, unskilled conscripts assigned unimportant duties like guarding monasteries.

Dan smiled behind his helmet and stopped the bike, *They've got no clue who we are.* They took off their helmets, stored them with the bike, and hiked the rest of the way uphill on foot. None of the JNA ever suspected that enemy forces were just a few miles away. Dan and Karol continued to climb the hills, using the thick brush and trees as cover in the darkness. As they made their way past Irig, the lights of the town dimmed and they had to use their night vision goggles the rest of the way. By 1:00 AM, Dan and Karol reached their target location. They were less than a half mile from the two monasteries. They used a depression in the ground and large fallen trees to cover themselves if a runaway cruise missile missed its mark. Dan switched his cell phone to monitor mode while Karol kept hers on cell phone. Karol pressed the numbers for the JSTARS and a radar operator answered the call.

"This is Wizard 86. Go ahead, Dodger 22."

"Wizard 86, this is Dodger 22. We're in position. Do you have our coordinates?"

"Standby, Dodger." There was silence on the cell phone earpiece for a few seconds then the voice came on again.

"Dodger 22, this is Wizard 86, will you ident for us?"

Karol pressed the ident button on her cell phone.

"Dodger 22, this is Wizard 86, you're in radar contact. Maintain your position and stand by."

Karol knew the JSTARS had their GPS position corroborated and the information relayed to DIA headquarters back at Bolling. She was wondering if Hal was monitoring their position.

Dan, listening to the NATO aircraft in the sky, came back and said to Karol, "Take cover! The B-52s just launched their cruise missiles."

The sound of air raid sirens could be heard in the

distance immediately followed by a barrage of antiaircraft fire accompanied by search lights. They were surrounded by triple-A sites hidden in the Fruska Gora hills. Some of the sites were just a few hundred feet away. The Serbs were throwing up a hail of ack-ack to protect the SAMs hidden near the monasteries. The sounds of jet engines could be heard roaring overhead, then huge, thundering explosions all around them shook the ground. Dan and Karol were right in the middle of a cruise missile attack. The barrage seemed to last for an eternity, but was only a few seconds. Dan could see fires burning near Staro-Hopovo monastery but heard no secondary explosions. The cruise missiles hit the trees surrounding the monastery, but as near as he could tell, the monastery was still intact. Then the sounds of more jet aircraft overhead, followed by a barrage of SAMs fired from the other monastery at nearby Novo-Hopovo. Again, the sounds of explosions shook the ground under them. More SAMs fired into the sky from the nearby monasteries along with ack-ack. The noise was deafening all around them. This barrage lasted slightly longer, with more ack-ack fire going up into the night sky all around them. Then there was silence. The call came through on Karol's cell phone.

"Dodger 22, this is Wizard 86, do you copy?"

"Affirmative, I read you loud and clear."

"Could you give us an update?"

"We have visual confirmation that one cruise missile hit just a few meters outside Staro Monastery. I'll put my laser designator on it. Massive amounts of triple-A fire from several locations around us. They appear to be mostly mobile sites. No visual confirmation on whether Novo was hit."

"Roger, we have your report. Remain in your present location. There are more aircraft on the way."

"We copy, standing by."

All Dan and Karol could do at this point was stay close to the ground and wait. Day two of Operation Allied Force was just beginning. So far it seemed that no enemy SAMs hit any NATO aircraft, and all aircraft were reporting operations normal.

* * *

AT THE SAME TIME, to the north near Novi Sad, Mike and Karen near the Mali Kanal were watching NATO bombs rain down on the oil refinery. Two five-hundred-pound bombs were dropped on the bridges that connected Petrovaradin and Sremska Kamenica south of Novi Sad.

After Karen transmitted her report to Wizard, she switched off her communications gear and headed back to the motorcycle. Because they were traveling on open roads, Mike and Karen decided to take one bike rather than two. As they approached the motorcycle, Karen heard the sound of dogs barking followed by men shouting. Mike immediately grabbed Karen and threw her down to the ground. They could see several men talking to some of the local villagers near the Mali Kanal. The locals had obviously gone there to watch the aerial fireworks display from a safe distance. Mike raised his head and could see the men were not JNA but rather paramilitary forces dressed in civilian clothes. They were questioning the locals. Each of the men was carrying high-powered rifles mounted with scopes and all had their faces cloaked by black ski masks. They were obviously looking for someone.

"They're not regular JNA forces; they're paramilitary. Looks like four, maybe five, all equipped with Russian-made sniper rifles. They could be looking for a downed airman or possibly us."

The Balkan Network

"What are we going to do?" Karen asked in a worried voice, obviously still concerned after her last fight with paramilitary forces. "We can't use our cover stories this late at night."

"We can't engage them in a firefight because they'd bring in the whole Yugoslav Army on us. We can't sit here and wait for them to find us because sooner or later the dogs will pick up our scent and we'd be discovered anyway. Our orders are to avoid paramilitary forces at all costs." Mike thought for a moment then said, "Ditch the equipment here in the fields by the motorcycle. Turn your jacket inside out. We'll have to stay low and out of sight; hopefully the dogs won't pick up our scents. We'll just have to talk our way out and hopefully come back for our equipment later. I don't think they'll suspect anything because there's already civilians out here watching the fireworks display. We'll come across as ordinary people watching the bombardment from the distance."

"What if they start asking questions about us?"

"We just tell them that we're husband and wife."

"That's nice, but what if they're smarter than that and start asking *specific* questions like where do you live and work? What will happen if they do a physical check and determine we're U.S. military personnel?"

"I don't think these guys are that sophisticated. The only way to determine if we're Americans is to look into our mouths and check our dental work. I don't see them doing that out here in the field. If we're caught, we'll tell them we own a restaurant in the city. I saw a pizzeria in an advertisement yesterday. They were advertising that they would be open during the war. I remember the name of the place, Cezar Pizzeria. The paramilitaries won't even question it if they ask."

"I hope you're right."

"If they're specifically looking for U.S. Special Forces, then they're expecting us to act in a particular way. Remember what Karol said about predictability? Just think and act like a Serbian."

The two got up from the ground and started casually walking toward the paramilitary forces. As they made their way to the men, the dogs immediately picked up their scent and started barking. The men turned around, pointed their rifles at them and shouted, "Halt!"

Domonic Slavo shouted at Karen and Mike, "Don't move another meter, or I'll take your heads off!"

Mike and Karen froze in their tracks. Four men and Slavo approached them and spoke in Serbian.

"What are you two doing here?" asked Slavo.

Karen replied in perfect Serbian, "It's better to be out here than in the city when the bombs start falling."

Slavo replied, "Why don't you just go to the air-raid shelters?"

"We did that on the first night, but we wanted to take a look from here. We can't understand why NATO is doing this to us. We've done nothing wrong."

"Come closer."

Mike and Karen walked slowly toward Slavo. They caught the first glimpse of him: pocked face with long black greasy hair. He was the only one not wearing a ski mask. He wore a black utility jacket and black military style pants. He was heavily armed with a Russian sniper rifle, two pistols on each hip, and several rounds of ammunition stuffed into pouches around his waist.

Slavo sizing up Mike said, "You seem like a healthy man, why are you not fighting for your country?"

Mike replied in Serbian, "I fought in Croatia and Krijana. I saw enough people killed."

"Who's the woman?"

"She's my wife."

Slavo stared at Mike, "We're looking for downed enemy pilots. We've been told a German aircraft was shot down and the pilots ejected. Have you seen anything?"

Mike and Karen both shook their heads.

"Come with me then. You two can join the rest of the group searching for the German pilots! They could be in our midst us as we speak."

Chapter 33
KUKUJEVCI FARM, SERBIA

It was sunrise when Dan and Karol returned to the farmhouse. Both were completely exhausted after being in the middle of the aerial bombardment. They had to make their way down the Fruska Gora hills away from the monasteries, taking the longer route that paralleled the southern slopes. It took them well over two hours just to reach the motorcycle and another hour to reach the ATV. When they got inside the kitchen, Karol said, "We've been so busy, I haven't contacted Karen and Naomi. I wonder how they made out last night."

Dan said, "I'll call Mike. You can talk to Naomi—she likes talking to you anyway."

"That's not funny, Dan. I have a better idea. Why don't we both get on the call and talk to everyone all at once? That way we can get to bed sooner."

Dan placed the call to Naomi and she answered on the first ring. "Hello, Lombard here."

"Get Speeder on the line. I want to conference everyone together."

Nick got on the line and said, "Speeder here, everything went smoothly last night. No trouble to report on our end."

Dan said, "Hold on while I get Grant and Eden on the line"

Dan called Karen but there was no answer. Next, he called Mike's number and after four rings he finally answered, "This is Grant, sorry for taking so long to answer, but we ran into some trouble out here."

Karol interrupted, "Are you all right?"

"Yes, ma'am, we're back at the safe house. We just arrived a few minutes ago. We were recruited at gunpoint by paramilitary forces looking for foreign invaders."

"How did you get free?" asked Naomi?

Karen came on the line, "We talked our way out of it. All of our training paid off. We acted like Serbians instead of U.S. military operatives. The paramilitaries looked us over and determined we were locals. One had me take off my boots and show them to him. Another had Grant strip down to his underwear. It's a good thing I had on Serbian boots and Grant had on his Serbian underwear."

"What can you tell us about the enemy forces?" asked Dan

Mike replied, "There were five men, all civilian types, heavily armed. The leader of the group went by the name Slavo. The others took orders from him. They forced us to search along the Mali Kanal in the mud looking for downed enemy pilots. Needless to say, we didn't find any."

"Okay, we'll all laugh about this later. It sounds like these men weren't the sharpest tools in the shed. I want a detailed report sent to me as soon as you can. I'll see if we can find more information on this Slavo guy. In the meantime, what can you tell me about the oil refinery?"

Chapter 34
DAY 4 OPERATION ALLIED FORCE

At 9:15 P.M. an F-117 using the call sign Mira 33, piloted by USAF Lt. Col. David Elko was turning outbound to an egress heading to return to Aviano Air Base. Elko had reached his target over Novi Sad and dropped his two precision-guided bombs. Both munitions hit their target, the oil refinery outside Novi Sad. As Elko was heading west-northwest, his routine was suddenly shattered by indications that Serbian air defenses near the Fruska Gora hills had targeted his aircraft. The 3rd Battalion of the 250th missile Brigade fired two SA-6 missiles at Mira 33. The explosions from the missiles temporarily blinded him and threw shards of jagged steel into his aircraft. The F-117 began to roll violently left then right. Elko knew his stricken aircraft was uncontrollable. He had no choice but to bail out if he wanted to live. He reached down and pulled the ejection handles. The canopy separated from the aircraft and the ejection seat fired, thrusting him into the night air. The force of the ejection seat carried him safely away from the stricken aircraft. As he was descend-

The Balkan Network

ing, Elko went through his descent procedures checking his parachute canopy and life-support equipment. He was shocked to see that life-support personnel at Aviano had not packed his parachute with camouflage material but was still packed with the bright orange and white training panels clearly visible in the night sky. He knew enemy forces would be on the alert to capture him—and the orange and white panels didn't help. It was just after 9:45 PM when Elko took out his survival radio and transmitted on Guard, the UHF emergency radio frequency.

"Mayday, Mayday, Mayday, this is Mira 33 on Guard, out of the aircraft, out of the aircraft! Mira 33, my beacon is on!"

Elko knew the Serbs would be monitoring the frequency, so he stopped the beacon after three seconds. He knew it was important to get a signal out as quickly as possible so SARs forces could respond. U.S. reconnaissance satellites orbiting Earth would pick up his emergency broadcast and triangulate his position to give an exact location. A few seconds later, a crewmember onboard the AWACS responded over his emergency radio, "Mira 33, this is Magic 41 on Guard, we copy your mayday."

Elko did not respond in case the Serbs were monitoring the frequency. All he could think about while dangling from his harness was to land safely. He put away his survival radio and concentrated on the terrain below. He descended through several cloud layers before he could make out the features of the ground. He could see he was drifting down south of the town of Ruma in an area of open farm fields with nothing to hide in. There were many vehicles on the roads below, and he was concerned somebody would spot his brightly colored orange and white parachute falling from the sky. Elko decided on a landing spot near a field and a railroad track. He turned his canopy toward the field and landed. As soon as he landed, he quickly hid his parachute and moved to a hiding spot off the road. There he opened his survival pack and smeared camouflage makeup over his face, neck, and hands—and waited.

Back on board the JSTAR, Wizard 86, Mission Commander USAF Colonel Frank Owens got the message that an F-117 was shot down inside Serbia. The time was 9:50 PM local time. He went over to one of the radar operators and said, "Contact friendly forces in the area and put them on alert that we have a downed airman. Give them the GPS location and tell them to implement Op Plan 22-7."

Dan's cell phone rang. It was 10:00 P.M. local time. He and Karol were still asleep. Dan looked at his caller ID and saw the JSTARS was attempting to make contact with him. Dan remembering to use his tactical call sign answered, "This is Dodger 23, go ahead."

"Dodger 23, this is Wizard 86, we have a confirmed downed NATO aircraft, call sign Mira 33. Implement Op Plan 22-7, GPS coordinates to follow in text message."

"Copy Wizard 86, we're on our way." As he was receiving the text message with Mira 33's GPS coordinates, he leaned over and kissed Karol on the cheek and said, "Wake up, sleepyhead, we're up to bat."

Op Plan 22-7 was simple. They were to make contact with Mira 33 and attempt to secure the airman until SARs could get him out. They were to use their tactical call signs for all radio and cell phone transmissions during the rescue operation to prevent any confusion. The GPS readout on Dan's text display showed the pilot's position was just outside the town of Ruma, less than a forty-five minute ride by motorcycle. In order to speed

The Balkan Network

things up, Dan and Karol decided to ride double and take highway E-70 from Sid to Ruma. At this time of night, they would look like ordinary vehicular traffic traveling on the highway. They were armed with pistols and AK-74 assault rifles stuffed into their backpacks. According to Op Plan 22-7, they were not going to rescue the airman but only make contact with him. If the rescue mission should be delayed or cancelled, they had to protect him until the next search and rescue mission could be mounted.

As Dan and Karol approached Ruma, they could see roughly eighty people comprised of police, military, paramilitary, and local villagers combing the nearby fields. Dan could see firsthand what Mike and Karen went through the other night. The enemy had a position on the downed pilot, and it would be a race against time to get him safely before their dogs sniffed him out.

Dan speaking in a low voice to Karol through his headset, "According to the last GPS position, the airman was hiding in an area off the main road near the railroad tracks." He parked the motorcycle off the main road, and he and Karol began to walk in the fields the rest of the way toward the airman. So far, it looked like the enemy forces were still searching the area to the northwest of the airman's location. They reached a point not more than hundred yards from Mira 33's last known position. From there, they would have to move cautiously because the airman would be scared and might fire on them as they made their approach. Dan decided to take a chance.

"Karol, I'll stay here and cover you. I'll call Wizard and relay a message to the airman that friendly forces are approaching from the west, and to be on the lookout for you; stand by to authenticate using tactical call signs. If the guy's sharp, he should have that information from the daily

SPINS. Please be careful. Approach slowly. I'll have you in sight the whole time."

Karol nodded her head, "He's going to be shocked when he hears my voice."

"Yes, I know, I'm counting on it."

Karol turned and made her way to Mira 33 while Dan contacted Wizard 86.

"Wizard 86, this is Dodger 23. We are in position and ready to implement Op Plan 22-7. Contact Mira 33 and tell him friendly forces are approaching from the west."

"Dodger 23, this is Wizard 86, we copy. We'll relay message."

Crouched down in the mud hiding from the enemy forces, Colonel Elko's radio quietly crackled to life again with a call from Wizard 86.

"Mira 33, this is Wizard 86, be advised, friendly forces are approaching from the west. I say again, friendly forces are approaching from the west!"

Elko did not respond but understood the message. He was surprised to hear that friendly forces were already in place. He would have expected them to appear much later and only if the rescue was delayed or aborted. Elko raised his head slowly as he heard movement coming from the west.

Karol kept low to the ground and crawled toward Mira 33. When she got to within voice range from his location, she whispered in a strong voice. "Mira 33, this is Dodger 22, can you hear me?"

There was silence from the airman probably because he was not expecting to hear a woman's voice, so she repeated her words again, "Mira 33, this is Dodger 22. I'm approaching your position from the west."

Then Karol heard his words, "I hear you, Dodger 22, authenticate Charlie."

The Balkan Network

Karol replied, "Purple! I say again, authentication Purple."

Elko responded, "I copy Purple. Dodger 22, make your way slowly," as he pointed his pistol toward her position.

Karol, still crawling, made her way to him. When she was within visual range, she did as instructed in the daily SPINS, stood up slowly with her hands above her head and said, "Lt. Cdr. Koskov, United States Navy."

"Holy Shit!" was the only reply from Elko, then he said, "I'm Lt. Col. Elko, U.S. Air Force, what the hell are *you* doing out here?"

"We don't have time for any bullshit, Colonel! Do exactly as I say if you want to live. There's enemy forces all around here looking for you. If they find you, you'll be in deep shit." Karol picked up her cell phone and called Dan. "I've made contact with Mira, he's all right. Now get over here!"

When Dan heard Karol's words, he sprinted the distance not worrying about the noise. Elko was stunned to see two Americans deep inside enemy territory. Elko could not make out their faces because they both wore black ski masks concealing their identities.

Elko raised his pistol at Dan and said, "Authenticate whiskey."

Dan knew this meant to authenticate the code word of the day, which was Boxcar. Dan replied, "I'm Dodger 23, authentication Boxcar."

Elko put down his weapon and said, "Lt. Col. David Elko. I've already met Commander Koskov. I'm glad to see both of you."

Dan replied, "I'm Major Radivich, U.S. Air Force. We'll be staying here until the rescue force arrives. For the time being, Colonel, this is a good spot to wait. You've done your homework well. However, time is running out.

We may have to move you to a different location if the enemy moves closer to our position. You will proceed with your rescue procedures and act like we're not here. I have a secure radio, and I'm monitoring all communications with the rescue forces. If there's any confusion or questions, Commander Koskov has a secure satellite cell phone and can talk directly to anyone on the planet. It's important you not reveal our presence or our location to anyone over the radio for obvious reasons. SARs don't even know who we are or our locations. Now, remain still and transmit your GPS location to Magic 41. There's some confusion as to your exact location. They think you're thirty miles to the northwest!"

Elko picked up his radio, called Magic 41 the NATO AWACS, and transmitted his GPS position using a special code directed by the daily SPINS.

Aboard the JSTARS, a young Air Force sergeant received the message from the NATO AWACS, Magic 41, and wrote it down and handed it to Mission Commander Colonel Frank Owens. Owens immediately knew what the message meant. Both friendly forces and Elko's GPS equipment confirmed Elko's GPS position. His location was two miles outside the town of Ruma. Colonel Owens immediately passed the information on to SARs stationed at Tuzla Air Base.

Dan and Karol stayed with Elko. As the time passed, Dan monitored several radio frequencies and said to Elko, "Enemy forces are looking for you twenty miles to the northwest of our present position. Your ejection seat and some boot prints were found in that area, and they seem to be concentrating their search in that area. Two A-10s are on their way and should be overhead shortly."

The A-10s would provide close air support and act as command and control aircraft for the rescue mission.

The Balkan Network

They could hear the distinct whine of A-10 jet engines above.

Karol spoke to Elko, "Don't make any movement until the rescue force arrives. The enemy forces will realize they're in the wrong position when they see the A-10s circling above us and start repositioning toward our location. The A-10s should be able to take them out. Continue with your rescue procedures. My partner and I will take up position and cover you. Luck was on your side tonight. We usually don't get out in the field until after midnight, and you were a short distance away. We have an off-road motorcycle in case we need to move you."

Dan and Karol took up positions a few feet away, in front and to the rear from Elko, and waited.

An hour and a half later, a flight of two MH-53J Pave Low III helicopters, one MH-60G Pave Hawk II helicopter, and two A-10 Thunderbolts escorting the rescue formation approached the valley where Elko was waiting. The weather pattern was changing as the evening progressed, and there was now a light overcast over the valley.

Dan, still monitoring the command and control frequencies, told Elko, "There were some problems with the rescue operation, and that's why it's taking so long. There was some confusion about your exact location as well as some in-flight refueling problems. The choppers had to refuel in-flight along the Bosnian border before continuing, but it looks like they're finally on the way."

Elko began talking on his radio as instructed from the daily SPINS and contacted the lead command and control A-10 circling above.

"Sandy 30, this is Mira 33, I hear the rotor blades!"

Dan, still monitoring the command and control radios, could hear the A-10 pilot voice his concern. The pilot no longer had visual contact on the ground because of the cloud layer, and he needed to maintain visual contact with the rescue force during the extraction.

Elko's radio came to life again with the pilot of Sandy 30.

"Mira 33, this is Sandy 30, I've lost visual contact with you. Is it okay to come in?"

Elko was not ready for that question, and he did not answer. He knew the enemy was all around him, but he did not know how close or with what kind of weapons. He turned to Dan and asked, "They want to know if they should proceed with the rescue without visual contact. How far away do you think enemy forces are, and what weapons will they have?"

Dan could only guess at this point. They had been lucky so far.

"My guess is they're lightly armed, perhaps fifty to eighty men scattered within ten to fifteen miles from our location. With the overcast coming in, the enemy will move closer to our position as every minute passes. If we abort the mission, we'll have to take you with us until another mission can be mounted."

Several minutes passed as Elko pondered the questions and answers. More jet aircraft could be heard above along with sounds of rocket engines igniting in the distance. This was a sure sign the Serbs knew the rescue force was approaching and were trying to shoot the aircraft with SAMs and antiaircraft artillery. Explosions followed with more jet noise from above. Elko knew that time was running out.

To make things worse, a visitor arrived, startling Karol as she turned to the noise in the tall grass. She put on her night vision goggles and saw the outline of a dog walking toward them. The animal was moving slowly. Dan and

The Balkan Network

Elko were twenty yards away, so she did not want to risk shouting in case enemy fighters were in trail of the animal. She had to think quickly and without emotion. She attached the silencer to her pistol and pointed the weapon at the visitor. She used her night vision goggles and took careful aim. If she missed or hit the animal in the wrong place, he would bark or make a sound that would compromise their location. The dog was now less than ten feet away from her. Carefully she aimed, held her breath, pulled the trigger, and fired off two shots. One shot hitting the animal in the neck the other in the forehead. The animal fell to the ground.

Sandy 30 called Elko again on his tactical radio, this time with more urgency in his voice, "Mira 33, if you don't answer we're going to abort the mission and come back later. I say again, can we come in?"

Elko replied, "Sandy 30, let's go for it. I say again, go for it!"

Sandy 30 immediately replied, "Execute, Execute, Now!" over the command and control radio committing the helicopters to the rescue mission. With that order, the helicopters moved closer to Elko's position.

The rescue plan called for the MH-60 Pave Hawk to land and make the extraction while the two Pave Low MH-53s would orbit above and provide fire support. The helicopters called in their location. They were less than two miles from Elko.

The Serbs, now fully aware that a rescue was going on, were tracking the intruders with their air defense radar systems located in the Fruska Gora hills. They turned on all their air defenses in the hopes of shooting an aircraft down. The A-10s circling above also picked up the threats and began deploying chaff dispensers and jamming pods and maneuvered to evade the incoming missiles. SAMs were screeching across the sky from all directions. The rescue helicopter formation was now overhead Elko's location but could not make visual contact with them because of the overcast cloud layer.

Dan turned to Elko and said, "The Pave Hawk can't interrogate your signaling device. Do you have an alternate?"

Dan, Karol, and Elko could now see the incoming helicopters through the cloud layer. They were practically on top of them, but the helicopters crews could not make visual contact with Elko. The rescue helicopter had to make *positive* identification of the downed pilot in order to proceed with the extraction.

Elko contacted the rescue forces on his radio and told them to stand by. He was using an infrared signaling device that would not give off his location to enemy forces. This device gave off a light that could only be picked up and seen by rescue forces with interrogation equipment onboard the rescue helicopters. He tried the device again then transmitted to the rescue helicopters, "What about now, can you pick up my signal?"

A reply came from one of the helicopters, "Negative, Mira 33. I say again, negative contact on your position. Just give us a signal, any signal!"

Karol looked at Elko and finally yelled, "For Christ's sake Colonel, just give them a signal, any signal, we're running out of fucking time! We're all going to get killed!"

Elko reached for his signaling flare and ignited the end. The whole area lit up like daylight giving off their position to everyone, including enemy forces.

"Bingo, Bingo, kill the flare, kill the flare!" was the call from one of the rescue helicopter.

This caused some confusion for Elko, because for fixed winged pilots, *bingo* means low on fuel and returning to

The Balkan Network

base. Elko turned to Dan and said, "They're *bingo*. Just my luck when I'm about to be rescued they run out of fuel."

Dan knew what was going on. He remembered his first assignment with the Special Operations Command and the language they used working with the rescue forces, so he screamed at Elko. "Put out the flare! They have you insight. They're coming in for you!"

Elko immediately crushed the flare with his boot as the MH-53s began setting up a protective orbit just as the MH-60 was touching down.

Karol gave Elko a salute and said, "Get going, you're on your way home now, sir."

Elko smiled at Karol, returned the salute, and without saying a word, turned, walked a few feet, knelt down and folded his arms behind his head as instructed by the daily SPINS. Two 'PJs' jumped out from the MH-60 with their M-16s ready for any close-in combat, grabbed Elko, and hoisted him aboard the waiting helicopter. The rescue force had been on the ground for less than forty seconds. The rescue helicopters and A-10s headed west toward friendly airspace with the rescued F-117 pilot safely aboard.

Dan stumbled through the grass to Karol's location, "The Serbs will be all over this place in seconds, let's get back to the motorcycle."

They two ran back to their hidden motorcycle next to a culvert. Luckily, the motorcycle and helmets were still in place. Karol and Dan took off their ski masks and turned their jackets inside out. Dan started the bike, and they got on the bike and headed to the main highway. All around them they could see cars, trucks, and people everywhere moving along the road. Some were JNA, and others were motorists stopping to take a look. Dan and Karol didn't realize how lucky they were. Enemy forces were less than a mile from the rescue point. They continued following the main road, swerving around cars and people who gathered to watch the event, and headed back to the farmhouse. The time was 2:00 A.M., and of the dozens of people on the road, none of them suspected they just helped rescue an American F-117 pilot.

* * *

A FEW MILES south of Dan and Karol's location, Nick and Naomi were hiding in an irrigation ditch southwest of Verna. They had seen the rescue formation of helicopters, A-10s, and F-16s thundering by toward Tuzla Air Base. They had been directed by the JSTARS to record the location of SAMs and antiaircraft artillery sites firing on the formation. Naomi pointed her laser designator at a mobile SA-6 site that had just fired a SAM at one of the escorting F-16s and relayed the coordinates to Wizard 86. The missile sites would be targeted on the next wave of air strikes that night. Then Naomi got the call from Wizard 86.

"Dodger 26, this is Wizard 86. Be advised we have a downed NATO aircraft near your vicinity. Coordinates to follow. Advise when ready to copy."

Naomi replied, "Go ahead Wizard 86, I'm standing by for info."

"Dodger 26, we have NATO aircraft call sign Bandit 7 downed by enemy fire. Coordinates to follow in text message. Proceed to location and implement Op-Plan 22-7. Advise when you're on your way; stand by for further instructions."

"We copy, Wizard 86." Naomi secured the call then downloaded the text message from her cell phone. Two Luftwaffe aircraft were shot down near Koceljevo. One

The Balkan Network

aircraft was destroyed on impact by SAMs, the other was damaged, but the crew ejected. The coordinates of the downed Luftwaffe aircraft put them over twenty miles to the south. Naomi turned to Nick, "There's a downed Luftwaffe crew twenty-miles south of us. How long do you think it will take us to get there?" as she pointed the coordinates on her GPS display.

"That location puts the downed aircraft somewhere between Draginje and Koceljevo." Nick switched his cell phone to GPS mode and looked at the map display. "That's extremely rugged and remote terrain. The quickest way to get there is by heading south on E-75 to the town of Valjevo, then we'll have to cut across remote terrain to get to his GPS location. I don't think we can make it all the way by motorcycle. The best we could do is get within a few miles of his location then try to reach him on foot. Maybe thirty-five to forty minutes if we're lucky."

"Let's do it!"

Nick and Naomi made it back to their motorcycles and headed south on E-75 toward Valjevo.

Twenty miles to the south in the remote area near Draginje, the pilot of Bandit 7, Major Olef Lundbar, German Air Force, was hanging from a tree still in his parachute harness. Two miles to the south of his location, enemy forces surrounded his weapon system officer, Major Daug Paulsen. Major Paulsen was severely injured with a broken leg suffered during the parachute landing. Fortunately, Major Lundbar was able to contact Paulsen before the enemy closed in on his location and transmitted the information back to the orbiting NATO AWACS. Major Lundbar was piloting his Luftwaffe Tornado, Bandit 7, along with his wingman, Bandit 8, when they received a call that a rescue operation was taking place and needed close air support. As the formation was climbing through 24,000 feet to join with the Sandy 30 flight, several SAMs struck both aircraft without warning. It had been a lucky shot for the Serb SA-6 missile crews. Fortunately, Lundbar and Paulsen ejected from their crippled aircraft, unlike their wingman.

Lundbar struggled to free himself from the parachute harness that kept him suspended from the tree. As he finally released the harness lever, he dropped several feet to the ground and rolled down the steep slope of the mountain. Lundbar was in excellent physical condition at the age of 27. He was medium build with short brown hair and blue eyes. He was trained by the U.S. Air Force at the Joint Euro-NATO Training center at Sheppard AFB, Texas, and he knew that SARs would be mounting a rescue. His emotions went out to his weapons system officer, who was surrounded by enemy forces with a broken leg, and pondered his fate. He knew from intelligence briefings that if a Luftwaffe crew went down, they could expect the worst from the Serbs, many of which still had a deep hatred for the Germans from World War II. Lundbar grabbed some of the rich Serbian soil and smeared it across his face then heard his survival radio come to life.

"Bandit 7, this is Magic 41. Be advised friendly forces are on the way to your position; stand by for further instructions."

Olef did not reply to the transmission for fear it would give off his location to the Serbs. Instead, he turned on his beacon for ten seconds so the AWACS could get a GPS fix on his exact location. All he could do now was wait for friendly forces.

Nick was traveling on E-75 at over eighty miles per hour; Naomi riding behind and keeping up with him. She had become very good at riding the motorcycle.

"Dodger 26, this is Wizard 86. Be advised, attempt to

The Balkan Network

contact Bandit 7 on emergency preset frequency channel 6."

With one hand on the handlebars and the other on her cell phone Naomi switched to emergency radio and selected channel 6. This was an emergency UHF frequency different from the standard 243.0 MZH used internationally as the emergency distress frequency. This UHF frequency had the ability to automatically hop from one UHF frequency to another, making it impossible to trace or intercept the call. This is known as HAVE QUICK communications.

It took Nick and Naomi less than an hour to reach the town of Draginje. From there, they made their way to the mountain passes as they climbed steeply to 4,000 feet elevation. From this location, Naomi could easily call the downed airman directly by cell phone. She contacted the airman to get a better fix on his location.

"Bandit 7, this is Dodger 26, do you copy?" There was no reply from the pilot.

Naomi tried again, "Bandit 7, this is Dodger 26, do you copy?" Again, no reply so Naomi signaled Nick stop alongside the road near a pullout that overlooked the mountain ranges to the south. It was well after 3:30 AM local time and the road was empty. From this location, she could get a clear line-of-sight signal to the downed airman as she tried one more time.

"Bandit 7, this is Dodger 26, do you copy?" There was still no reply.

"Do you think he's injured and that's why he can't reply?" asked Nick.

"I don't think so. We would've been told he was injured and couldn't speak. No, I think he's just not replying for some reason. Maybe there's enemy forces surrounding him or he has his radio turned off. Let me try something. Naomi switched from English to German.

"Bandit 7, this is Dodger 26, please say something or I'm returning to base!"

Within seconds, Lundbar replied in heavily accented English, "I copy, Dodger 26. I didn't reply because I thought it was the Serbs trying to get me to answer my radio. Just to be safe, authenticate Charlie."

Naomi responded, "Bandit 7, this is Dodger 26, authentication Purple."

Lundbar replied in German, "Can you speak in German?"

Naomi replied back in German, "I'm Staff Sergeant Naomi Markof, United States Air Force. My German's perfect."

Speaking now exclusively in German, Lundbar informed Naomi that his navigator was captured by the Serbs and in enemy hands. He asked Naomi to pass the information on to NATO. Naomi was able to get an exact GPS fix on the Lundbar's location, and she determined that it was too remote to make physical contact. He would have to move to a better location in order for her and Nick to get to him or for SARs to mount another mission. Several minutes passed when Lundbar spoke again to Naomi once again in German.

"You're a brave woman to have come this far to try to save me; however, I feel this wasted time could be better spent with my fellow aviator. There is a chance they will not torture or mutilate him if I'm with him. I am making my way down the mountainside to surrender. They are probably looking for me as we speak."

"Don't be a fool, Major! We can get you out of here, that's our job!"

"No, you listen to me, Sergeant. I'm ordering you.

Don't attempt to make contact with me any longer. I'm turning myself in."

Naomi thought out loud, "You stubborn son of a bitch!" Then her phone went dead.

Nick said, "What shall we do?"

"There's nothing we can do. Under the circumstances, I think he's right. The Serbs will not treat them kindly."

Nick and Naomi got back on their motorcycles and headed toward the Tenderloin. It was just after 4:00 AM. Naomi would send a report off to Dan when she got back to quarters, and he would probably want a detailed verbal briefing as well.

* * *

TO THE NORTH NEAR TEMERIN, Mike and Karen were hiding alongside an irrigation canal. They could hear the sound of aircraft above making their egress runs out of Serbia, searchlights pointing upward to the night sky. All they could see to the south were searchlights and tracer rounds streaking upward toward the retreating aircraft. The salvos were intense. Most of the SAMs and triple-A fire were coming from the Fruska Gora hills, to the south of Novi Sad. NATO aircraft knocked out the three main bridges that crossed the Danube at Novi Sad and were targeting the remaining bridge at Backa Palanka and the Danube near Ilok. They were now completely cut off from the rest of the Prospector circuit.

Mike was listening on his communications radio, "Looks like they just rescued a downed pilot south of Fruska Gora. There is no word on the status of Dan or Karol. They were right in the middle of things."

"There shouldn't be, our locations and existence are

confidential. You could try giving them a call directly and see if they're safe."

"I'm sure they're both okay, otherwise I would have heard some chatter on the radios. We'll get a report by noon today." Mike and Karen continued to hide in their location, waiting further orders from the JSTARS.

Chapter 35
DEBRIEFING

Dan and Karol rode to the farmhouse and parked inside the barn. The JSTARS instructed them to head back to base and wait further orders. NATO headquarters could not take the chance of having them exposed after a rescue for fear the Serbs would be on the lookout for them. Dan and Karol were extremely exhausted from the stress of the evening. Karol went upstairs to take a bath while Dan stayed in the kitchen and filed his report on the secure Web site. Just as he sent his report off to NATO, his cell phone rang. The number on the caller ID indicated the call was made from Naples and by Group Captain Snell, and Dan answered, "This is Specter."

"Specter, I'm calling to let you know the F-117 pilot is on his way to Aviano as we speak. The rescue operation went well; congratulations, well done."

Dan responded, "I noted some problems with the procedure, but I'm sure NATO will get a full debriefing on the operation."

"Luck was on our side tonight. CNN reported early in the evening the pilot was captured."

"That information could have been deliberately leaked to the media networks in the hopes of causing confusion with the rescue forces. Or it could be there was indeed a NATO crew captured. We honestly don't know for sure, do we?"

"Well, the main thing is that we were able to rescue the F-117 pilot. You can take the rest of the night off, and I'll call you back tomorrow with more tasking."

"Good night, sir," and Dan hung up the phone.

As Dan secured the call from Snell, Naomi called. She gave Dan a detailed report on the downed Luftwaffe pilots. Her report confirmed his suspicions that indeed there was another NATO crew shot down and that was why there was some confusion on the news media networks.

"You're right, I think if I had been in the same situation, I'd do the same thing as the German pilot. There is a remote possibility they'll both survive the ordeal."

Karol was still in the bathroom upstairs. She just took a bath. She felt a little better today but still not one hundred percent. Her stomach had been upset for days—and she was late. She thought she might be pregnant, but it was hard to tell when it actually occurred. More than likely, it happened back at Bapska or there in the farmhouse. That's when they were tired and careless. She should have at least accepted the contraceptives from Dr. Reed, or maybe Naomi was right all along. Maybe they should have switched partners then none of this would have happened. In any event, she couldn't tell Dan. If she told him, he would be obligated by the UCMJ to inform Washington, and she would be recalled from the mission to face court martial. Dan would be held accountable as well. That would be the end of her career in the Navy; perhaps his too. Their mission would be canceled. The whole team would be let down. She couldn't let this happen. Too many lives were at stake now. She had to go on. She would keep it to herself as long she could. Hopefully, the war would be over by then. She thought, *"Shit, it's my fault. I'll just have to deal with it when we get back to the States."*

Chapter 36
BACKA PALANKA, SERBIA

It was midmorning on Day 5 of Operation Allied Force. Commander Vecili Vorchek was at his field headquarters outside Backa Palanka. He was getting word that NATO bombers were still targeting the dummy armored divisions outside Novi Sad. In addition, the missile brigades were reporting that NATO bombers were continuing to strike at the dummy SAM sites. Moving the SAMs and deactivating the Soviet-made radars systems and installing homemade cameras inside the systems as a way of tracking aircraft appeared to have been successful. The NATO military tactics up to this point had been predictable. First came the Tomahawks and ALCMs. The JNA forces let them through, only firing during the final trajectories using their antiaircraft guns. Then came the bombers, usually in groups of fifteen to twenty aircraft. The plan was to let the bombers hit the empty barracks, dummy air defenses, and armored divisions, and only fire triple-A artillery using cheap worthless shells. The high tech NATO fighters would then automatically respond with their own antiradar missiles revealing the coordinates of the fighters that had

The Balkan Network

just launched their missiles. This was the tactic used in last night's raid that brought down one of the American F-117s. An air defense radar operator guided his missile using a monitor with a joystick and aimed the camera at the light emitted by the attacking jet aircraft's engines. Vecili could not wait for the report coming in that night. He called Belic.

Belic, just getting up from bed, answered, "Good morning, Vecili."

"Have you seen the news reports from last night?"

"I was about to read the paper."

"It appears we were successful in shooting down one of the American F-117s, unfortunately the pilot was rescued. Their SARs picked him up within hours after he ejected—right from under our noses. What can you tell me about this?"

"I was going to send you a report tonight as scheduled."

"I don't have time to wait. The F-117 pilot was rescued outside Ruma. We had nearly a hundred men and several dogs looking for him. My men were no more than five kilometers from the position of the downed airman and were unable to find him. He had to have had help from the ground."

"Very well, Vecili, I'll tell you what I know. The information I'm getting from Langley is there is a team of six operatives working in the Srem District. Two are working north of the Danube River near Novi Sad; the others are south, possibly near Ruma. It would make sense the downed pilot had help from the ground. I don't have physical descriptions of the operatives because the CIA is not providing that information. I believe they are working in pairs. As the air war progresses, the operatives must continue to make daily reports. Sooner or later, one of them will slip up, make a mistake, be careless, and divulge more information on their locations and identities. When that happens, I will pass that information on to you.

"See that you do; you've already been paid handsomely for you efforts." He hung up the phone and contacted Slavo.

Domonic Slavo, still in the field near Glozan, answered his phone, "Yes, comrade?"

"Most of the invaders are in the south near Ruma. That leaves possibly two near your position. If they have two operatives north of the Danube then they have been cut off from the others. I just received word that NATO aircraft bombed all bridges across the Danube in the Srem District. I want you to leave the area to local militia forces. They should be able to find the two Americans. Take your men across the Danube and search the area near Ruma. An F-117 was shot down last night and the pilot rescued. We believe the pilot had help from operatives on the ground. As usual, you are authorized to use whatever means at your disposal."

"Please, Commander, I only need another day or two. I've picked up a trail near Temerin."

"That's too far to the north. I need you to search further south. NATO aircraft are now starting to egress south of the Fruska Gora hills to avoid the SAMs. Besides, I've given you enough time to find the invaders. You should have picked them up by now."

"I wish you would have given me this information earlier. I picked up two locals the other night near Novi Sad. They were a man and a woman, supposedly husband and wife. They looked like ordinary citizens and spoke to us in Serbo-Croatian. I had them search the canals with my men. You don't suppose they could have been the two Americans you're talking about?"

The Balkan Network

"Of course not, you fool. Do you think the Americans are that stupid to send in a man and woman! They probably have another arrogant SEAL or Delta team working in the area. Leave it for the local militia. I need you south of the Danube."

"Yes, comrade, I'll have my men get ready. I'll have to secure a boat to get across the river. I should be across by nightfall."

Back at his apartment in Belgrade, Belic sat down at his kitchen table. He took out the cell phone that he kept in his jacket pocket and hooked it up with a special connector to his laptop and pressed the numbers to make the secure satcom connection. The screen read: U.S. Central Intelligence Agency Secure Web site. He entered his username and password, and he clicked on the DIA Reports link. This took him to a page that detailed all Defense Intelligence Agency reports. He chose a sublink that read, "Balkan Network." Belic saw a new link he'd never seen before titled "Prospector Circuit." He clicked on that link and began to read the reports originating from an operative code-named "Specter."

Chapter 37
TRAITOR

For the Prospector Circuit, Operation Allied Force continued through April. Each day, Dan received his tasking orders from Naples. Each day, the routine was the same except the air strikes were earlier in the evening, sometimes during daylight. Just as Hal and Josef had predicted, the air campaign was lasting much longer than a few days as NATO headquarters originally planned. To the south near Varna in the Tenderloin, Naomi and Nick's tasking orders changed to more threat analysis. Each night they would receive target information from the JSTARS, and they would get a laser designator on the targets. Each night, NATO bombers would hit the targets with little or no effect on the air defenses. Mike and Karen did much the same back in North Beach. The only exception was Dan and Karol. They had very little threat analysis and more search and rescue. More and more NATO aircraft were returning to base either shot-up or with mechanical problems, requiring them to fly at lower altitudes. As a result, they were put on maximum alert in case one of the crews had to eject. To everyone's surprise, no additional

The Balkan Network

Serbian MIGs were shot down, with the exception of a few on the opening night of the air campaign. The Serbs were borrowing a tactic learned during the 1991 Iraq war. It was better to hide and save your fighters and pilots for another day rather than go up against a superior adversary.

It was now the last week of April 1999. The air campaign had lasted for a month with little or no end in sight. Karol woke up at 11:00 AM and began writing the daily report to send off to NATO. She had not slept well that night. Even though she was tired, she could not sleep more than a few hours every night. She decided to let Dan sleep in a while longer. There was a lot of material she had to send to NATO, and she could use the quiet time to get some work done. When she finished her report and sent if off, she decided to go back and do some more research on the mysterious telephone number originating from inside Belgrade. She pulled up the page that had all the numbers listed and then highlighted the ones originating from Belgrade. She was surprised to see that each night a phone call was made from Belgrade using a cell phone to log onto the DOD Web site. Karol still had access to the NSA database from her assignment as a Naval Intelligence officer. She logged onto the NSA Web site and began doing a cross search on the Belgrade number. This would take several minutes because the NSA Web site would not give the information instantaneously. It would eventually kick out a name or location of the person that made the call. She started a search using a name. After several minutes, a message came up that read, "No names for existing number." Then she tried a search on location. Within seconds, a message came back written in Serbian Cyrillic. Karol translated the words: Overland Air Freight Company. Next, she did a simple Internet search using the white pages and came up with a physical address for the

Overland Air Freight Company. It was located at 23 Bulevar Kralja Aleksandar, Belgrade, not more than three city blocks from the city center. She quickly raced upstairs and awakened Dan.

"Dan, get up. I've found something you need to take a look at. I found some more information on the mysterious caller from Belgrade." Dan got up and followed Karol downstairs to the kitchen table.

"I was able to access the NSA database, and I found a physical location of the person making the calls from Belgrade. I didn't get a name, but I was able to get a company, The Overland Air Freight Company located on Kralja Aleksandar."

Dan recalled the conversation he had with Josef back on the train. He remembered Josef mentioning something about a CIA contact working in Belgrade who ran an air freight company.

"You say these calls came from someone at the Overland Air Freight Company?"

"Yes," said Karol. "The calls are made each day after midnight local time and the calls are routed to a secure satcom data link similar to the one we're using. It's safe to say that someone else is passing or receiving information the same way we are. Do you think it could be another circuit or cell operating in Belgrade?"

"No, I don't think so. To the best of my knowledge, we have no assets in place in Belgrade, at least no DOD assets. Strange the data links are established about the same time we receive our tasking orders from Naples. Can you pinpoint the exact location of where the calls are being made?"

"I don't have clearance to go that deep into the NSA network. If I had a name, I could try doing a search on cell phone numbers assigned to that person."

The Balkan Network

Dan thought for a long moment and tried to recall the name of the CIA contact in Belgrade.

Give me a second Karol. Professor Kostinic said a name to me during my briefings aboard Amtrak. He mentioned his name a couple of times to me. Wait a minute—Josef said the CIA contact working in Belgrade used to be the station manager for Pan American World Airways."

"That's a start. Let me do a search on Pan Am and try to access personnel records. It could take a few hours, but I think I can do it." Karol went to work on the computer while Dan fixed breakfast.

It was well after 1:00 P.M. when Karol said, "I've got a name. Does the name Milan Belic mean anything to you?"

Dan smiled from ear to ear and kissed Karol slightly on the cheek. "You're a genius, that's him! I just couldn't remember his name until you mentioned it."

Now that Karol had a name, she could go back to the NSA database and try to find cell phone numbers belonging to that name. After a few hours, Karol was able to trace another number belonging to Milan Belic. All she had to do now was cross-reference this number with numbers originating from the other number. This was simple because Belic's cell phone only made calls to one other cell phone. Karol ran a cross-reference on that number.

"You're not going to believe this Dan, but Belic's been calling someone with a cell phone registered to the Serbian Defense Ministry."

"We have a possible traitor in our midst. I want you to keep an eye on his activity. There was always the possibility of being double-crossed on this mission. Hal, Josef, and I discussed this back in Washington. In fact, I was not happy to hear that Langley would be getting all our reports from the field."

"You mean all this time CIA has been getting our reports?"

"I'm afraid so. We were told the CIA needed this information to keep their database updated."

"God knows what they'll do with it."

"We didn't have a choice. CIA dictated the rules to us. We had to go along with them. We did agree to hold off up to six hours before the DOD passed information on to Langley. That way, if there is a double-cross, we'll have some advance notice. I think you may have given us the upper hand. This could also be the reason why the Serbs have not discovered our locations and why Mike and Karen escaped the paramilitary forces."

"What about our locations? Does the CIA have that information as well?"

"No, that was our only condition. We've kept our locations confidential just in case this sort of thing happened. We didn't want Langley to know our specific whereabouts. They didn't have a need to know if, in fact, they only wanted the information to update their database."

"I think we should break protocol and contact Mattingly and inform him of what we've discovered."

Dan thought for a moment then said, "As usual, you're right. Let's make the call."

Chapter 38
THE PENTAGON, WASHINGTON D.C.

It was nine in the morning back in Washington when Mattingly saw Dan's number on the caller ID. He thought to himself, *Why's he calling?*

"Hello, Specter, how can I help you?"

"I'm sorry to break protocol, sir, but Sutter's come up with something I think you should know about. Let me get right to the point. I think Milan Belic is passing information on to the Serbs."

Mattingly obviously recognized the name because he didn't delay in his reply and immediately said, "Milan Belic—what made you come to that conclusion?"

"Sutter traced several phone calls originating from the Overland Airfreight Company going out to a cell phone registered to someone in the Serbian Defense Ministry. Belic is the owner of the Overland Airfreight Company. He's also the CIA's only human asset in Belgrade. He's using another cell phone to access secure sat-com data links similar to the one we're using. I don't know how he got that particular phone, but it's all adding up to a traitor."

"This is extremely sensitive information. Have you discussed it with anyone else?"

"No, sir, no one else knows of this except Sutter and me."

Karol interrupted the conversation, "Sir, we just want to make sure the circuit is not in jeopardy. I thought you told us there were no other assets in Belgrade."

"You're right, we have no DOD circuits in Belgrade. If it's Belic, then he's working on his own. He was one of the reasons why CIA wanted DOD to come up with the assets to man this mission. Just to let you two know, we have a DOD cell in Kosovo and another in Tuzla. All of our circuits coordinate from one central location in Bosnia. Belic could be placing routine traffic calls to give him the benefit of the doubt, but just to be on the safe side, I'll follow up on my end. If it looks like your circuit will be compromised, I'll have you extracted by the choppers. As a precaution, I want you to go about your everyday routines. Don't let NATO know about this and do not contact me further on this matter. I'll let you know if we find something."

Dan secured the call with Mattingly. "Up to now our circuit has been either very lucky or very good, and we've managed to stay one step ahead of our adversaries. I think the time delay in our reports to Langley has, in fact, bought us more time. Can we tell what sort of reports Belic was transmitting to his Serbian contact?"

Karol went back to her computer and pulled the history on Belic's reports. All the files were written in text format and in Serbian Cyrillic. Karol copied the files and began translating the material. "The first report details a deception plan. You were right about the armored division in Novi Sad. It appears they are decoys to lure NATO aircraft into a trap. Also, there's an aircraft model maker who made fabricated MIG 29s out of balsa wood to fool NATO planners. There's more Dan, Belic reports over 90 percent of the NATO air strikes are hitting wooden rockets staged to look like SA-2 missile sites."

"This explains why Naples has the targeting information so screwed up. Copy everything and send it directly to Bolling. It will be a race against time to get this information to NATO headquarters before it's too late."

Chapter 39
THE END OF OPERATION ALLIED FORCE

May 2, 1999

Jazak monastery in the Fruska Gora hills, founded in 1736, was dedicated to the Holy Trinity. The construction of the church lasted from 1736 to 1758 and was constructed in the traditional design at that time: chapel in the middle and dormitories surrounding the main structure. By 1741, the monastery was ready to receive the brethren. A baroque bell tower was added to the site on the west side and completed in 1803. The monks' quarters, surrounding the church on three sides, was built between 1736 and 1761. By 1926, the monastery underwent general construction to further strengthen the structure. It was the perfect military fortress. During World War II, the monastery was heavily bombed by Allied forces because Jazak was used by the Germans as the Balkan headquarters for all military operations in Yugoslavia. After World War II, it was repaired to its original luster, complete with fortifications to the monks' quarters. Now the monastery housed the Command Center for Vecili Vorchek and his

The Balkan Network

paramilitary forces. At 9:00 PM, Vorchek received a phone call from Belic.

"Vecili, I have good news for you. As I promised, the American operatives have been careless and have given off their locations. There are two operatives working close to your vicinity. Their last known position is a few miles to the east, in the area near Irig. They seem to be passing information back to NATO headquarters on the location of your SAM sites and most importantly, they are helping the downed airmen. They are two U.S. military officers, male and female, working as a team."

"This is splendid news! Can you give me the exact location?"

"All I can tell you is that they have been using an area near Novo-Hopovo and Staro Hopovo monasteries and are using off-road motorcycles and ATVs to get around."

"Thank you, Milan, you will be handsomely rewarded for this information. We expect another NATO air strike tonight on the monasteries, except this time JNA will be targeting aircraft and hopefully tracking down the American terrorists assisting the airmen."

Vecili turned to his lieutenant, Domonik Slavo. "We have the NATO scum you've been searching for. You were right all along my friend. It *is* a man and woman. Take your men to Staro-Hopovo and find them. They're using off-road motorcycles. Do what you must to track them down. I want their heads on display in Belgrade by tonight, especially the bitch." Slavo smiled showing off his crooked teeth, nodded his head and then left the room.

DAN RECEIVED his tasking orders for the night. They had been routine for the past week. NATO was intensifying the air strikes on the SAM locations in the Fruska Gora hills, and they were still needed in the area. Dan and Karol rode from the farmhouse to their location near the primitive campsite outside Irig. The Irig location was perfect for hiding their equipment and supplies, and because of the almost nightly air strikes on the hills, there were no campers or hikers using the National Park. When they got to the hiding place near the campsite, Dan and Karol turned their jackets inside out, showing the night camouflage pattern. Next, they put on their black ski masks, concealing their identities. Tonight, there would be a new moon and thus little light to aid them, so they decided to bring their night vision goggles. Next, they loaded their AK-74s and extra rounds into their backpacks. The past two nights saw increasingly more and more JNA and paramilitary forces operating in the area, and they had to make sure they had plenty of ammunition in case they got in a firefight. As usual, Dan switched his cell phone to aeronautical radio mode and monitored all NATO aircraft transmission. Karol kept hers on cell phone in case she had to reach someone directly. Dan rode the motorcycle and Karol rode the ATV. They separated by several hundred yards and headed into the thickly wooded areas surrounding the monastery at Novo-Hopovo. No sooner had they separated when Dan detected several JNA forces moving toward them. He suspected they'd seen him. Quickly he contacted Karol, "Enemy forces ahead. I think they've spotted me. Turn around and head down the hill toward Irig. I'll try to lose them."

"Be careful, Dan."

Dan accelerated the bike and headed deeper into the thicket trying to work his way down to Karol. His night vision goggles limited is peripheral vision, but they gave him a slight advantage over the enemy. Three men on motorcycles peeled off from the main group and followed

The Balkan Network

him. His only thought was to get as much distance from the main JNA force and the three motorcycle riders, then try to engage them so they wouldn't go after Karol, who was riding the much slower ATV. He turned and accelerated down the hill, going in and out of the brush. The three men following were obviously not skilled riders because Dan easily increased the distance between them. He found a clearing with some fallen trees, then slowed the bike down, got off, and knelt below the tree stumps, waiting for the three riders to appear. To further confuse the enemy, he left the engine running. He pulled out his pistol with silencer and took aim at the clearing where the riders would be coming, his night vision goggles giving him the edge. As soon as the riders came into view, he fired and emptied his twelve-round magazine. All three men fell from their bikes with a loud crash, not knowing what hit them. Dan slapped another magazine into his Makarov then shouldered his AK-74 and took aim at the clearing. He heard nothing, so he fired several rounds into the fallen motorcycles disabling the bikes. He switched his cell phone to GPS and tried to get a fix on Karol. Her location was less than two miles away to the left. He got back on his motorcycle and headed for her location. Dan switched to walkie-talkie mode, "Sutter, I think I've lost them. I'm making my way to your position, are you alright?"

"I'm okay. I'm headed down the dirt road back to the campsite."

As she said this, both Dan and Karol could hear the sound of rocket engines igniting not far from their location. They could see the light from the rocket thrusting upwards toward the moonless sky. An explosion immediately followed, and the distinct sound of a crippled jet engine. Dan knew immediately the Serbs had shot down another NATO aircraft.

* * *

DOMONIK SLAVO also heard the explosion. He was trying to contact the three men who had peeled off and followed the lone rider into the woods. There was no reply from them, so he called Vorchek.

"Comrade, I sent three of my men after a lone rider on a motorcycle, but I've lost contact. In addition, a NATO aircraft was shot down not far from my location. Which direction do you want me to go?"

Vecili replied, "Send more men after the lone rider. He's probably by himself and your men should be able to handle him. I want you to follow the trail of the NATO aircraft and the downed pilot. That'll take us to the other operative, hopefully the bitch."

Slavo acknowledged the order and sent two more of his paramilitary forces after the lone rider. He got on his motorcycle and headed toward the location of the downed aircraft.

ABOVE THE FRUSKA Gora hills at 29,000 feet, the pilot of Gordo 54, an American F-16 yelled, "Mayday! Mayday! Mayday!" over his emergency radio before he ejected. The distress call let SARs know he was in trouble and prevented the Serbs from keying in on his location. Captain Mark Williams drifted down over enemy territory. Williams was in his mid twenties with short blond hair and a boyish face. He had been physically and mentally preparing for this event his entire Air Force career, hoping it would never happen, yet here he was, drifting down safely to earth. He watched as his aircraft hit the ground in a ball of flames. His F-16 had been shot down by a Serbian SA-6 SAM. Captain Williams had just finished an air strike against a Serbian SAM site nearby when the missile exploded close to his jet. He never saw the incoming missile or had any cockpit indications he was being targeted. It all happened at once. As he was descending to the ground, he was wondering what enemy forces were waiting for him below. He reached for his Beretta but discovered it was not in his holster. He must have lost it during the ejection sequence.

Almost directly above her, Karol could see the orange and white canopy of the downed pilot drifting to her location. She called Dan using the walkie-talkie function of her cell phone.

"Dan, I think I've got a downed pilot about to fall on top of me. What should I do?"

"Don't approach him until I can get confirmation it's one of ours. It could be a Serbian jet".

"I don't think you need to worry about that. I can see the American flag on this right shoulder from here!"

"Okay, if he's that close try to make verbal contact using your authentication call sign. I'll contact Magic or Wizard to get confirmation."

CAPTAIN WILLIAMS HIT the treetops of the wooded area outside Irig. He broke tree branches and limbs as he made his way down to the ground. Hitting the soft earth, he rolled over and released his parachute harness. He quickly hid the parachute and life raft and began running down the mountainside. He could hear vehicles all around him, and he knew the Serbs were alerted to his location. He would run some distance, then stop, then run again and stop, listening for the approaching enemy.

Dan was now concerned the entire missile brigade managing in the Fruska Gora hills would come out looking for the downed pilot, so he quickly called Wizard using secure cell phone.

"Wizard 86, this is Dodger 23, I have a downed pilot in my vicinity. Can you give me his call sign?"

"Standby, Dodger 23," was the reply from the JSTARS.

Dan could hear more vehicles approaching and men shouting, probably more motorcycles or other ATVs.

"Dodger 23, this is Wizard 86. We have confirmation that Gordo 54 broadcast a Mayday call with no other transmissions. You are a go for Op-Plan 22-7. I say again, you are a go for Op-Plan 22-7."

"Dodger 23 copies; go for Op-Plan 22-7."

KAROL WAS NOW off her Honda Rancher ATV and within a few meters from Captain Williams. She still had her night vision goggles on so she could see him clearly. She moved toward him slowly so she could get close enough to authenticate using her voice. She could see that his holster was empty and he was looking around for something to throw in her direction. Karol, now ten feet away, stood up and began to whisper loudly when the pilot started sprinting away from her like he was in a track meet. Karol, three months pregnant, would never be able to catch him. "Damn that stupid son of a bitch," she said out loud. She had no choice but to get back on her ATV and follow him.

Karol contacted Dan. "Dan, I lost him. I was within ten feet from the guy and the son of a bitch just took off running like he'd seen some wild animal. I must have scared the hell out of him. I couldn't keep up with him on foot. What should I do?"

"Go after him on the ATV. I'll contact Magic and relay

The Balkan Network

to the pilot that friendly forces are approaching trying to make contact."

Dan called the NATO AWACS directly to avoid confusion, forwarded the request to contact Gordo 54, and advised him that friendly forces were in the area.

WILLIAMS HAD BEEN RUNNING for almost an hour. He couldn't believe that someone or something had found him so quickly. He guessed that some creature about five feet tall with big red eyes was descending on him and was about to bounce on him like a wildcat when he made the sprint downhill. Little did Williams know what frightened him was none other than Lt. Cdr. Karol Koskvo, United States Navy, and the big red eyes were her Viking night vision goggles. William's radio cracked to life.

"Gordo 54, this is Magic 41. Be advised friendly forcers are attempting to make contact with you. They should be approaching from your rear on an ATV."

Williams did not answer his radio, but listened intently and could make out the sound of a vehicle approaching from the distance.

"Roger, Magic. Gordo 54 copies your message." Williams heard the sound of an approaching ATV, and then the sound stopped. He could hear footsteps and branches breaking in the distance, then a female voice said in English, "Gordo 54, this is Dodger 22, I'm approaching your position".

Karol did not hear a response from the pilot—again, because he was surprised to hear a woman's voice. She repeated the words again, "Gordo 54, this is Dodger 22, Authentication Bravo. I'm at your two o'clock." Karol authenticated the code color of the day: blue.

Finally, when Williams was convinced the voice he

heard belonged to friendly forces, he repeated, "Dodger 22, this is Gordo 54, I copy."

Karol came out from the brush her hands raised above her head and showed herself to the pilot. All Williams could see was a human figure about five-foot-six wearing a camouflage jacket, a black ski mask, and night vision goggles.

Karol took off the heavy goggles and ski mask then said, "I'm Lt. Cdr. Koskov, United States Navy. Do exactly as I say if you want to be rescued. I've got to get you out of here and to a secure location. There are enemy forces all around us, not to mention thick vegetation. You'll never be rescued from this location. I want you to contact Search and Rescue using your radio. Don't tell them I'm with you or mention my name over the radio. Our existence in the field is extremely classified. Not even SARs know of our locations. We'd like to keep it that way because we still have to operate in the area once you're picked up. Tell them you're all right and that you're searching for a better location, and you'll check back in an hour with a new location. Do you understand?"

Williams nodded his head and did as instructed, and then followed Karol back to the ATV. Williams got on the back of the Rancher with Karol. They headed down the mountain for the general location of the farmhouse.

Karol contacted Dan. "Dan, I've got Gordo 54 on my ATV and we're heading down the mountain. Any suggestions on locations?"

"I got your GPS location. There's enemy forces everywhere. I engaged three awhile back, and I just engaged two more. There's something else. I think they know we're helping the pilot. The enemy forces seem to know my exact location. It's almost like someone is directing them toward me."

Karol said, "I need to keep moving for another hour before we reach more favorable terrain. I can stay off the main roads and use the secondary farm roads, but eventually I'll have to get back on one of the main roads."

"Make your way to Chinatown. There's a small creek just outside Kukujevci. We've reconnoitered the area before. You'll know it when you see it. Make your way there, and I'll catch up to you within an hour. I need to shake off enemy forces and direct them away from you and the pilot."

"Dan, please be careful!"

"You be careful too. Nothing's going to happen. If I have to, I'll stop and engage the pursuers just as I did before. Just get that fighter jock to a secure area so he can be rescued. I understand rescue forces are on the way."

Karol and Williams reached the flat fertile farmlands of Vojvodina. It was still pitch-black outside, and no enemy forces were following them. They found the area outside Kukujevci next to the small creek. Just as Dan had said, there were plenty of places to hide alongside the creek. The creek was used for irrigating the fields nearby, and once the rescue forces committed to the rescue, they could use the farm fields as a landing platform. The two got off the Honda Rancher, hid in the tall grass next to the creek, and waited.

Karol told Williams, "Captain, go ahead with your rescue procedures. Contact SARs and give them your new location. They'll be able to get a new GPS fix on your position."

DOMONIK SLAVO ARRIVED at the original location where the downed pilot landed. He saw the ejection seat and parachute harness thrown carelessly to the bushes, but there was no sign of the pilot. The area was too wooded for the rescue operation to take place, and he decided the airman must have worked his way downhill to flat ground. After a month and a half of tracking the invaders, he was finally on their trail. If luck was on his side, tonight he would have a downed enemy pilot and at least one, maybe two, covert operatives as his trophies. He got back on his motorcycle and headed for the JNA outpost near the town of Besenovo. There, he would gather more men and vehicles to make his way toward Vojvodina.

Still shaking off enemy forces, Dan killed two more enemy fighters. Somehow, they knew he was not a local farmer helping search for a downed airman. He reflected for a moment at the information and phone calls made by Belic to someone in the Serbian Defense Ministry. Then it became apparent to him that Belic could have set a trap for them, and he remembered how Karol went deep into cyberspace trying to find Belic's location. He could have used that opportunity as a way of luring in the location of the operatives. Dan did not have time to reflect long. His radio came to life with SARs moving into Serbia from Tuzla Air Base in Bosnia. He could hear the sound of F-16s overhead providing Combat Air Patrol (CAP) and the distinctive sound of A-10 Thunderbolts maneuvering over the flat farmlands near Kukujevci.

He called Karol again, "I'm off the mountain heading toward you on the main road. I should be there in fifteen minutes."

Dan could hear the sounds of the two Pave Low and Pave Hawk helicopters approaching from the distance. It was a sure bet the Serbs knew the rescue maneuvers and procedures by now. He switched his cell phone to aeronautical radio and began monitoring radio transmissions of SARs. The lead helicopter was looking for Gordo 54 near

The Balkan Network

the original position where he ejected. They had obviously not gotten the word the downed pilot was moved closer to the flat farm fields. At that moment, Dan saw the Pave Hawk helicopter make an immediate turn in the opposite direction away from Dan's position and the original position of Gordo 54. It looked as if Karol and Gordo were able to transmit the new location to SARs. This, unfortunately, would give off the new location to enemy forces on the ground as well. Dan cursed under his breath and thought, *if they know the rescue force is repositioning, then it's a sure bet they know about Karol's location too*. He contacted Karol on walkie-talkie. "Karol, the rescue formation is repositioning to your location, what's your status?"

"I can hear helicopters and aircraft circling above, and there's search lights pointing in our direction!"

"Hold off a few minutes longer until I can back you up!"

Karol could now hear and see the helicopters approaching from the west. She also saw a small truck loaded with ten to fifteen paramilitaries and JNA forces moving into position to take aim at the approaching helicopters. *Crap*, she thought to herself. Then she said to Williams, "You stay here and follow your rescue procedures. I'm going to move between us and the enemy forces and try to delay them until they get here."

Karol moved in to the tall grass toward the truck. She thought about her unborn child and wondered if she was doing the right thing. She knew they had a job to do, and she needed to concentrate on the tasks at hand. She could not let the team down now. If she could delay the paramilitary forces until Dan could get to her, the rescue could be accomplished successfully, and she and Dan could escape on the motorcycle. In addition, she knew the A-10 Thunderbolts would be targeting the forces once they came on scene. She took out her AK-74, pulled back on the bolt, and fired at the truck. Men screamed in agony as Karol's AK-74, riddle the side of the truck, taking out a half-dozen men. She gritted her teeth, slapped in another thirty-round magazine and continued to fire into the truck, then another.

Dan heard the sounds of automatic gunfire and knew Karol was in trouble. He had to get to her and help until the Pave Lows could get the airman out. He never had the chance to tell her how much he cared for her. He was too busy running the mission. He switched to walkie-talkie on his cell phone and called Karol once again.

"Karol, I'm just across the field behind you at your two o'clock position. Do you copy?"

There was no reply and he tried again.

"Karol, do you copy? I'm just across the field at your two o'clock position."

Finally, she came back. "Dan, I'm surrounded. I took out one truck but another one followed, and I think there could be more behind that as well, please hurry!"

"Karol, listen carefully to me. I want you to switch to hot-mic and keep the line open." Dan could hear the sounds of automatic gunfire in his headset and knew Karol made the switch. The Pave Lows were now over station, and they began to fire at the positions around Karol. Dan got off his bike and began running to Karol's location. He did not want to waste precious time contacting Wizard 86 and relaying information to the lead A-10 on the location of friendly forces. His only concern now was to get to Karol.

Three more troop carrier trucks arrived between Karol's position and Dan's, and the troops began unloading and firing their weapons at the Pave Lows and Karol. The Pave Lows returned fire using onboard Gatling guns. Dan could see the Pave Hawk maneuver between the Pave Lows and land in a clearing just to the West of Karol and the downed airman's position. Another A-10 made a pass and strafed the troop carrier trucks in front of Dan. Screams could be heard from the trucks as the A-10 fired 3,900 rounds per minute of depleted uranium armor-piercing rounds into the trucks and cut into the men's bones and flesh to pieces. As the Pave Hawk lifted off the ground with the rescued airman, Dan heard the words he hoped he would never have to hear, "Dan, I'm hit, I'm hit!"

Dan shouted as loud as he could into his headset. "I'll be there in less than two minutes!" Dan could hear the sounds of sobs in the background over Karol's mic. His rage was now in full gear at the thought of losing her. He raced to one of the blown-up troop carrier trucks and fired his AK-74 into the back. There was no sound. He took every weapon he could see and any extra ammunition in sight and headed for Karol. He could see two more vehicles approaching Karol's position. He shouted again into his headset, "Karol, I'm less than a hundred yards away. Just hold on!"

Another A-10 made a strafing pass and knocked out more vehicles—too little too late. Then Dan saw one of the trucks near Karol's location speed away.

"Karol, if you can hear me say something?" Dan heard a slight moan over his headset then the line went dead. Another A-10 made a strafing pass and took out the remaining trucks and troops, then there was silence. All Dan could see in the distance was a lone truck moving at full speed away from the scene. Dan reached Karol's last known location. He missed her by just a few seconds. All around him, he saw dead bodies, body parts, and burning vehicles. He could see blood on the grass where Karol had been hiding. The Serbs had tried to ambush the rescue forces but instead had captured or killed Karol. He tried to run after the fleeing vehicle, but it was useless. He would never catch them on foot. Exhausted, he fell to his knees, dropped his weapons, and then shouted, "Damn you, Belic!"

Several minutes passed. Dan stood up, picked up his AK-74, and fired all thirty rounds into the burning trucks. There was an eerie silence in the farm fields as he stood alone. He contacted the JSTARS using the emergency number Karol had given to all the operatives. A radio operator, aboard the JSTARS answered the phone, "This is Wizard 86".

Dan replied, "Wizard 86, this is Dodger 23. Be advised Dodger 22 is missing-in-action. I say again, Dodger 22 is MIA."

Aboard the JSTARS, Mission Commander Colonel Frank Owens received the message and replied to Dan directly, "Dodger 23, this is command one, we copy Dodger 22 is MIA. I'm sorry to hear that. We'll pass it on to headquarters. Return to base and stand by for further instructions."

Chapter 40
ESCAPE

Dan made his way back to his hidden motorcycle and rode back to the farmhouse at Chinatown. Ironically, he was less than fifteen minutes away. Once there, he raced into the kitchen and logged onto his computer. He got a fix on Karol's GPS position. She was traveling on E-70 toward Sremska Mitrovica. He was hoping she was still alive, but then again, if she was alive, the Serbs would torture her to get more information out of her. His thoughts turned again to Karol and his true feelings—how much he cared for her and not telling her so. Now, it didn't matter. Soon Hal would be getting word that Karol had gone MIA or KIA, and he would be working on extracting the entire circuit. He stayed at the kitchen table and monitored Karol's GPS location. When her position was at Sremska Mitrovica, for some reason the GPS icon stopped transmitting. Dan continued to stare at the screen and lost track of time. The entire rescue had lasted just over four hours. Daylight was approaching with Dan still watching the computer screen in case Karol's position reappeared. The farmhouse seemed quiet, lonely, and empty without her.

They had lived together here for over a month as if they were husband and wife. Now, none of that was to ever happen again.

Dan's thoughts drifted back to Josef and what he had told him about leaving behind the SOE operative, Penelope Walsh, in the hands of the Gestapo. He also thought about the promise he made to him. He secured the Internet connection on his computer and called Naomi.

"This is Lombard."

Dan immediately replied solemnly, "Naomi ... Karol's gone. She's been shot."

"No! Dan, please tell me you're joking."

"I'm afraid it's true. They shot her as she was providing cover for the rescue formation, and I saw the Serbs take her body away. I was monitoring her GPS location until just a few minutes ago."

Naomi was stunned and speechless over the phone then continued, "Can you give me more details of what happened? I heard over the radio there was a rescue going on."

"We got the pilot out, but Karol didn't make it. I lost contact with her in the firefight. Her last words to me were that she was hit. No one else on the team knows about this." Dan pounded his fist on the table, then said, "Naomi, if it wasn't for Karol, the rescue helicopters wouldn't have landed and rescued the pilot. She took out a whole truckload of enemy paramilitary forces by herself."

Naomi detected the sadness in Dan's voice. "What about you? Are you all right, sir?"

"I'm okay for the time being. I was told to return to base and stand by. My guess is Finder is working on extracting the entire Prospector circuit. Naomi, I want you to listen carefully. Karol and I believe that our circuit had been compromised long before tonight. Karol found some information on the computer a few weeks ago that suggested our locations may have been tipped off to the Serbs. They were waiting for us tonight. It was a total ambush. They knew our exact locations at all times. Five paramilitaries came after me on motorcycles. Several others chased me down by truck. That's how Karol and I got separated. I was trying to put distance between me and her and the enemy fighters. By coincidence a SAM shot down a NATO fighter and the pilot ejected over our heads. Karol went ahead and implemented Op Plan 22-7 by herself." Dan paused for a second more remembering what Josef told him about not waiting until it's too late. "Listen, I'm not waiting for Hal to arrange an extraction. I want you and Nick to carry out your escape plan. Use the emergency *Goalpost* escape route. I'll feel much better when you two are back in Croatia. Our mission is over anyway."

"How soon do we have to leave? We just got into the safe house an hour ago. We've been up all night."

"Get a few hours sleep then head out."

"What about you? What will you do?"

"I'm going after Karol, dead or alive. I'm not leaving her behind."

There was a long silence on the phone, then Naomi said, "Dan, can I ask you something?"

"Sure, go ahead."

"Why did you call me and tell me about Karol? Why didn't you call Eden? She's the next senior ranking member of the circuit."

"I needed to talk to you first. I want you to know something about Karol before anyone else finds out. She was taken by paramilitary forces, not JNA. They won't take her to a POW camp. If she's still alive, they'll probably take her to a death camp or some other miserable place and torture the information out of her. I can't have her go through that. I'm going looking for her even if it's the last thing I do alive."

"You really do care for her, don't you?"

"Yes, I do, along with the rest of you but I never got a chance to tell her so. Now you know the real reason why I wouldn't let you switch partners with me back at Bapska, even though you were right about everything."

"I'm sorry, Dan, for both of you. I'm also sorry for treating Karol the way I did throughout this mission. I was not kind to her at all from the beginning. I knew she cared for you. I want you to know that." Naomi became more confident and serious then said, "Don't worry, sir, Nick and I'll be ready to move out this morning. I'll tell Nick what happened to Karol and file my reports as soon as I get to Croatia."

"Thank you for everything you've done on this mission. You served your country with pride and honor. If I don't make it back alive, I want you to know that." Dan secured the line with Naomi then called Karen's number. She answered the phone and said, "This is Eden."

He briefed her on what happened.

Karen was stunned. "Hold on a second while I get Grant on the line."

Both Mike and Karen were on the line now, and Dan continued, "I already spoke to Lombard and broke the news to her. I want you two to be ready for extraction. I was told to stand by and wait for further instructions, but I'm not waiting for the extraction orders. There is a real possibility that our circuit's compromised. They were waiting for us last night. We were ambushed. I want you two to go ahead with your escape procedures and get back to Croatia. Use your primary escape route. I'll stay here and look for Karol."

The Balkan Network

Mike spoke up immediately, "I'm staying with you, Major."

"Calm down, Mike. I'll be all right. Karen needs you to get her back into Croatia. The escape plan calls for the two of you to work together. Besides, I know this area, and there's an excellent chance Karol is still alive. I might be able to get her out."

Karen spoke up, "Don't worry, sir, Mike will do what you tell him because he'll do what I tell him!"

"Thank you, Karen. Now I want you two to listen to me. Karol discovered a few weeks ago that our circuit locations may have been tipped off to the Serbs. We could be in jeopardy right now. That's why I'm not waiting for the extraction orders. Time may be critical at this point. The sooner you head out the better your chances of escape. I've already given orders for Nick and Naomi to move out this morning."

Karen spoke up, "I understand, sir. We'll see you back in Croatia."

"Good luck to both of you. No matter what happens, I'm proud of all of you."

Dan hung up the phone and went upstairs to the bedroom. He saw the bed where he and Karol slept every night and made love. His resolve only got stronger. If it was Belic that tipped off the Serbs and caused Karol's death, he would make sure Belic paid dearly. He took a shower and changed clothes. He took all the cash they had hidden in the bedroom. He took two magazines for his Makarov and put them inside his coat pocket. Dan looked in the mirror. He looked just like an ordinary Serb traveling on business. He placed his cell phone in the other pocket and went downstairs. He went into the barn, opened one of the sacks of grain, and took out a package of plastic explosive, detonator, and timing device. Next, he filled the motorcycle with the last of the fuel. His cell phone rang. It was Mattingly.

"Dan, you and Karol were right, your circuit has been compromised. All of Karol's information checks out with NSA. I also received word about Karol going MIA. I ordered the extraction of your entire circuit. Unfortunately, the Serbs launched an air strike on Tuzla Air Base this morning and destroyed three helicopters and two C-130s, evidently in retaliation for the rescue assault last night. Eleven casualties were reported, which included pilots and ground personnel. They've ceased all operations from Tuzla until they can secure the airfield. I'm afraid we're going to have to wait a few hours for replacement choppers to be flown in from one of the carriers."

"What about the emergency escape plan?" asked Dan.

"That plan calls for the escape of each element separately. There's no guarantee we can get everyone out successfully."

"It's a chance I'm willing to take, especially if the Serbs know of our locations."

Mattingly thinking the scenarios through said, "All right, go ahead and execute escape plan Bravo. If they can get a chopper out sooner, I'll cut the re-tasking personally and have them pick up the team members in route. There's one other thing I want to pass on to you, Dan. We tracked Karol's GPS location. She never left the Srem District. That was an hour ago. She could still be alive."

"Can you tell me her last known position?"

"Dan, I can't risk that. I need you to get out with the rest of the team. I can't have you wandering all over Yugoslavia looking for her."

"I understand, sir. I'm packing up as we speak."

Dan hung up the phone and heard the sound of vehicles approaching the farmhouse. He looked out from the

The Balkan Network

barn and saw two truckloads of Serbian militia forces. He thought, *that didn't take them long*. They all looked like paramilitary with no distinct uniforms and wearing black ski masks. Some were carrying sniper rifles. They knew he was here. Karol could *still* be alive; only she could have provided his location to the Serbs under torture. Dan started the bike and rode out the back door of the barn and headed across the farm fields. He never looked back. All he could think about was Karol.

Dan cut across open farm fields and made his way to the main highway E-70 toward Sremska Mitrovica. Once inside the city center, he parked his bike and walked two blocks to the bus and train station, which were co-located. He looked at the schedule on the wall to determine whichever form of transportation left for Belgrade first. It was after ten in the morning. A bus was scheduled to leave in fifteen minutes. He bought a one-way ticket and climbed aboard the waiting bus.

The bus trip to Belgrade took less than one hour. They made stops along the way at Batajinica and Zemun before arriving in Belgrade. The bus passed by the *T* in the road where he and Karol helped rescue the F-117 pilot. He was surprised to see just how close to the main highway they were. The bus pulled into the downtown Belgrade bus terminal at 11:10 AM.

Chapter 41
VARNA, SERBIA

It was now 11:00 A.M., and Nick and Naomi were about to leave to carry out their escape plan, when Nick heard a car approach the safe house and screech to a stop. Nick looked out from the window and saw a police car. Two plainclothes police officers got out holding AK-47s.

"Oh shit! Naomi, get our things! We'll have to go out the window! They're after us!"

Naomi grabbed their backpacks, weapons, and cell phones as Nick looked out the window at the parked police car below. Naomi thought to herself, *Karol might be alive*. If that was the case, she couldn't imagine the things they were doing to her.

Nick thought that if they followed standard procedures, they would leave the keys in the ignition. Then he told Naomi, "Our only chance is to use the police car as a getaway vehicle. We've only got one shot. We'll have to do it while they're inside. Jump!"

Nick and Naomi jumped from the second story window and landed on the pavement below. The sounds alerted the two officers who immediately reversed direction

The Balkan Network

and headed back downstairs. Nick went to the driver's side while Naomi went to the passenger side. They both climbed inside the police cruiser. As Nick had suspected, the keys were still in the ignition. He started the car, put it in gear, and floored the accelerator. The sound of screeching rubber filled the air. The two police officers were running out the front door of the inn just as Nick and Naomi were heading onto the main road.

Nick yelled, "Duck!"

The sound of automatic gunfire erupted from the rear, and the back windshield shattered as Naomi ducked below the dashboard. The two men started running after the car. More bullets riddled the car as Nick tried to swerve to avoid the burst. Naomi returned fire out the back windshield with her AK-74 flinging spent cartridges everywhere, still thinking about Karol's fate. Nick continued to accelerate as the two men behind them disappeared in the distance.

Naomi said, "We've got to get across the Sava River. NATO bombers have taken out both bridges at Sabac. We'll have to continue toward Sremska Mitrovica. There's one bridge still standing. It's our only chance by car."

"Just tell me which way I need to go. We don't have a map, so you'll have to read the road signs!" Nick glanced on the seat between them and noticed another AK-47. A big smile appeared on his face, and then he started to laugh.

Naomi shouted, "What's so funny? We just got our asses shot up trying to escape!"

"All throughout this mission, I've been saying that I wish I had a full-size AK-47. Well one just appeared."

"Pay attention to the road, stupid! This is no time for jokes. Sooner or later the two cops are going to be calling for reinforcements. We're an easy target with the back windshield gone."

They reached main highway E75 and turned left toward Sabac. They had to go the opposite direction for a few kilometers before they could pick up the secondary road toward Glusci and Sremska Mitrovica.

"We need to stay away from the main city. They'll be expecting us to try to cross the river there," said Naomi. She turned around and looked out the back windshield to see if anyone was following them. So far, the area was clear, just regular vehicular traffic traveling on the road. As she was turning around, she saw blood on the seat between her and Nick.

"Where did this blood come from?"

Nick turned to Naomi, "I think I have a little scratch here," as he pointed to his left side.

"Let me see." Nick's left side was dark with blood. "That's no little scratch, you've been hit!"

Naomi looked frantically around the car for a first aid kit, but there was none.

"Quit jumping around the car like a monkey! I'm trying to concentrate on the road!"

"You idiot, I'm trying to find a first aid kit. If we don't stop that bleeding, you're going to bleed to death!"

"I feel fine. Like I told you, it's just a little scratch."

"Pull the car over! There might be something in the trunk."

"Are you nuts? I'm not stopping this car!"

"If you don't stop this fucking car right now, I'm going to put a bullet in your other side!" Naomi took out her pistol, pointed it at Nick's side, and shouted, "Now pull this fucking car over—now!"

Nick knew he lost the argument with Naomi. He was starting to get light-headed as he slowed the car to a stop.

The Balkan Network

Naomi opened her door, ran to the back, and opened the trunk. Inside, she found a first aid kit, another AK-47, and several rounds of ammunition. She took everything from the trunk and got back in the front seat and said, "Drive faster until we can find a better place to pull off the road."

Nick drove another five miles before he saw a group of trees and pulled over to a stop. Naomi got out, came over to the driver's side. Nick was bleeding profusely now. She took off his jacket and tore his shirt. She could see a round went through his flesh. Luckily, the bullet did not make its way into his abdomen, but it was still a bad wound. She bandaged him up as best she could.

"This will have to do until I can get you inside Croatia. Can you still drive?" Nick nodded his head and said, "I think so."

Chapter 42
NORTH OF THE DANUBE RIVER

Mike and Karen waited until 11:00 AM before they left the Hotel Jet. They rode double on one bike and took the road from Temerin toward Despotovo. There they could cross the Mali Canal to the east of Despotovo and travel off-road from that point on to the Danube River and Croatia. Their escape route was risky because it took them around the dummy tanks and SAM sites which were heavily bombed every night. The area would be teaming with JNA forces. Their only hope was that the JNA would decide to stay indoors because NATO aircraft were still patrolling the skies above.

"Mike, do you think Karol's alive?"

"It's hard to say. Dan didn't give us a lot of information on her wounds. She could still be alive. I'd be doing the same thing Dan's doing if it were you."

"Yes, I know that."

As Mike and Karen approached the Mali Kanal, they noticed a roadblock set up by three paramilitary men. They were stopping every motorist crossing the canal near

The Balkan Network

Despotovo. Mike slowed down as they passed several cars that stopped waiting to clear the roadblock.

"Can we get off the road?" asked Karen.

"It's too late, they've already spotted us. There was a bend in the road. If I had seen them earlier, I could have gotten off. They obviously knew about the blind spot."

"Remember what Dan said: we could be compromised. In fact, they may be looking for us."

As they got closer, Karen remembered her tactical exercise back at Quantico, which seemed like eons ago. She wasn't going to get stuck in the same position as Karol. Karen knew Mike would have both hands on the handlebars and he was not in a position to do anything. She had both her hands free, and she had her Makarov fully loaded with silencer attached.

"I can take them all out if you can get a little closer."

"What are you talking about?"

"You know we've got no choice. You're driving, but I'm back here doing nothing. Remember our rules of engagement? We're enemy combatants."

"As usual, you're right. Let me get closer. The closer we get, the less useful their weapons. You'll have to make a clean shot to the head. If you hit them anywhere else they'll be able to return fire."

"I know, just say *now* when you think we're close enough, and I'll start firing."

Mike cut in and out of several vehicles then finally reached the front of the line. They were five feet from the three paramilitary men. They were large and strong, probably militia ready for a firefight. They had their weapons pointed at Mike and Karen with their hands facing them signaling to stop. Karen responded immediately at Mike's signal. She pulled out her pistol from inside her jacket and fired all twelve rounds at close range. The three men crumbled headfirst to the ground. Mike accelerated past the fallen men and raced across the canal toward Despotovo.

Chapter 43
THE HUNT

Dan was at the terminal in downtown Belgrade. He'd been here several times traveling with his family. He walked out from the bus terminal, turned left, and walked a block and a half to the post office. He crossed the street and entered the lobby of Hotel Posta. *This would do*, he thought. The hotel was perfect, basic necessities and no credit cards accepted. "Cash only," the sign on the hotel door window read. Dan checked in and paid the clerk cash. He told the old man at the front desk that he would only need a room for a couple of nights; he was on his way to Romania, but the train service was unpredictable with the war going on.

The motel clerk said, "You could be here longer than a couple of days if you're trying to get to Bucharest. Sometimes the train leaves on schedule, other times the train never arrives from Vrsac. NATO aircraft are targeting the railway bridges, but so far, they have not been able to destroy them. You're better off taking the bus. The buses leave on schedule for the most part."

"Thanks for the advice. I'll take the bus then." Dan took his room keys and walked up the two flights of stairs.

The room had a single twin bed, nightstand, and small bathroom. He took off his jacket and turned on his cell phone. He could see on the caller ID that Mattingly had been trying to contact him. A few seconds later, Hal called.

"Dan, are you all right?" There was a break in the background of the transmission.

Dan knew the NSA was cross-referencing his GPS location with the cell phone. Then the line was clear, and Dan said, "Yes, sir, I'm all right."

"Dan, you're heading in the wrong direction. You should be near the Croatian border by now, what's wrong?"

"I'm not leaving until I find her."

"Don't be a fool, son. You can't do anything about her by yourself."

"Yes, I can do something. I'm going after Belic. If I find Belic, I find Karol."

"I know what you're feeling now, Dan, truly I do. I went through the same thing myself fifty-five years ago."

"Yah, but this time I'm not in London like you were. Before he died, Josef told me the whole story about Penelope Walsh. He regretted leaving her behind until he went to his grave. I'm only a few miles away from Karol. I'm not making the same mistake he made. I *can* do something about it."

"It's too risky, Dan. Belic is a dangerous man. He's a professional. He's been doing this line of work since before you were born."

"I've got to try even if it means getting killed. It's a risk I'm willing to take. You said from the beginning there was the possibility of getting killed on this mission."

"Dan, wait; we'll send in our own team after Belic."

Dan hung up the phone and went into the bathroom. He took out his shaving kit, disassembled the razor blade, and went to the sink. He raised the hair from behind his head and felt for the GPS transmitter implanted under his scalp.

On the other end of the line in Washington, Undersecretary of Defense Harold Mattingly closed his eyes and let out a sigh. He knew Dan was right. If he'd been in Yugoslavia in 1944 and not in London, he would've gone after Penelope as well. He pressed another number on his cell phone, and NSA spy satellites rerouted the call. After several rings, someone answered the phone.

"I've been anxiously awaiting your call. What did you find out?"

"I just got off the phone with him—luckily he's still alive. You were right all along. He *is* in Belgrade. He's going after her. We've talked about this possible scenario before. You know what to do."

"I'll take over from here and bring him in." Yuri Pavol hung up the phone with Harold Mattingly.

Dan used his fingers to feel for the device then took the small blade from his razor and began to slice the skin and hair away from the transmitter for its removal. He cleaned and dried the device then came back into the bedroom and opened the small nightstand. He found what he was looking for. He placed the device in the envelope and sealed it. Then he wrote an address on the envelope he remembered from his childhood. His aunt still lived in Podgorica, Montenegro. He went downstairs and bought a first-class stamp from the hotel clerk and attached it to the envelope. He walked across the street and placed the letter in a mailbox at the post office. He walked past the post office and across the train tracks to the Danube River. He got as close to the river as he could, with the damage from NATO aircraft, then stopped a few feet from the water's edge. He reached into his pocket and took out his cell phone. Dan thought for a second about throwing the phone into the river, but decided not to because the NSA could not track the location unless a call was made. He elected to keep the phone in case he had to alert friendly forces of his location. He put the cell phone back into his pocket and walked back to the hotel.

Chapter 44
STREMSKA MITROVICA, SERBIA

Nick was still losing a lot of blood. The squad car was approaching the city limits of Sremska Mitrovica when Naomi shouted, "How could I have been so stupid! We have a police radio!" She turned up the volume on the radio and started listening to the chatter. She concentrated on the transmissions then said to Nick, "Turn around and go back. They've got the entrance to the whole city blocked off!"

The Serbs made a crucial mistake. They assumed the Americans could not speak the language and were transmitting their exact moves and locations over the radio in clear communications. Naomi's Serbo-Croatian was better than the police officers chasing after them, and she was monitoring all transmissions from pursuing police and dispatchers. Because of the many farm roads, it was impossible for the police to block all roads into the city.

"They've got all roads blocked except the unmarked farm road near Glusci. We can take that road and cut across to the road along the Sava. There's a bridge still standing on that road. They're not expecting us to cross there."

Nick said, "We've got to switch cars. The first car we see coming at us, we'll carjack."

No sooner than Nick said this, a small Yugo came into view with a young couple driving. Nick swerved and blocked both sides of the road. He and Naomi got out from the police cruiser with their weapons drawn. Naomi held her Makarov pistol at the driver and shouted in Serbian, "Get out of the fucking car!"

The young couple, seeing fire in her eyes and ice in her veins, did as she told them.

"You can take the cruiser, but we need your ride," she told them. The couple could see the blood dripping from Nick's side and knew they were serious. Nick was now feeling weak because of the loss of blood and said, "I don't think I can drive any longer. You'll have to take over from here."

They got in the Yugo and headed toward the Sava River. Naomi said, "I wish we had the police radio. I could still monitor the transmissions." They approached the Sava River and, as expected, found the crossing unattended. Naomi floored the accelerator, and the Yugo sped across the bridge heading into Sremska Mitrovica.

"We're safe now. The police will still be looking for the cruiser. My guess is the young couple will get held up and questioned for some time before they realize they have the wrong people and see the blood on the floor. Nick, how are you feeling?"

"Tired, I need some rest and water."

"Don't fall asleep. It's from the loss of blood. You've got to stay awake a little longer."

She reached over and slapped him on the cheek.

"My side is starting to hurt now."

"That's a good thing. The pain will help you stay awake. The Croatian border is sixteen miles away. I can make it to the border crossing near the minefields at Bapska. From there we can get to the winery." Naomi could see more police and military vehicles moving in the opposite direction toward Sremska Mitrovica. She decided to get off highway E70 and head for the Fruska Gora hills. She could still make it to the safe area on that highway.

"Nick! Stay awake. I need you to stay awake!" Naomi knew Nick was continuing to lose a lot of blood. She didn't know how much longer before he bled to death. She had to take a chance and cut straight across the farm fields instead of using the main roads. She found another secondary road and turned left toward the Croatian border. The area was starting to look familiar. She could see the vineyards up ahead.

"Nick, we're almost there."

This area was flat, and the only thing that distinguished the border was the overgrown vineyards littered with mines. She found the area she was looking for and stopped the car.

"Nick, we're here. Can you get out of the car?"

Nick only moaned and turned over in the front seat.

"Don't quit on me now! Get out of this fucking car, you little twerp!"

Nick tried his best but couldn't.

Naomi shouted, "You've got to get out and walk!" Naomi opened the door for Nick and could see the pool of blood on the floor. She knew he was in trouble. She took his arm and placed it around her neck then heaved him to his feet. She tried to walk him across the border, but he fell every other step, and she had to get him back to his feet. She looked across the vineyard and the minefields and said, "I think I remember the safe route through the minefields, but I'll have to carry you." She bent over and placed his arm around her then lifted Nick on her back like a fireman. She couldn't let him walk by himself through the minefield.

"I'm going to have to carry you across, so don't move, and for God's sake don't die on me now that we're this close!"

Slowly they made their way through the minefields. The afternoon sky was overcast and the light was not as bright as it could have been. Naomi struggled and fell several times along the way. Each time they fell she closed her eyes waiting for a mine to explode, but nothing happened. She kept going with Nick on her shoulders, each step a little closer to freedom, each step carefully placed to avoid the mines. Military discipline and obedience kicked in now as she struggled with each step. She could now see the warehouse and barn of the Bapska winery and knew they were just a few steps away to safety and freedom. Nick could see the winery too and moaned, "I can make it from here. Just drop me here, and I'll walk."

"You stupid jerk, you're in no condition to walk. You think I carried you this far so you can step on a mine and blow us all up to pieces."

They reached the warehouse and Naomi dropped Nick to the ground. She opened the large warehouse doors and took a peek inside. It was dark and quiet. The only thing inside was the EU truck they left behind. Everything seemed to be in place just as they left it almost two months ago. She bent down and got Nick to his feet and walked him into the warehouse and closed the doors behind them. Once inside, their eyes still not adjusted to the darkness, Naomi heard the distinct sounds of rifle bolts as lights came on in the warehouse. Standing at the top of the stairs, were paramilitary soldiers wearing black ski masks

The Balkan Network

and holding AK-47s. Then a voice said in perfect French, "So, young lady. It looks like you're not who you said you were after all. Turn around slowly and place your hands behind your head."

Naomi placed her hands behind her head and turned around slowly and saw inspector Sergi Boraviko standing with an AK-47 pointed at her head.

"I see your French is as good as your German."

Naomi fell to her knees and began sobbing.

Chapter 45
THE WAIT

Mike and Karen were riding on their motorcycle southwest toward Backa Palanka. They had gone off-road several times to avoid more roadblocks and JNA forces. Despite the NATO fighters patrolling the skies above, the Serbs deployed forces throughout the area. They were obviously fully aware that two Americans were on the loose in the area who just killed three men.

Mike said to Karen, "You did well back there. Not many women could have done what you just did. I'm proud of you. Now, how about contacting Wizard and seeing if you can get any word on the status of the rescue helicopter?"

Karen thought about the four men back at Ilok and how they almost raped and killed her. These three men were no different. Had they been given the opportunity they'd have done the same thing. She made a direct call to Wizard using the emergency number Karol had given them. After several tries, a radio operator answered the phone.

"This is Wizard 86. Can we help you?"

"This is Dodger 24. We are executing escape plan Alpha, heading southwest toward the pickup point. Can you give us an update on the extraction?"

"Dodger 24, standby we'll check."

Mike had to get off the main road again because he could see more JNA forces ahead. He turned right and headed toward the farm fields. Karen was still on hold with the JSTARS. They were probably cross-checking their position and identities. The radio operator came back with, "Dodger 24, be advised, your pickup time is delayed two hours. Can you hold off until then?"

"I guess we don't have any choice. We'll get as close to the pickup point as we can and wait."

"We copy two-four. We'll contact you and authenticate when choppers are inbound."

"Thanks, we'll be standing by." Then she secured the call from the JSTARS.

"They want us to hold out for two hours, can we do it?"

Mike looked over the surrounding area then saw several haystacks in a farm field ahead and said, "Perfect."

Chapter 46
PREACHER

Sergi Boraviko lowered his AK-47 and ordered his men down from upstairs. Two medics attended to Nick, placed him on a stretcher then moved him to another room. Behind Boraviko, another figure moved forward from the shadows. The man was about six-foot four, heavily built, and wearing a dark overcoat. He approached Boraviko and spoke in English.

"This is Staff Sergeant Naomi Markof, United States Air Force. She's the one I told you about. She survived the detonation of the IED. You met her several weeks ago here at the winery."

Sergi nodded his head in acknowledgement, moved closer to Naomi and said in a soothing, reassuring voice in English, "You can get up now, young lady. We're not going to hurt you."

Naomi got up slowly from her knees and looked up. She could see inspector Boraviko in black military style fatigues standing next to the man that appeared from the shadows.

The man in the shadows replied, "Sergeant Markof, I

The Balkan Network

am known as Yuri Pavol in this country. That, of course, is not my real name, but I'm working with inspector Boraviko. My real name is Aleksandar Radivich, codename *Preacher*, otherwise known to you as Dan's father. I'm the organizer for the entire Balkan Network. I've been monitoring the network from Tuzla Air Base. Inspector Boraviko is organizer for our Croatian circuit."

* * *

IT WAS past 4:00 P.M. when Dan walked the four blocks to Bulevar Kralja Aleksandar. The streets of Belgrade seemed normal despite the night bombing attacks by NATO aircraft. Taxis were operating, stores and restaurants were open, and people were on the streets going about their business unaffected by the air campaign that had being going on for over a month. He found the address he was looking for: number 23 Kralja Aleksandar. It was a five-story office building located near St. Tasmajdan Park. Dan recalled that Josef told him that Belic did not have a large office. It was just a small establishment, probably only two employees. Dan walked up to the building and read the Cyrillic lettering on the directory. The Overland Airfreight company was located on the fifth-floor suite 510. He entered the building and walked the five flights of stairs. Suite 510 was located next to the stairway entrance. The office complex was in true communist style, basic with no décor, walls painted in a light cement-colored gray. Dan could see in the light beneath the door that someone was still in the office. It was just after 4:15 P.M., and most people were finishing the day's business and making their way to their homes in preparation for tonight's NATO bombings. Dan went back to the stairway and listened for someone to exit Belic's office.

By 4:30 P.M., Dan heard someone exit Belic's office and could hear the sound of keys locking the door. Dan gave the figure a few minutes as he locked the door and headed to the elevator. Dan concluded that Belic would habitually take the elevator down to the first floor. He was right. Belic walked away in the opposite direction. Dan opened the door of the stairway and got a look at the man who was responsible for Karol's fate. He was in his late sixties, stocky build, wearing a Soviet-style gray suit. Dan followed Belic out of the building and shadowed him to the Trandafilovic Restaurant. He waited outside for Belic to finish his dinner. When he finished, Dan followed him out of the restaurant. Belic was walking to the northeast and started picking up the pace, obviously anxious to get home before the first NATO bombs fell. His apartment was in a modest district of Belgrade overlooking a cemetery. Dan watched him enter his apartment. The building was a ten-story apartment complex. Dan elected not to follow him inside. Instead, he looked at the directory located on the outside of the complex. It was too simple: Milan Belic lived in apartment 306.

Chapter 47
NEW PLANS

Inspector Boraviko helped Naomi to her feet. "Don't be afraid, Naomi. You're safe now. The Croatian circuit has been working out of the winery since the start of the war. We've been monitoring your situation in case any members of the network needed to use the escape route."

Naomi, having difficulty believing the words she heard, got to her feet and said, "Can you help Nick? He's lost a lot of blood."

"My medics are working on him now. There is a NATO helicopter scheduled to land and pick you up within the hour. If he's safe for travel, he'll be on that helicopter."

"Thank you, Inspector."

Aleksandar Radivich spoke next. "Young lady, how did you find your way across the border? You surprised us as you came into the winery from that direction. That whole section is covered with land mines."

"We reconnoitered the area before we left for Serbia. It took Nick and me several days to find a safe passage."

Sergi said, "That was a brave thing you did. I doubt

some of my men could have pulled off the same feat. Is it a safe route all the way across into Serbia?"

"It's about a mile of minefields, but once you're through the area, you're fewer than one hundred yards to a road that leads directly to Kukujevci."

One of the medics came up to Sergi and whispered something in his ear.

"I have good news for you, Naomi. Your partner's wounds are no longer life threatening, we've stopped the bleeding. He is out of danger now; however, he has lost a lot of blood, and we have him on an IV. Also, there's a single NATO Pave Hawk helicopter en route. He should be here in fifteen minutes. Your partner will be on that aircraft."

Aleksandar Radivich put his arm around Naomi's shoulder and said, "Come, take a seat, have some water."

Naomi sat down on a stool and gulped down s bottle of water.

Radivich now spoke in Serbo-Croatian. "Naomi, there's been a change in plans. I want you to listen to me carefully. We don't have time to explain everything; it's very complex." Radivich grabbed a crate and sat next to Naomi. "I've been working with the Balkan Network since the beginning. Dan doesn't know this. Secretary Mattingly and I kept it from him for fear he might jeopardize the security of the entire network. I also received word from my sources inside Serbia that the naval officer on your team is still alive. She's held captive at Jazak Monastery. It's practically a fortress itself. The Gestapo used it as a prison during World War II. The naval officer is being held by a notorious warlord named Vecili Vorchek. He's the same man who ambushed and murdered twelve of Sergi's fellow policemen back in 1991. He's nothing more than a well-financed terrorist. The Croatian government has been trying to apprehend him for several years, but he has eluded them so far."

"What about Dan, any word on him?" asked Naomi.

"You will not be going on the helicopter with your partner. We need you to escort us across the frontier. Dan is trying to rescue the naval officer by himself. He doesn't know what we know. He's in jeopardy of being killed unless you help us. The route across the minefields is the quickest way into Serbia and Jazak Monastery."

Naomi took a deep breath, the information too overwhelming to process.

Sergi knelt down, faced Naomi, and said, "Vorchek is a bad man. He kills for sport and pleasure. He will think nothing about killing an American military officer. To him, there is no such thing as the Geneva Convention. He's not a member of the Yugoslav armed forces, so he can do as he pleases. He might even cut her head off and display it as a trophy. He's the same man that sent terrorist insurgents across the border. Four of those men tried to rape and torture the other female of your circuit. Remember, I conducted the investigation myself. I have a team of special forces ready to cross the border to try and rescue both Commander Koskov and Major Radivich, but we can't unless you show us the way."

Naomi's thoughts went out again to Karol and Dan. She recalled how Dan called her and told her about Karol getting shot; possibly tortured and he was staying behind to find her. She would never be able to live with herself if she didn't go with Sergi and his plan.

"All right, Inspector, I can do it. I can get you across the border. When do we leave?"

"The helicopter should be here in ten minutes. We'll leave as soon as the helicopter is airborne. We want to be across the border before dark."

Aleksandar Radivich looked at Sergi and said, "Get your men ready to move out. We don't have a moment to spare if we're to pull this off."

He then turned to Naomi and asked, "Can we get the EU truck through the minefields?"

Naomi nodded her head. "Yes, I believe we can. We tried to find an area where we could drive a truck or small vehicle through, but you'll have to follow me every step of the way."

Chapter 48
EXTRACTION

The USAF MH-60G Pave Hawk helicopter touched down in the open field just outside the Bapska warehouse. Two USAF pararescue men jumped from the chopper to meet Nick and get him onboard. Once he was safely aboard, the Pave Hawk lifted off the ground and headed for Tuzla Air Base. As the helicopter vanished in the distance, Aleksandar Radivich took out his cell phone and called Hal Mattingly.

"The chopper is airborne with the Army corporal onboard. They should be in Tuzla in twenty minutes. We're on our way across the border now."

Mattingly replied, "Good. When he gets to Tuzla, I'll have the chopper turn around and go after the other two."

Mike and Karen found the haystack to be a perfect hiding place. The haystacks looked like something out of a children's storybook. Karen called Wizard to get an update on the extraction.

"Wizard 86, this is Dodger 24, can you give us an update?"

A voice came back over Karen's cell phone and said in

a plain voice, "The rescue helicopter had to make a stop in Croatia to pick up one of your wounded team members. That's the reason for the delay. When the chopper is safely back at base, it will be returning for your extraction. They'll wait for the cover of darkness because they're going in single-ship. Three MH-53s were destroyed in an air strike earlier today."

"Thanks for the update. We'll be waiting for them."

Karen told Mike about the chopper making a stop in Croatia to pick up a wounded team member and the air strike on the base.

"I wonder who could have been injured. It was either Naomi or Nick. They're the only two that were using the northern escape route," said Mike.

"I hope they both got out okay."

Dan returned to the Hotel Posta at 6:00 P.M. The first wave of NATO aircraft would be dropping their payloads within an hour. Dan reflected on Karol and wondered if she was alive. He regretted having never expressed his true feelings to her. If she was still alive, he couldn't imagine the things they were doing to her to get her to reveal information. His thoughts turned to rage once again. He began to plan his next move.

Darkness fell over the Serbian countryside. Mike and Karen were still hiding in the haystack, their faces now blackened with face paint and their jackets turned out to display the night camouflage and military markings, waiting for the rescue helicopter to arrive. They had not reviewed the SPINS for the day so they would have to rely on the ISOPREP information that was on file back at Aviano Air Base if SAR wanted to authenticate. They heard the sound of jet aircraft above. Mike and Karen knew the rescue helicopter would be close by. Karen looked at her cell phone and switched it to GPS tracking

The Balkan Network

mode. The small CRT screen displayed a topographical map. Their location was two miles outside Backa Palanka and 150 feet from the Danube River. The rescue helicopter would be making its approach over Bosnia and Croatia and would only enter Serbian airspace to drop down and make the pickup. Mike's cell phone beeped with a text message. A flight of two A-10s was attempting to contact him. Mike switched his cell phone to emergency radio and answered the call.

"This is Dodger 25, go ahead with your message."

"This is Sandy 51. We're providing CAP for the chopper, call sign Jolly 24 on tactical frequency. They should be overhead in five minutes. Prepare to signal so they can make the drop."

"We copy, Sandy. Tell Jolly 24 to look for my beacon."

Mike switched his cell phone to beacon. They could hear the sound of rotor blades approaching from the west. Karen said, "They're less than three minutes away, coming in low."

"Dodger 25, this is Jolly 24. Prepare to signal in five."

Mike heard the words in his headset, "Five, four, three, two, mark!" Mike turned on his signaling device. Only rescue helicopters had the equipment onboard to properly interrogate his signal.

"We have you in contact. Prepare for extraction."

Mike and Karen prepared for extraction as directed in the rescue plan from the daily SPINS. They were to approach the helicopter with both hands behind their heads then go down on both knees while the PJ approached and authenticated them. The Pave Hawk came in low just above ground level and crossed the Danube river and into Serbian airspace. The chopper landed approximately twenty yards from the haystack. Mike and Karen came out from the haystack and approached the helicopter as it touched down. Mike and Karen fell to their knees, hands behind their heads. A PJ came up to Mike and held an M-16 to his head and said, "Say your call sign and your authentication number."

"Dodger 25, authentication 112957."

The PJ nodded his head then asked Karen, "What's your call sign and authentication number?"

Karen replied, "I'm Dodger 24, authentication 1281."

The PJ gave a thumbs-up signal to the pilots then hoisted the two on board. Five seconds later, the chopper was crossing the Danube River safely in Croatian airspace.

Chapter 49
THE APARTMENT

It was 7:30 P.M. in Belgrade when Dan heard the air raid sirens go off. He grabbed the small bag with explosive charges and his Makarov pistol and walked the five blocks to Belic's apartment. He entered the garage parking lot located beneath the apartment complex and used the stairs to access the building's rooftop. "Any spot will do," he said to himself. He selected an air-conditioning unit toward the middle of the building and placed the plastic explosive charge next to it. He attached the detonator inside the explosive and armed the remote control. The explosive was set to go off on his command, using the small remote-control unit. He walked back to the stairway and waited. He could hear the muffled sounds of NATO bombs exploding in the distance. He had to wait until one landed closer to the city limits. He knew the bridges were a constant target in the city and sooner or later one would drop. At 8:00 PM, Dan heard an explosion near the Dunav railway station. It was now or never. He pressed the remote, and the explosive charge went off, shaking the building. This was exactly what Dan was looking for. He went to the fire alarm and pulled it. The alarm sounded and people started to open the doors to their apartments. The fire department would be there in a few minutes. He went to the third floor and waited for the fire escape door to open. Within minutes, people were filing into the stairway to evacuate. Dan stayed in the stairway, watching through the open doorway as people came by him. A figure walked out from apartment 306; it was Belic. He glanced up and down the hallway watching people exit through the fire escape. He closed and locked his door and walked to the exit, holding a briefcase in his right hand. Dan continued down the stairway with the rest of the people but exited on the first floor instead of ground level. He raced to the opposite end of the building and used the fire escape exit to go back up to the third floor. Once there, Dan went to apartment 306. More and more people were exiting the building now. Dan reached into his pocket, pulled out a lock pick, and started to work on the keyhole. Within a few seconds, the lock opened, and Dan was inside Belic's apartment.

It was modest, to say the least. There was a small living room with a small couch and television, small kitchen, and a single bedroom with bathroom. Dan slowly entered the darkened apartment. He used a flashlight to guide his way. He didn't have much time. Soon the fire department would declare the building safe, and residents would start returning to their apartments. He entered the kitchen and noticed a laptop computer on the kitchen table. He turned on the computer but the system was password protected. There was a simple solution: Karol had taught him how to bypass the user lock codes on any personal computer. Within seconds, Dan was on Belic's personal desktop page. Nothing seemed out of the ordinary, mostly office documents and shipping expense records. He decided to check

The Balkan Network

the Internet browser. He could not log on for some reason. Belic was not using a dial-up service, but he was logging on somehow. He tried to find a cable or other high-speed device, but there was nothing like that in the kitchen. He checked the living room and still no high-speed outlet was in his apartment. Dan knew his time was limited. He went back to the kitchen and searched for a junk drawer. Every bachelor had one, and he was no exception. He opened all the drawers and found what he was looking for: a junk drawer that kept pencils, pens, stables, paper clips, bottle openers, and yes, computer cords. He saw a cord that he recognized immediately. It was the same computer cord Hal Mattingly gave to every member of his circuit to connect their personal cell phones to access the secure sat-com data link. Dan took out his cell phone. If he turned it on and dialed his access number, the NSA would surely be tracking him. He connected his cell phone to Belic's computer and dialed the local Serbian number to access the data link. To no surprise, Belic's Internet connection was established, and a message appeared in English on the screen: "U.S. Department of Defense Web Site. Secure Sat-Com Data Link Established." Belic's computer was programmed to access DOD secure Web sites. How he was able to do this remained a mystery but explained everything. Karol was right, there was a mole in the system and Belic was the criminal. But why would a twenty-five year CIA operative commit such an act of treason? Dan didn't have time to investigate further. He found a box of blank CDs in Belic's junk drawer and copied all the files onto the disks. He was about to turn off the system when he noticed a link he hadn't seen before: Secure Data Transfers. Dan opened the file and saw thousands of text files, most with cryptic information written in Cyrillic. Again, he didn't have time to go through them, but he did recognize one word written in Cyrillic: Prospector. Dan copied these files and then turned off the computer and his cell phone. He was online for less than five minutes, but it was enough time for the NSA to trace the call's location. Dan still didn't see anything in Belic's kitchen or on his computer that would lead him to Karol. He went into the bedroom. Moving in semidarkness, he turned on the light. On the nightstand, something caught his attention. To the right of the lamppost was a cell phone that looked exactly like the one Dan had. But this phone did not have a multifunction mode; it was strictly a cell phone. He picked it up from the charger and hit the call log icon. He spotted a telephone number he immediately recognized. It was the same number Karol had showed him that belonged to someone in the Serbian Defense Ministry. He switched off the device and placed it back on the charger. Now all he had to do was wait for Belic to return. He returned to the kitchen. Behind the small refrigerator was an electrical panel. He opened the door and shut off the power to Belic's apartment. Everything went dark and quiet. He closed the panel door. As he walked out of the kitchen, he noticed something he hadn't noticed before. On the sink was a bottle of scotch whiskey. It all fell into place as Dan recalled the strange request from Josef onboard the train not to drink. Perhaps Josef knew all along that there would be a mole in the system. Dan took out his night vision goggles and the 9 mm with silencer and sat on the couch with the bottle of scotch and started to drink.

Chapter 50
TUZLA, BOSNIA-HERZEGOVINA

The trip back to Tuzla Air Base took over thirty minutes. Aboard the chopper a combat medic attended to Mike and Karen. Both were in good shape except they were in need of water, so the medic gave each of them a bottle. The MH-60G Pave Hawk helicopter touched down at 6:00 P.M. As the helicopter made its approach to the airfield, Mike and Karen noticed the damage from the Serbian air strike and realized the significance of the delay in their rescue. All around the flight line were the remains of three burned helicopters and two C-130s still smoldering. When the Pave Hawk touched down and came to a stop, the PJs opened the door, and a man approached the chopper from the tarmac. He was dressed in an RAF flight suit and came up to the helicopter and addressed Mike and Karen,

"Sergeants Crisko and Karl?" My name is Squadron Leader Tony Cannes. I'm with the Tuzla Circuit of the Balkan Network. Welcome to Tuzla Air Base, or what's left of it. Come with me to Base Operations. We need to debrief you and send you off to the infirmary."

Mike and Karen followed Cannes to Base Operations

and entered a secure room next to the weather station. Inside, Squadron Leader Cannes had them sit at a conference table.

Cannes said, "I'm sorry for the delay in your pickup, but as you can see, we came under attack this morning, and we had to pick up one of your colleagues who sustained injuries during the escape. I am happy to report to you that Specialist Belleu is recovering in the infirmary and will be flown to Germany as soon as we can get an air evac. You'll have a chance to talk with him once we're done debriefing."

Karen said, "What about the other person on our team? Was she able to get out as well?"

"Did you say *she*? I was not aware there was another person. We got the tasking orders directly from Washington, and we were only told to pick up one survivor, the Army specialist."

Mike and Karen looked at each other and immediately thought of Naomi.

Mike said, "Do you think she made it out on her own without Nick?"

Karen thought for a moment, "It's hard to say. Somehow, I think Naomi can look after herself. She usually gets what she wants. She's had no trouble doing that on this entire mission. She might even be on her way back to Serbia to try to find Dan. You know, both women were in love with him. Maybe Nick can give us more information on her fate."

* * *

DAN WAITED in Belic's apartment for over an hour when he heard voices coming down the hallway outside. The fire department obviously had declared the apartment safe and

The Balkan Network

allowed people to return. Dan could hear keys entering the lock and the door opened slowly. The light from the hallway briefly entered the room and temporarily blinded Dan through his goggles. Belic entered holding a briefcase in his right hand and closed the door. He went to the light switch to turn it on, but nothing happened.

Dan said to Belic in Serbo-Croatian, "The lights don't work."

Belic froze in his tracks, then Dan said in English, "Turn around slowly and face me."

Belic turned and faced Dan in the darkness, still holding his briefcase.

"So, you understand English. Then let me make this simple. Where is Commander Koskov?"

"I don't understand you or know what you're talking about," Belic replied in Serbo-Croatian.

Dan fired one shot from the Makarov and hit Belic in his clenched fist. He immediately grimaced in pain as the bullet took off the top of his knuckles and dropped the briefcase. Dan continued to speak in English, "You were very foolish in leaving all your toys here. I found everything."

Belic, holding his right hand in pain, spoke in broken English, "If you want money, I have some in my briefcase. I can give it to you, and you can leave before the authorities get here."

"Don't play games with me, Belic. I was told how clever you are. If you want to live, just tell me where Commander Koskov is!"

Belic went to his knees in pain. Dan got up and walked toward him. Dan kicked the briefcase away from him and picked it up. He opened the briefcase, took out the loaded Beretta and emptied the magazine.

"You know damn well who I am. I'm all over your

computer. You double-crossed our network, the U.S. Government, and NATO. Now, one of my officers could be dead because of you. I'm going to count to three. Just tell me where Commander Koskov is. If you don't tell me where she is on the count of three, I'll shoot both of your knees out, and you'll be crippled for life. Then I'll leave and take all the files I downloaded from your computer and kindly hand them over to the Russians since you have the names of all their GRU agents working in Eastern Europe. The choice is yours."

The thought of dealing with the Russians obviously got through, and Belic knew at this point Dan wasn't joking. He immediately replied in good English, "I'm sure we can come to some sort of an agreement, Major."

"One."

"You'll be killed the moment you leave here."

"Two."

"I have the entire Yugoslav Army looking for you."

"Three." Dan fired one round toward Belic's knees hitting the floor, and he went down on all fours grabbing his right hand in pain. "I'm not messing with you, Belic. I don't care if I kill you or if someone kills me. My only concern is Commander Koskov and her fate. I don't care if I die trying to find out. Now tell me where she is?"

"I can't tell you. I can only show you the way. But, in return, you have to give me all the files you downloaded."

Dan reached into his pocket, pulled out the CDs, and said, "Here's the files. Show me the way and they're yours."

"I'll have to drive you there. It's an hour drive outside town, but we have to wait until the air raid sirens go off. The local authorities will not be letting vehicles on the road during an attack. I have a car in the garage. We can leave as soon as we get the all-clear sign."

"Good. Now that we have an agreement, we'll wait." Dan, still operating in darkness, got Belic up off the floor and tied a towel around his wounded hand. Then he bound his hands behind his back with a set of flex cuffs and seated him on the couch.

"That was clever of you, Major, to turn the power off and use night vision equipment. However, sooner or later, my eyes will adjust to the light."

"I'm impressed; you even got my rank correct. I was only recently promoted to Major, and that was a temporary promotion known only within the DIA. So, tell me, Milan, how long have you been selling information to the highest bidder?"

Chapter 51
FRUSKA GORA, SERBIA

Sergi Boraviko, his team of twelve Croatian Special Forces, and Aleksandar Radivich loaded onto the EU truck. Naomi walked in front, retracing her footsteps across the minefield. The process was slow as darkness fell over the countryside.

"How much further?" yelled Sergi.

"I don't know, maybe another kilometer at the most." Naomi could see the abandoned Yugo a few feet ahead but couldn't remember how she got to her location from the Yugo. Only a few feet remained of the minefield. "I can't remember how we came over to here. This is where I had to carry Nick. He fell a few times, and I had to get him up. I wasn't paying much attention to the ground here."

Aleksandar Radivich said, "Just take your time, Naomi. We don't want to rush you. It will come to you, just be patient." Aleksandar was right, Naomi saw the blood on the ground from Nick's wounds.

"I think I found it! Right this way!" Naomi thought that Nick had provided something useful after all. The EU truck was now safely across the minefields and into Serbia.

The Balkan Network

Sergi yelled to Naomi, "Get in the back of the truck now."

Naomi climbed aboard, and they headed for the Fruska Gora hills. Sergi motioned to some of his men to take the Yugo, "We might be able to use another car as well as the weapons." Looking up at Naomi, he asked, "How much fuel is in the tank?"

"I'm not sure, but I think there was at least a half of a tank when I left it."

Aleksandar Radivich called Hal Mattingly on his cell phone. "We crossed the border, and we're on our way. We're using two vehicles, the EU truck and a small Yugo. Get a fix on our location and inform the JSTARS. You should still be getting a readout from mine and Sergeant Markof's GPS location. We don't want NATO aircraft to mistake us for a target of opportunity."

Mattingly replied on his cell phone, "I'll cut the tasking orders directly with NATO Headquarters. Your team will have fighter CAP for the entire operation. Good luck, Yuri," then he secured the cell phone connection.

* * *

DAN WAITED in Belic's apartment for over an hour. NATO aircraft would be returning to base now, and he felt there would be no further air strikes for the night. He turned to Belic and said, "This is long enough. It's time we leave. You'll live with your injuries. I chose my shot with care. You'll have a little pain, but you should be able to use your other hand to drive."

Dan got Belic to his feet and tied another set of flex cuffs around his ankles. Then he searched Belic. As he suspected, Belic had several weapons hidden on him. He had a knife around his ankles, another small pistol on his thigh, and various small needles that could be use as puncture weapons hidden in his clothing.

"You must think I'm stupid if you think I'm going to drive in your car without searching you."

Dan cut the flex cuffs off Belic's legs and led him downstairs to the garage and to his car. He had a small, white, Yugoslav-made sedan. Not the best for escaping, but it would do under the circumstances. Dan said, "Is there anything you want to tell me about that's hidden in your car before I find out?"

Belic replied, "There's one in the glove box and another under the driver's seat."

"My oh my, you must be afraid someone's after you. Perhaps it is the Russians after all?" Dan suspected that Belic worried someone would be trying to kill him. They got inside the car, and Dan held the gun to Belic's side and said, "Start driving."

* * *

BORAVIKO'S TEAM was dressed in paramilitary clothing similar to the Serbs. The only thing that distinguished the Croatian commandos from the Serbian paramilitary forces was the small Croatian flag attached with Velcro on the chest of every soldier. The truck carrying the strike team used the road that followed the ridgeline of the Fruska Gora hills. They made their way slowly up the mountain ridges carrying the heavy load of men and equipment. Along the way, they passed several JNA forces patrolling the hillside. Each time they passed a group, Naomi grabbed Sergi's arm.

"Don't worry, they won't even question us. We look as if we could be Serbian paramilitary. Most of them are teenagers, young JNA conscripts with no desire to be here anyway. If we get in a firefight, it will be no match for my men."

After an hour of driving, they stopped in a wooded area outside Jazak Monastery. Aleksandar spoke to Sergi, "Get the men together so I can brief the assault."

Sergi gathered his men around the hood of the truck while Aleksandar unfolded a map and drawing of the monastery and said in Croatian.

"The latest information I have is that Commander Koskov is being held in an isolated room beneath the infirmary here," he said as he pointed to a room on the map. "The monastery is built like a fortress. The residential area surrounds the chapel. The main entrance to the monastery has one huge wooden door heavily guarded by Serb paramilitaries. The entire compound, however, is lightly guarded, perhaps three or four at the most. There's a service entrance near the kitchen. We'll enter the monastery there. Sergi, you and I, with two other men, will enter the building there. The rest of your men will take up positions on all four posts of the compound and secure the area. Vorchek will have guards posted on the perimeter. Your men will take them out and assume their positions while we enter the monastery and get Commander Koskov. Once inside, we'll make our way downstairs to the room where the naval officer is being held. At this point in time, we do not know her condition other than she's still alive. She's being guarded by two paramilitaries with two monks caring for her injuries. The guards are posted outside the door and the monks are with her inside. We'll take out the two guards then enter the room and extract Commander Koskov. When we get back to the kitchen, we should be able to get her outside and safely out of here."

"What about Vorchek and Slavo? Do we have any information on their location?" asked Sergi.

"My contacts inside the monastery informed me that during the air strikes, Vorchek and Slavo move to the northeastern section of the building and hold out in one of the dormitories there. This part of the building is the strongest since it was rebuilt after World War II. Once the air strikes are over, they move back to where Commander Koskov is being held."

Aleksandar Radivich took out a bible from his overcoat and continued, "We'll need an element of surprise so our team will dress up using the monk cassocks I provided and each will carry a bible. You'll have the hoods down so no one will recognize your faces. We'll place a loaded pistol inside the bible. Once inside, we'll use the pistols to take out the guards."

"NATO aircraft will be dropping their bombs any minute now. We move at the first sounds of an explosion," added Sergi.

Naomi spoke up and confronted Aleksandar Radivich, "Let me go with you, Mr. Radivich. Dan saved my life when I stepped on a land mine. I might be of use to you once we're inside. I can wear one of the cassocks and gain access just as easy as any of you can. I owe it to Dan and Karol. I was not kind to Karol either. I was mean to her all the time because, frankly, I was jealous that Dan cared for her more than me."

Sergi looking at Naomi and seeing this remarkable woman, said, "No, it's out of the question. It's much too dangerous. You're safer here with my men."

"I've already been in one firefight today. It's nothing I can't handle."

"She's right, Sergi, we'd better bring her. I have an idea. I'll brief you as we go along," said Aleksandar.

Chapter 52
JAZAK MONASTERY

Dan and Belic were heading outside of Belgrade on the main highway leading toward Novi Sad. NATO aircraft were patrolling the skies above, and Dan could occasionally see an explosion far off in the distance. Judging by the direction Belic was heading, Dan presumed they were heading back to the Fruska Gora region. Dan suspected all along that this was an area of intense JNA and paramilitary activity, judging by the number of SAMs and the number of NATO air strikes. He decided to take a chance and turn his cell phone on. This would enable the NSA to track his location. He reached into his pocket without Belic noticing and turned on the cell phone. He made a call to Mattingly's number using the preselected speed dial number 2. Once the connection was made, Dan turned the volume to mute and left the line open. He knew that Mattingly would be trying to talk to him, but with no contact, his next move was to trace the location. This would at least put rescue forces on alert that he was no longer in Belgrade. Dan pushed his Makarov pistol in Belic's side and said, "Keep driving."

With the sound of the first explosion less than three kilometers away, Sergi's men assumed positions on the perimeter of the monastery. The young paramilitary guards were no match for Sergi's elite commandos—they never knew what hit them.

"It's show time," said Sergi.

Sergi, Naomi, Radivich, and two other men dressed in cassocks headed toward the service entrance. Aleksandar Radivich took up the rear. Everyone except for Aleksandar had their hoods drawn over their faces. He was a familiar sight at these monasteries, and if someone recognized him, he could act like he was escorting some of the monks back inside the monastery during the air raid. They made their way into the kitchen and downstairs to the room where Karol was held.

Sergi said to the unit, "You two men stay here and guard our escape route. Radivich and I, along with Sgt. Markof, will take the doorway."

Naomi and Sergi walked in front. Radivich took up the rear as they approached the door. Immediately, two Serb guards came to attention on seeing the three. Aleksandar Radivich spoke up in Serbian, "I'm here to swap out the two monks inside with these two."

One of the guards, presumably the leader, spoke up, "I was not briefed there would be a change. I'll have to call Vorchek." He leaned down to pick up his walkie-talkie, but Sergi pulled out his pistol from his bible and fired two shots hitting each man in the forehead.

"Quickly, get our other two men down here to take up their positions while we get these two bodies inside. We don't want blood all over the pavement," said Sergi.

Aleksandar returned up the staircase to get the two men while Sergi and Naomi opened the door and dragged

The Balkan Network

the two bodies inside the small chamber. Once inside the dimly lit room, Naomi could see two monks sitting next to a stretcher. Sergi held his pistol at the monks and said, "Get down on your faces you two!"

The two monks got down on the floor and put their faces to the pavement. Aleksandar returned with the two men and placed them outside the door to stand guard. Naomi hurried to the stretcher and saw Karol laying there with her eyes barely open. She had several IVs going into her arm and was wrapped in bed sheets. Her head was wrapped in bandages covering her hair, and her face was badly beaten. Her skin was as white as the sheets. Naomi bent down and said to her in English, "Karol, it's me, Naomi. We're here to get you out. Can you understand me?"

Karol, obviously in pain from the beating and gunshot wounds, nodded her head and began to speak softly. "Is Dan here? How did you know where to find me?"

"No, ma'am, he's not. We don't know where he is. We were hoping he was being held here with you."

Karol closed her eyes and struggled with each word and said, "I was shot in the leg and hip, and I couldn't get to him. They took me away and beat me. I tried to hold out but they penetrated me with sharp instruments to give them answers."

"You'll be okay now, ma'am. We're going to get you out of here. These men will take you back to Croatia. Ma'am, I'm so sorry for treating you horribly these past few weeks; please forgive me."

"Is Dan still alive?"

Naomi pretended like she didn't understand her; she just smiled at Karol then turned to Sergi and said, "Please get her out of here."

Aleksandar and one of the other monks pulled the IVs from Karol's arm, and they both picked up the stretcher and carried her out of the room. Two more of Sergi's men, along with the two monks that were originally in the room, were now in the corridor outside. One of the men was also a medic.

The medic said to Radivich, "She's lost a lot of blood, possible internal injuries and is in shock. She's in bad shape. I've got to get her back outside and on some more blood right away or we'll lose her." They placed Karol on another stretcher and moved her back upstairs to safety. Naomi, Sergi, and Radivich remained in the room.

"Here's my plan, Sergi," said Aleksandar. "We'll need Naomi to fill in for Koskov. Naomi, I want you to lie back on Commander Koskov's stretcher and pretend you're her. Sergi and I will assume the positions of the two monks guarding over her. If my hunch is correct, after the bombings, Vorchek and Slavo will make their way down here where it's safe and continue their torture-interrogation session. We'll leave two of our men stationed outside the room covering the door. They're dressed exactly like the paramilitary guards that were stationed here originally. They'll hide their faces with black ski masks."

Sergi helped Naomi get undressed and wrapped her in a bed sheet. Next, they placed a bandage around Naomi's head similar to the way Karol had around hers. Naomi got on Karol's bloodstained stretcher and Radivich placed the IVs on her arm and secured them with adhesive tape.

Sergi received a call on his tactical radio from one of his commanders outside. "Inspector, I'm sorry to bother you, but I received an urgent message for you from Washington. It appears Major Radivich's GPS location has been received and is heading in this direction."

"Make sure you secure the perimeter. When he approaches the monastery, let him in the compound."

Sergi turned to Radivich, "Yuri, it appears your son is approaching the monastery."

Naomi said, "He's trying to get Karol."

"We know—we're counting on it," said Aleksandar.

Chapter 53
BRAVE AND BEAUTIFUL

Dan recognized the countryside. They were outside the town of Maradik, heading toward the monastery of Jazak. It was hidden and tucked away in the thickly wooded area of the Fuska Gora. The single road leading up to it was secluded and unattended. As the sedan approached the main entrance to the compound, a group of paramilitary soldiers wearing black ski masks met them. Belic slowed down as they approached the guards. The guards immediately took up positions surrounding the sedan. One of them approached the driver's window with an AK-47 and pointed the weapon at Belic, "This is a restricted area. No one is allowed here, especially during an air strike."

"My name is Milan Belic. I'm here on official state business to see Vecili."

"Just a moment," said the young soldier as he turned and then talked into his walkie-talkie.

"You may proceed."

Belic drove to the main entrance of the monastery where two monks opened the large wooden door and let him drive through. Once inside the monastery, he parked the car near the main chapel in the cobbled courtyard.

"We need to get out here and walk the rest of the way."

"Don't try anything foolish," said Dan. Dan followed Belic to the northeastern section of the monastery. They entered the building on the ground floor and walked up to the second floor to one of the offices used by the ministry. In front of the office were two armed paramilitary soldiers. The two soldiers, on hearing the two men approaching, immediately held their weapons up and shouted, "Hold your positions!"

Belic spoke up. "I'm Milan Belic. I've come to see Vorchek."

One of the men came up to Belic and began searching him. Then he went to Dan and found the pistol in Dan's pocket and the floppy disks and cell phone. The guard took the pistol, but he gave the floppy disks back to Dan and said, "I'll have to take this. You can get it back when you leave." He then opened the door and showed the two men in. Vecili Vorchek and Domonik Slavo were sitting at a table. The two men were eating and drinking. There were empty beer bottles and loaded pistols strung about. The men had obviously been drinking for some time.

"This is a surprise visit, comrade. Who is your guest?" said Vecili.

"I brought you the other American criminal you're searching for. His name is Major Dan Radivich."

Dan interrupted and spoke in Serbo-Croatian, "Let's cut the crap, gentlemen. I'm here to offer you an exchange, your piece-of-shit traitor for my officer."

The two men seated at the table began to laugh loudly then Vecili spoke, "You stupid fool, do you think you're in a position to bargain with us!"

The two armed guards entered the room guns drawn and taking aim at Dan. Vecili stood up as Belic and Domonik broke out in laughter. "Are you as dumb as you look, boy? Did you think you could actually waltz in here and make demands on us? Well let me tell you something, stupid. You're not leaving here alive. I have your *officer* downstairs. She's practically dead. In fact, we thought she was dead, but we found the bitch still breathing. I decided to spare her life a while longer because she could provide us the locations of the other operatives. We shot her ass up pretty good, and she's lost a lot of blood. In fact, if she's doesn't get a blood transfusion soon, she will be dead. We also found out the little bitch is pregnant—or should I say, *was* pregnant."

Again all the men in the room broke out in laughter as Dan lowered his head in defeat. He couldn't believe what he was hearing. "Let her go. Give her the blood transfusion and in exchange, I'll take her place."

Vecili, still laughing, walked over to Dan, "I have a better idea. You can sit and watch your little bitch die in front of you as we torture her to death. After that, we'll do things to you to make you give us the information she wasn't able to provide us."

Slavo rose from the table, walked over to Dan with a big smile on his face and punched him in the stomach as hard as he could. Then Vecili hit Dan in the face. Dan dropped to the floor and the two of them began kicking and beating him in the face and body. Slavo took out a small club and started hitting him across the shins, elbows, and ankles, concentrating on the bony parts of his body, inflecting maximum pain. They did this for several minutes until Dan was at the point of unconsciousness. They raised him to his feet and continued to beat him. Blood gushed from his face and nose, and he fell to the floor, the men laughing with each punch.

Finally, when he was almost unconscious, Belic spoke up laughing, "Let me have his hand. So, Major, you like to shoot people in the hands. I'll show you what it's really like to get shot in the hand."

Belic took Dan's left hand, put one of the loaded pistols to the back of it, and fired a round through his hand. The pain went all the way up Dan's arm.

"Get him to his feet and get him downstairs. The last thing that little bitch will see before she dies is his ugly face," said Vecili.

They lifted Dan to his feet and dragged him downstairs to the room below. As the group approached the room, the two armed and hooded guards came to their feet.

"Open the door and let us in," said Vecili.

The two guards opened the door and let Belic, Slavo, Dan, and Vecili into the dimly lit room and closed the door behind them. Dan dropped to the floor on seeing the woman on the stretcher. Dan felt at peace in his mind knowing he had finally seen Karol—the last thing he would do alive. Blood was now running down his face stinging his eyes and obscuring his vision. Blood from his hand was dripping to the floor. He crawled to the stretcher on one arm and tried to get up to look at Karol. Vorchek, Belic, and Slavo stood around the body on the stretcher and Slavo kicked Dan again in the forehead. He fell to the floor in defeat. Vecili pointed at the two monks seated behind Karol and said, "Get away from her! You can't do anything for her now, not even pray." The monks got up slowly from their chairs—faces covered under hoods—and began backing up to the wall.

Vecili continued laughing and said to Dan, "Get up,

stupid! Look at what you've done. Not only will you die, but your little whore will die as well."

Slavo grabbed Dan by his left hand and pulled him to his feet. Dan cried out in pain as Slavo began twisting Dan's wounded hand. Naomi, hearing Dan's cries, couldn't stand it any longer. She remembered her training a long time ago back at Quantico. She remembered her mistake in not taking action when the time was right and thus risking the life of one of her teammates. She was ready now. Nothing was going stop her; none of them suspected her presence. She raised her silenced Makarov and pointed it under Slavo's chin. She didn't even have to aim; she just raised the weapon and fired. Blood and brain matter splattered all over the walls, and Slavo dropped to the floor like a hunk of meat, blood poured from behind his head like a faucet. Then she sat up from the stretcher and pointed the pistol at Belic, ready to fire again. He stood in shock as he watched the killing in front of his eyes. The two monks behind the stretcher lowered their hoods, revealing Boraviko and Aleksandar Radivich. Then Sergi yelled in English, "Naomi, put the weapon down, it's all over!"

Naomi lowered her Makarov as each of the men pointed their pistols at the remaining adversaries. Boraviko said, "Hands behind your heads, you two."

Vecili Vorchek yelled to his guards outside.

The two guards outside the room opened the door slowly with their AK-47s pointed behind Vecili and Belic and shouted in Serbo-Croatian, "Croatia! Croatia!"

Aleksandar Radivich spoke up. "So we meet again, Milan, but this time under different circumstances. We suspected a traitor among us but, we had no proof. Now we've got the proof. The intelligence community is not kind to traitors."

Belic, still in shock and disbelief, said, "How can this be happening?"

Boraviko walked up to Vecili and grabbed him by the collar. "You can't hide for long. God has a special place for people like you. I watched you kill twelve of my fellow police officers in cold blood. You ordered the mass murder of two-hundred and sixty innocent men, women, and children in a hospital outside Ovcara. Some of those people were patients and medical personnel working in the hospital trying to save the lives of Serbs and Croats. You ordered insurgents to cross the border and wreak terror and havoc onto the streets of innocent Croatians. I'm not going to kill you, Vecili. That would be too easy. As Chief Inspector for Croatian Interior Ministry of Police, you're under arrest! I'm taking you back to The Hague to face charges for crimes against humanity."

Naomi took off the bandages and sheets, rolled off the stretcher, and crawled to Dan, not worrying she was half-naked. Dan was now almost unconscious laying face down on the cold concrete floor in a pool of blood. Blood was running down his badly bruised face and hand. His eyes were practically swollen shut from the beating he had just taken, but he could make out the features of Naomi's angelic face and half-naked body. He sensed it was a dream or he was dead and this must be what it's like to die.

Naomi gently put her hands around his face, "Danny, can you hear me? It's me, Naomi. It's all over. Your father is here with us. We got Karol out safely. She's going to be okay. Nick and the rest of the team are safely out, too."

She leaned over and gently kissed him on his battered and swollen lips. The last thing Dan saw before he lost consciousness was Naomi's beautiful face.

Chapter 54
TUZ;A AIR BASE, BOSNIA-HERZEGOVINA

May 9, 1999

The U.S. Air Force C-17 touched down at 7:00 A.M. local time and taxied to the main ramp area of Tuzla Air Base. Preparations began for a turnaround flight to Ramstein Air Base, Germany. At 8:00 A.M., the aeromedical staging unit was ready to transport Lt. Cdr. Karol Koskov, Major Dan Radivich, and Corporal Nick Bellou to the waiting aircraft. Sergeant Major Karen Criskos and Gunnery Sergeant Michael Karl arrived at the aircraft unassisted. Staff Sergeant Naomi Markof was still at Base Operations debriefing Lt. Gen. James Hamilton, Commander in Chief of the Defense Intelligence Agency who had flown in onboard the C-17. She would be accompanying the team back to Wiesbaden Air Base, Germany and eventually on to Washington.

General Hamilton said, "So let me get this straight, young lady, you stole a police car and drove it deep through enemy territory with a bleeding soldier in the front seat? You negotiated your way through a minefield carrying that wounded soldier on your back? And you helped rescue, not one, but two of your fellow officers held captive deep inside enemy territory?"

"Yes, sir, but it was a team effort."

"Team effort my ass. I doubt if some of our special ops guys could have pulled off what you did. I'm recommending you for a citation!"

At 9:30 A.M., the C-17 was ready for departure. Aboard the aircraft, the entire Prospector circuit was getting ready to head back home. Karol was heavily sedated and was being attended to by a flight nurse. She lost a lot of blood and needed to be transported immediately back to Ramstein Air Base to undergo more extensive care. Nick was actually back to his old self, complaining about how he should get a medal instead of Naomi. Mike and Karen were standing off to the side, glad everyone was safe and going home. Dan was laying on a litter with a cast on his left hand and two black eyes. Naomi leaned closer to him and said, "Danny, do you mind if I call you that in front of everyone?"

Dan, barely conscious and still in pain, moved his lips slowly, "Sure, why not, we're all practically a family anyway."

"Remember when I asked you way back when if we would ever see one another again, and you said to me we'd all meet again at Tuzla?"

"Yes, I do remember saying that, but I only said that to calm your fears."

"I know that now, but look, here we are. We're all here together."

"Yes, but Karol is still not out of the woods."

Naomi continued, "You said to us back at Bolling that your biggest fear was leaving someone behind and you'd do anything to bring everyone back safely. It looks like you've accomplished what you set out to do."

"Thanks. It's a promise I had to keep for someone."

Chapter 55
SIX MONTHS LATER

Captain Daniel Alexander Radivich returned to Travis AFB shortly after he returned to the States and resumed his position in the 75th Airlift Squadron flying C-5s. He fully recovered from the gunshot wound to his left hand and returned to flight status. No one in the squadron ever knew about his secret mission into Serbia. His injuries and bruises were simply explained as a broken wrist suffered from slipping in the shower while TDY at the Pentagon.

Lt. Cdr. Karoline Anne-Marie Koskov received a Silver Star and a Purple Heart while single-handedly engaging the enemy under heavy fire, contributing to the safe rescue and recovery of U.S. Air Force Captain Mark Williams. She spent three months at Bethesda Naval Hospital recouping from her wounds and fully recovered. However, her injuries were too severe and the loss of blood too massive, causing her to miscarry. Because of her heroic efforts in support of Operation Allied Force, the Navy did not pursue UCMJ charges against her. Instead, she was promoted to full Commander and assigned to the

TACMO facility at Travis Air Force Base where she is chief of unit intelligence.

Sergeant Major Karen Criskos and Gunnery Sergeant Michael Karl retired from the Army and Marine Corps. They live in Salinas, California, and have become close and dear friends to Dan and Karol. Nikola Belleu was discharged from active duty because of the wounds he suffered and received the medal he so dearly wanted. He was awarded a Purple Heart. For her part on the mission, Staff Sergeant Naomi Markof was awarded the Air Force Cross, the second highest award given to Air Force personnel. This award is normally accompanied with full military honors. However, because of the classified nature of the assignment, her award was presented at a simple ceremony at the Pentagon. She was promoted to Technical Sergeant and given her assignment of choice. She took Karen's advice and chose the Defense Language Institute in Monterey, California. Majors Lundbar and Paulson, the two Luftwaffe tornado pilots, survived their capture by JNA forces and were repatriated on July 4, 1999. They are still on active duty with the German Air Force. Vecili Vorcheck was taken to The Hague to face charges for crimes against humanity. He died of *natural causes* waiting trial by the World Court.

Epilogue
EMERYVILLE, CALIFORNIA DECEMBER
1999

Dan was sitting on the same park bench Josef Kostinic sat on almost one year earlier. It was a beautiful Saturday morning in the San Francisco Bay Area. The sun was out, boats were sailing, and the seagulls were as annoying as ever. Dan saw a car approaching the park from a distance with a woman driving and a passenger in the rear. He could not make out the identity of the woman or her passenger. The car stopped behind him and someone got out and closed the door. Then the vehicle drove away. Dan could hear footsteps on the soft grass approaching from behind, but he decided not to turn his head and look back to see who it was. The figure approached and came in front of Dan.

"It's a beautiful day, Dan. It's good to see you. Thank you for meeting me today."

Hal Mattingly was wearing the same dark-blue, pinstriped suit he had on the day Dan first met him onboard the Amtrak Coast Starlight.

Dan stood up, shook Mattingly's hand, and said, "I hear you have a new job, congratulations. I understand you've been appointed president of the Golden Gate Institute for Strategic Studies here in San Francisco."

"Thank you, Dan."

"I was just thinking about Professor Kostinic and everything he told me, especially the part about the SOE agent, Penelope Walsh. I made a promise to him not to leave anyone behind. When I first met you onboard the Coast Starlight, I could tell you had suffered a great loss. I saw it in your eyes. I'm sorry. She must have been a very dear and special person to you."

"Yes, Dan, she was, but that was a long, long time ago. I was a young man then."

Mattingly and Dan took a seat on the bench and looked out at the Golden Gate Bridge.

"You know, Dan, this is where it all started. Right here on this same park bench. I asked Professor Kostinic to meet me here that morning just as I did you today."

Dan threw a piece of bread from his sandwich at the seagulls as Mattingly continued, "By the way, Dan, if it wasn't for your father and the Croatians, you, Karol, and the rest of your team would have never gotten out."

"Yes, I know that."

"Then why are you so upset at me and the Network?"

"Why didn't you just come right out and tell me from the beginning that my father was involved instead of giving me hints about his past?"

"It wasn't that easy. Your father was the Defense Intelligence Agency organizer for the entire Balkan network. I was just the facilitator. I brought the personnel together and handled logistics. The whole operation was the mastermind of Professor Kostinic and your father. When Josef passed away, your father was left to run the operation by himself. Luckily, we had inspector Boraviko on our side. If we had told you in the beginning that your father was involved, number one, you wouldn't have believed us, and number two, we didn't know if you'd go along. Remember, we were running out of time and options. By the way, it was not my idea to bring you onboard in the first place, it was Josef's. He was the one that recommended you. He had no idea about who Preacher was until we started planning the operation. It was by pure coincidence that you just happened to be Aleksandra's son. When your father discovered Josef specifically requested you for this assignment, he agreed, but only on the condition you volunteered on your own free will. That was another reason why I had you aboard Amtrak—to give you time to make this decision uninfluenced."

As the two men looked out over the bay, Dan said, "Whatever happened to Belic? Because of him, I almost lost Karol as well as the rest of my team."

"He was a contract CIA operative. He was not a US Citizen. There was not a lot the government could do. It turned out Belic was a triple agent working for the Russian GRU passing on valid information to them, presumably at a price. However, the system has a way of taking care of itself. I don't think we'll have to worry about Belic destroying the intelligence communities of the world anymore. The CDs you provided to us were sensitive in nature."

"How was he able to get away with so much?"

"Evidently, Belic used a cell phone and cable adaptor that was used by a U.S. Special Forces unit killed in Serbia before the war. Belic was in charge of recovering the bodies. It's believed this is when he found the phone and used it against us. He had a lot of information on his computer, not only on the CIA, but on the former KGB. Of course, we didn't waste any time in sharing this information with those agencies. Belic had too many enemies looking for him. They eventually caught up with him and gave him due payback. His body was found in a dumpster outside Belgrade not long after the war."

"There will be others just like Belic."

"There always are. If Belic hadn't double-crossed us, you'd have been totally successful on this mission. Anyway, Dan, you surprised us. You did better than we expected for your first time. Josef would have been extremely proud of you. Your intuition served you well. In fact, if you hadn't ordered the extraction on your own when you did, there's a good probability Naomi and Nick would have perished along with Mike and Karen. You stayed one step ahead of them all the time."

Mattingly changed the subject and said, "It appears that Operation Allied Force inflicted less damage to the Yugoslav military than originally thought because of the use of ingenious camouflage and misdirection techniques to disguise military targets. You found some of those targets, but NATO did not want to believe your reports. NATO believed they had destroyed about two hundred Serbian tanks, but only twelve were subsequently confirmed destroyed by United Nations Peacekeeping forces. We even discovered MIG-29s made from Balsa wood. Despite complete NATO air superiority, the Serbs mounted a massive air strike on the Tuzla Air Base and knocked out the entire Coalition Combat Search and Rescue force. Thank God, we still had naval assets, and we didn't lose any more aircraft during the remaining days of the war. Milosevic survived the conflict and declared a major victory for Yugoslavia and Serbia, and he's still at large being indicted on war crimes charges. So, Dan, who really won the war? More importantly, was it necessary and worth it?"

Mattingly continued to look out onto the bay for

several minutes then said, "You know, Dan, the U.S. Intelligence community is in complete shambles. It's only a matter of time before this country realizes it. It might happen tomorrow or ten years from now, but eventually our country is going to have a serious intelligence meltdown. One morning we'll wake up and find our country under attack. Why? Because each agency doesn't share information with each other. They say it's because of the current laws, but that's all a bunch of crap. Stop and think about it for a moment. For starters, we had a secretary of defense who was incompetent. We had NATO planning an entire war based on information provided to them from the CIA. We had the DIA providing information to the CIA who in turn misdirected the information to NATO. The FBI knew all about Belic but said nothing to any of us. When the Defense Department tried to provide information directly to NATO, they ignored it and went with the information provided to them from Langley. That information turned out to be inaccurate or bogus. The NSA intercepted Belic's transmissions years ago but never said anything to the FBI or the CIA. This is even more reason why we need a single national intelligence network. I will say one thing about the Soviets—they had the right idea with the KGB, but they still had to deal with the GRU."

"What's all this got to do with me? I'm back on active duty."

"All I'm saying, Dan, is keep us in mind. DIA is starting a new rival intelligence service focusing on counter-terrorism and counterespionage, code-named *Nimble Dodger*, based out of Mc Dill Air Force Base. They could always use a good man. There'll be more conflicts and more wars, except the next time the DOD will conduct their own covert operations independently from CIA, and Special Operations will play a major role in that conflict."

Mattingly let Dan think about it for a moment. Then he saw a woman approaching the park. As the woman came closer, he recognized Karoline Anne-Marie Koskov. He did not expect to see her.

"She looks great, Dan. She healed nicely from her wounds."

"She took a hit in the right cheek of her buttocks and another to her upper leg, severing an artery, plus a few broken ribs thanks to Vorchek and Slavo who beat the crap out of her. Probably because she put up a good fight and they weren't expecting it. Much of her body was badly bruised and of course, abused. The doctors tell me she could still have children again.

As Karol approached the two men, she recognized Hal and said, "Hello, stranger. It's good to see you. Dan told me you called and asked to see him today. I thought this would be a good excuse to get out and see San Francisco again."

Mattingly said, "You look great, Karol. I'm sorry for your loss though. You're still young. There'll be other opportunities."

Then the vehicle that dropped Mattingly off came back and stopped alongside the curb. The woman in her late fifties was still behind the wheel. Finally, she opened the door, came out, and spoke with a well-educated British accent, "Dr. Mattingly, you're wanted back at the Presidio."

"I'll be right there."

Mattingly turned to Dan and Karol and said, "By the way, you two. You do remember my personal assistant, Ms. Sara—Sarah Walsh? I adopted her shortly after World War II. She's been working with me for over twenty-five years now. Penelope was her mother."

About the Author

Gregory M. Acuña is an emerging author. *The Balkan Network* was his first book in a series and the sequel to *Credible Dagger*. He is currently writing his fifth book, a Cold War Thriller about a US Army officer who tries to sell Pershing II Missile deployment information to the Soviets. However, his beautiful East German contact is also a double agent working for the Americans and East German intelligence.

Gregory M. Acuña is a former USAF pilot and current B-777 Captain for a major U.S. air carrier.

f

Other Books by Gregory M. Acuña

Credible Dagger

Nimble Dodger

Knight To King 6

Available in ebook, paperback and audio

Made in the USA
Las Vegas, NV
09 March 2024